SOUL SURVIVAL

A BOY IS THE BATTLEFIELD OF GOOD AND EVIL

CRAIG FLEMING

fifth story
PUBLISHING LLC

Copyright

1

JACOB, 2015

For some people, solitude is a blessing. For others, it is an abject curse.

During part of my childhood, I would spend the very early hours of many mornings walking the length of the rows of cornfields on our family farm. The sweet, pungent smell of the rich Kansas soil, freshly planted and tilled, the misty morning air, the sound of cicadas singing seemed to run together and bleed away. The vividness of the thoughts injected into my memory as I walked remain to this day.

On those mornings, I'd wake up earlier than the sun and sneak downstairs before anyone else was up. This was a bit of a challenge as my dad was the epitome of a Midwestern farmer, the quintessential "early to bed, early to rise" type. Which is why I was never able to keep anything from him—I knew he was aware of what was transpiring from the very beginning.

He knew. I knew. But neither of us talked about it—at least not at first.

What I don't remember is exactly why this exercise became such a ritualistic part of my life. Part of my entire family's life, actually. It was as if I was shrouded leading up to this hard-left turn that was dropped unannounced into my daily routine. It sucked for a kid who didn't know what was happening. (Would have sucked for anyone, quite frankly, especially for a kid whose grand plan for his life certainly didn't involve physical limitations and social indifference.)

Childhood memories get distorted with time, the true and false get subtly mixed. The good is a bit amplified, and the bad slides back into the subconscious.

But that didn't happen for me.

My morning ritual lasted for most of my formative years, throughout middle school and into my freshman year of high school. And then it stopped. Abruptly.

It is very strange and complicated, that story, an epic spiritual battle, a series of events that changed my entire life. It's too much to get into now. We'll discuss it all later, I promise.

But, before we get start down that path, I probably need to tell you about myself.

My name is Jacob Ross, and I'm 35 years old. I grew up in Perryton, Kansas, but I have lived most of my adult life in Phoenix. I will not be going back to Kansas anytime soon. Probably ever.

Perryton is smack-dab in the center of the state and smack-dab in the middle of nowhere. From downtown Perryton, you could drive west in a straight line for about 10 miles on Highway 40 and hit our farmhouse. A tiny, insignificant map dot, a place few would know from any other little town across the Midwest, but it was home for me.

Of course, my geography expanded as I got older. When I was 10 and part of Cub Scouts den number 10, I discovered the Smoky Hill River to the south, and when I got older and got my driver's license, the towns of Ellsworth and Black Wolf drew me in with movie theaters and fast-food restaurants. Ultimately, I moved to the grand metropolis of Wichita after high school. I lasted one year at WSU.

My best memories, and my most horrific ones, are set in Perryton. Starring the same set of characters—my older brother and sister, my parents and my best friend Marcus. My sister and I still reminisce about those days during our sporadic phone calls, occasionally broaching some tough subjects, while intentionally leaving others alone, wishing our brother was there to share in our select memories. He may come back to us yet. There's still hope.

I haven't spoken to my brother in years. It's actually a real shame because he was one of my heroes growing up. I looked up to him, respected him, loved him. But the two of us, we changed. I now know for sure that the same last name does not guarantee lasting, like-minded relationships.

My dad and mom are still married and living in south Texas. Refugio, to be exact. I do my best to be a good son. I call them regularly, catch up on the latest football news and my mom's book club. But perfunctory is the best way to describe our phone calls. I find myself hoping mom answers and dad is not home. I guess some of what happened in Kansas still stands between us.

As you can see, none of us stayed in our home state. It's better to flee the scene of the crime.

There are just some things no one will ever forget.

2

DAVIS JOHNSTONE, 1974

Fifty years, 18,250 days, every day the same.

Except one. The day that changed my life. The day Lydia was abducted.

I am the third generation in my family to grow up in Perryton. My father, Thomas Johnstone, had been the pastor at the First Baptist Church on Jefferson Avenue since the day he was called to the pulpit just weeks after he married my mother. I was born in the Church's parsonage back in '24 and spent my first hours in its musty narthex being passed from one parishioner to the next, old women clucking over me and pulling those blankets just a little bit tighter, because after all, it would be a shame for the pastor's firstborn son to catch a cold on the day he was born.

It was in that same narthex that I would later play hide-and-seek with my brother on eerie, empty Saturdays and stand straight and tall in my best brown wool jacket on Sunday mornings when the very same room that was abandoned the day before became electric with crowded energy.

Fifty years of Kansas sunrises, that flaming orange ball throwing light over the wheat fields as I carefully buttoned two jackets—both mine and my brother's—over my trembling body because, even though it was just 200 feet from our front door to the front of the church, it was a cold 200 feet, especially at 6:30 a.m. when my mother sent me over to tell my father the oatmeal was on the table.

Fifty years of Kansas sunsets, the bright day slinking away as my father and I raked leaves in front of the church steps, talking about the weather and Jesus' ministry and just about every other thing fathers and sons talk about on windy autumn afternoons.

Fifty years of walking through those front doors into that same narthex that protected me from catching my death on the day I was born, where I raced every day after school, spending those afternoons in the administrative conference room doing my homework, just waiting until dad was done with his work so he would walk home with me, quizzing me on the Bible and debating theology and hearing the stories of his day, slamming into the house and inhaling the rich scent of whatever it was my mother had put on the table that night.

I loved those 50 years, those 18,250 days.

It was on one of those days that my dad joked that he "looked at me and realized he was now looking up instead of down." I remember him staring at me and calling out to my mother that I apparently forgot to stop growing. My dad joked that his biggest regret was the fact that he had peaked out at a few inches shy of six feet, a respectable height as long as you didn't want to play basketball for Kansas State. I shot past dad at 13 and, by the time I started 10th grade, I had settled in at 6'4" and weighed a very athletic 240 pounds. No one in the Johnstone family had ever come close to achieving those proportions, so I was the first male on either side to have the adjective "athletic" attached to their name.

A few of those 50 years were filled with both academic and athletic trophies, with a Salutatorian sash, a framed certificate on my wall naming me Kansas Athlete of the Year, letters from colleges asking me to go to exotic places like California and New York to play ball. But I never went. Instead, I found myself in even more exotic places like Normandy and Paris and the Italian Coast, places far from my Kansas wheat fields and the old church that was now being repaired by a group of eager parishioners who wanted to help my father while his sons were off at war.

And yet, even those days, those ones spent far from Kansas, I remember them as part of the same big picture. I remember the sunrises and sunsets, running in heavy boots across seemingly familiar fields on the other side of the world, the popping of gunshots ringing in my ears, a light misting rain soaking through my shirt, the terror of possibly losing my own life, of my friends, the hope of a better tomorrow, the yearning to go back to that old, creaking church on Jefferson Street, to spend an afternoon with my dad, who was yearning for the same.

Everyone assumed I would follow in my dad's footsteps and join him as a pastor and, in some ways, I did. But, in many other ways, I didn't. Because, while I grew up to love Jesus and serving others just like dad, I also grew up to spend my days doing different things than my dad did. I opened a prosperous insurance practice. I got married and loved on three children. I coached sports. I worked tirelessly within the First Baptist Church, saying yes to almost anyone who needed help. Still, even with all those accomplishments, I never forgot where I came from.

Fifty years of ups, downs, highs, lows, tears, smiles, and hot coffee on the front porch with my wife joining me as a sounding board, confidante, and friend. Fifty years of laughing kids, conversations with my dad, talk of war and peace, theology and history, what to do with little Charles Whitaker who absolutely refused to go to school, how to take care of Widow Smith who wasn't sure she could pay her rent, of everything expected and typical and normal... until...Lydia.

If you ask most anyone, my age or older, to describe the most defining social moment in Perryton, you'd get the same answer from eight out of ten interviewees. It was a hot and sticky August afternoon in 1959. The day started like any other. We had set a big white box in the hallway by the door to the Missions department and asked everyone to bring cans of food and gently used clothes to help some of the families who were struggling.

Many of the poor were black, not that I really cared. I knew the racial history of Kansas. I had learned some of it from old Mrs. Hoagland, my sixth-grade teacher, who had still been bitter about her great-grandfather's loss of his stately plantation in the years following the Civil War. She taught us about a series of violent and bloody conflicts, driven by the Kansas-Nebraska Act in 1854, conflicts that ultimately forced Kansas settlers to decide on the issue of slavery, and more importantly, to decide whether Kansas would enter the Union as a slave state or a free state.

Horace Greeley, the famous editor of the New York Tribune coined the term Bleeding Kansas. The violence born out of this conflict, and fanned by the Kansas-Nebraska Act, indicated that there was to be no compromise for Kansas, and ultimately helped to set the table for the Civil War, a war Mrs. Hoagland was still fuming about, 90 years after it ended, a time that still caused her to call the black families who lived down by the creek "filthy" and mumble under her breath that the only thing they were good for was getting back into the fields and helping things get back to the way they should be.

My father told a different story. I had reported this history lesson to him one afternoon when he asked me to help him scrub the old wood plank floor in the narthex and then watched his face as it turned red and his jaw clenched in anger. "Davis," he had said through gritted teeth, "sometimes the things you learn in school are not the truth. They are opinions based on human emotions, human feelings, and human prejudices."

He had explained that, contrary to Mrs. Hoagland's history lessons, there was another side to the story, a side that involved entire families brought up in captivity, told they were sub-human, unworthy. A side that told of freedom won, freedom deserved, yet of slaves breaking away from captivity only to find Bleeding Kansas left them in another, and equally evil, set of chains. Of racism and violence and cruelty that lasted for generations, of people who still believed, in spite of 90 years of abolition, that blacks should be enslaved.

It was based on this history that I worked hard to collect food and clothing for the poor in Kansas each month. And it was based on this history that I made absolutely no differentiation between whom I served. Poor was poor, hungry was hungry. And so that August afternoon, like so many other afternoons before, I loaded my truck up with canned goods and headed to New Richland, the oldest and most rundown neighborhood in Perryton.

I had known Leon and Coly Williams for years now. Leon was the janitor at the high school and Colleen, or Coly, was a mom to three boys and one girl. Leon had lived in New Richland his entire life, as had his family for as long as anyone could remember. To say the Williamses were my favorite family was an understatement. Leon and I had quickly become best friends, sharing stories over hot chicory, realizing we had much more in common than one would think at first glance.

I had spent many afternoons with the Williamses and Johnstones flipping burgers on the barbecue, singing hymns and playing horseshoes. I had held their sweet daughter, Lydia, as she was baptized. I had watched her blossom from a shy, quiet child to a confident, outgoing, and intelligent adolescent. She was a bright, shining star. She was the reason I loved my ministry and the one who made it easy for me to wake up early on Saturdays to make the trek out to New Richland.

She was also the reason my entire life changed.

Because that day, that stifling, hot August day, stands out as the one, dark, evil day amongst 18,250 others.

It's the one day that was different.

And it's the one day that would change everything for me and so many others who spent their days in Perryton.

3

JACOB, 1990

Doesn't everybody everywhere traipse off to school on the first Tuesday after Labor Day? I assume this set-in-stone date is a long-time social edict kept under lock and key and hidden away in the basement of the county jail. That the school year revolved around the farmers' planting and harvesting schedules never dawned on me, even as a child who grew up on a farm amidst cornfields harvested each autumn.

But, in 1990, aside from the same start day and the same old brown loafers my mother bought me every year from JC Penney's, I somehow knew fifth grade was going to be different.

Before that year, no one had really cared what I looked like (pretty average, to be honest), what my dad's income was (again, average) or how athletic I was (the fastest runner in our grade, thank you very much). Everyone was basically the same, except for Stevie Walker, the new kid, who showed up in fourth grade with a new pair of Air Jordan shoes and a Transformers Trapper Keeper.

For whatever reason, I had been warned that social edicts would change in fifth grade.

The teachers in the Kansas Public School System were mostly well-meaning, spending their days focused on their united interest in furthering the educational opportunities for the next generation of Kansas leaders which, in layman's terms, basically means their days were boring. The biggest problem was that the teachers were held back by untenable bureaucracy and a bland curriculum that made it impossible for them to do anything to hold my attention for more than six-and-a-half minutes. Homeschooling hit the Kansas market too late for me, I guess. Mom would have been an extremely good teacher. I could have learned more in less time. I try not to think about the if-onlys.

The one unfettered arena in which the teachers were more than competent was the application of discipline. We may not have been spending our time learning interesting things, but we surely learned the boring things in a quiet and well-behaved manner. As a result, we had no choice but to learn the basics—reading, writing, and arithmetic with a healthy dose of Kansas history mixed in.

I had plenty of acquaintances but, due to the fact that I lived way out in the country and had to help with the farm chores after school (and certainly not because I tended to be a bit awkward and odd), I only had one person whom I would have called a true friend.

When I think back on my time at Perryton Elementary School, I waver between warm memories and wanting to throw up in the trashcan. Periodic catharsis is a good thing.

"It is 7:15, Jacob. Get rolling!" Mom had yelled up the stairs on that first morning of fifth grade. Her yelling never came across as threatening. It was always received with a mixture of love and instructional care.

"I'm ready, Mom, just tying my shoes."

"Did you eat anything? You need to be sure you don't get hungry before lunch."

"I ate. I'm good. Is my lunch bag made?" My mom didn't seem to know that I had gotten into the habit of grabbing a bowl of cereal after my morning walk in the fields. I had just started the ritual a few weeks earlier so maybe she wasn't aware of what I was doing. (Of course, looking back, I now know the refrigerator was Mom's sacred domain and she absolutely knew every item in it, when it was bought, what shelf it was set on, and when it would go bad. I probably didn't fool her. Never did as it turned out.)

I bounded down the stairs, trying to descend two or three steps at a time, still able to take them without falling or tripping, a skill I hardly recognized as significant at the time, but would later realize as one of those accomplishments defining my carefree youth.

"Bye, Mom. See you this afternoon!" I had yelled as I pulled the front door closed.

"Bye, sweetie." Mom smiled as she wiped her hands on her ever-present apron. Over the long term, I think moms are sad to see their children grow up and bound out of the house, but maybe in the short term, they are just happy for a quiet house and a hot cup of coffee in peace.

Out the front door and down the drive I ran, pausing for a few moments to enjoy the smell of the morning and the feel of running the winding road to the bus stop, imagining what it would be like to see Vernon again after a long summer. I was the Flash reincarnated. I had picked up speed during the last twenty-five yards and then jammed on the brakes so I could slide to a stop by the mailbox. I immediately looked back to see how long my skid mark was at the end of the dirt road. A PR, once again. I dismissed the nagging thought that Mom wouldn't like me wearing out my shoes.

I waited for the school bus where Route 40 intersected with the long, winding dirt road up to our house. It was probably a 200-yard walk, or run for the Flash, to and from the house. Since Vernon was always prompt, I learned to be prompt as well. Life lessons, courtesy of the world's best bus driver.

Smiling at my success, I looked right and saw the very top of the school bus breach the rise in the road. The black roof, then the flashing light panel that was about to be turned on and finally the yellow hulk of the bus. That yellow too gaudy for anything but school buses. As quickly as I could see the 346 emblazoned on the front left side of the bus's hood, the lights started flashing. I loved it. I was the only one at my stop, so I was convinced the lights were only for me.

Vernon McKinley was my bus driver every year from the day I started first grade until the day he mysteriously disappeared.

He wore the same uniform every day: putty grey work pants and a matching grey short-sleeved shirt. Probably purchased from Dickies; Carhartts were too expensive. The shirt was always stressed against his ample belly where the material only met at the buttons. Thankfully, he wore a belt, or he probably would have exploded. This is particularly true when we drove down the tractor-rutted farm-to-market roads. As we picked up speed, his entire midsection would start bouncing in a seemingly incongruent fashion. Then, as we hit the bus's top speed limit, everything came into harmony. His belly moved in one synchronous motion with the tremors of the bus. A thing of beauty to watch, for a kid that is.

Vernon gracefully lumbered the bus to a halt as a small puff of dust rolled off the tires, ascended to about hubcap height, and then settled back. He started opening the door a tad early so, when he came to a complete stop, the door landed fully open at the same second. A real pro. And there he was, sitting high in his big leather seat, looking as huge as a grizzly bear, his giant hands engulfing the bus's steering wheel.

"Howdy, Jacob!"

"Hello, Mr. Vernon." He always asked us to call him by his first name. He was just like that, one of those adults who seemed more like a friend than anything else.

Vernon never failed to earn our respect. He broke up fights, made the bullies sit in the back of the bus, and was never, ever late for his route. I liked him. A lot. But, interestingly, I never knew much about him. I just assumed he came with the bus when it was purchased by the school system.

Either way, Vernon was my favorite, and while I knew he followed the same routine at every stop, I couldn't help but wonder if he smiled extra big for me. I was the Flash reincarnated. I was special.

"How was your summer, Mr. Vernon?" I said as I jumped onto the first of three bus steps.

"Not bad, not bad at all. Looks like you had a good summer. You're about a foot taller." Vernon's voice boomed.

"Yep, great summer." Of course, I hadn't grown over the past three months. Not even a half-inch. But that was enough idle chit chat. After all, he was an adult and probably didn't really care for boring details of a kid's summer vacation and I certainly didn't want to admit how boring my days were on average. I'm sure he knew though. As I found out later, Vernon was actually a kid once.

I rumbled back to the middle of the bus, dropped my backpack, and hit the seat exactly as Vernon shot forward. Perfect timing was another one of his skills.

As he drove off, I sunk into my seat and couldn't help but think about what had happened to Jaime Brockton.

Jamie was two years older than my brother, so four years older than me. I did not know him, only *of* him. In this part of Kansas, it is not unusual for each bus stop in the morning to be manned by one kid, two if they had a brother or sister. The route was geographically large, spread out across farmland, with miles and miles of wheat fields spanning each stop.

Our school had only about 200 kids from K through 12. Three-fourths of these kids lived in town or close enough not to be on one of the rural bus routes. Jamie was on one of the more suburban routes, although the word "suburban" is stretching it.

Our school was located on the southwest side of Perryton, specifically facing Roosevelt between 102nd and 103rd streets. Not too far from downtown, but then nothing is too far from downtown in a rural metropolis like Perryton. It consumed the entire block and stood in judgment over every person who ever grew up in Perryton. At the end of the school day, all six buses picked up in the same area outside the school at the far end of the front-circle drive. It used to be a very chaotic area with buses coming and going as well as parents' cars lining up to pick up the few kids that did not ride a bus. The general afternoon drill was to line up behind the designated yellow line painted on the arced sidewalk. Specific lines marking the two rural routes and the four suburban routes. Each line was uncreatively numbered one through six, which in turn matched a number printed to the left of the bus door.

(At least the powers-that-be had decided on simple identifying numbers versus matching animals or flowers like many other schools use, otherwise known as Bus Garanimals.)

On the day Jaime Brockton died, he had been standing first in line as the kids waited for the bus. Jamie, all 4'8" and 90 pounds of him, was never near the fastest or strongest but, on this day, he was certainly the unluckiest. Jamie merely turned around and set his feet in front of the almost invisible barrier and waited. Not three seconds later, Tommy Martin and Rex Garcia, two of our high school varsity football players, ran smack dab into Jamie's back. Three hundred sixty pounds hitting 90 pounds at the end of an imaginary football play. Jamie did not see them, and they did not see Jamie.

The laws of physics took over.

The story goes that Jamie was catapulted ten feet into the air and landed in a balled-up thud on the exact spot the bus's front right tire was soon to occupy. The bus driver did not see Jamie. Jamie did not see the bus either. (Which, in hindsight, was the only good thing about this entire terrible story.) He was immediately flattened from head to pelvis. Most all bones broken, and organs crushed. Blood squirted in a tight 360-degree pattern. More ended up on the asphalt than was left in his frail, lifeless body. But what really got everyone's attention was the moist popping sound of his insides forcing their way out of his insubstantial body. His skin was no match for the strength and weight of a standard Type B school bus. This was a wet, guttural sound that you feel in your stomach more than you hear.

To this day, most of the kids at the bus stop still have nightmares. Tommy and his family have moved away. Rumor has it they put him in a mental hospital. I think that was probably more urban legend than fact. Rex Garcia is still at our school for his senior year, although it has been a struggle. He no longer plays football and small-town gossip says he hardly talks anymore. Understandable. Not real sure about the bus driver. I just know it wasn't Vernon. (I never had the nerve to ask Vernon about the Jamie incident.) I can't imagine that poor bus driver's grief. He disappeared shortly after he was cleared of any wrongdoing. I guess this fell under the caption of "accidents happen." Apparently, Jamie's parents moved soon afterward as well.

My brother Luke had been at home sick on that disastrous day, and I was to be picked up by Mom, but she was late. Thank God Luke was under the weather. Hearing the stories is horrific enough for him. It affected him far more than it did me. I was far enough away that I did not see the accident. The ensuing mass of entangled humanity prevented me from working my way to a vantage point. I was probably lucky in retrospect. That said, I can still hear, or should I say feel, that popping sound.

This sudden, freakish accident left one seventh grader dead and two other students' lives, along with a bus driver and their related families, in a shattered mess. Never to recover. Add to this the ripple effect among the kids at the bus stop, the families in the crowd, and even me and half the other kids who still, two years later, have a hard time stepping onto a school bus and thinking of anything else.

Hundreds of people have never been the same.

This is why I always step back two paces when the school bus is arriving. Don't even think about it, just happens as sure as breathing.

Vernon breaks to an abrupt stop at the next pickup in front of the Polanski's farm. I'm jolted from my horrific thoughts. I thank Vernon under my breath. I also wipe the thin glaze of perspiration off my forehead. I'd like to never think about Jamie Brockton again.

I will not be so lucky.

But, for today, I have something else to distract me. Or, rather, someone else.

Susie Polanski.

She hops on the bus with the enthusiasm you only have on the first day of school. Jimmy, her brother, sulks his way onto the bus behind her. Life never gets better for him. Vernon asks them the same question he asked me. They both sit in the seat directly in front of mine, and Susie looks back at me and smiles.

I liked Susie a lot more than Jimmy. She was nice. He was not. In fact, he was a complete and utter a-hole. To this day, I have no idea how someone as kind and sweet as Susie could come from the same gene pool as Jimmy.

A few more stops and we arrived at school only to file off the bus. I struggled a little, my knees aching. My agility was not what it once was, but I do not think anyone noticed. We stepped through the opening in the steel fence and, sure enough, I got a little queasy.

And so, it began.

The year that would change my entire future.

4

JACOB

Fifth grade didn't feel too much different than the other four grades. Same teachers, same faces, same smells wafting from the cafeteria. My classes were not any harder either, so boredom set in by the end of day one.

At least I was prepped for the grind.

Every class was an average, unexciting extension of the prior year. Math, English, Science, and of course, Penmanship, which was a disaster for me. My teacher told me I should consider being a doctor, which I didn't understand but laughed at anyway.

The one subject—if you could call it a subject—I excelled at was Conduct. I generally got great marks—at least until fifth grade when a mixture of apathy and angst seeped into my countenance.

Mrs. Hutchinson was my teacher. I barely remembered her from fourth grade because she was at the other end of the hall, and we fourth graders never went down to that part of our wing. I did, however, remember her being old, and when I walked in that first day of fifth grade, my memory proved correct. She was ancient.

"Okay, everyone, wrap up your cursive practice sheets and get ready for recess," Mrs. Hutchinson said from the front of the class. She was a very slight person, frail even. It's ironic I would think that, because I was smaller than she was, but regardless, I remember feeling like I was looking down on her. Her brown hair was cut short, she wore overly large glasses, and her dresses always seemed a little off, as if they were one size too big. One shoulder would be lower than the other, and the hem was never straight. I'd catch her periodically straightening her outfit only to have it misalign itself shortly thereafter.

"Drop your papers into the basket on my desk on your way out. Have fun and be safe on the playground!" she yelled over the din of chairs scraping the floor. Waves of pent-up energy exploded from 14 students racing out the door. She'd be lucky if half the papers made it into her basket. I can still picture her bent over at the waist gathering papers as we ran by.

Recess was either 30 minutes of heaven or hell, depending on whether or not you were athletic enough to be passable at kickball, baseball, or Capture the Flag. By fifth grade, this reality was crystal clear, and the pecking order had been set, a pecking order that would last until high school and beyond. But I was one of the lucky ones, at least at the start of that year. That would change, but on that blissful day, I was still King of the playground.

People called me wiry, which is code for small and skinny. But I was fast. Probably the fastest kid on our side of 10th grade. The playground was L-shaped, bordered on the inside of the L by the elementary cafeteria and gymnasium. Grass was hard to find in the fall, which made rainy days interesting. The outside of the L was completely surrounded by a four-foot hurricane fence.

I spent my recess time on the ball field, the farthest space from the school, bordering Grant Street. We were always hopping the fence and running across Grant to retrieve our ball. This was followed by a stern reprimand from the attending teacher which we never heeded. To my knowledge, no one was ever hit by a car, although Tommy Johnson did fall in mid-stride once and took a good three-fourths of the skin off his left knee. Bled like crazy. He wore it like a badge of honor for at least two weeks. I didn't understand how clumsiness was an honor.

I get it now.

I loved kickball. No one could ever throw me out. Once I started running around the bases, I was unstoppable. The guys behind me would crush the ball, and off I'd go. Running like I did to the bus stop, the feeling of an all-out sprint around the bases was euphoric. The Flash strikes again.

Even though recess lasted 30 minutes, it felt like 10. Unlike class time where 10 minutes felt like an hour, maybe two. And so, when recess was over, I'd drag myself back into class with beads of sweat running down my flushed cheeks, already thinking about the next recess. "All right, everyone," Mrs. Hutchinson said. "Get out your favorite pencil; we're having a quick pop quiz in Math."

A pop quiz on the first day of school? What madness was this?

I wasn't the only one upset, as evidenced by the chorus of collective groans. My 13 classmates and I slowly reached into our backpacks to retrieve our pencils and lined paper. As if we all had one massive ESP event, everyone was moving in slow motion trying to delay the inevitable. It didn't work. With hands on hips, Mrs. Hutchinson waited patiently. We were doomed. I aced the test anyway. I had switched gears quicker than even I thought I could.

Oh, how I long for those days!

***

The first week went as expected. The first day repeated five times, although Fridays always had a special feel. TGIF before I knew what that meant. Recess seemed better, the teachers were noticeably calmer, and the day felt much shorter. When the 3:00 bell sounded, school finally let out with an explosion of kids hitting every known exit. The older kids headed to football meetings, band, or some other high school activity. The rest of us ran for the buses or our parents' cars, knowing we'd be back by 7:00 to settle into the stadium to watch the inevitable beat-down routinely delivered to the Perryton Bearcats on any given Friday night.

Since the Jamie incident, as we called it, I waited for Mom on the west side of the main entrance. She picked me up whenever she could, but on Fridays, I had to ride the bus because Mom volunteered at our Church's weekend food truck. She and 20 other ladies spent the day spreading peanut butter and jelly and assembling baloney and cheese sandwiches. And sharing juicy tidbits of gossip about the crazy folks in town.

That day, the ride home was without incident. As should be expected. We were the third stop before school in the morning and the third stop on the way home. Usually 15 minutes in all coming and going. There's no rush hour traffic in Perryton. I sat in my usual seat in the fifth row to be exact. Susie got on just after me. She hit the bus on a dead run, her long blonde hair flying around her head in total chaos, no Jimmy in sight.

Susie smiled as she tamed her hair and started to walk toward an open seat in the fourth row. She stopped mid-descent, rose up, smiled even broader, and pirouetted into the seat next to me. I felt her heat. I hoped she couldn't feel mine. We touched hips as Vernon gunned the engine and pulled out of the school's front circle drive.

"Hi, Jacob."

"Hey, Susie." Wow, how creative. I think, when her hip touched mine, my brain went into preadolescent lock-down. It's hard enough to talk to a girl under normal, standing-in-the-hall circumstances, but when there is physical contact, game over.

"How was your first week?" she said with a smile. Ice started to melt.

"Okay, I guess." Ice melted a little more. "Kind of like last year. Same teachers, students, and lame homework." I was able to mutter double-digit words!

"I get that," she said, looking right at me, eyes sparkling Then she touched my shoulder. If the game hadn't been over before, well, that was the moment I lost my heart. I froze up like a cup of water in December. I literally did not know what to do or say. So, I did nothing. From that point, until Vernon stopped in front Susie's farm, I think I managed maybe two words. Luckily, she seemed not to notice as she bounced up from our seat, glided down the aisle, and jumped off the bus. I gathered the nerve to look out the window as she passed her mailbox, just in time to see her turn and wave at me.

(I remember that day on the bus as if it happened yesterday. It was a jolt of electricity, a zap of lightning, or whatever else you want to call it. Fact is, I knew there and then that Susie was the girl of my dreams. Funny, I was both right and wrong.)

The walk from the bus to my front porch that day was like a dream. Thankfully, there was no YouTube back then. Mom must have seen me though, because she was grinning when I reached the front porch.

"Are you feeling good this afternoon, Jake?" I wish everyone would call me Jake, but Mom was the only one.

"Not bad, Mom," I said, blushing. "How long have you been standing here?"

"Oh, just a few seconds," she lied. "How about a snack? Dad will be in shortly, and we can have dinner. We need to head to the game around 6:30."

"That works. Is Luke home? Hey, wait a minute. It's Friday. I thought you were making sandwiches?"

"We were, but we had a lot of help, so we finished early. I got home about five minutes before you did." Fate is funny.

"Will you help with dinner?"

"Sure. What are we having?"

"Chicken and dumplings. Dad's favorite. Yours too, right?"

"Yes," I said pumping my fists. Hard to think of a better feeling than the complete love of your mom. I really don't think she ever did anything that didn't have one of her kids in mind. Chicken and dumplings were my love language. One of them anyway. "Is dad home yet?"

"No, haven't seen him since lunch. I think he's out on the north end of the wheat field. He said he was heading out there to set up for soil samples."

"He'd better hurry or he'll miss the game, dinner too. More for me." Although we both knew I'd never dare eat dad's share of his favorite food. (The last thing I'd ever do was eat into dad's portion, of course.

If I did, I know I'd need to have my fast shoes on, that's for sure.)

Dad finally showed up as we were about to serve dinner. He took a quick shower and returned wearing his standard football watching clothes—his best Lee jeans, a Bearcat polo, and a matching ball cap with "1990-91 Football Booster Club" embroidered on the left side. I'd see about 50 of those that night. Make that 100.

We have pointless hats like that strewn around the house and barn, mementos of annual $100 donations to the athletic endeavors of our high school jocks by overzealous dads. "That was great, honey," Dad said, wiping his chin as he slammed his napkin onto his chair. "Let's go, or we'll be late." For the record, we'd never been late. But, when dad says go, we go. Mom and I were the first to react, Luke trailed as always. My sister Mary was nowhere to be found.

"Come on guys. Let's go, or I'll leave all stragglers!" Dad called over his shoulder as he hit the side door, one step on the porch, then the driveway. Also, for the record, he never once carried out his threats to leave us behind. We piled into dad's '85 LTD, tan with a brown landau roof. Oh, how cool that look was back then.

The 10-minute drive to the stadium was uneventful. As a family, every car trip was the same. Dad smoked—the entire time—holding the cigarette against the slightly cracked driver's side window, as if that was the cure all for the ills of second-hand smoke. Mom stared straight ahead in an eerie silence, the radio played music I hated, and of course, Luke and I tried our best to define the imaginary boundary that divided the back seat. I owned the right side behind Mom and Luke the left side. We constantly fought over the boundary, most often with our fists, and Luke won more often than not.

Mom hated our bickering but rarely intervened. I don't think dad cared either way, but it was good opportunity to drive with the left hand (holding a cigarette, mind you) and swing at us blindly with the right. Luke and I got very good at dodging dad feigned attempts. Ninety percent of the time the turf war ended after Luke got bored hitting me and resorted to the headlock. That's when Mom did intervene. Protecting her baby boy, I guess. Regardless of the drama that happened en route, we always arrived in one piece.

5

JACOB

At a quarter to seven, we pulled into the caliche-covered parking lot adjacent to the Fighting Bearcat's stadium. Dad parked the car in the usual spot, a lot like Presbyterian Church pews on Sunday, and we piled out. Luke ran immediately to his group of friends. I walked with a slight, but painful, limp to meet mine. I assume mom and dad gathered with their friends as well, but I never paid much attention honestly.

The stadium held about 250 people on the home side. Fewer for the visitors as they had the luxury of movable stands. The number of stands lined up correlated directly with how much we liked the opponent. I heard "Make me stand" was our motto. Parents sat in a bell-shaped pattern at their respective 25-yard lines. The band occupied the far-left side of the stands and the remaining spots were filled in randomly by any students who cared to show up.

Like most small-town football games, the scene was always caste-oriented. The middle schoolers roamed the "Pit," a fenced-in area off the east end zone, away from the school and locker rooms. We elementary kids either sat with our parents—how embarrassing—or roamed around under the stadium searching for dropped candy or foam hands.

That's what I did that night, all while looking longingly at the Pit. One more year and I would be there, longing to be on the field. I only remembered that night because it marked the last game before I knew—*really knew*. We lost by six touchdowns. Most people had checked out of the game by halftime. The grownups seemed to linger under the stands longer than normal, probably five minutes into the third quarter. Good for the concession business, which was in turn good for the Booster club, which I guess was good for everyone.

Except for our players.

Oh, and for my family, it turns out.

The night was also warmer and more humid than normal. The air felt weird, almost thick as it wrapped you in an uncomfortable embrace. Everyone was noticeably lethargic, even the football team. Not only was I feeling strange, there was a building soreness in my legs, and my mouth was so dry. About halfway through the third quarter, I decided I needed a Dr Pepper. Not wanted, *needed*.

"Guys, I'm dying for something to drink," I told my friends as I turned to head under the stands and up the ramp to ask my parents for money. As I bee-lined it to where they sat for every game, I caught a glimpse of my dad standing under the far end of the stands talking to Mrs. Ryan. I remember it striking me funny—my parents never socialized with the Ryans—but that lasted about one second as the mission at hand reengaged my brain.

I had almost forgotten about my dad's little conversation by the time I made it up the ramp, turned 180 degrees to the left, climbed 10 steps and landed next to my Mom.

"Hi, Jake. What's up?" Mom asked, startled. "What are you doing up here?"

"I'm thirsty, Mom. Can I have a dollar for a drink?"

"*May* I have a dollar for a drink?" Mom shot back. You can take the teacher out of the school, but…

"Okay, okay, maaaaay I have a dollar, please?"

"Well, since you asked so nicely, sure," Mom said, laughing along with her friends. She dug a wrinkled dollar out of her purse, placed it in my hand, and kissed my cheek. Money and kisses always came in pairs. I felt a little redness hit my face. I was getting too old for kisses on the cheek, but clearly, she disagreed. Deep down, I did too. I was just self-conscious in public.

As I stood up to leave, I caught a glimpse of my dad through the cracks of the bleachers.

"Mom, why is dad under the stands?" I asked. "Not sure, sweetie. Just lagging behind, I guess."

It didn't look that way to me.

"Thanks for the dollar. I think I may come back and sit with you and dad. I'm a bit tired." I left the word "achy" out on purpose.

"Sure, Jake." She looked at me as if I had asked to quit school and join the circus. "We would love to have you join us. I'm sure dad will be here when you return."

Dollar in hand, I ran to the concession stand. I passed dad on the ramp. Thinking back, I realize he looked sheepish—guilty, almost—but that day I didn't think of it. Not for two more years. That night I had cold Dr Pepper on my mind.

"Hi, Mrs. Polanski. May I have a large Dr. Pepper?" I remembered my mom's grammar lesson.

"You bet, Jacob," she said, smiling. "Ice too?"

"Yes, ma'am." I was the lone patron at the concession stand. "Tough game again," I added.

"Ninety cents, please, Mr. Ross," Mrs. Polanski said with a sparkle in her eye and that same grin. The sparkle reminded me of her daughter. "Here's a dollar. Throw the change into the booster jar." I felt very grown up.

I quickly added, "Tell Susie hi!" I immediately regretting my mouth leading my brain into action. I quickly ran up to my seat, half hoping she would heed my suggestion and half hoping she wouldn't.

But, alas, I'm sure she never said a word to Susie. She had much more pressing concerns on her mind that night. This was the last time Mrs. Polanski worked at the concession stand. In fact, it was the last Friday she ever spent in Perryton.

But that's a story for later.

6

DAVIS, 1959

I drove up to the Williamses' home, the smell of my wife's fresh-baked cherry pie filling my truck with a warm cinnamon scent. But the clothes and cans of food and the pie were a secondary reason to be at the Williamses' house that day. Mostly I just wanted to visit. The pie never made it to the table.

As I turned into the caliche driveway, I saw cars parked at all angles on the front lawn, fenced in by two Perryton police cars, red lights flashing. A wave of dread crept over me as I slammed on the brakes. Forgetting what I was carrying as I jumped out of my truck, I rounded the corner of the garage into a vision of utter chaos. I sprinted into the mass of neighbors huddled around the front porch.

"Leon! Leon? What in the world is going on?" I shouted over the expanding din of voices, frantically searching for the face of my old friend. When I caught sight of Leon, the look on his face cemented my fear. My imagination ran wild. Was Coly injured? Had one of the boys broken an arm? Had they been robbed? But, as quickly as those thoughts jumped into my head, they fled. None of these fears were serious enough to cause this much commotion. The reality was far worse.

"Davis, Lydia is missing." Leon slunk into my arms, tears streaming down his cheeks. "She's...gone. She was...out front playing and then she just...disappeared."

Leon was joined by a uniformed officer with a small notebook. "Mr. Williams, you said your son saw a car driving north right after your daughter disappeared?"

"Yes...yes, he said it was sky blue," Leon said, then gave a little half pause. "A Chevy. My boy knows his cars. He says it was shiny and nearly brand new."

"Is he sure?" I couldn't help myself. "No one around here drives a Chevy, at least not a nice one."

"I'm...I'm positive," Lee firmly added as he moved from behind his dad. "It was a light blue Chevy. Heading right there that way." Lee pointed up the road.

"Officer, how long ago did this happen?" It was all I could muster. My chest was tightening, and my fists were clinched, aching to do something, to find Lydia. The wave of dread had thickened into a paralyzing weight. I took a deep breath. I had to pull myself together. I had to find a way to help.

"Sir, the Williamses called our department about 15 minutes ago. We were here in less than five minutes."15 minutes ago. We were here in less than five minutes."

"Well, can I help? Can we go look for her, too?" I was desperate now, incapable of standing back and doing nothing. Can we go look for her, too?" I was desperate now, incapable of standing back and doing nothing.

The officer shrugged. "Be my guest. Just know, we have our full force on this case, so don't get in the way of our investigation. And the parents, they must stay here. You know, so we can communicate with them as things progress."

Leon's eyes looked desperate. I grabbed Leon's arm, knowing that, as a father, he certainly would be unable to stand there doing nothing. Ignoring the officer's request, I said, "Let's go, Leon."

The deputy shook his head sternly. "No, I said Lydia's parents need to stay here. In case they find her."

Leon gritted his teeth. "You will have to shoot me to keep me here. Are you prepared to do that, sir?"

The deputy looked at him with sad eyes and whispered, "Go. We will follow you. Make sure Lydia's mama sits tight."

Leon walked over to his wife and whispered to her quietly. She nodded, tears streaming down her cheeks.

We ran to my truck. I turned the key and started the engine. "What else did the police say?"

"There was nothing else to say, Davis," Leon said, defeated. "He only saw the fleeing car, and it may have nothing to do with us. He didn't see a sign of Lydia. It could have been a couple out for a joyride."

"That's bull and you know it, Leon," I said. We both knew better. "No one takes a joyride on this side of town. How many new Chevys drive through your neighborhood in a given month, much less a day?"

"None," Leon mumbled. He was shutting down under the pressure of the situation.

I yelled and, at the same time, punched his arm as hard as I could. "This is no time to power down, my friend. We are going to find Lydia unharmed and bring her home. I promise. You need to believe that. I need you to help me make it a fact."

Rubbing his arm, Leon straightened, and a look of resolve crossed his face. "She's...just a baby and...someone has her."

"I know, Leon, I know. She is very special to me as well. Let's make this night have a happy ending."

And, right then, I prayed in the only way I knew how. Desperately, earnestly, hopefully. Because, if anything happened to Lydia, it would wreck me. Completely and utterly wreck me. And if it would wreck me, imagine what it would do to her mama and daddy.

Leon and I sped up RR 160, followed closely by one of the Perryton police cruisers. I was stomping on the gas and straining the engine, exceeding 70 miles per hour because of a hunch. When I first heard Lydia was missing, I had asked myself why. Why would someone grab an 11-year old black girl from her front yard? Why Lydia? Why the Williamses?

And then I remembered the men in the white hoods. Twenty-five miles north of Perryton was the town of Dalton, which has always been considered the hotbed of the Kansas chapter of the Ku Klux Klan. Up until that day, I had been unaware of anyone from Dalton bothering to come to Perryton. But, for some reason that day, my gut told me that the KKK in Dalton was the source of this nightmare.

I had one shot at being correct and, as far as I could think, the Klan had the highest odds of being involved. Twenty minutes later, I slowed down and entered Dalton's city limits. My hands gripped the steering wheel so tightly that most of the blood had drained out of my fingers. I sat there, alternately shaking both hands to bring them back to life before I spoke to Leon for the first time in 15 minutes.

"Leon, put this hat on and pull it low. Slide down in the seat as well. Better if I'm the only one these fine citizens of Dalton see when they peer in our direction." I pulled a greasy, well-worn Jayhawks ball cap out from under the driver's seat and handed it across to the passenger seat.

If Perryton had the light air of welcoming acceptance, Dalton had the dank stench of xenophobia. Very few outsiders were welcome, and most locals knew to either drive around Dalton or not stop as you drove through town. Of the 900 or so people who lived with the city limits, easily 200 were active Klan members, and the rest of Dalton's citizens were scared to death of them. The sheriff, his lone deputy, the county judge, and the owner of half the town square's real estate were part of the KKK. Fear and hate ran the town.

"I heard from detective Watkins that the Sunoco station off the central square was one of the few meeting points for the local KKK activity," I explained to Leon.

"The…Klan?" His eyes widened.

"I don't want to scare you, but my gut says this is where we start. When I pull into the station, if there is anything of interest, I'll get out to investigate. You slide over to the driver's seat, so we can get away fast, but stay low. Okay?"

"You…you call the shots, my friend," Leon seemed to know he was mismatched when it came to the KKK. "I'm here to be your backup. I will be your backup. I will not fail." Leon seemed to be giving himself a pep talk.

"And here we are." I pulled into the station and screeched to a halt within 10 feet of the outside pump island. "You know what to do?"

"I sure hope so." Leon sank lower into his seat and closed his eyes, clearly in silent prayer.

JACOB

Our house was exactly the same as our neighbors', and their neighbors, and the neighbors beyond that. It was the quintessential Midwestern farmhouse, two stories and wooden, framed with white painted siding that turned grey over the years. The grey stood out against the vast green and gold fields of wheat, corn, and soy beans, just one tiny dot in the landscape across the plains.

I always wished I could fly over central Kansas and count the farmhouses that collectively acted as the nerve center for the production of the vast majority of the food the rest of America eats. I'm sure that, if I had kept tally, I would have found only two or three architectural layouts that were repeated, as if Henry Ford had had his way. Maybe he did.

All the bedrooms were upstairs. My parent's room was the hard left, Luke's and mine was the hard right and Mary's was at the top of the stairs. The bathroom between my room and Mary's was shared by all three of us kids. I'm sure Mary would have loved a bathroom of her very own. On the other side of the hallway, the master bath was entered only through my parent's bedroom. If their bedroom was generally off limits, their bathroom certainly was a no-go.

The hallway was L-shaped, connecting my parents' and Mary's rooms, as if the architect had been a huge fan of 1960s Motel 6. The railing that separated us from a 10-foot plunge onto the downstairs hardwood floor below never seemed too substantial in my daredevil eyes, but it kept me from breaking my neck several times throughout my childhood. Looks were deceiving. The railing ran the initial length of the hall until the right turn in the L, and then the hallway transitioned into a tightly-closed, wood-paneled corridor. I think mom and dad put Luke and me as far as possible from their room, allowing Mary to be the buffer between us and them. A smart move. For Luke and me, our bedroom was synonymous with punishment or sleep. Rarely did we elect to spend time there during the day. There was too much to do outside. For Mary, it was the opposite. For her, her bedroom was synonymous with sanctuary.

Downstairs were our kitchen, dining room, informal den, utility room, and small powder room as well as the waste of space known as a formal living room. An L on top of a rectangle, just like thousands of other houses scattered across the Midwest.

To me, it was just a home—a place to eat, sleep, and feel safe. In our family, a night after a Bearcats' loss was best spent in your room. Dad never got mad at much, but for some reason our high school football games set him off. He was never violent or destructive; he just yelled a lot. Mom had learned to zone it out early in their marriage. I saw her eyes roll enough to know her opinion of dad's tantrums. This is probably why I was never a big football fan, I was turned off and never fully got turned back on.

I woke up around 4:00 the morning after that six-touchdown Bearcat loss with a start. What 11-year-old wakes up at that ungodly hour? I didn't set an alarm; I just woke up. My eyes popped open as if attached to a timing mechanism buried deep inside my brain. To this day, I'm up by 4:00 every day, 4:30 at the latest. I knew immediately there was no use lying in bed, as I wasn't going back to sleep. My body—or maybe it was my brain? Or something else was taking over. I slipped out of bed, pulled on the old Bearcats sweatshirt and jeans I had dropped on my floor the night before, grabbed my well-worn Chuck Taylors, and slid out of the room. Tiptoeing down the hall was easy. The wood slatted floor was very solid. The stairs not so much, but I learned to walk along the outer edges of the planks, so the wood wouldn't give under my weight and squeak. I fancied myself the world's best cat burglar.

Down the stairs, across the entryway, through the living room, and into the kitchen. I would catch the swinging door, lead it to a resting position and call success. I was standing in the kitchen when a tangible change washed over me. It happened every morning at that point. I couldn't stop it if I tried. My emotions would switch from the artificial excitement of my cat burglar escapade to a very real, very pervasive sense of dread. This change was as visceral as a case of food poisoning. I'd almost double over as a wave of nausea would seize my stomach. It was never enough to stop me from moving forward and out the door, but always enough to question my sanity, or at least my decision-making abilities.

So, there I was, once again, standing in the middle of our kitchen, half bent over with the moonlight casting an eerie shadow across the linoleum floor, wondering why I couldn't just force my legs to walk back upstairs and hop back in bed. But I never could bring my legs to do it.

There was something in me—or outside of me—that seemed to control my every move.

Slowly, the nausea began to subside, and I straightened up and walked out the back door. The moon was waxing near full, so I could see clearly across the yard. I stood there breathing in the now cool, thick air, exhaling warm, damp breath that looked like smoke. Off I went, same as every other morning, walking up to the corn field on the back side of the drive way and turning to the left. This direction took me out to Highway 40 where I'd turn right into the field and onto the longest stretch of corn rows.

I'd like to be able to explain how I felt next, but it's hard to describe. I can say all my anxiety and the remaining nausea evaporated the instant I stepped into those rows. It was as if I was yanked out of my body, exiting with a swoosh that I could almost hear. From there, the walk was ethereal. I was straddling the feeling of an earthly stride. My feet moved robotically, one in front of the other, all the while slapping the earth. This effort was counteracted with an exercise in maintaining my balance while floating along the rows. I was caught in that thin place between here and there. Sorry, but description-wise, that's the best I can do.

Indescribable, but necessary, a part of me I could never quite escape, never quite avoid, and certainly, never quite explain. Yet, without explanation, without any real reason, I walked morning after morning, week after week, year after year.

Even as everything else changed, came crashing down on me, those walks stayed the same.

Cold, terrifying, and absolutely unstoppable.

***

The state of Kansas, located on the eastern boundary of the Great Plains, is an interesting state. Really it is. But, if you are from any state other than Kansas, you're probably questioning its impact on history. You think it's not important.

I disagree.

Kansas's early history is wrapped up in the crossroads of nomadic Native American buffalo hunters, early Spanish explorers, and French fur trappers. Kansas joined the United States in 1803 as part of the Louisiana Purchase. Some 50 years later, it became a battleground for what was the beginning of the Civil War. Kansas elected to remain a free state in the face of many of its settlers' opposing views on slavery.

See, there's some historical significance for you.

Postwar, Kansas became dotted with frontier towns and tiny Midwestern farmhouses like mine, crisscrossed with railroads that transported cattle driven in from Texas. As with any area of growth, immigrants began moving west and settled throughout the state, initiating the explosion of agricultural communities and family farms. Many originally tried raising corn, which was soon replaced with wheat due to a lack of rainfall. Even today, Kansas is about 90% agricultural, with wheat, sorghum, and corn leading the way for its cash crops. And so, my family's cornfields and wheat fields were just a few of thousands in Kansas. We had mostly wheat on the north and east fields and corn along Old US 40. Beautiful on one hand and depressing on the other.

Our farm was roughly one half a square mile. We lived on two acres that ran the length of the south side of the farmland, a nice rectangle perpendicular to the fields. In front of our house was grass, trees, and the driveway. Behind it was our garden flanked by two paths, one leading to Old Potato Creek and the other leading to the barn which sat on the very southeast corner of the wheat field overlooking the creek.

The long side of the cornfield was a little more than a mile. Took me about 40 minutes to walk that distance—at least in the early days. As I turned right onto the long run of corn, my head would clear, and the fog would lift from my insides. I then entered into a stretch of time where my thoughts were sharp and crisp, and my imagination seemly limitless. On that side of the field, I felt great. Unstoppable. I've never taken drugs, but this may be as close to that experience as I can imagine.

I also had a sensation of being pulled along the path. Almost as if I had tried to stop, I would have been dragged against my will. Except for the weather, every day was the same. Lots of mud, lots of cold, lots of sweat and rain. The moon was my only friend as it danced over the rows as if my partner at a royal gala. It never missed a walk with me, either, although it was, at times, muted behind the clouds. I always gained comfort in knowing it was there. The long tentacles of its light interrupting the shadows were a bit unsettling at first but quickly became cherished company. The only constantly changing factor was my imagination, growing ever wilder.

That was my life every day between 4:00 and 4:45 in the morning. I wandered back into the house almost immediately after reappearing on the driveway (or around 15 minutes later if I had to clean mud off my shoes or cool down from a summer sweat.) I would reverse course to my room, lie on the bed sometimes sleeping, most times not. Either way, I'd be up again at 5:30, give or take. Luke was none the wiser. Nothing disturbed that kid's sleep. A quick shower and I'd be back downstairs in the kitchen well before 6:00.

"Good morning, Jacob. You're up early." This was my dad's opening salvo most every morning. He was nursing his second cup of drip coffee by the time I arrived and halfway through the Wichita Eagle newspaper. Dad sat in the same spot at the kitchen table the entire time I lived at home. His aluminum chair was at the end of the oval wooden table closest to the kitchen door, so his back was the first thing you saw when you walked into the kitchen. Bad idea in a mafia movie, but it worked okay at home.

"Yeah, I need to do a few things before I leave for school," was my general response, which was true less often than not.

"Should have done all that over the weekend, I suppose. It would make your Monday morning easier."

"That's true, but I hate to ruin a good weekend with school work."

Dad would look up at me for the first time and slowly shake his head. I wasn't sure if he was agreeing with me or judging me. Probably a bit of both.

"Anything I can help with?" he asked. His voice was neutral, but his eyes were pleading.

With a bowl of Cheerios in hand, I sat at the table on dad's left. "No, I just have a couple of chapters in *Old Yeller* to read before English at 10:00."

That was the depth of our daily morning discourse.

But not today.

"Jacob," Dad said my name in such a way that it startled me. Both his inflection and the fact that he broke our usual pattern.

"Yeah, dad. What's up?" A hundred thoughts flew through my mind in the second it took for him to continue. None good. How could they be? My dad never talked to me over breakfast. Why now? Had to be bad news. Seeing dad talking to Mrs. Ryan under the stadium was the last tiny flicker in my brain before dad slowly set his readers on the table just to the left of the paper, picked up his half full coffee mug, took a sip, and looked directly into my eyes.

That look scared the crap out of me.

"Jacob," he said again, "is everything okay?"

"What do you mean?" So, bad news in the Ross family was not the topic. What was?

He took another sip of coffee and picked up his glasses, twisting them in a nervous manner. "Tell me why you leave the house every morning at 4:00."

I tried to look nonchalant. "There's nothing to tell, Dad," I said, hoping beyond hope that this would end the discussion, all while knowing full well there was no chance of that. I started to rise from my chair. Dad slowly lifted his hand like a traffic cop halting the crowds at a school crosswalk. It worked. I resettled into my chair, knowing escape was not an option. This conversation was only beginning.

A non-standard conversation was out of character for my dad. The last thing I wanted to do was talk to him about my morning adventures. How could I? I wasn't even sure what they were all about or why I felt trapped in this strange routine. How can I explain my daily event to anyone when I hadn't sorted it out for myself?

"Jacob Thomas." Dad threw out my middle name. He was serious. His eyes were squinting, and his glasses were still twirling. "You know as well as I do that's not true."

And I did know.

But that didn't mean I was going to tell him a darned thing.

8

JACOB

"Tell me, please, Jacob. No judgment, I promise." He paused. "I just want to understand what's going on and why." The concern on his face and in his eyes ratcheted up a bit. "Dad, I don't know. Really. I honestly have no idea. I know I get up early and walk the length of the corn field, but exactly why I do it, or why I can't seem to stop myself from doing it, is a mystery to me." I didn't mention my aching knees.

The look on my dad's face was one of extreme doubt. I know he thought I was dodging his concern. And maybe I was. Maybe I just needed to talk to someone about what was going on and that simple act would provide some level of clarity. But I just couldn't. Not with my dad. Never in my life did I think it would be him.

"Look, Jacob, I'm not buying that story. If you don't want to tell me, then fine. I've got chores to do anyway." With that, he set his palms on the table, slowly rose, and walked out of the kitchen. Did

I really see concern on his face? Did he truly care for a moment or two, or did I dream what I wanted to dream? I've asked myself those questions for almost 25 years, and I honestly don't know the answers. I will say, however, that to this day, I wish I had spilled it all out on the table that morning.

Maybe he would have understood. And maybe, in turn, I would have understood better. Who knows, maybe he would have had an answer, or at least moved me closer to one. I think it hurt him that I was not willing to open up to him in a rare moment of vulnerability.

It still pains me to know it was a moment I would never see again.

I sat there for quite a while replaying that back and forth with my dad. I ate breakfast. Cheerios with a thick layer of sugar. Pulled all my stuff together for school and sat in the living room reading my English homework. I left the house as if in a trance. I didn't stop thinking of it until I hopped on the bus, and my mind switched to hoping to see Susie and not her brother.

But, that day, even that went wrong.

It was Jimmy who hopped on that bus. Alone.

DAVIS, 1959

Sydney Allen Trisker was a third-generation Daltonite and a second-generation member of the KKK. He was the only son of Cyril Trisker, the reigning Grand Dragon of the Kansas chapter of the KKK. If Cyril was mean, Sydney was meaner. If Cyril was dumb, Sydney was dumber—by a mile. Since he was young, people had called him S.A.T. after the exam everyone knew he'd probably never take (and certainly never obtain a passing score). The fact that his nickname was also his initials was too much for most of our town to comprehend, much less figure out.

Sydney hated this nickname with a venomous passion. He had beaten several classmates to a bloody ending after overhearing them use this moniker. He had a reputation that expanded for miles. All the way to Perryton.

I had certainly heard stories of him.

And stories of his dad.

Neither S.A.T., nor his dad, were particularly tall or muscular, but both were sinewy and as mean as a beaten-too-often cur. They resembled each other—both with dark, stringy hair and small ears that stuck straight out, the left more than the right. Both had small, beady, murine-like eyes. The biggest difference in the two was S.A.T.'s smattering of swastika-themed tattoos on his arms and chest, along with a dozen or so cigarette burns on his back. Neither Trisker was a pretty picture by any stretch of the imagination. Their other common trait was a general dislike for their fellow man, in addition to a substandard IQ mixed vigorously with a lack of self-esteem, all of which resulted in a deep-in-your-bones hatred toward pretty much everyone.

Everyone knew S.A.T. energetically embraced his family's approach to life early on. As a child, stories go that say he victimized the unfortunate stray dog or cat, then moved to victimizing his fellow classmates, followed by his fellow high school dropouts (none of which, like S.A.T., ever attempted to sit for the actual SAT) and then finally graduated to victimizing his fellow KKK chapter members. None of this was a surprise to anyone, just a way of life for a Trisker.

The fact was that Cyril had victimized S.A.T. since he was a small boy. Even called him S.A.T. behind his back. Many people wished that just one-time S.A.T. would overhear his dad. That was a fight everyone wanted to see.

Cyril had bred the perfect Klan member.

The problem was that S.A.T. was never quite up to the task.

I'm not sure why S.A.T. chose Lydia.

Perhaps he felt like he had found the coup-de-gras when Beater Smith told him about the black kids that ran unsupervised up and down the street in the poor section of Perryton. Perhaps in his warped and twisted mind, this spelled a home run, a way to impress his father. Whatever their reasoning, their motivation, S.A.T. and Beater (don't ask how he got that nickname, but it wasn't from fighting) devised a plan to grab one of these kids to use as entertainment at the next Klan rally.

I'm sure they had planned their scheme (with the meticulousness of a two-year-old). After finishing off a fifth of Hiram Walker whiskey they sped south toward Perryton. Adding drunk to dumb is never a good amendment to any plan, but it fit the nicknames. And so, when Lydia skipped her rope across the street just as they crossed into the Perryton city limits, they pounced.

I'm sure they had no idea who she was, and I'm sure it didn't matter either. She was a child, she was black, she was who they needed. A boy would have sufficed, but a girl was even better.

What happened next has been part of local legend for years now. With unexpected skill, Beater slowed down in front of the Williamses' house, S.A.T. jumped out just as Lydia skipped over that pink rope and snatched her by the arm. While Beater was whipping an impressive U-turn, S.A.T. jerked Lydia into the air, stumbled two steps to his left, and fell into the car, dragging his right foot and both of Lydia's knees along the road.

With his left hand on the steering wheel, Beater grabbed S.A.T.'s t-shirt and pulled the two of them into the car. The door slammed as he hit the accelerator. A well-designed stunt team couldn't have choreographed an action scene any better. Blind drunk luck prevailed to Lydia's detriment.

I imagine they sat there for a few moments, unable to believe their luck. Beater hit 80 and left only a trail of dust behind him. The very same trail of dust Lee saw as he was frantically looking for his sister.

What happened next still makes me ill.

They crushed her down in the front seat.

Then they stopped the car and threw her in the trunk.

S.A.T. grabbed an oily rag from the floorboard and violently stuffed it into her mouth.

And so, she sat in that trunk, in the fetal position, blood seeping from the newly formed cuts to her lips.

She recalled S.A.T.'s harsh words. "Haul ass to the Sunoco!"

She remembered wondering why they would take her to Sunoco. Why they would take her at all.

She also remembers hearing a heated argument from the trunk.

"You fucking did what?" The voice said it over and over, amping up each time. "You dumb shit. How could you kidnap some coon's daughter and not expect trouble to follow? Where is she?"

"In—in the trunk."

Lydia later told me that was the moment when her fear reached its peak, footsteps echoing up in her head as they approached the car.

The trunk opened.

The words being shouted became clearer. "But, Dad, I thought it would be a fun side distraction at tonight's meeting."

"Distraction? What would we need a distraction for? That's the opposite of what we need tonight. Or any night. This is a serious business. S.A.T., get your ass out of here right now and take her back to where you found her. Dump her on the side of the road and get back here immediately. Take that shithead Beater with you."

Lydia remembers bile rising in her throat. Dump her on the side of the road? Would she be able to find her way home?

"Fine!" S.A.T. slammed the trunk shut and started toward the car.

The sound of his footsteps was cut off by the screech of eight tires breaking hard. What Lydia didn't hear or see was her father and me jumping out of the car to be greeted by a swaggering Cyril. A well-practiced look of pacification washed across his face as he emerged from the shadows onto the driveway. He leaned slowly against the full-service pump and turned to the 1955 Chevy 3100 that had just pulled in. "What's the hurry, guys? Can I help you?"

10

JACOB

Kansas designated Harney Silt Loam as the official state soil because it was an ideal prairie soil and recognized as prime farmland. The name "Harney" (which means "people") is a derivative of the Wichita Indian word for Pawnee Indian (Harahey) and originated from the explorer Coronado's journey through Kansas. Why have an official state soil? We Kansans recognize that soil is our life blood.

For years, farmers in central and south-central Kansas have battled low soil Ph. Because well-drained soils usually become acidic over time, farmers constantly battle to make sure their fields are well-drained. Sandy soil is generally more susceptible to acidity and is harmed by the application of high rates of nitrogen-based fertilizer, so farmers often add lime to the soil to raise the pH. Of course, this is expensive.

There is an easier solution: rotating wheat, corn, sorghum, or even sunflowers, without soy beans in the rotation, allows farmers to use a smaller dosage of lime as those crops can tolerate a bit lower pH level.

My dad taught me all this, and my most pervasive thought topic during my morning walks was my dad's agronomy lessons. Maybe it was the feel of the soil under my feet, the dirt becoming a trigger for these memories. Either way, I'm not sure if this is a good thing. The memories of one's father should be comforting, bringing a smile to your face. Thoughts, ideas, and examples of how to deal with life. Something tangible to grab hold of in trying times.

My memories are about dirt.

I woke up earlier than normal on a Friday in late September. Thanks to my internal clock, I immediately sensed it was not the usual time. I laid in my bed for a few minutes before I convinced myself that falling back asleep was not an option. I swung my feet out of bed and gathered up and slid on my clothes. I glanced at my brother and heard nothing but rhythmic breathing as I stepped out of my room and quietly pulled the door closed, holding the handle down so the latch didn't pop back into place. It's amazing how loud that metal on metal sound is on a dead quiet morning.

"What are you doing?"

I jumped. Mary was standing in the hallway.

"Just heading downstairs," I weakly replied.

"It's a bit early for your walk, isn't it?"

I was stunned to silence. First Dad, now Mary.

How did she know about my walks?

I stood there dumbfounded. A slow grin spread across her face.

"What? You didn't think I knew about you sneaking out of the house every morning?"

"But…how?"

"I caught you sneaking out about a week ago. I was in the bathroom and had just turned off the light when your bedroom door creaked open and out you popped. I took a step back into the bathroom as you walked by. I waited a few seconds, followed you down the stairs, and watched you from the kitchen window."

I stood there speechless.

She looked at me, head cocked to the side, hands on her hips, as if to say, "Spit it out."

"Look, Mary, I need to go, but I'll explain later. I promise." Maybe she would let it drop. Explaining something I didn't yet understand seemed like a waste of time.

"Sure, okay. But I will not forget. I want to understand." Worry crept into her eyes.

It made sense. What young boy wakes up before sunrise to walk the fields?

"Thanks, Mary," I said, as I turned and walked down the stairs. My relationship with Mary had just changed forever. But, at that moment, I wasn't sure if it was for the better or worse. But that day she changed from a relatively dismissed person who happened to live in my house to someone who would ultimately help me. Save me, even.

It was not the last time she would step up either.

I felt better than I had in weeks as I bounded out the back door, with a spring in my step. Maybe it was the fact that the weight of my secret had been taken off my shoulders? I hung a left and walked at a brisk pace to the end of the driveway, feeling happier than I had in months.

The moon shone bright, straight in front of me. The dirt path was illuminated by glowing shafts of light that snuck past the corn stalks and leaves. As soon as I entered the corn rows, my mind began to tingle and all my thoughts were crisp, flying through my mind at an ever-accelerating pace. My knees felt strong. The usual humming in my joints had abated. I imagined the Flash was back and gliding down the rows. My thoughts wavered between memories and prophetic images of the future.

As the pace of my thoughts accelerated, they went from clear to muddled. When I reached the end of the row, I slowed to a stop and bent down on one knee with my hands pressing against my ears. I needed to slow everything down—my stride, my anxiety, and the jolts through my brain. How do I make sense of my thoughts when they were so tangled and foggy? I'm not sure how long I was idled. I realized I was on both knees sweating profusely.

For the first time in my life, I prayed for understanding.

I prayed for sanity, or at least a halt to my slide toward insanity.

Mostly I prayed for help.

I had never turned to God for anything before, and that fact scared me as well. But, that morning, it was if I had no choice, no other place to turn.

What a mess.

I stood slowly, almost falling as my legs wobbled. The pulsating pain was fully back in my knees, worse than ever before. I turned and deliberately forced my feet toward the house. As I walked toward our farmhouse, the whirring in my brain seemed to waft away in the morning breeze, my mind solely focused on the trek home. By the time I stepped onto the back porch steps, I was limping worse than ever. I reached the back door and checked my reflection in the window. Wide-eyed with dirty shoes, wet hair, and scratches on my arms from the corn leaves, and in serious pain. As I reached for the doorknob, it flew open on its own. Well, not on its own. There stood Mary. And she was ticked.

"Jacob, what is going on? You look deathly ill. You will not walk past me until you tell me exactly what is going on."

I tried to push past her. She blocked me. "No, Jacob." She unleashed a stream of questions at me. I just stared at her, confused. She gave up. On the questions that is, not on me. "Go upstairs and take a shower," she said. "Dad's at the barn, so it will be better if you are upstairs when he gets back instead of standing here in the kitchen looking like a ghost. Geesh, you really look like shit."

It's funny, of all the questions and comments she spewed that morning, the word "shit" startled me the most. I guess I knew deep down all the other facts were just that, facts. Hearing my 12-year-old sister cuss broke the tension and made me laugh. First on the inside, then audibly. I felt a clean release as I walked up the stairs.

The shower was exactly what I needed. Purging the outside as well as the inside. Often, I couldn't remember a lot about my walks, almost as if they'd been a dream. But, that morning, my walk seemed clearer, sharper. I had no erosion of recall, no colors fading to grey, just a crystal-clear vision. My physical discomfort stood out the most. As I showered, I wondered why my knees had been devoid of pain for the first time in months, only to reverse course and become worse than ever. Pain that sent me to my knees in prayer, pain only exceeded by the turbulence in my head.

I poured shampoo in my hand and vowed to sort it all out later. The humming started off softly in the background, but within a few seconds it started building in my knees as if the vibrating feeling was trying to dominate all else. As vibrations built, the pressure built, then slowly expanded like fluid under heat. My knees began to vibrate.

For a few wonderful moments, I could literally shake my legs and the pain would magically disappear, then come crashing back.

That morning in the shower, I felt a sudden need to tell someone. Not about the walks, but about the pain. It was getting worse— more frequent, more severe.

I dressed for school as Luke was waking up. I glared at him across the room. Life was simple for him. Not caring if I woke him, half-hoping I would, I slammed the door on my way out.

I met Mary at the top of the stairs. I had no words, so I hugged her. I think that shocked her more than anything else that had happened.

"We'll talk tonight, Jacob."

"Okay."

She smiled a half smile, and we silently went about our days.

The day felt lighter, easier, knowing my burden would lift that evening. I couldn't wait to tell Mary everything.

11

JACOB

Friday was another standard day in elementary education.

(And in case you're feeling like it's getting redundant me saying that, let me remind you that I lived it. Day after standard day.) I swear I could have learned more in one hour of studying on my own than I did under the Kansas school system's curriculum. Teaching to the lowest common denominator deflated my momentum. It created tedium and boredom and what I now consider a form of pure torture.

Friday was also another standard day in that our beloved Bearcats got their heads handed to them in a one-sided game of football leaving Dad pissed the whole night. I spent the night in my room. Luke and I played blackjack for matchsticks. I fell to the same fate as the Bearcats.

Luke could light up the entire town with all the matchsticks he won.

But it didn't matter, we had fun. Even under the weight of the Bearcat loss, we laughed a lot as we snuck food out of the kitchen acting like ninjas trying to escape discovery by the evil overlord in the next room. We acted like friends. I really, really miss that. Friendship with Luke became far and few between after that evening.

Saturday started early. I was sitting in the kitchen devouring a bowl of sugar-laced Cheerios and a glass of orange juice when my dad walked into the kitchen. The temperature and tension notched up a bit. Okay, a lot.

"Morning, Jacob."

"Morning, Dad. What's going on today?" I replied, not knowing what to say.

"Same as always. I need to collect soil samples and prep the for the wheat planting, but first I have to fix Old Greenie. She's acting up again."

Old Greenie was our 1978 John Deere tractor. The tip of the spear in farm management. If your tractor breaks down, your farm operation breaks down. Not a good thing. No wonder Dad had been in such a foul mood the night before.

"I'll help, Dad. I hate to see Greenie not running right."

"I'd like that, Jacob. Thank you."

We spent most of the day working together. We never said much to each other, but that felt right. As the day warmed up, most of the ice between us also thawed. I truly enjoyed the day working with my dad. He was intuitive when it came to farming; he seemed to know the art side of the farm without a lot of effort. How much fertilizer and when? Chemical treatments? All balanced with the amount of rainfall. Fixing a tractor has a repair manual. Intuition doesn't. And the more I worked beside him, the more my respect for him grew.

He was also dogged in the maintenance of the farm and its equipment. We had Greenie running by lunch. Turned out she needed a new fuel line as the old one was partially clogged at one end and had a tiny pinhole on the other. How does that even happen, I wondered? And then I realized I probably shouldn't be asking questions about why things happen. Not with my morning habits, the humming in my knees.

Mom brought us lunch in the barn and we ate sitting on a few hay bales. Tuna salad sandwiches, Fritos, and Gatorade. To an 11-year-old, lunch on the hay bales was pretty awesome—beat any five-star restaurant I could imagine. Dad never spent more than 15 minutes eating, well, maybe 20 for Thanksgiving dinner, so we were up and at it shortly thereafter.

After our quick lunch, we headed out to the fields to take soil samples. This is a once every three years event that takes a few days to complete. We numbered the fields in a grid fashion on a Soil Map with each square being roughly 20 acres depending on the geography. We would then collect samples in a random zig-zag fashion while walking out and back on the grid. We took dozens of samples so one tainted sample wouldn't impact the test. I remember it being about 25 per grid square, or 400 to 450 total samples taken when the task was complete. The containers, which looked like the small, grey plastic canisters with black tops that 35mm film once came in. (Back when people actually bought film.) The caps had a number that corresponded with the numbered grid. We'd scrape off crop residue before sampling and push the soil probe about six inches into the soil. Not a small job, as you can imagine, but one I didn't mind as I did it with my father.

Strangely, walking those same fields in the light of the day, side-by-side with my father felt entirely different from my morning walks. It was as if I was in a completely different place, a completely different farm. While my pre-dawn walks were hazy and humming, these walks with my dad were steady and strangely satisfying.

At the end of the job, we had four or five boxes full of ordered soil samples. Dad stacked boxes in the bed of the pick-up and that was the last I ever saw of them. I assume all was well with each and every one of those samples, because we kept on farming. Same as every year. I am sure the results augmented my dad's intuition, or vice versa, but I never asked. To me, once the job was done, it was over.

We completed two grids, and then a few more minor chores, before we headed to the house for dinner. I loved it. I felt a huge sense of accomplishment. I also felt tired. My knees were singing. A limp had worked its way into my gate by late afternoon. I tried my best to hide it. I also felt comforted by a hard workday alongside my dad. A son should always feel rewarded when he spends time with his dad. I know I did, at least at this point in my life.

"Jacob, thanks for your help today," Dad said with a pat on the back as we stepped onto the front porch. The day was quality time for him, bonding time, which is kind of sad when you think about it. But for me it was a treasure of a day, aching knees and all.

12

DAVIS, 1959

I leapt out of my truck just as Winston McCall, Perryton's three-time elected sheriff, and his deputy pulled up behind me in their black and white Dodge cruiser. I furiously ran toward Cyril, stopping within two inches of him, planning to use my size to intimidate. It didn't work. Cyril had spent three years in state prison so he wasn't easily intimidated. I was a good 5 inches taller and 70 pounds heavier, but Cyril held his ground and his innocent grin.

"A young child was taken from Perryton about an hour ago," I said. "You guys know anything about it?"

"Not a thing." Cyril twisted his lips into a sneer.

"They were headed this way," I said.

"So? Who fucking cares? What does that have to do with me?" Cyril said.

"I happen to care," I spewed back.

"So? You're just some washed-up jock. We don't know nothin' about any kid missing from your piece of crap town." Cyril said. "You best be heading out of here. Accusations like that will get you a night in our fine jailing facilities."

A flicker of guilt in his eyes told me they were involved. When his eyes darted to the left, I noticed the sky blue '56 Chevy parked in the shadows of the Sunoco's far garage bay.

"What the hell? There's the car!" I said, sprinting toward the Chevy. "That's the car Lee saw!"

Sheriff McCall pushed Cyril out of the way, He stumbled to gain his footing, guilt all over his face. The next 60 seconds felt like an hour as the Sheriff and I raced toward the car. Cyril stood there in disbelief.

A hundred thoughts exploded in my mind. Like: "How many of the Klan members are packing?" With each stride, I was sure death was writing up my exit papers. But, to my surprise, four of Cyril's so-called friends turned and bolted out the garage's back door, slamming it behind them.

My odds quickly improved.

Winston and his deputy fanned out with guns drawn and at their sides. Within three strides of the car, I heard two sounds that scared me to death.

The first was the whimpering cry of a young child.

The second was the metallic sound of a live round being loaded into the chamber of a fire arm. In a split second, I decided to deal with the latter. I swiveled left in time to see S.A.T. six feet from me, in all his crazed glory, level a 45-caliber Colt revolver directly at my face. I swear to this day that the devil was looking at me through ugly, scarlet eyes. S.A.T. grimaced and extended his swastika-laden forearms, but he was a bit slow. Just before he could pull the trigger, I pressed hard with my trigger finger to fire off four rounds from my semi-auto 38 Ruger.

I was a good shot. All my days in the military.

Two hit S.A.T. in the forehead and one in the neck. The fourth was a center shot on an old Pennzoil sign which was just now repainted with S.A.T.'s brain matter. Life left S.A.T. well before he collapsed into an expanding pool of his own blood.

"Sydney, my boy! You shot my boy!" Cyril wailed about the son that, not two minutes earlier, he was going to beat to a pulp. He moved toward me, gun drawn. He pulled the trigger.

Three additional shots rang out simultaneous to Cyril's lone round, and the moment was over. Cyril's shot ricocheted off my left shoulder. Damn, that stung. The subsequent two shots were from different directions and both ended their journeys firmly embedded in Cyril's skull. Winston stood with his arm still extended. Wide-eyed with dropped jaw, he was noticeably shaking.

It's rare to shoot another human being, even a vile one, and not have it bother you. That is, if you are a compassionate person, which Winston was. The other bullet originated from the gun held at arm's length by Leon Williams. He was not shaking. If shooting Cyril ever bothered him, he never let on. Saving your daughter's life trumps everything.

I turned to Beater, the brave Klan member with urine-soaked pants. "Give me the damn car keys. *Now.*" Beater complied at light speed, highly motivated by my pistol pointing squarely at his face. He tossed the keys to me just as Leon ran up to the Chevy.

"Lydia baby!" Leon cried. "Are you in there? Are you okay?" Tears were streaming from his face. All we heard was a muffled voice, but I popped the trunk, and Lydia's eyes met Leon's. He gently pulled the tape from his daughter's face and the filthy rag from her mouth. She gasped for fresh air. Their simultaneous cries were like the sounds of angels.

I stepped back from the car and leaned against the wall to catch my breath just in time to hear Beater say, "stupid niggers."

I snapped. I spun around and slammed Beater square in the jaw. My hand was sore for a week; his jaw was wired shut for three months. I wish it had been three years.

The other three Klan members were frozen in place. Like Beater, one had urine stains down the front of his pants.

"What the hell is going on here?" Sheriff Malcolm Wilson yelled as he was stepped out of his squad car. Winston, having regained his wits, walked over to Malcolm and put his arm around his fleshy shoulders.

The two sheriffs knew each other professionally.

They hated each other personally.

Winston leaned over and sternly whispered into Malcolm's ear for a good two minutes. His hand continuing to clamp down ever harder as he spoke. He finally released him and walked away.

Malcolm gathered himself and cleared his throat and called for the local county coroner. His buddies scattered.

The Trisker bodies were left to lay on the Sunoco garage floor for 30 minutes before they were taken away. There was no need for a crime scene investigation. The eight living Klan members, who fled the scene at different times, were never charged. Small town justice decided two dead Triskers was enough to settle the score.

***

I drove Lydia and Leon home. They held each other tight, both alternating between crying, trembling, and laughing. I remained silent the entire drive home. It was their moment, not mine. I did wipe away a few tears. I walked Leon and Lydia halfway up their drive before they were joyously spirited away by the entire Williams family.

And then I turned to go.

I was just grateful that the Lord had put me in the right place at the right time. All I wanted out of life was to serve God and others, and today I had done that.

At that moment, Lydia smiled and waved goodbye over her dad's shoulder. I didn't wave back, just continued to my truck, climbed into the front seat, and settled behind the wheel. And started to cry.

When I got home, I was greeted by my family like any other day. My kids gave me a quick hug, my wife smiled and asked how my day was. Everything was…normal. Without a word, I headed to the bathroom where I sat on the toilet and cried for half an hour.

These tears were not for Lydia.

I had cried those tears in the truck. These tears were for myself. The day's shock had already worn off, and I was left thinking of all the pain and evil in our world. Winston and I rarely ever mentioned our time together in Dalton. And Lydia seemed back to her normal self within a few weeks. At least outwardly. She never played alone in the front yard again. All the members of the Williams family saw to that. The events of the *Davis Raid* never vanished fully, but they became almost like a dream—a nightmare—to her.

She lived with nightmares the rest of her life. The worst part of her dreams were the hidden events she had never shared with a soul. On those nights, she woke up in a cold sweat.

Lydia only revealed these events to two people during her lifetime. Once after she had been married for a few years. It's hard to hide secrets from the man sleeping next to you.

The other came later during a time of crisis.

13

JACOB

The smell of Mom's fried chicken enveloped me as I walked in the back door. I ran up the stairs, took the fastest shower of my life, and was sitting at the table in less than 10 minutes. I beat my dad, but not by much. Luke was helping Mom with the final touches of our special dinner and plopped down in his usual spot. Mary was nowhere to be found. Mom and dad had long ago given up hope of her being a regular participant in the family, particularly dinners, so no one expected to see her. She often snuck down after we ate and filled up a plate of leftovers from the fridge. Even with Mary missing, the world was in balance. Mom's fried chicken had a way of doing that.

"Where were you all day?" I asked Luke in a not-so-kind voice that clearly indicated I worked my tail off and he did not. He heard me loud and clear.

"Football practice at school all morning," he snorted as he reached across the table for the pitcher of tea.

"So, when did you start practicing on Saturdays?" I said. "You're on the 8th grade team. That's not even real football."

"Shut up, Jacob. You wouldn't know football if it bit your ass." His quick glance at Mom showed a look of regret. Probably not for what he said to me, but the fact that Mom rebuked him. (I think Dad liked his fight, but that was to be expected.)

"It is the first step to the varsity team, Jacob. Luke has four years of high-level football in his future," Dad said with an air of transferred superiority.

"Big deal." It was the best I could come up with on such short notice. "Besides, based on what I've seen, it's anything but high-level."

"That's going to change," Dad trumpeted. "You wait and see. The middle school team is loaded, and Luke is leading the way."

My day with my dad was fading into the past. He was visibly excited with the prospects of his number one son being the star football player. All else paled. "He'll set the table for you. You guys will be teammates during your sophomore year."

"Who cares? I'm never going to play a down of football and don't really want to. You sucked the life out of that years ago." I didn't actually say that out loud, but sure wanted to. No guts, no glory.

Dinner was great, and the conversation was civil, which was surprising based on the preamble. I darted immediately to my bedroom. It was definitely Luke's turn to do the dishes.

I forgot to say goodnight to Dad and Luke. Halfway up the stairs I ran into Mary as she was descending into the kitchen. She had that look on her face of a prisoner heading to their execution. Well, maybe not that dire, but close.

"Jacob, is dinner over?"

"Yeah. It was great. You should have some."

"I will, I guess. Time to run the gauntlet," she said half joking. "Hey, Jake, let's get together after church tomorrow."

"I'd like that, Mary. Are you going to church with us?"

She smiled slowly and turned away. I knew what that meant.

Long after Luke was snoring, I stayed awake thinking about tomorrow's visit. What would I say to Mary? Should I take the lead and just spill the beans or let her lead with questions? I didn't realize it initially, but I was rubbing my knees, making them red and chaffed. Bad sign. When I sleep at night I need a pillow under my knees. It's all that keeps me from a painful morning, both in my legs and in my lower back. There I was, an 11-year-old boy, and feeling like I was 60. Strange. Scary.

It was almost ridiculous that I couldn't sleep without a prop. (Interestingly, I sleep better now in my 30s than I did then. Thank God. Things like that don't normally get better.)

But, that night, it wasn't the knees that kept me awake, but my racing thoughts. Because, tomorrow, everything would change.

Because I was going to tell Mary.

14

JACOB

"Let's go, guys. Pastor Thompson is not going to wait on the Ross family!" The fog of sleep slowly faded, and I realized it was time to get up.

"It's 8:30. Church starts in an hour." As soon as I heard Dad's last comment, I realized I was still in bed and had not woken up all night. How could that be? I had awakened at 4:00 in the morning every day for weeks now, instinctually, unavoidably. Why not that day?

My next thought was just as hopeful: Maybe if there was nothing left to explain, then I didn't have to have that little talk with Mary.

Tossing back the covers, I swung my legs out and sat on the edge of the bed. I was too stunned to move. I just sat there, watching in a daze, as Luke rolled out of his bed, dressed, mumbled a few unintelligible comments as he lumbered out of the room. My feeling of hopeful elation was mixed with disbelief.

Then I started to doubt. My legs felt better on my previous walk, at least for a while, but that walk did not end well. This had to be one of those things that was too good to last. Even so, I was awash with hope.

"Come on, Jacob, we're leaving in five minutes!"

"Okay!" I responded, hopefully loud enough to be heard.

I jumped out of bed, taking care to notice every muscle, every twinge, every movement of my legs. Man, I did feel good. Dressing quickly, I bounded down the stairs. So far, so good.

We, of course, were in our self-assigned pews at the First Presbyterian Church of Perryton prior to the opening hymn.

***

My expectation of normality was quickly shattered. We were home from church by noon and at the lunch table by 1:00. (How was Mom able to make a fantastic lunch of pot roast, veggies and my all-time favorite, mashed potatoes, even when we were at church all morning? To this day, it's all I can do to make myself a grilled cheese sandwich in the hour after I get home.)

The conversation was fun—the way Sunday dinner with the family should be. It was my turn to clean the dishes and, for once, I was happy to do them. I still felt great, my knees were almost tingling with the sensation of wellness, and my stomach was comfortably full. But, by two o'clock, a deep-seeded fear began to shove my hopes aside.

More than shove, actually.

It was closer to a beat-down with a bloody stick. It was as if an imaginary switch was flipped and my knees begun to hum like a florescent light. Only this time, it was a painful, wretched hum. I was standing alone in the kitchen and I swear I could see my legs vibrate. The feeling that came over me was horrific. I was tearing up. Not in pain, not yet at least, but in realization. A realization that the morning had been an anomaly.

And the last few months had not.

The pain came later. The hum very quickly accelerated to acute pressure at the core of my bones. The pressure then built to a point where I was physically on my knees and, with the palms of my hands flat on the floor, trying to keep from splaying in front of the sink. Sweat broke out on my forehead and back, spreading quickly to most parts of my body. My teeth began chattering. The doctor would later say I had a vicious (he really used that word) onset of the flu. I knew better. Even then, I knew it was no flu.

Time seemed to move in slow motion. I don't fully remember the events of that afternoon, but the haze was lifted and I saw both my parents standing over me. They had heard a plate shatter on the floor. I didn't hear a thing. Dad was trying to help me to my feet, and Mom was crying.

"Jacob! Jacob! What happened?" My dad tried to pull me up to a sitting position.

"No, Dad, no. I can't sit now. My knees, my legs really hurt." My parents told me what I said later. I do not have any memory of the conversation.

"Susan, call Dr. Morton. Get him over here. Now!" Dad barked. He may have been tough on me, but the tremor in his voice told me he really did love me.

My next memory was lying flat on my back in Room 301 of the

Russell County Hospital. Mom was still crying. Dad's face was still twisted in misunderstanding.

And I knew by the look on his face that he was asking, *"Does this have anything to do your morning walks?"*

Of course, he already knew it did.

15

JACOB

The Mercers' farm sat empty for more than two years. For a good reason, too.

No one wanted to live in it after what old man Mercer had done.

The Mercers were one of those families that went back four generations in Perryton. Always farmers, always farming the same 350 acres known conveniently as *The Mercer Place*. Nathan Mercer moved to Russell County in the late 1800s from the northeast. I can't remember which state, although I'd guess Massachusetts from disparate conversations I'd overheard now and again. Nathan and Norma had three children. The oldest son, Jackson, stayed on the farm his entire life. Their daughter died at an early age, and the youngest son moved back east. Jackson begat John and John begat Wilson. Wilson is the Mercer who was farming the land just across the creek and north up the hill when we moved into our place.

To my recollection, I first met Mr. Mercer in town at Thompson's Seed and Hardware store. He sure seemed old then. But he was nice enough. He bought me a Gilliam's Old-Fashioned Candy Stick that Mr. Thompson kept in the display jars next to the front cash register. Root Beer flavor, my favorite. I never set eyes on his wife, something I am still thankful for.

As the story goes, Norma Mercer fell hard into Alzheimer's back in 1983. It hit old Mr. Mercer like a runaway freight train. He refused to let anyone take care of his wife and managed all her care by himself. How he managed, I'll never know, considering the fact that he also had to oversee his wheat farm. He quit socializing and was rarely seen around town.

By 1985, Mrs. Mercer was really bad off. Her Alzheimer's had progressed into its latest stages, and her related physical deterioration had rendered her virtually inanimate. To make matters worse, Mr. Mercer began showing signs of the same disease. Maybe it was just the strain of caring for his wife, maybe it was a strange coincidence, but either way, his mental acuity was clearly worsening. Only his disease seemed to be advancing at a much slower pace. Such a pace, in fact, that he had plenty of time to plan out his endgame. He wasn't about to follow his wife down the same path.

The farm began to show serious signs of decay. How could it not? When 1987 rolled around, Old Mr. Mercer was struggling mightily. Of course, no one knows what really happened, but most of the story was based on what the police could piece together. That and some good old-fashioned small-town gossip.

The story goes that Mr. Mercer, in what was probably one of his final lucid moments, just said, *"enough is enough."* He then dressed his beloved wife in her Sunday finest and propped her up at the kitchen table. She had no idea what he was doing, of course. He, too, was dressed in his church clothes. This all made sense based on their faithful 50-year membership to the First Saints Lutheran Church of Perryton. What didn't make sense was what he was about to do as his last living statement.

Mr. Mercer loaded his father's very rare Browning BSL side-by-side 12-gauge shotgun and stood behind his wife's chair. He then placed the end of the barrel at the nape of Norma's neck and pulled the trigger. I assume he couldn't bear to face her? When that little job had been successfully accomplished, he proceeded to perform the time-tested exit plan of the gun barrel in the mouth. The police found two not so cleanly decapitated bodies. Hers was face down on the table and his was on its back on top of the chair, which must have flipped backwards upon discharge. (The story goes that they never recovered all the pieces of their heads which were strewn in two nice geometric patterns across the linen tablecloth, onto the fleur-de-lea wall paper, and up to the ceiling. A nightmare for the low man on the CSI totem pole, I'm sure—a piece of town gossip that was repeated year after year on Halloween by school children for decades.)

The Mercers were buried in the county cemetery with only a few good Lutherans and Mr. Thompson in attendance. Murder and suicide tends to keep the crowds down. It was a very sad ending to a longtime Perryton family line. No one ever heard if anyone claimed the remainder of their estate. No one dared enter the house for years. No looters went through Mrs. Mercer's jewelry box or stole Mr. Mercer's old black-and-white TV. The house just sat abandoned.

Finally, in early 1989, the place sold. Created quite a buzz in town too. The Ray family moved to Perryton from Wichita and into the farmhouse in the summer. They owned the property for six months prior to occupying the house, but that time was wisely spent cleaning, painting, and performing a myriad of very needed repairs. The farmland was also cut, plowed under, and prepped for the winter wheat season. The only time I ever heard Mr. Ray mention the purchase, his response to an inquiry was, "I don't believe in ghosts or jinxes, but I do believe in a good deal."

And that farm was a good deal.

The Rays were good people too. They were the first black farmers anyone could remember in the entire county. This probably mattered to a few Perrytonites, but not to me or my family. My mom, being Mom, took a homemade apple pie to the Rays on the day after they moved in. She and Celina Ray ate a piece of pie, drank some coffee, and were close friends from that point forward. The Holy Spirit bound them together tighter than thieves, my mom always said.

(As a side note, Dad, being Dad, was a little more withdrawn. He did spend a lot of time with Mr. Ray in the context of farming, but not so much in a social setting. Still, I think they would have called each other friends. I'm sure of it, actually.)

The Rays had three children. Marcus, who was a year older than me, Cynthia, who was a year younger than me, and Maggie, who was two years younger than Cynthia. Their fourth child died a few years earlier after struggling with a rare debilitating muscular disease.

Why am I telling you this?

Well, of course, they were a wonderful family. A pillar of the Perryton community.

But also: knowing them saved my life.

16

JACOB

My mom's friend, Mrs. Celina Ray, was one of the first people to visit me in the hospital. Mom and Dad were sitting quietly in my room, Mom with a hand on my leg when Mrs. Ray raced into my room early on Monday morning. As normal, Mrs. Ray was dressed as if she was headed to a formal dinner with the Governor of Kansas. Conservative dress, high-heels, and a perfectly selected hat. (I swear she wore the same thing when she was cleaning the basement. I can't prove it though.)

"Jacob Ross, you scared me to death." She wagged her finger at me. "How are you?" She immediately took my hand, the one not stabbed twice with plastic tubes, and patted it with such vigor you'd think that was the medical answer to the entire set of my physical problems. Even with her stern words, she exuded care and comfort.

"I'm okay, I guess."

"Well, baby boy, you just rest and let the doctors care for you. I'm making a basket full of food for you and will bring it to you when you get home. We'll put some meat back on those bones. We will." She then leaned forward and said, "Or I smuggle it into the hospital. Your call."

I tried not to laugh. It accentuated my headache when I did, but I couldn't help it. The thought of her doing anything close to illegal was chuckle worthy.

"Your mom and dad told us what happened. Very strange. I never heard of anything like that. How are your legs?"

"Okay, I guess." (I didn't tell them, but I didn't need to guess, I knew. They were anything but okay.) I also had a raging headache centered over my eyes. Felt like my forehead was on fire from the inside and something was trying to put it out with a pickax.

"Mr. Ray and the kids send their best," she concluded and then kissed me on my cheek. An immediate and sudden shock snaked across my face and down into my chest. Not a painful shock but a soothing current that seem to lessen my headache. If I didn't know better, her kiss also seemed to lessen the vibrating pain in my knees.

At the time, I figured it was just a figment of my imagination, wishful thinking. Later, I would find out it was anything but.

"Thanks, Mrs. Ray. I'm looking forward to the dinner. Be sure Mr. Ray, Marcus, and the girls come over, too. I'd love to see them." Even sick, I knew to keep my manners.

She smiled and threw another kiss over her shoulder in my direction. She left and, with her, part of the air in the room seemed to disappear, too. Very few people in my life had that presence. It was as if her presence brought extreme pleasure that immediately shifted to extreme displeasure when she left. She had an aura of divine intervention.

At the time, I figured I was hazy from my illness.

Later, I found out that God was working a miracle through her.

17

JACOB

I returned home after two days in the hospital.

True to her word, Mrs. Ray and Marcus were waiting in the driveway when I got home, clutching the best meal I had eaten in a long time. No offense, Mom, but two days of hospital food doubtlessly amped up the taste buds a bit. After lunch, Mom chased everyone out and sent me to the living room couch to relax in front of the TV. Not a bad afternoon. Truthfully, I slept more than I watched television. I got in about one-and-a-half episodes of *Leave it to Beaver* before I sacked out. My headache was all but gone, and the pain in my knees had subsided to a low-grade hum. Manageable.

I woke up late in the afternoon shocked at how long I had slept. The sun was already low, and the living room was more shadows than not. I sat up on the couch trying to clear my head, realizing that I felt pretty darn good. Was I…better?

Just as I was about to stand up, Mom and Dad burst through the kitchen's swinging door with enough force that it seemed the door would never settle back to its resting position. I quickly sunk back down into the couch cushions, knowing what was coming. The quintessential Kansas Inquisition. Dad looked pissed and Mom looked frightened. I understood both emotions.

"You're awake," was all Dad could come up with.

"Yeah, I'm a bit fuzzy, but I feel good," I responded mid-stretch. My whole body was tight.

"Jacob." Mom's eyes grew serious. "What happened? What is wrong with you?"

"I don't know, Mom." I was telling the truth. I didn't know.

"Well, can you try to explain it?" She looked so worried and scared that I wished I could.

Dad, ever the pragmatist, had an expression hovering on the worried side, and Mom, the anti-pragmatist, was clearly terrified. They both kneeled down right in front of me at the same time. Mom folded her hands in her lap, as if she was anticipating a full disclosure, as if I had this all figured out and was about to reveal my cards.

Mary burst into the room. "I guess I'm right on time."

"Hi, Mary," I said tentatively.

"Well, I've been wondering if the hospital thing was just an act to get out of our discussion. Was it, Jacob?"

"What does that mean?" Mom and Dad said in perfect tandem.

"Mary and I had plans to discuss…what was going on…after

85

church." I tried to explain, knowing full well this was not going to sit well with them. In fact, it didn't.

Dad's face turned red and the veins on his neck began to jut out. "I gave you every opportunity to talk this through not a few mornings ago and you declined. Then I find out you're more comfortable having this discussion with your sister. That disappoints me, Jacob. Why would you blow me off like that?"

Dad had swung from worried to upset in moments.

I understood my dad's disappointment. For all the past and future issues we had, I always knew, in his own abridged way, he loved his kids. I think his anger was a way to cover up the concern and emotions that followed.

"We can tell you're mad, Brian. It's pretty obvious," Mom interjected. The interjection lasted but a few seconds because of my dad's withering look. Mom sat back quietly.

"It should be obvious," Dad said. "Jacob, start talking. I'm tired of this whole situation. There is something clearly wrong with you, and I want to hear about it." He looked at Mary. "Sit down if you want. Seems you're on the inside, so I guess you have a right to the facts." Calming down a notch or two, Dad adjusted his gaze back to me. "Let's go."

I realized I wasn't going to get by with just brushing them off.

"Okay, you guys, I will at least try to explain." I knew I had to say something.

I talked for the next hour straight. I really did try to be as forthcoming as possible, to tell them what I knew. But how do you describe a humming in your legs? An unquenchable urge to go on walks in the corn fields? It all sounded absurd to me, and I was living it. How did it sound to my family? Still, I tried to tell it all. The only piece of the story I omitted was the kiss on my cheek from Mrs. Ray. That was too weird, and I was sure I'd figure out an explanation for that someday.

Wouldn't I?

I slowly looked up after I told my tale and scanned my family's faces. Mary looked calm and sympathetic. Mom looked like she was about to get sick. Tears where running out of her puffy eyes and down her flushed cheeks. I felt very bad for her, to the point I could hardly look in her direction. Wasn't she supposed to be feeling sorry for me?

But then I looked at Dad. He just looked pissed. Almost as if he couldn't believe what I was saying, as if he was wondering how this strange child with the strange stories could be his son.

I found myself wishing—not for the last time—that the conversation had been just between Mary and me.

That would have made all the difference.

I promised myself right then and there that all future conversations would not involve my parents.

I just couldn't take that again.

18

JACOB

While every school day up to that point had been routine and boring, every school day after that point was anything but. From that day on, my school days and studies were regularly interrupted by visits to the doctors. The constant procession to general practitioners, specialists, and wackos didn't throw me too far off course, although it did result in me barely pulling a B+ in old Mrs. Linder's math class.

Even with regular visits to specialists, and the best in pain management, no one could find anything to abate the pain in my legs. It didn't get much worse, but it certainly didn't get better. Instead it ebbed and flowed, some days where normally incessant low-grade pain was almost nonexistent and other days full of intense discomfort. The pendulum of pain and no pain swung back and forth, day in and day out, almost as if everything needed to even out into a nice bell-shaped curve.

I found myself wondering *who*. Who decided whether it was going to be a good day or a bad one? Truthfully, I would trade the good days to eliminate the bad days. Spending my free time on all fours getting battered by waves of nausea was not my idea of fun. Hiding every moment from Mom and Dad in order to avoid the worry and fretting was a big ask as well.

Perhaps hardest for me was that no one picked me anymore for kickball. I guess that happens when you limp around school as if you're the old man who has worked in the cafeteria for 40 years, but I still missed the game. I tried to sit outside and watch my friends and Susie play during recess, but being an observer instead of a participant was so painful I decided to stay in the classroom. With that decision, my social status headed down a slippery slope.

Soon, I could swear people were leering at me as I hobbled around the school, holding their derision back—kind of. I felt their stares. I saw the way their eyes avoided me. I saw the pity.

Maybe that was the hardest part.

Or maybe it was the kickball.

After a while, most of the other students just ignored me. That actually hurt the worst. Kids who were once my friends all but moved to the other side of the hallway as I limped past. I was fading away as if I was that kid that moved away two years ago. I used recess time to catch up on homework I missed during my many unsuccessful trips to the doctor. Mrs. Hutchinson, God rest her soul, was willing to spend some of her free time keeping me up to speed.

I continued to ride the bus to and from school, even though the Flash had officially been retired. Getting up the three steps onto the bus was the hardest part, but getting off was still easy. Gravity is a great thing. All I had to do was concentrate, as the last thing I needed was a face-plant in the school parking lot. Whatever social status I still retained would have disappeared along with my dignity. Even with my rapidly declining social status, Jimmy continued to be a complete asshole to me. He laughed in my face and called me names. It only got worse over time. I guess some kids are just born mean and stay mean. Eventually, that worm turned hard. That's a story for later.

Susie, on the other hand, continued to be who she always was. Her kindness was often muted by her brother, but she generally stood in my defense. She had a built-in kindness, a way of showing me she was kind and caring, even on the toughest days.

I still remembered one of the first days I went back to school after my hospital stay. My mom had dropped me off, so I had avoided the bus ride, but I was still walking into the gauntlet. The pre-first period crowds were already gathered between our car and the front door of the school. "You're welcome, Jake. Have a good day."

"Yeah, right," I mumbled under my breath.

I gathered myself out of the LTD and headed towards the school's front doors. My legs were aching quite a bit, the pain only surpassed by my social anxiety. The racket of the crowd lessened. Was this my imagination? I looked in front of me and saw a part in the sea of students open up just like a scene from *The Ten Commandments*. I tried my best to walk normally and act like everything was great, but to no avail. The leper had arrived! And, clearly, the masses wanted no part of him. My emotions sunk to a new low.

Had the Flash really come to this?

"Hey, Jacob." I heard it but thought it was my imagination. I cautiously looked up. It wasn't. A familiar arm wrapped around my shoulders. Susie's warmth was tangible. "Want to walk with me to first period?"

"Ummm…I mean, yes!" I stuttered.

We walked the remaining distance to our class in silence as the other students returned to their morning routines. My tattered morning had been partially repaired. Other rips in my fabric were to come, but today, well, today, Susie had saved me.

"Um, thanks, Susie." I whispered to her as we walked into class.

She merely smiled that Susie smile.

***

Then came that freezing cold November day when I had the misfortune to be one of the last students on the bus. Even though I raced to grab my backpack and get outside, I was the last one to get to the schoolyard where the buses were lined up. As I wobbled toward the bus stop—and wobbling was an apt description as it hadn't been a good day for those throbbing knees of mine—I was afraid Vernon would not see me waving my arms. He was closing the bus's folding doors when he turned his head and heard me screaming. Luckily, he quickly flung open the door and smiled.

"Jacob, get your sorry butt on board. I almost left you behind," he said without an ounce of venom in his tone. All his venom was saved for Jimmy. Once my physical issue became public, Vernon amped up his care and concern for me. Good guy.

"Thanks, Vernon. I'm sure I could have run all the way home." Joking sometimes helped. "But Mom would have been really upset to have me all hot and sweaty at the dinner table."

My relief at not missing the bus quickly turned to dread. I took not more than two steps down the aisle when I looked up and saw

Jimmy sitting in the fourth row, staring directly at me. His grin was part stupidity and part evil. I'm not sure which I feared more. I tried to rise up and walk as if nothing was wrong. But the tremor in my lower lip gave me away. That and my limp, which was too noticeable commensurate with the pain coursing through my legs. I was not ready to mix bad knees with bad Jimmy.

"Hey gimp-shit, come sit next to me." It was the first educated comment out of Jimmy's mouth. It went downhill from there. "You wobble just like a Weeble, but I bet you'd fall down." He said as he was slowly balling up his fist.

I started to walk past him, planning to park in the sixth or seventh row when he leaned into the aisle all but blocking my way.

"I said sit with me, Dickhead." The cold chill that ran through me was on par with the pain in my knees. How in the world are Susie and this lump of steroid-infused badness even related? I've asked myself that same question a hundred times and still have no answer.

Either way, I was One-A on Jimmy's list. I figured his hatred of me was two-fold. It was partially because that I was skinny and gangly and half his size and partially because I was the proud owner of the gimps. (I found out later that I was wrong, because 99% of his hatred of me was due to the fact that his sister liked me more than she liked him.) Either way, Jimmy hated me, which resulted in a periodic confrontation. Okay, a regular confrontation.

This confrontation surfaced only when I was riding the bus without my brother. Luke would beat the crap out of him, and he knew that in spades. Between Luke and Vernon, I survived most unplanned Jimmy assaults.

Jimmy topped out at a tall 5'9" in fifth grade and was still a short 5'9" when he disappeared from Perryton. That said, I was petrified of him in fifth grade and specifically that day on the bus when he insisted I join him in row four. "I'll pass, need to stretch out a bit." Would that get him to leave me alone?

Nope. He grabbed the right strap on my backpack and pulled me hard into the seat next to him.

"You know, Gimp, your parents should either drop you in a well or cut those worthless legs off you." He said it with a clinched jaw and spit flying every which way through his crooked yellow teeth. There was a self-satisfied gleam in his eye. Seriously, what was he even saying? Did he think it would hurt my feelings if he told me Mom was going to cut my legs off? Fat chance.

At least Jimmy would never win a war of words with me. Fists, sure, but his words were laughable.

I shrugged, trying to get him to let go of my backpack. I looked desperately up at Vernon, who had suddenly stopped again to reopen the door for another straggler. Bad timing. Jimmy jerked forward as the bus lurched to a stop. It only made his mood darker. How dare someone interrupt his fun. The look on his face immediately morphed, his sneer bouncing back and forth between hatred and the fear of being caught red-handed. I looked away from him and up to the front in time to see not one, but two, last riders bound up the steps and onto the bus.

Susie and Luke.

I was saved.

Jimmy's face changed once again to fear.

"Get your gimpy ass off my row." He pushed me toward the aisle and rolled his eyes as if I had some nerve to even speak to him.

93

Fate had intervened. Looking at those two walking down the aisle, I could have sworn they both had halos above their heads. Even with Jimmy's innocent look and rolling eyes, Luke knew immediately what Jimmy was up to. The realization spread across his face at the same speed it spread across Jimmy's, only in opposite directions. Luke's stride widened and he reached the fourth row in record-setting time.

Susie was right behind him, and I wondered for a second if her brother was more scared of her or Luke.

The answer was neither, because just then Vernon came lumbering down the aisle. He could smell what was coming from a mile away. Luke grabbed Jimmy by the front of his tattered jacket. Susie grabbed Luke around the waist, although halfheartedly and ineffectively, and Vernon was engulfing all of them. With Vernon interceding, the frenzy of activity came to an abrupt stop.

Leaning forward at a 45-degree angle under the tension of Vernon's vice grip, Luke threatened, "Jimmy, if you ever, and I mean ever, touch my brother again, I will grind you into a pile of steaming dog shit. Do you fucking hear me?" Luke yelled in a cadence where each succeeding word was louder than the previous one.

Man, he was pissed.

Man, this bus ride had turned fun.

"Everyone spread out and sit down," Vernon bellowed. Every one of you in a different row. Do it now." He stood firm to be sure he was heeded, then returned to the driver's seat, adjusted his cap, and put the bus in gear once again. He glanced frequently into the rearview mirror to make sure his command was under constant compliance. It was.

As I sat on the sixth row, I could still hear Jimmy grumbling to himself. The rabid dog's collar had been reaffixed. Luke patted my shoulder as he walked past me to a row further towards the back of the bus. He smiled and winked at me. I looked up at him as if he were a conquering hero. Blood is thicker than water for sure. (It was at that moment that I realized that regardless of Luke's clear annoyance of me, he loved me. He really did. And I think he still does, even though things are so different now.)

But I quickly forgot about Luke's kindness when Susie covertly rubbed up against my shoulder as she too passed me. I wasn't sure if it was intentional until I caught her quick smile. This was turning out to be perhaps the best bus ride of my life.

As we rode over bumpy roads, many, many thoughts rattled through my head. I was proud of my brother, I loved my brother. I still do to this day. I was worried for Susie's safety. Would Jimmy blame her? Would he dare lay hands on his sister? If Jimmy was this way in public, what was he like at home? More importantly, why was he so mean?

I know now, but I sure didn't have a clue back then.

Luckily, Jimmy and Susie's stop was before ours. He slunk off the bus behind Susie, who sprinted down and out the door and up the driveway to their house. Jimmy's shoulders were hunched over in his best whipped dog impression. Just before his head disappeared through the bus door, he slowly turned and stared straight at me with a slight grin.

A second round of chills ensued. Luke moved up to my seat and plopped down next to me.

"What's up, Jacob?" He put his arm around my shoulders.

"Thanks for that, Luke. That could've hurt." I tried to laugh.

"We're brothers." That was all he said, but it spoke volumes. "He'll leave you alone from now on." Luke spoke with the confidence of a star football player. Little did he know, I had none of his confidence.

Vernon pulled to a stop in front of our mailbox and we stood up together. I was still a little shaken so it took me longer to descend the stairs. Luke put a steadying hand on my shoulder. I overheard Vernon say to him as he was about to close the bus door, "Luke, nice job."

They exchanged a look that appeared to be a silent vow to protect me. I should have been offended, wondering why they thought I couldn't take care of myself, but I wasn't.

I knew I needed them. Both of them.

19

JACOB

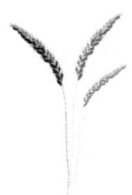

Even as everything changed around me, my morning walks remained the same.

Same time of day, same duration, same tingling in my legs, same over-arching strangeness. But there was one small change. I moved locations.

It wasn't a strange, spiritual awakening that made that change, but instead, due to the harvest, I no longer had the ability to walk in seclusion down the third row of the corn field. The stalks had been cut, leaving that row in plain view of US 40. So I made the very rational decision to start walking in the wheat field.

Ruddy, newly-plowed rows and the same smells of dirt and morning air mixed with a healthy helping of anxiety continued to greet me day after day, week after week, after I moved to the wheat field. The typical rows in our wheat field were narrower than in the corn field, with the wheat generally planted on 10-inch spacing, too narrow to walk between with any steady grace. Dad typically plowed a single, wider access row in order to walk down the heart of the field. This row, about twice as wide as the other rows, would be my morning path as I walked the wheat field.

I've already explained that, from the moment I woke up every morning, it was as if some unwanted force took over my efforts, my thoughts. During the ordinary course of any day, run-of-the-mill thoughts seem to form in a normal brain with no sense of time or direction. They're just present.

But during my walks it was different.

The best way to describe my thoughts as I walked was that they arrived on a bolt of electricity. I could almost see them coming and recognize the thought before it completely formed in my head. The more bolts that attacked me, the more muddled my thoughts became, yet the more clear-headed I felt. Looking back, I would describe it as awakened thoughts recolored as awakened dreams, but at the time, none of it made sense in my mind.

Instead, I felt like a freak show with an overactive brain that couldn't make sense of itself.

Periodically, I would try to find a way to rationally line up the thoughts in some congruent pattern. I would sit and make a silent mind-map just like Mrs. Hutchinson had taught me, creating a logical explanation for my clearly illogical brain. But it never worked out. Just as I thought I had figured out the patterns of thoughts, those patterns shattered quickly as if they were glass rods smashed with one giant swing of a steel bat.

By Christmas, I was a teetering who was dealing with painful legs and chaotic dreams and a very real feeling of imminent death. Not suicide, no, not by any means, but a feeling that death was coming like a freight train, and I was standing squarely between the rails. Death had entered my body but was having too much fun to finish the deal. Sometimes I felt like acquiescing, but most of the time I was in a fighting mood. I was very hopeful that 1990 was an aberration, but of course it wasn't.

**

That winter was one of the coldest and wettest on record, especially January, February, and the front end of March. The weather made most everything more difficult, from traffic to working the farm to my early morning walks.

They were brutal.

The temperature most mornings hovered around zero and that was before the deduction for the wind chill factor, which was significant. The wind blew unbuffered down from Canada, often carrying snow or sleet. The plowed rows were filled with snow. I bundled up the best I could before I hit the mud room—at least I had some logical sense left in me—and Mom was there every morning to see me back and to make sure her son had not been converted to an ice sculpture. She'd be at the back door with a cup of cocoa and a dry blanket.

After a few months, she started adding coffee to my cocoa and I've been a coffee junkie ever since. Dad was up most mornings too but not waiting anxiously at the back door. He'd be in his usual spot at the kitchen table, with his cup of coffee, plowing through the news of yesterday's events. His simple acknowledgment was a brief glance up to catch my eye and then he'd return to his ritual.

I took this as an act of caring. I had to. I have always wondered what he would have done if, one morning, I failed to walk back into the house. I should have hidden in the barn to find out. Probably a good a thing I didn't test those waters.

My parents had entered into a phase of acceptance. I'm sure my morning walks drove them crazy, but I think over time they had become almost numb to the fact. I wasn't any worse for wear (aside from rosy cheeks and shivering lips), and Mom took comfort in planning and executing any number of cures for my limp.

Some were stranger than others. I overheard them talking about letting me have some rope and maybe this would fade as quickly as it seemed to appear. Truthfully, I think they were afraid to stop the cycle of my walks for fear that the potential result might be much worse than the current situation.

The cold wind would hit me as soon as I walked out the back door and, by the time I returned home, I was near frozen and very uncomfortable. Yet, strangely, the in-between was lost on me. I don't remember the debilitating cold that should have made it a very painful 40-minute walk while traversing the wheat field. I don't remember sleet biting my face, snow seeping into my boots.

I do, however, remember the treacherous footing. My physical limitations coupled with the frozen, uneven path notched up the slip factor. I have come to the conclusion over the years that my mind deflected the brutal effects of the weather as my thoughts and, to a degree, my actions were hijacked. An undercurrent of foreboding tension settled into our house.

When I was with my parents, and sometimes Luke or Mary, you could feel the air pressure in the room change. Breathing was noticeably more difficult. The best way to describe the feeling in our home was that it was like the pall that settles over a funeral.

Mom appeared to be the most affected by my situation. When she met me upon my return to the back door in the mornings, I felt nothing but concern and care but, as the day went on, she became more tense and agitated. This cycle was repeated every single day. I'm sure she was not sleeping well. I'm sure she dreaded hearing my door squeak open in the night. You don't realize the stress a parent feels for their children until you become a parent yourself.

As much discomfort as I felt in my legs, I still tried to help Dad with the farm work. The blanket of snow made it challenging, as did the fact that he usually refused to let me help. He was too worried about me. Still, Dad and I spent many weekends in the barn working on Greenie, cleaning up and organizing the tools, pulling out the old hay from the lofts, and generally tidying up the joint. It was probably a lot of unnecessary busy work, but the end product was nice. It was the best the barn ever looked. Greenie was at the top of her game too. By the time the snow melted, we had a pristine barn filled with sharpened tools and equipment that purred like a herd of cats.

It felt great to work with my dad, to get closer to him, to bond.

Ironically, the closer I got to Dad, the further I drifted emotionally from Luke. It was a drift that never fully reversed itself. Not even to this day, although I'm working on that.

It was strange that, after the heroics on the bus with Jimmy, that Luke and I never felt that brotherly bond again. That was our pinnacle. Maybe the closeness was one-sided, and he was just doing his brotherly duty. Maybe it was the fact that he was a healthy athlete with an accelerating social status and I was the exact opposite. Either way, it stung. I was his brother and brothers take care of each other, don't they?

Yet that was the winter I noticed Luke taking a wide berth in the hallway at school, as if he had no idea who I was. It was the winter he began looking away as he passed me on the bus. And it was the winter that he stopped talking to me about football. About anything. I have since forgiven him, but forgiveness and acceptance are two very different things.

As Luke and I drifted apart, Mary and I built a bond that lasts to this day. I spent more time talking to my sister that winter than I had collectively in my lifetime up to that point. I had always viewed her as this weird, out of touch, big sister. Had I treated her the same way Luke treats me? The answer was an absolute yes. I regret that still.

One extremely cold January night, I was lying in bed wrapped in too many blankets, trying in vain to stay warm when this reality dawned on me. It hit me hard. I made a promise that I would take the time to get to know Mary.

And so we spent many hours that winter playing cards, talking. I quickly learned that she was gifted with an engaging personality, tremendous insight into people, and particularly our family, and was clearly the brightest of the five members of the Ross clan, by a mile. At the time, she was just my fun big sister who never judged me.

Mary was my prized possession. She still is. Mrs. Ray is a close second.

20

JACOB

The mother of all winters loosened her grip on Kansas and begrudgingly gave way to a glorious spring. Whether it was all the rain that sourced a never-ending stream of nutrition, or the expanding days of sunshine everyone thought was a thing of the past, the wheat crop escaped from under the layers of melting ice and snow to shoot out of the soggy ground. Of course, both the rain and the sunshine were the driving factors—as always. Corn and sunflowers were fun to grow and, in most years, brought in a nominal profit, but it was wheat that was the make-or-break crop in the majority of Kansas. Bad wheat crop meant bad farm year. One bad farm year meant struggling economics. Two bad farm years most likely meant foreclosure. Simple as that. Sad as that.

As Winter faded, the rows between the planted wheat slowly morphed from solid alleys of ice to some of the gummiest mud known to man. Walking transitioned from an exercise in maintaining one's balance to an exercise in merely lifting your leg while having the corresponding shoe remain attached to that foot. My morning walks proved to be difficult for much of the Spring once the Winter's ice and snow melted. Footing was in constant flux as the weather alternated between clear skies with sunshine and low clouds with rain showers.

Interestingly, I was not compelled to walk every morning. For months, my body or my mind woke me at more-or-less the same time every day. Once winter broke, it seemed my biorhythms changed. At least one morning a week, and sometimes two, I would not wake up until after 7:00 a.m. This break in my routine was not consistent from week to week, only consistent in that I stopped walking every day. That was the good news. The bad news was that I started having bothersome dreams on the days where I did not wake up. When I did wake up early, the ritual was the same all the way until the first few steps in the wheat field. But now the wheat was about thigh high. It was a beautiful gold color that lit up on sunny days as if the light was emanating from deep in the plants roots. I will always love the morning view of a rolling plain carpeted in Kansas wheat. This etched-in-my-mind memory is from the normal parts of my life such as walking to the bus stop or driving into town with Mom. It did not come from one of my walks.

Under my newly adjusted schedule, I probably averaged five or six walks a week. As I mentioned, they were never in the same order. The days skipped were random and unpredictable. I had to prepare every evening for the expectation of a walk the next morning. It was frustrating. As time wore on, my walks actually became a bit monotonous. The newness had worn off. I was now used to the feeling of being propelled by some external force through the 40 minutes, the myriad of thoughts that invaded that time. Even the feeling of being zapped with electrical thought currents became ordinary. How is that possible?

Week in and week out I trudged through the fields. Early on I expected a continual physical deterioration of my knees and an amplification of pain. This didn't happen. I had leveled off. I wasn't sure what to think of this change or lack thereof. Was this it? Was this the way I was going to live the rest of my life? On one hand, I was hopeful and, on the other, petrified. The hopeful side of my brain told me that I was used to this level of pain and anxiety. The petrified side wanted nothing to do with this debilitated state with zero chance to regain normalcy. The hopeful side tried to convince me I could live the rest of my life with a small limp; who needs athletics anyway? The petrified side wanted the Flash back, wanted the social status back, and certainly wanted the return of a strong, healthy body (and mind). I wasn't sure whether the hopeful side or the petrified side would win the longstanding internal debate. Little did I know that, by mid-summer, we'd all know the answers to these questions. The debate would be settled, just not to my liking.

21

JACOB

"Jacob, let's go. We've got errands to run," Mom implored from the bottom of the stairs.

The third weekend of April brought beautiful clear skies and an opportunity to get out of the house for something other than my morning walk, school, or the limited help I provided around the farm. I was actually looking forward to spending a Saturday with Mom running errands in town. I really didn't care what they were. I was along for the ride.

"Coming, Mom!"

"Are you really running errands with Mom?" Luke rolled his eyes to match his condescending tone.

"Sure. She needs the company." I didn't mention that I was feeling stifled inside the house day after day.

"Gee, have fun."

No retort was forthcoming, fuel to the fire and all that.

I tied my shoes and ran out of the room. My legs were feeling good. I had slept in that morning, which helped. Grabbing my wallet just in case, I swung into the hall with the assistance of the door frame. Both feet left the floor. A tiny hint of the Flash reappeared, then disappeared just as fast. Three steps and I was turning left past the bathroom and to the top of the stairs.

"Hey, Jake, watch where you're going!" Mary squealed.

She had stepped out of her room at the same time I was bounding by. She backed up a half a step, and I zigged slightly left. Both moves were enough to avoid a head-on collision.

"Sorry," I said.

She glared at me. "Where are you going in such a hurry?"

"Just out with Mom." I felt a little embarrassed that I was so zealous to spend time in public with my mom. Not exactly a ramp-up in the cool factor, but with my ever-eroding social status, I didn't really care. Mom could be fun. And sometimes she stopped off at B&R and bought me a cappuccino blast.

I had settled into a new paradigm that was clearly not cool.

"I'll go, too," Mary said.

"You will?" I narrowed my eyes at her. Why in the world would she want to run errands?

"Okay, I guess. But you'd better hurry. Mom's getting impatient."

"I'll be down in a second." She spun into her room.

With my last three steps off the stairs, Mom appeared out of the kitchen. "Let's go, Jake. Lots to do."

"Wait a sec. Mary wants to go."

"Okaaay." Mom said, perhaps both shocked and amused. Not just one, but two, of her pre-teen kids were running errands with her?

A few minutes later the three of us were out the back door, into the LTD, and heading toward the highway. Mom took a left onto 40 and into town we went.

It was very strange, and a bit awkward, to have the three of us together without Luke or Dad. The conversation was stilted. But as we settled into the strangeness, I realized it was kind of nice. There was less pressure in the air. And more space in the car. The short drive to the town square was mostly silent. For Mary, silence was normal. For Mom, it wasn't. I think we were all trying to process this unique situation.

"Where to first?" I said, interrupting the quiet.

"Sun's Drugstore. Then we need to then go to Emory's, Binger's, and the Ace Hardware."

Binger's was the local grocery store. The Binger family had about 20 stores in small towns in mid-Kansas. They were always clean and friendly. The food was fresh and well-priced, or so Mom would say. The family lived in Perryton, and Susan Binger was in my grade. She was one of four Binger kids. You would never know they were rich by talking to any of them. They wore average clothes, drove hand-me-down cars, and socialized around town as if they were a typical middle-class family. I found out later that most city fundraisers were funded, at least in part, by one or more Binger. "Look, Mom, there's a parking spot where that Jeep is backing out," Mary pointed. These were her first words of the drive.

"I see it, thanks."

Mom slowed and waited for the Jeep to drive off before she pulled into the vacated spot. We could run all our errands within the town square, so this was our Ford's resting spot for the day.

I never paid too much attention to my hometown while I was living there. Like so many other small towns, Perryton was planned around a town square that was anchored by a large brick and limestone courthouse. The Russell County courthouse sat on two acres and was bounded to the east by First Street, to the west by 101st Street, to the North by Elm Street, and to the south by Washington Street. The balance of the town radiated out from these four main streets, either numerically, alphabetically by tree type, or chronologically by dead presidents. Rather archaic, but easy to remember. Also, easy to find addresses. The courthouse, or the Court, as most everyone called it, was constructed at the turn of the 19th century. A limestone base and porches were the horizontal elements and standard Midwestern red brick provided the vertical support. Each corner was architected with silo-shaped towers. The Court was capped off with a domed copula, the highest point in the county which provided an endless 360-degree view of central Kansas, or so it seemed.

The Court had its share of dramatic trials, but mostly was home to civil proceedings, small claims disputes, and the payment of traffic violations. North of the courthouse and across Elm sat the Jefferson Memorial Library, which was constructed soon after the Court and in the same late Victorian style with a splash of Romanesque Revival. Same architect too. They made handsome companions and anchored the downtown both geographically and visually. The library was flanked by two five-story office buildings that provided an endless procession of attorneys moving back and forth to the Court. On most days, it looked like someone had poked a hornet's nest. How in the world was there that much need for legal work in a single agrarian county?

As I stepped out of the Jeep, I glanced over at Johnstone's Freedom Park named for Davis Johnstone. The park sat just south of the town square and was completely surrounded by the state tree of Kansas, the Cottonwood. In the center of the park was the requisite bandstand, the focal point of every 4th of July celebration I can remember. Even back then, I knew how important Davis Johnstone was to our town's history. Mom led the charge down Elm toward the drugstore. Lord knows what she needed there. I certainly wasn't going to follow too closely in case she needed to load up on female stuff. I slowed my walk as we approached the front door and decided to sit on the bench which was conveniently located under the forest green awning, aptly emblazoned with a graphical image of a sun and the words "Sun Drugstore...your needs are our cares." My legs had felt great all morning, but I could also feel a twinge of that deep-seated discomfort rearing its ugly head. It was almost as if my knees had overslept, too.

"You guys go on in. If it's okay, I'll hang out here until you're done." The look on Mom's face told me she knew both reasons for my request.

I sat in the shadow of the Court. What a huge structure. I had no concept of its goings-on at that point in my life, but even so, I appreciated its size and stature. It was a very busy day downtown and I watched passers-by and realized that I only knew about half of the people milling around. Perryton often attracted shoppers from other towns, which was good for business and good for me, too. I liked to see new sights, notice new people. I counted cars, too, and was over 75 by the time Mary and Mom reappeared. Anything to distract me from the slowly evolving discomfort in my knees.

"We're going to run into the bookstore before we head to Emory's," Mom said. "Want to come?"

I shrugged. It was nice sitting there in the shade. "I'll just stay here. Come get me when you're done?"

"Sure."

As Mom and Mary walked away, I found myself wishing for what must have been the millionth time that I could just have a normal day doing normal things like a normal kid.

That wish was not coming true any time soon.

***

"Hurry up, Donnie, I don't have time to wait on you as you slog along behind me. This is exactly why you need to lose some weight."

My head snapped hard to the left at the demeaning comment. Walking straight toward me was a mother who was way overdressed for a Saturday shopping trip in Perryton. Honestly, she was overdressed for shopping anywhere, except maybe 5th Avenue during Fashion Week. High heels, pearls, and a flowing chiffon dress; she was June Cleaver reincarnated. In one hand she was carrying her purse and, in the other, a small package that, based on the bright pink wrapping paper, must have come from Emory's. She was young and beautiful, but the tortured scowl painted on her face was enough to make you look away, which is exactly what I did, right after her piercing eyes caught mine. As I quickly averted my eyes, they landed directly on the object of her disaffection: her tow-headed, messy-haired son. I'm guessing he was about my age and the exact opposite of his mother. He was frumpy at best. And, by frumpy, I mean every part of him was dirty and rumpled from his stained pants, to his untied shoes, to his hair that looked like it was cut with a weed eater. Disdain bled from his mother and engulfed his posture, the posture of a child who has been verbally reduced for years, further weighed down by the myriad packages he lugged around for his mom.

I felt sad for him.

There I was, a kid the same age, hardly able to walk, but I felt sorry for him. It was my first instinct. He slogged with every step so devoid of grace I fully expected him to fall flat on his face at any minute. Luckily for him he didn't. He just slogged ahead, pulled forward by the unsympathetic leer of his indifferent mother.

That was when it hit me.

I was a slogger too. I slogged every morning through our family fields. I slogged as if pulled under the weight of an incriminating force. I slogged as if the only grace I'd ever know again in my life was that which was unemotionally offered prior to dinner.

I slogged.

That was the perfect definition of the ever-expanding and overwhelming part of my life. As soon as my counterpart slogger disappeared around the corner onto Elm Street, I caught Mom and Mary out of the corner of my eye.

"Did you get what you needed?" I asked.

"We did," Mary winked as she responded. She knew exactly why I was nervous.

"Where to next?" I said.

"Let's go to Emory's," Mom said. "I'd like to visit with Liz."

Liz was Malcolm Emory's youngest daughter who had managed the family's local print shop ever since I could remember. She was a few years behind Mom in school, but they had been friends in elementary school. Mom always made an effort to visit Liz and buy a few items. She once said that if she was going to take up some of her time during the work day, she should at least pay for it. I doubt Liz looked at it that way.

"Mom," I said, "card shops are not really my idea of a fun destination. Do you mind if I jump into the diner for a Coke? You can come get me when you're done yakking."

"Sure, Jake. I understand." She fumbled in her purse and pulled out a few dollars that she tucked into my hand. The kiss quickly followed, of course.

"Me too, Mom." Mary said. "I'd rather go with Jacob and let you visit with Miss Liz."

"Fair enough." She handed me a few more dollars and reminded me to treat my sister. "I'll come find you both in a little while."

We parted ways.

"Hello, Mr. and Ms. Ross. Welcome." James' loud voice didn't match his formal tone. "Take any booth. It's still too early for the lunch crowd, so you'll get the VIP treatment." I never knew James' last name. I'm not sure who did, but I supposed someone in Perryton had access to this tightly held information. I never heard anyone call him anything but simply James, the guy who owned and ran the Downtown Diner. He was head chef, head waiter, head dishwasher, and head cashier.

James had that knack for making everyone feel special, as if they were the only customer, which we were at that moment. Between James' effusive personality and damn good food, he had a gold mine at that diner. He clearly loved his diner and obviously loved the people of Perryton. They loved his food in return.

"What can I get you?" James asked.

"Two Cokes on ice please," I responded.

"Coming up."

Mary and I sat in silence for the next few minutes in anticipation of our cool drinks. Either that or we were both desperately searching for that perfect conversation starter. I know I was. She finally looked straight at me.

"Spill the beans, Jacob." Her smile wasn't a conniving smile, but it also wasn't sympathetic.

I shrugged.

"Tell me what's going on, Jake. You can trust me." With these few words, all the tension hanging over our booth vanished into thin air. I felt a huge wave of relief.

Maybe Mary would understand.

Maybe this burden would no longer be mine alone.

22

JACOB

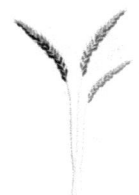

"Okay, Mary. You asked for it."

"I did." Those were her last words for the next 30 minutes. You would have thought a dam burst based on the endless stream of semi-incongruent thoughts that poured out of my mouth. For some reason, I felt free to be much more forthcoming with Mary than I had been with my parents. "So, that's it," I finished.

Everything was still clear as mud in my mind.

Mary lowered her head and lightly touched her cheek with her left hand. She sat like this for 10 or 15 seconds, then shifted her eyes up to me. That's when I noticed tears in her eyes.

"I—I don't even know what to say."

I shrugged. I obviously didn't either.

"Tell me you'll be okay," she said. "You'll get over this." I could hear the tremor in her voice.

"Of course I'll be okay." I was the Flash. I was invincible. Wasn't I?

Mary clearly wasn't convinced. Two tears landed on the diner's table. And I sat there wondering if I really was, in fact, going to be okay. It's hard to gauge something like that when the symptoms were so bizarre.

"We need to go find Mom. Are you done with your drink?" I figured both of us needed a break from the emotions.

But Mary stayed seated. "Jake, you said you've had days where you sleep in, that you don't go for a morning walk. Did I hear you right?"

"Yes, that's true."

"Are you sure?"

"Of course I'm sure."

"But…okay, I have a confession to make." Mary paused and looked at me intently. "I've been so worried about you that I've started waking up every morning to see if you pass my bedroom door. I usually even stay awake while you are gone just so I can make sure you come back. But here's the thing: I can't think of any mornings in the past few weeks where you did not head out at more or less 4:00 in the morning."

"No, Mary, not every morning. I slept in twice last week. I think I would know."

"No, I'm positive. You got up every morning this week." Mary's voice was almost accusatory.

Did she think I was lying?

Mary frowned. "Could you have been sleepwalking? You know, like Dad did that one time he went out on the front porch in his pajamas?"

Sleepwalking?

That seemed so odd since I was hyper-aware on the mornings I did go out. Maybe Mary was wrong. Maybe her days were all blending into one.

"No, I think I would know if I went out. It's not like this is a short, friendly jaunt. They hurt! What if you're just not waking up every morning? Forgetting?"

"No, I'm positive. Look..." She pulled a slip of paper out of her purse that had a list of dates and times. Monday. 4:26 am. Tuesday. 4:08 am. Wednesday. 4:13 am.

So strange.

I was positive Tuesday had been one of the days I had slept in.

The bell hanging above the front door dinged, breaking the tension. We both turned to see Mom walking toward us. I quickly stood up and followed her out the door.

I needed a break from the tension.

I also needed some time to figure out what was going on.

23

JACOB

The conversation with Mary wasn't over.

But neither of us got back to it for a few weeks. I think we needed some time to sort things out in our minds.

And so we waited, skirting around each other, pretending everything was normal. But then she cornered me as I walked past her room one evening.

"What's going on, Jacob?" She had her arms crossed.

"I…don't know. I promise I don't remember some of those walks, Mary." I was frightened to my core and admitting that fact out loud made it worse, if that's possible. I was lost. I was completely and utterly confounded.

I would know if I were taking long walks in the middle of the night, wouldn't I?

At least that was my logic. But Mary's revelation at the diner, coupled with her positivity that she was telling the truth, confirmed my biggest fear: no one was at the helm of my badly listing ship.

"Come in and sit down." Mary waved me into her room, scooted over on her bed, and patted the mattress.

"Thanks," was my mumbling response. I took a few steps forward and sat on Mary's bed. She quietly pushed the door shut and turned around. As soon as I hit the mattress, I realized this was the first time I had been in her room in what seemed forever. Mary's room was the extreme opposite of Luke's and mine. No piles of dirty clothes, no junk strewn everywhere, and not a speck of dirt or dust. Everything was neat and in order. As I was discovering, her room was exactly like she was. Neat and thought through. I started talking before she could. "Mary. I want to tell you something I purposefully left out of all the discussions we've had so far. Nobody else knows this. Can you keep a secret?"

She shrugged. That was as good as I was going to get.

"Remember when I passed out in the kitchen and ended up in the hospital?"

"I'm pretty sure I remember that, Jake," she said as if that was the dumbest comment she'd ever heard. She turned her desk chair around to face me and sat down softly.

"Well, Mrs. Ray came to see me just after I got home."

"I remember that. She brought us that great dinner the next day."

"Yes!" My taste buds started watering. Pavlov would be proud. "Anyway, before she left the hospital, she came right up to my bed, leaned over, and kissed my cheek."

"Aaaanddd?"

"Well, this sounds strange, okay?" I was having trouble getting the words out. "But she leaned over me and placed her left hand on my right shoulder so she was looking directly at me. She did it so gently that I felt none of her weight on me. In fact, I couldn't even feel her at all. Almost as if she was floating over me."

"You were a bit out of it, Jacob. I'm sure she was just being really gentle."

I held up my hand. "But wait…"

"Oh-kay," Mary said with a tone that indicated she was ready for the punch line.

"But, at that moment, Mrs. Ray's eyes lit up. Not like a flash of recognition, but a real flash of heat. As if flames had ignited behind her eyes and the brightness flared out of her pupils. I swear I could feel heat."

Mary definitely thought I was crazy now.

"I know it sounds stupid, but as her eyes flared and she smiled slightly. Her back was facing the rest of the room so only I could see her face. She then bent forward and lightly kissed my right cheek. As soon as her lips touched me, a shock-like current exploded into my skin and rushed across my face, down my neck and into my chest. It worked its way into my skin, if not deeper. It didn't hurt or anything, but even after she left, I felt better. Good even. It was like she had healed me a little with that one touch."

"Are you sure, Jacob?"

"Mary, I swear, I have thought about this a hundred times since then. This is exactly what happened." Mrs. Ray's voice, her expressions from that day, had danced in my subconscious.

"That's really weird Jacob. Are you sure you weren't hallucinating? I mean, between your condition and the drugs the hospital was giving you, maybe you dreamed it up."

"Maybe, I guess. But I don't think so. The feeling was too real. I think it happened just as I described."

"I can see why you have never told any of us. We'd lock you up. Dad would for sure."

"I still don't know what to do about it. But...it sure feels good telling someone."

Mary looked up at my eyes and took my hand. "I believe you, Jacob."

I was too choked up to speak.

"What if...what if you go to the Rays' and ask her? Maybe she felt something, too."

I hadn't thought of that.

But what if?

What if Mrs. Ray knew the answers?

"I think I'll do that, Mary."

"Tomorrow?" she pleaded or, more likely, commanded.

"Yes." The idea grew on me each second. Maybe she would have some answers. Maybe she would tell me I wasn't crazy.

Then Mary said something I hadn't thought of before. "What if she's expecting you to come see her? What if her kiss was some sort of a signal?"

What if.

I wondered about that for the rest of the evening.

24

JACOB

Early spring faded into late spring which then gave way to early summer. It was a wonderful time in Kansas. The corn fields had been planted, the wheat was stretching toward harvest, and the weather was generally ideal.

Life continued on.

Not better, but not worse.

More of the same, same, same.

I was more convinced than ever that life had hit a stasis. I did everything I could to convince my family that my walks were still dull and random, insignificant. My parents seemed to believe me. Mary acted as if she believed me, too. The clock rounded 4:00 a.m. on the 25th of May, and I woke with a start. I was having one of those dreams that felt all too real and I was (for once) thankful to be awake. Even if it meant being awake at 4:02 a.m. Even awake and unable to remember the details of the dream, I couldn't let go of an intense feeling of dread. I felt as if life was escaping and death was overwhelming. My world became twisted and contorted. I was glad for the opportunity to throw on clothes from the various piles scattered around the floor and escape the clutches of my bed. Out the back door and into the wheat field I fled. I was walking with determination. I was escaping a nightmare.

Or at least I thought I was until it struck again.

Only this time, it was real.

As soon as I stepped into the field, my ever-random thoughts began arcing across my brain, driving deeper with each successive bolt. I tried to slow my pace, but could not. The invisible hand was firmly planted in my back and taking great pride in shoving me forward in spite of my fading resistance. At the turn, nausea joined the fun. Halfway back and I felt like puking my guts out. Bile had coated my throat and was threatening to exit through both my mouth and nasal passages.

I tried to fall to my knees but was lifted each time to slog forward, each time spitting up a small mixture of viscous yellow phlegm and pale green bile. With my head in a haze, I finished the walk and burst out of the wheat field onto the dirt road that ran perpendicular to both fields.

The helping hand disappeared, and I was finally allowed to fall with a thud onto my screaming knees with such force that I performed a Tommy Johnson, only without the pride of missing flesh from my kneecaps. A few violent heaves later, and the balance of the bile in my throat spewed out my mouth and nose. I'm not sure which was worse, the taste in my mouth or the burning in my nasal passages. I remained on all fours looking disgustedly at a puddle of greenish yellow liquid as it absorbed itself into the hard-packed dirt road.

I waited there for what seemed like hours.

Slowly I rose to my feet, wiped the remnants from my mouth and face, and pushed forward to the house. Each step brought some relief. When I reached the back porch, my headache had cleared, my stomach was mostly settled, and the pain in my knees had partially subsided.

I sat on the top step of the porch, planted my face in my hands, and mumbled a tiny prayer. "God, I can't do this anymore. I need help. Please." Just as the last word was spoken, the back door flew open and Mom exploded out onto the porch, her face twisted in some strange combination of anger and worry. "Jacob, where have you been? Do you realize it's already 6:00 a.m.? What is going on? I've been worried sick."

All this was said in a staccato that would make a late-night TV pitchman proud. Mom was petrified and had every right to be. I had no idea I had been outside for so long.

And it dawned on me: I had lost it. My sanity had completely disappeared.

The story just kept getting better. Or worse.

25

JACOB

Saturday morning. And a beautiful, perfect Saturday at that. There was still a cool crispness to the air. Dad was up and out working the farm. Luke was still snoring. And I woke up at 7:30 for the first time.

Or did I?

I had set a little trap for myself the night before. I had lined my clothes up on the edge of the old rug that partially covered our wooden floors. I put them in a perfect row, just on the edge. That way, I'd know if they had been touched.

I took a deep breath and peeked at the rug.

The clothes had moved. They were no longer in a straight line, but instead, tossed in a pile.

Of course, someone could have kicked them or something. Maybe

Luke had gone to the bathroom in the middle of the night. My mind immediately went into justification mode, as if my wet, muddy shoes weren't proof enough.

I planned to talk to Mary as soon as she woke up.

I also knew I had to go see Mrs. Ray.

There had to be an answer out there somewhere, and she seemed like the best starting point.

"Good morning, Jake." Mom said. "I was wondering when you were going to get out of bed again."

"Again?" Did my mom know something, too?

"After your walk." She was nonchalant, as if it was obvious.

"I didn't walk this morning, Mom. Just woke up after a good night's sleep."

"Yeah, you did, Jacob. I woke up early and came down for a cup of tea. I was sitting at the kitchen table this morning when you walked in the back door." She glanced at her watch. "It was about two and a half hours ago."

And then that look washed over Mom's face as if a mask was set in place that made her instantly look 10 years older. I've seen the change many times throughout this ordeal. The look of guilt-ridden fear. The look of someone racked with a raging internal struggle of a mom's love that is arm-wrestling with the fear of the unknown, or even the fear of something supernatural. I get it, I really do. Especially after all these years and knowing Mom through the eyes of an adult.

"You don't remember going for your walks, Jacob?"

Just then, two things struck me. One, despite my denial, Mary was absolutely right. I was walking in my sleep. Which meant that my overly bizarre dreams maybe weren't dreams after all, but strange memories of an actual morning slog.

But the second thing was even more surprising to me than the first. Why had no one from my family ever followed me out the back door and down the driveway to watch out for me during one of my mornings slogs? If they were so concerned, I would have thought at least Mom or Dad would trail me outside and into the fields.

"No, Mom, I don't." I'm sure I looked like a deer in the headlights. "Did Mary see me this morning?"

"I'm not sure, Jacob."

I rocketed out of the kitchen chair and spun 180 degrees back though the swinging door. Running as fast as I could, taking stair steps two at a time, I landed in front of Mary's room. "Mary, wake up!" I shook her awake wanting, no *needing*, an immediate answer to my question. I needed a fourth party to confirm what I already knew. "Mary, get up!"

Mary slowly opened her eyes, just awake enough to be pissed.

"What are you doing, Jacob? I'm sleeping in case you didn't know."

I ignored her and jumped in. Almost yelling. "Mary, did you see me go on a walk this morning?"

"Geesh, calm down, Jacob."

"Mary! Did you see me get up this morning?"

"Yes. Yes, Jacob. You left just after 4:00."

Well, there it was. Confirmation.

I turned and walked to my room. Each step harder than the next. Not because of any physical pain, this time, but due to mental anguish. Anguish over the realization that my affliction had not leveled off, certainly had not lessened, but instead, I was getting worse.

Up until now, I knew what I was doing when a walk was happening. I couldn't necessarily control it or myself, but I was awake, or should I say aware, during my morning slogs. Not anymore. I placed the toe of my left shoe on the heel of the right, pushed down until that heel was free and kicked my shoe as far across the room as possible. I repeated the process. Luke didn't even wake up when the shoes hit the wall. I threw myself onto my bed, tucked my legs under the covers and slowly pulled myself into the fetal position.

I felt like crying, but I didn't. Sleep came too quickly.

26

JACOB

I now know that saying *"You never know what goes on behind closed doors"* is often very true. In fact, it's true more often than we'd like to admit for many of our neighbors, school friends, and the people with which we share a community. A fact that becomes one of our harshest adult realizations. Evil often wears a convincing mask in public.

This was especially true for the Polanskis.

The family wheat farm on which the Polanskis lived was significantly bigger than our family farm. It covered close to 1500 acres or 2.5 square miles, which meant that their front drive entrance was a good mile and a half from our driveway, closer to the Perryton city limit sign than it was to our property line. It was almost too far to walk, which never in my life had dawned on me, up until the morning of June 5th.

At the time, I didn't know the history of Susie's family.

Now I do.

During one of Susie's confessional moments, she told me the sad history of her dad's regression.

Abel Polanski inherited the family farm from his parents. He was the third generation Polanski to farm wheat in Kansas. The funny thing was, he never wanted to stay in Perryton and farm wheat for a living. Abel pined for the big city. He pined for big adventure. He pined for anyplace but central Kansas. Ever since he was in junior high, he had dreamed of leaving his hometown in the rearview mirror as soon as he graduated.

Abel would often zone out in class and fantasize about attending a school on the east coast where he could learn business as a career and sophistication as a way of life. The complete transformation of a rube. He wanted to be an employee of a large industrial company with a global presence so he could travel the world working hard on their behalf as well as his.

The template was in place as both of the older Polanski boys left Perryton after high school and never returned. Abel's oldest brother roughnecked on drilling rigs offshore Africa and on land in the Middle East, and his middle brother worked as a sales rep for a lumber company with holdings in Russia, South America, and Indonesia. He read and reread their sporadic letters home and dreamed of all the places he would visit. Abel was proud and jealous at the same time. He knew his time was coming.

It never did.

Jimmy's granddad died of a massive heart attack when Abel was a senior in high school. The infamous widowmaker struck again. His coronary artery was completely blocked and he went from standing in his steamy bathroom, casually shaving the morning stubble, to face down dead in a matter of seconds. His wife of 30 years found his stiffening body folded over the side of the bathtub. Instantly, she became completely lost, both on the farm and in life.

Abel's father had been her world.

He had managed everything related to the business of the house to the business of the farm. Abel's choice was to leave Perryton to start his great undertakings and watch his family lose their farm or stay and help his mom.

He chose what anyone would have—he stayed.

His brothers never came back, and he never left. The pride he once had in them and their high adventure was quickly reduced to resentment. His lot in life was now a poisonous thorn festering in his side, getting worse every year. Ultimately the poison spread throughout his system, and the resulting bitterness never waned. He tried several business ventures, hoping for success at the level that would allow them to sell the farm and live happily ever after in any town but Perryton. All his ventures failed, heaping misery onto misery and debt onto his balance sheet. By the time he was 28, terminal resignation had set in. There was going to be no leaving the farm or Perryton. It was a sadistic, twisted version of *It's a Wonderful Life*. Sadly, for Abel, there was no Clarence, Mary, or Zuzu's petals to make this story a happy ending.

And then came Jimmy and Susie.

Over the years, Susie and Jimmy were sucked into the vortex of their dad's depression. As it turned out, Jimmy was a conduit for his dad's anger and he had a lot of anger. He felt the wrath of his dad's failures on a regular basis. Unable to cope with Abel's descent into constant verbal, and sometimes physical, abuse, their mom left them and Perryton in the dark of night.

This was the last straw for Abel.

Everyone had left town and he was left in town. I sort of felt sorry for Jimmy when I learned about his home life. Sort of. It also seems that Susie was the apple of her dad's eye. Abel treated her like a queen, most of the time, which only further ate at Jimmy. You can only kick the dog so often before it permanently turns feral. Jimmy was kicked way past the number of needed times.

And so the cycle continued: Jimmy beating Susie, Mr. Polanski beating Jimmy, and Jimmy hating everyone in the world. Like father, like son. What do they say about the infamous descending acorn? Susie ultimately suffered from a form of post-traumatic stress disorder which makes sense based on her living in, and coping with, a war zone.

And, to make a long story very short, this is why she missed so much school at the end of fifth grade. This is why I never saw her on the bus that Spring, why she never brushed against my shoulder or looked at me with those big green eyes.

***

Boredom will make you do a lot of things that an otherwise occupied mind would never dream of. And I was very bored on the Saturday morning of June 5th. I was sitting at the kitchen table facing a day with literally nothing to do. Luke and Dad were off to some Jr. High football love-fest and Mom was at the church.

I was not ready to go see Mrs. Ray.

I was determined to do it sooner, as opposed to later, but wanted a fully vetted plan. Well, maybe that wasn't it. What I really wanted was the nerve to walk from our back door to her back door. I didn't have the nerve on that day.

I flipped the TV on and off several times, quickly dismissed reading a book. (After all it was summertime, and no one in their right mind reads in the summer.) I settled on a few games of Solitaire. How bored do you have to be to settle on Saturday Solitaire? The cards held my interest for about three losing games and then Susie popped into my mind. Not just the thought of her, but her feel and her smell. My brain quickly bounced from our rides home together on the bus, to her absences from school, to the fact that I hadn't seen her in weeks, and from there hatched the totally insane idea of walking to her house to check on her.

What was I thinking?

Obviously I wasn't. Hindsight is 20/20, or so they say.

I pulled on my best Levi's, laced up my new sneakers, and set off without a single thought as to the downfalls of my idea. My legs felt pretty good so I assumed I could make the walk without much effort.

I never thought about having to retrace my steps for the mile and a half home.

I never thought about Jimmy.

And I never thought about the state of Susie's home life or the mental state of her father. The idea that Jimmy could have been home should have stopped me in my tracks and sent me home. But out the door I went, up the driveway, and left onto the shoulder of Old US 40.

The shoulder along 40 was more of a wide drainage culvert dividing the road and the very edge of our property and then the Polanski's property all the way to their front drive and beyond. The grassy culvert was set a few feet below the grade of the road and was fairly smooth due to years of rain runoff, which was its only significant use other than catching the random, recently drained beer bottle. Compared to walking in the tight furrows between the corn and wheat rows, it seemed like a perfectly paved sidewalk.

It was a mild June morning, and there was still a bit of crispness to the breeze. My walk was easy. I made good time. Very few cars passed in the 30 minutes it took me to walk to the entrance to the Polanski drive. The coolness in the air, and the coolness in my steps, abruptly ended as I ascended the side of the drainage ditch and landed on the gravel entry road that twisted out of sight towards the Polanski's house.

My stomach fluttered; I was going to see Susie.

Then real life slapped me in the face. I remembered Jimmy's harsh scowl as he had hopped onto the bus the day before. What was I going to do if Susie wasn't home and Jimmy answered the door?

Just then, I caught a glimpse of the rusty red truck through the trees. My heartbeat picked up. Jimmy and his father were probably coming for me! Hunting me down! They knew I was there, knew I was coming to see Susie. I whirled around and dove into the culvert, lying flat up against the corrugated metal drainage pipe that connected that side of the driveway with the other side. The pipe was too small to crawl into, otherwise I would have. I pressed so tightly into the grass and dirt that it felt like I would have permanent creases in my skin. I quit breathing and waited for the truck to drive by. I could hear its speed slow as it approached 40 and then accelerate to head into town. I rose up quickly to peer over the level of the road with just enough sight line to see two heads through the back window of the pickup. I had my confirmation. Both Polanski males were off the property. The coast was clear.

I was going to see Susie.

I exited the culvert and stood on the entry to the Polanski's front drive. I took inventory of my state. Not good. The clean shirt I had picked out to wow Susie was now wrinkled, dirty, and grass stained. Oh well. I rubbed the grass and dirt out of my hair and wiped the leaves off my face.

It was as good as it was going to get.

I finally rounded the last curve and stopped in my tracks 20 yards from the Polanski house. Did my jaw drop? It sure felt like the proverbial slack-jawed moment. I could not believe what I was looking at. My initial thought was I had landed in an overdone scene for a B-level horror movie. The two-story farmhouse was not too different architecturally from our house, but it looked like a brown wart on brown landscape. It needed paint so badly that I couldn't tell what the original color was. The shutters were akimbo, and a few of the windows were covered up with plywood. This seemed like the epicenter of decay. All the vibrant green of the outer wheat field slowly turned to a pale yellow to a dingy brown before terminating at their home. There was not a living blade of grass within the 20-yard perimeter.

I'll be honest—it scared me.

I was sure there were cannibals chained in the basement ready to dine on my flesh and bones, or maybe *The Texas Chainsaw Massacre* redux. I shook my head to rid myself of these thoughts. I remembered Susie and could not reconcile this house with her. I was in the wrong place. I had for sure stepped into a horror movie.

"Hey, Jacob. What are you doing here?" The sound of the front door slamming shut jolted me out of my fog. Embarrassment replaced the feeling of dread. I went from scared to elated. Susie looked like a diamond sitting on a pile of coal.

"I came to see you. You've missed a bunch of school and I was… worried." I blurted the truth. I'm glad I did. A stupid excuse would have been just that.

"I'm fine, Jacob." Susie's eyes darted down the road and back to me. "But you should go."

"I saw your dad and brother leave as I was walking up to your driveway. They didn't see me."

"Jacob, I don't know when they are coming back." She looked scared.

I shrugged. "So, I'll leave as soon as we see them coming up the drive." I hope that sounded more confident to her than it did to me.

Susie stepped off the porch and began to walk toward me. She was a beautiful as always. Thick blond hair, blue jean shorts, and a Led Zeppelin t-shirt. That moment sealed the deal. I loved her. I always have. I always will.

"Jacob." She smiled that Susie smile. "I'm glad you came, and I'd love to talk to you on Monday at school. But this…isn't a good time."

She stopped two feet from me. Her smell followed close behind and overwhelmed me. I would have taken a beating just to spend the rest of the day with her. I didn't understand what she would have to endure if her father or brother caught me there.

It was later in life, in very private moments, that she opened up to me. If I had known then what I know now, I may have been inclined to be her knight in shining armor. To have stayed and conquered her demons.

Or maybe that would have made me her *dead* knight in shining armor.

"I'm...I'm glad you came, Jacob." She was pushing me down the road. "We'll talk on Monday."

I was relentless as only an 11-year-old boy can be. The last thing I wanted to do was walk all the way home empty-handed. We were both too young for the all-out emotions of lust. That would come later. But I was old enough to have that feeling of deep friendship, maybe on the precipice of first love. I started to argue my case again, begging her to just let me stay a few more minutes.

Susie would have none of it. She stood there with her fist on her hips, unwilling to budge. The look in her eyes made me realize she wasn't changing her mind.

"Okay, Susie. I'm glad you're okay. I'll see you later." It was all I could muster. I turned and headed back out the way I arrived.

The road was mostly shaded, thanks to a line of Cottonwoods planted years before down both sides. I'm sure it looked majestic at some point, probably when Jimmy's grandpa was still alive and kicking. The current Polanskis cared for these trees like the balance of their property, so there were periodic gaps where a random tree had died and had never been replaced. A majestic drive to a well-kept farm house had turned into a gap-toothed drive to a hovel.

I was at the halfway point between the Polanski house and 44 when I saw the ever-present, trailing cloud of dust as the red truck exited the rural route onto the windy drive.

I was trapped.

My stomach sank and my pulse accelerated.

A million fruitless options raced through my brain, a brain seizing up with fear at an alarming rate. I couldn't run home without running past the truck. I couldn't hide in the ditch because it was still 200 yards in front of me. I had nowhere to go. My knees began to sing in pain almost as a precursor to the way the rest of me was about to feel. My feet felt like they were mired in a molasses puddle. The pain in my knees continued to ramp up. I think, in retrospect, whatever alien authority had overcome me during these past nine months was telling me what to do.

It was as if a voice in the sky whispered, *"Connect the dots, Jake."* I had painful knees every time I walked in the rows of the wheat field by my house. A wheat field exactly like the one that was 10 feet away. Suddenly my brain seizure abated, and the path to safety became obvious.

I half ran, half dove through an unintended opening in the Cottonwood trees and into the Polanski's wheat field. I was far enough from the house that the wheat was relatively healthy and provided more than enough cover. I pushed lower than I had in the culvert, trying to disappear into the dirt. I lay there completely still as the pickup truck ambled by.

Jimmy and his father were driving without a care in the world, not knowing that a prone invader was just three yards from them in a state of unbridled fear. After the pick-up truck had driven well past where I was, I stood up for hopefully the last time that day and brushed off the dirt and leaves covering my entire front side from head to toe.

As quickly as I could, I limped off the property and back into the drainage ditch along RR 40. After being in the Polanski's wheat field, that roadway felt like a familiar blanket, like Mom's kitchen, like homemade apple pie. Whatever corny euphemism I used to describe it, the fear was released and replaced with a feeling of safety.

I did not fully realize until later how much danger I was actually in by going to Susie's house. I thought my only risk was Jimmy, but later learned his dad should have been my biggest fear. If Jimmy was a walking time-bomb, his dad was an incendiary device.

Yes, I had put myself into danger but, worse, I had put Susie in danger.

I vowed to never do anything to possibly hurt her again. I suspected Mr. Polanski was the source. Certainly, the ruinous state of their farm could not be solely laid at the feet of Jimmy, but I did decide that the ruinous state of his son was no accident. Fear crept back into my consciousness. Fear for Susie and that ever so slight and fleeting feeling of sympathy for Jimmy. Mr. Polanski was a bad man and had created a son in his image. Susie escaped some of the collateral damage but not all. She dealt with the effects well into her adult life, as did I.

27

JACOB

Standing on the front porch of our house never felt so good.

The front porch had never *looked* so good either. Painted railings and shutters, flower pots teeming with pansies, Gerber daisies, and trailing rosemary. Yeah, the paint was scuffed off the floor planks between the steps and the front door, but that was to be expected.

My dad and I had fixed it up over the past few weeks, made it nice.

And, as I stood there, staring at the beautiful farmland where I was fortunate to grow up, I glanced in the direction of Susie's farm and shuddered. I was so fortunate.

I vowed right then to never take my parents for granted. For all the issues we had, and all the issues we would continue to have, they paled in comparison to others. My dad was not perfect, would never be close, but at least he was a man of compassion with a moral compass that pointed in the right direction most of the time.

He battled his demons like lots of other men, maybe more often than other men, but right then standing on the front porch, a mere hour after I had traipsed across our wheat field after hiding from Mr. Polanski, I would have sworn he was a saint.

Compared to Mr. Polanski he should have been canonized by the Pope himself.

My reverie was broken by my mom peeking out the door. "There you are, Jacob! Come and have some lunch."

I turned toward the railing and tried to hide my grass-stained clothes from my mom's probing eyes. "Be there in a second, Mom. I just have to wash up."

I raced upstairs and into the bathroom to wash my hands and face. My neck and arms too. I should have taken a full-blown shower, but Mom would have noticed. I ran my fingers through my hair and then quickly changed into clean clothes. I jammed the grass-stained clothes under my mattress. I'd figure out what to do with those later.

I was back down the stairs within three minutes.

I plopped down at the table just as my mom set a soup bowl and spoon on the placemat. The room felt brighter and the furniture seemed newer than it had just that morning. All was good in the Ross household. I wondered why.

The ceramic bowl was light brown on the inside and deep red on the outside with four roosters evenly spaced like they were marching in a never-ending circle. The dishes we had owned for my entire childhood. Some were cracked and re-glued, and all were chipped, but they had held every meal I can remember. (My office is the final resting place for the last remaining dish, a soup bowl of all things, sitting on the end of the credenza. I made a conscious decision not to give it to Goodwill. It reminds me of Mom, and it reminds me of all her wonderful meals, but mostly it reminds me of the fact that I grew up in a household full of mealtime conversations, kindness, and sage advice. At least most of the time.)

"Where are Dad and Luke? Not home yet?"

"Still at the football whatever, I assume," Mom said, rolling her eyes and shaking her head. She felt a lot like I did about the sacred game of high school football. I had to chuckle.

"More power to them."

"We're having chicken noodle soup. Made it from last night's leftovers." She held up a ladle from the pot, noodles heaping from the sides of the spoon. "I made the noodles just now. But I can also make you a sandwich if this is not enough."

"A sandwich sounds good. The soup sounds better. I'm starving."

I stood up and walked to the cabinet and grabbed a plastic cup. I poured myself a glass of milk. Mom already had her tea on the table. I also snatched a few paper towels, fancy enough for an ad hoc lunch, and sat down.

There was dead silence in the room for about two minutes after she put the bowl in front of me and I scarfed down half of my lunch.

Mom shot me that *"slow down or you will choke to death"* look that is universally required whenever a kid eats too fast, or what is deemed too fast by a parent. Message received. I set my spoon down, wiped the soup off my face, and leaned back in my chair. I sat completely still for 30 seconds under a glare of inquisition from Mom. She didn't say a word. She didn't need to.

I knew exactly what she was thinking. *"Where have you been all morning?"*

Slowly a slight smile broke across her face and the conversation began. Mom was not direct. She liked to work her way into the big question by softening up your midsection with numerous meaningless jabbing questions.

"Why are you so hungry? Why'd you head upstairs when you got home?" Okay, so those were pretty direct.

And then, just as you were focused on her right jabs to the abs, she swung the strong left upper cut. "Where were you while I was at church?"

I tried to dodge it, to come up with an answer that would satisfy her, but she caught me directly in the jaw. TKO. Match over. For a split second, I thought about making up some crazy story about working in the pasture or in the barn, but decided, wisely, to lay out the truth.

"I walked down to the Polanski farm to see if Susie was okay. She missed a bunch of school this last month." Relief filled me as soon as the words came out. Maybe Mom would have some answers? I sure had some questions.

With each successive word, Mom's mouth gaped a little more, her eyes opened a little wider, and her face twisted into a mixture of fear and pain. This was not what she had expected me to tell her.

"You what? You went to that…that house?" It was all she seemed able to come out with. Her other words stuck in her throat.

Her reaction answered a lot of questions.

Finally she began talking. "Honey, Susie's dad is…not a very nice man. And, sadly, from what I hear, her brother is turning into a mirror image of him."

I just nodded.

"Jacob, I know what happened on the bus with you and Jimmy Polanski. Luke told me the story. Do not ever go over to that house again. I know you like Susie. Everyone does. The poor girl, living in that crazy house. But I won't risk your safety."

Man, I had been so in the dark.

Mom talked about the Polanskis as if Susie's difficult home life was common knowledge throughout Perryton. Small towns do not hide much, if any, of the truly juicy gossip. Abel's view on the world slowly bled over to Jimmy, as it was apparent to most of the elementary school teachers that Jimmy was emotionally charged, to say it kindly. Most hoped he'd grow out of it, but deep down they knew better. Too many of Abel's genes and influences. The social theory of nature vs. nurture didn't apply here; it was both. It became worse with every year. To the point where having Jimmy in your class meant you lost the informal lottery that was held every August in the teacher's lounge.

(Most everyone in Perryton would also have agreed with my assessment of Susie. *"How in the world did she survive the situation? How was she such a delight? How did she rise above her brother and Dad?"* The truth to the first question, as I found out later, was she didn't. Not entirely. The answers to the other two questions were both difficult and complex. Years later, I was privy to some of the emotional struggles she had with a deep-seated anger, but that's a story for later.)

I glanced up at Mom and saw the terror in her eyes.

"Jacob," she shook her head and bit her lip. "Just promise me you'll never go over there again. Never. Is that clear?"

How could it not be clear?

"Jake, promise me."

"Yes, ma'am, I promise."

28

MARY DOUGLAS, 2014

The heart of winter in London is a thing of beauty on one level and a thing of brutality on another. It is always wet, it is always windy, and it is always cold, always. Bone-chilling cold. The kind of cold that makes the inside of your ears ache if exposed to the frigid air for more than a few moments. The kind of cold that makes fingers tingle, toes burn, bodies shiver. It's no wonder Londoners drink so much hot tea.

Most people hate winter in London, but Mary loves it. She has ever since the day she stepped off that plane seven years ago. She says she loves the vibrancy of London, the teeming diversity, the colorful blend of humanity mixed with the grey of London's foggy sky. And I believe her, but I also know that Mary mostly loves London because it is the antithesis of central Kansas. There are no wheat farms sprawling down highways as far as the eye can see, no rusting pickup trucks pushed into driveways and all but forgotten, no tiny farmhouses dotting the landscape one after another, no Perryton and its endless cast of characters.

Instead, she lives among wonderfully crowded streets, where she attends the theater whenever it strikes her fancy and afterward chooses between a lovely little Indian bistro owned by a couple from Mumbai or a classic French café that serves the most amazing chocolate croissants. There aren't chocolate croissants in Kansas, that's for sure. Unless, of course, you count Little Debbie chocolate cupcakes as French pastries.

Mary escaped Perryton—as she often describes her departure—within months of graduating number one in her high school class and acing the SAT. She was only 17, but more than ready to leave Kansas to start her college career. With numerous options, she chose New York University or, really, they chose her. The relentless admissions team recruited her, offering a full ride scholarship into the College of Liberal Arts, where she dove head first into a BS in Art History. Again, top of her class. Who from a farm community in Kansas does that?

Four years in New York City cemented the deal: Mary was never coming home. She was the exact opposite of Oliver Wendell Douglas in *Green Acres*—she wanted tall buildings and city streets and crowds. In her third year at NYU, Mary met Jackson Douglas at an Art History lecture. She fell hard for him, and truth be known, he did the same. They married shortly after graduation. Jack, a third-generation New Yorker, came from a family that never worried about money. They were very well-heeled as New Yorkers put it.

Jack and Mary quickly fell into busy lifestyles. Mary went to graduate school by day, quickly earning several PhD tracks with a combination of outstanding grades and an infectious personality. Jack jumped head first into the family business. On weekends, they window shopped 5th Avenue, dined in tiny restaurants where owners served them dishes like Egg Plant Parmesan and salted Bronzini that Mary could never have tried back in Kansas. They saw every Broadway show, walked hand-in-hand through Central Park, falling more in love under the city lights.

Once Mary graduated with a Masters Degree, she began to interview and (not surprisingly for anyone), she had about a million offers to extend her education. Okay, so it was more like seven, but she really could have gone anywhere in the world. She chose the Royal College of Art and embarked on a doctorate in Art History. Jack's family import/export business had its European and African headquarters in London so (as Mary's ever-growing luck would have it) he simply transferred to London. If only life were that easy for all of us.

Mary's glowing academic career ended with dazzling commendations and resulted in job offers she didn't want. Full-time teaching, even at a top university, sounded absolutely stifling. Art history research sounded horrific to her. She needed lots of people and lots of space, and so she landed softly into art restoration. She spent her days either traveling Europe to consult on oil paintings that needed repair, teaching an Art History class once a week at her alma mater, or writing books on her love for art history and restoration.

Her home and professional life was a fantasy. The cherry on the sundae was the birth of their son William, or Liam, as he was called for the remainder of his life.

She says, at that point in her life, she nearly forgot Kansas. It was a dream world to her—so long ago and so far away. She rarely thought of it and certainly didn't miss it. Or us, for that matter. (Okay, I confess she missed me and Mom a little, but I'll get to that in a minute.) Her childhood, her family, was such a small, small part of her life now. Sad as that is.

I suppose that's what happens when you have a childhood that's worth escaping.

29

JACOB

Three months is a lifetime.

It's also a split second.

But, that summer, each day seemed like two or three, and the month of June took forever. *The Elementary School Time Warp*. It's not a theory, but a proven fact. If only that elongation of time never changed. Tragically, it not only changed inversely as I got older, it changed with a heartless vengeance. A true cruelty of life. I'm sure even Einstein couldn't fully explain this phenomenon. I guess we, as frail-minded humans, are never quite happy. We frantically grasp for the opposite of what we actually have. We want time to accelerate when we're young and to decelerate as we age. What person, in the final throes of their life, wouldn't love for *the Elementary School Time Warp* to reappear?

I was about to come out of the eternity that was summer for a

12-year-old. Other than my flirt with danger, otherwise known around our house as *Jacob's Polanski Death March*, I had a boring summer. I suppose that's what happens when it hurts to walk and your brain and body are doing crazy things. I had one fantastic evening and one monumental event wrapped in many layers of tedium.

(It is well known that boredom is a significant factor in the calculus of the *ESTW* phenomenon, which is why Luke, who spent his days playing football and drinking Cokes in the diner with Jennifer Morris, felt like summer flew by.)

I saw Susie twice after mid-June. Once, I spotted her in town while I was running errands with Mom. She was with her dad so I quickly moved to the other side of the street and waved from a distance. Her quick smile was a like a salve to an open wound. I swear she was lit up as if the sun was setting directly behind her.

The second time I saw her was at Johnstone's Freedom Park on the 4th of July. Thankfully, there were no signs of the rest of her family, so I slid onto her blanket next to her.

"Hi, Susie."

She beamed. "Jacob. How's summer?"

"Lonely. Terrible. Almost worse than school. Almost."

"That bad?"

"How's it for you?" I glanced at her, hoping she was looking back.

She was. Her eyes looked dark, stormy. "It's been hard, Jacob. I can't wait for school to start again."

We sat and talked for an hour, all the while missing the majority of the fireworks bursting overhead. Susie was as engaging as always.

Her hair was pulled back in a ponytail and she wore a *Pink Floyd, Dark Side of the Moon* t-shirt, replete with the triangular prism and fractured light. Where does she get these shirts broadcasting 70's rock bands? Her shorts covered only a small bit of her long, tan legs. They were folded gracefully underneath her body. My senses were overwhelmed.

(I never did ask how she ended up at the fireworks show without her family. I guess I just didn't care as long as I got that time with her.)

She did spend the first few minutes of our conversation dressing me down for showing up at her farm 3 weeks earlier. Was I ever going to live this down? She once again made me promise to never do that again.

I promised. Anything for Susie.

(I did, however, break that promise before high school was over. Many times, as it was.)

Sitting in the grass on that hot evening was the highlight of my summer. Of my year, for that matter. Susie's bright, happy, calm energy stayed with me for weeks. Of course, *ESTW* reversed its course and the evening flew by. In what seemed like a few moments, the fireworks show was complete, we both stood up to go our separate ways. I attempted to give her a hug, awkward at best, but at least I tried. She appreciated it. We smiled and parted, or at least she did.

I stood frozen in time and space, watching until the crowd engulfed her.

***

As if to add to the monotony of my summer, my early morning slogs continued as if they were part of a normal life. By the end of the summer, I had been enmeshed with this ritual for almost a year.

Life was almost ordinary at the Ross house. Repetition breeds contentment, I guess.

The pain in my legs was a little worse than at the start of the summer. What was better was the roller coaster pain I experienced early on in this craziness. The daily and weekly pain was consistent. The inflow of ideas, thoughts, memories, etc. were on an even keel too. Everything was…the same.

Things were good. Relatively, for sure.

To the rest of the world, my daily experiences would probably have been on the cutting edge of freaky, but over time, I'd been lulled into thinking the current state would be the future state and the future state would be the same as the current state. I was wrong.

I eventually learned to not try and predict the future.

I supposed you are wondering about my one monumental event of the summer. Here it is: I finally found the nerve to go visit with Mrs. Ray. Of course, Mary and I had numerous discussions leading up to it—often with me arguing, her pressing, me refusing—until finally on the afternoon of July 20th, I just decided to get it over with.

That morning, Mary and I talked about how I would approach Mrs. Ray. Since her visit to the hospital, I had worked her into The *Wizard of Oz* status. A person who was daunting, and yet magical. A person whose true self was hidden behind a façade. I had elevated her in my imagination to a person who—I'll be honest—scared the crap out of me.

(Now I know she did embody many of those characteristics. She was daunting in presence because she was, in fact, magical.)

Even as I tied my shoes, I tried to get out of it. "I just don't see the point of going over there. She's not going to remember."

"What's it going to hurt, Jacob?" Mary said. "She is one of the nicest people in this hick town." She did have a point.

"I guess the whole electrically-charged kiss was weird. What if it was a figment of my overactive imagination and she knows nothing about it?"

"We've been over this a dozen times. I think it was a sign, a message. What if she was asking you to come investigate and you don't go because you're scared?"

"And what if she had no such message and she ends up thinking I'm completely crazy?"

"So says the guy who entered the dark confines of the Polanski's farm." Mary smiled. "You can't say this is scarier, can you?"

Talking to Mary was like trying to catch a ricocheting bullet in a steel room. She organized her thoughts, made a pragmatic decision, and moved on to a different topic before most people could even understand the issue at hand. She wasn't really going off subject; she had just laid it to rest.

I finished lacing my shoes and resigned myself to a visit to the Ray house.

"Go, Jacob. Get out of here." Mary said. "Mrs. Ray is the key. I know she is. You know she is. It's why she gave you that signal. Now get out of here." She was opening the back door of the kitchen and half pushing me out onto the porch. It turned out Mary was right.

Once across the creek, you were standing on the border between the Mercers' (now Rays') farm and the Merkle's farm. Most people in town still called the Rays' farm by its former owners' names. The Mercer family had owned that property for longer than every lifetime in the county, so it took a bit of time to reorient most people's thinking.

I again tried to find a reason to head back. I was scared.

If I saw a possible downside in proceeding, I absolutely saw a downside in retreating. Mary was likely playing sentinel on the back porch in case I chickened out. Smart girl. I selected the possible over the guaranteed. On I walked.

The border of the two farms was not marked with a fence, rather with a series of overlaid, scalloped formations etched in the soil where both families turned their tractors 180 degrees as they crisscrossed their farmland. This impromptu road provided a straight shot into the Rays' farm and close enough that a left turn provided a quick jaunt through a section of their field to their house.

The winter wheat was now harvested so the field was wide open. This is the time of year when you can stand at most any place in Perryton and see to the horizon. All the fields were cut to the ground, and a sea of the brown and gold colors of the dying leaves and uprooted crowns dominated the view across the landscape. It was an appreciated beauty, a reminder of a successful harvest.

Walking along the tilled rows was strangely familiar. Three steps into the field and a familiar tremor radiated from my legs. The flow of energy pulsed as I walked, peaking at the midpoint of the field as if this was the source point of the emanation. The rate at which the vibrations modulated upward in intensity was exactly, as best I could tell, the same rate as it modulated down as I crossed the imaginary half-way point.

What was going on?

Why was it that, every time I was near Mrs. Ray, my brain started doing crazy things?

I popped out of the field onto a small stretch of mowed grass that ran along the back of their barn. My pain and the strange buzzing instantly ebbed. Now I knew for sure that the source of all this craziness was not some magical generator buried by a long past alien race underneath our fields. Location was not the key. So, what was the key then? Wheat? Mrs. Ray?

A turn right, then 20 steps and a left, and I found myself standing next to a patch of sunflowers lazily enjoying the warm summer day. Mrs. Ray's garden was immaculate. Straight rows, healthy plants teeming with summer vegetables of all kinds and, of course, not a weed in sight. The wind began to pick up and the sky was quickly turning slate grey. I slowly walked the 50 or so feet between the Rays' garden and their back porch. Each step was easier physically, harder emotionally. I had this foreboding sense that my day wasn't going to end well, that I was staring into the face of a George Romero remake of The Wizard of Oz, only this wizard did not dispense hearts and brains; he ate them.

(How could I have ever made the leap from the kindhearted Mrs. Ray to a zombie Tin Man? That just shows you the state of my mind at that point in my life.)

I stepped onto the first riser up to the back porch, moving about as slowly as I possibly could, praying she wouldn't be home.

With a bang, the back door burst open, and there she was. A smile exploded across Mrs. Ray's face as she wiped her hands on a bright red dish towel and tossed it back into the darkness of her kitchen.

"Jacob Ross. I have been hoping you would come visit me. Come on in, please come in. I just pulled an apple pie out of the oven. Care for a piece? We have vanilla ice cream too." She stepped aside and I was engulfed with the sweet smell only a freshly baked pie can emit. Even if I had wanted to say no, I couldn't now. My stomach would have none of that negativity.

Mrs. Ray slid a plate with a huge slice of pie in front of me. "Milk, Jacob?"

"Yes, ma'am. Please."

She turned back to the fridge to pour me a big glass of milk.

My eyes had fully adjusted from the bright light to the darkness inside her kitchen. I quickly decided it was not a dungeon of death, but just an ordinary farmhouse kitchen. In fact, it was a superb kitchen. They must have completely redone it before they moved in. It looked nothing like our kitchen at home. What had surely been crusty, yellowed linoleum had been replaced with hardwoods and, where most of my friends had 20-year-old GE appliances, the Rays' had matching, high-tech appliances of an unknown origin.

This was a kitchen for a master chef. I took a bite of the pie and realized that Celina Ray deserved a kitchen for a master chef. It was delicious. The ice cream was quickly melting as it nestled up against the still hot slice, but I ate it all so fast that the pie never had a chance to fully complete the job.

Mrs. Ray walked—or, rather, floated effortlessly—and sat next to me. There was something different and special about her. I knew right then and there that the electricity-charged kiss was real.

"Mr. Ray and the kids just left for town, so it will be quiet for a while. I need that occasionally," she casually remarked.

I pushed my plate aside. "That was delicious."

"Thank you, Jacob. I'll send a few pieces of pie home with you."

I wasn't going to argue with that.

She grabbed my empty plate and took it to the sink, saving me the embarrassment of licking the plate. (I admit: I was tempted.) With her back still to me, she broke into the subject we both knew was coming. It was the reason I was sitting there. It was the reason she had summoned me here.

And it was the reason I am alive today.

30

JACOB

"Jacob, how are your legs feeling?"

"Fine," I lied. Fine was relative.

"Oh, really?" She turned around toward me, her eyes almost accusatory.

I heard a little voice inside me whisper, *tell her the truth, do not omit anything.* This was the counsel my sister gave me. Mary was always right.

"Actually, ma'am, they're not fine. But they are the same as they've been for the last year, more or less."

"Are they still hurting?" It was more of a statement than a question.

"Yes. Quite a bit sometimes."

Mrs. Ray stood behind the chair to my right looking down at me.

"Are you still getting regular bouts of nausea?"

"Yes, but not as bad as before. I think I'm almost getting used to it."

"And what about your daily walks?" she asked as she sat down at the kitchen table.

How did she know this? She surely can't see me from her house. Did Mom tell her?

"Still the same. It's almost like I'm…um…sleepwalking. Or sleep slogging." Boy, did I sound crazy.

"Slogging, huh? I like that term," she said with no conviction.

I took a deep breath as the air in the room seemed to change. The prelims were over; the warm-up questions were asked and answered. It was now time for the change-up question that sent me reeling.

"So, Jacob, what about nightmares? Or frightening dream-like episodes?" She stared intently into my eyes as she walked around her chair and elegantly sat down. She folded her hands into her lap as if this was the most comfortable situation possible. It wasn't for me.

I hadn't told anyone about those. Not even Mary. "What do you mean, Mrs. Ray?"

"You know what I mean, Jacob. Do you have strange dreams at night? Or strange dreamlike episodes while you're walking, like numerous random, often chaotic thoughts that seem to come out of nowhere and scramble in your mind?"

Could Mrs. Ray read my thoughts?

I think she knew she had scared me because she put a hand on mine. "It's okay, Jacob. I understand. If anyone understands this all, it's me."

I responded in a frantic, high-pitched voice reminiscent of a late-night TV pitchman. "H-how do you understand?" Hold it together, Jacob.

"Jacob, I'm not really sure. I think it had to do with the time I came to see you in the hospital. Do you remember much of that visit?"

So she did remember the kiss. "Yes ma'am."

"Do you remember when I bent over you and kissed your forehead? Just before I left?"

I flinched. "Ye-yes. How could I forget?"

This was nuts. Was I really going to tell her about the kiss that felt like an electric shock? She'd think I'd lost my mind.

"It felt a bit like an electric shock, didn't it?" she said as her eyes bore even harder into me. She was looking for any sign of truth to her statement. No problem; it was printed on my face.

"Yes." I got out that word, no problem. Yes, the kiss had felt like an electric shock.

"I felt it too. It was as if a small current ran down my face and leapt onto you. I knew right then that we would be having this talk one day."

"That—that's right, Mrs. Ray. It was like the current ran all the way down my chest and then back as if it boomeranged. The weirdest part was that, after that, I felt better."

It was Mrs. Ray's turn to look shocked.

"It was like you healed me, for a bit at least."

"There's more, Jacob. Immediately after that kiss, I began to have visions. At first, I wasn't really sure what I was experiencing, but over the course of the following weeks, I realized the current had carried the knowledge of all your pain and confusion into my conscious. Basically, I can feel what you're feeling."

I looked at her, stunned. After that, she certainly wasn't ever going to be able to call me crazy. "Is...is this something that has happened to you before? Can you feel for other people?"

"That's a story for another time, Jacob."

Another time? All this and she wanted me to wait for another time?

"How about now? My last year has been a living nightmare. I'm scared to death and now I know you have some answers. Please, tell me."

"I understand, Jake. I do. But today is not the day."

I was being dismissed. She stood up and walked to the kitchen counter to wrap up some pie.

I pushed back my chair and rose. I started to rebut her decision but quickly thought better of it and turned to walk out the back door.

"Jake."

"Yes, Mrs. Ray?"

"Jacob, my only conclusion is that I was saved all those years ago so I could save you. You are the one that Evil and Good seem to be fighting over."

"But, why?" I stammered, hardly able to breathe.

"I don't know why, but I think I'm right. I think they are."

This shook me to the core. Good and Evil are fighting over me. For the first time ever, I wondered if Mrs. Ray was off her rocker. Unfortunately, she wasn't. Not even close.

"Come on, Mrs. Ray. That's Hollywood stuff. I mean I've only seen that movie a hundred times."

Her mood immediately changed. A pall fell over her. "Jacob, I am right about this. For some reason, you are focus of Evil's emergence and Good's efforts. Is it either because Evil wants you to lead its charge or because Evil wants to stop you from being allied with Good. I'd like to think it's the latter. Either way, we need to find out."

That last bit of information was a bit disarming, to say the least.

Her demeanor lightened a bit and she leaned forward, drilling me with her eyes, as only Mrs. Ray could.

"Evil doesn't want you to be evil; it just doesn't want you to be good. Evil realizes it just won't work to make the masses purely evil—it would destroy the world. Plus, it's too much effort and too much noise. And so Evil chooses subtlety. It chooses to enter with a whisper so you may not even realize it's there."

"There are three types of people in this world, Jacob—good people, bad people, and those who are indifferent. Sadly, the last category is by far the largest. Evil needs only to focus on the good people. The bad people of the world are already on Evil's team, and the indifferent sorts have already removed themselves from the game. And so, without much effort on Evil's part, the playing field is significantly tilted, and the numbers start to stack in Evil's favor. That leaves just a few truly good people to stand up to Evil, to stand in the way of Evil's progress." A slight pause, and Celina Ray asked me. "What is the definition of good, Jacob?"

I thought this was a story, not an exam.

"I don't know. Doing the right thing, I guess."

"To some degree, you are correct, Jacob. But good as I am referencing

161

is far deeper than just doing right. Good, in the truest sense, pushes back on Evil. Good protects the soul from Evil's reach. True Goodness is what is needed to survive. One of my favorite Bible verses comes from Romans 12: "Do not be overcome by evil, but overcome evil with good." Paul was correct then, Jacob, and he still is today."

I certainly had failed that one-question test, hadn't I?

I took a deep breath, and she handed me two pieces of her amazing apple pie Saran- wrapped on a paper plate. "You might want this later."

"Thank…you."

Her smile broadened. "Good bye, Jacob. Come back soon, and we will talk some more."

There are three things I remember about the walk back home that afternoon. The first was that I felt nothing as I traversed the Ray's' field. Strange. The second was that it was darkly ominous due to the sun beginning to set behind the low, building rain clouds. And the third was the torrential downpour that hit as I was crossing the creek.

I ran up the path and onto the back porch. I was soaked to the core.

With the covered pieces of pie balanced on my lap, I sat on the old wooden bench that had been living at our house when we bought the farm. The solidness of the oak slats felt good. They felt reassuring. It was the first time since I walked into the Rays' kitchen that anything had felt solid. Everything else felt like shifting sand that was about to pull me under, engulfing me in madness and not thinking twice about the consequences.

After 15 minutes of hard rain, the weather began to ease; the wind behind the storm calmed, dropping the air temperature below that of a normal July afternoon. I began to shiver as the remaining wind lapped across my soaking wet clothes. I'm sure this was the cause of my shivers. Or could it be the remnants of my afternoon at Mrs. Ray's?

I was never able to decide.

31

JACOB

As you can imagine, the following week was torturous.

I spent my waking hours alternating between the dissection of every last word of my discussion with Mrs. Ray and nervously wondering when I would see her next.

What would I ask her?

What would she reveal?

I had, of course, told Mary everything Mrs. Ray told me. She listened attentively to every detail but was just as stumped as I was about what Mrs. Ray had meant. We both agreed to not speak a word of any these discussions with Mom or Dad. Leave them in the dark. Best for them and definitely best for me.

(That said, Mary did flinch a few times when I detailed some of the weirder revelations, particularly in regard to my thoughts and memories moving on an electrical trail into Mrs. Ray's conscious. Looking back, I'm amazed Mary didn't immediately dismiss me as crazy.)

I was determined to find answers. My plan was to spend the remainder of the summer visiting with Mrs. Ray as often as necessary until I figured out exactly what was going on. I figured, if anyone could figure out a way to cure me, it was her.

The good news was that she was receptive and amazingly forthcoming every single time I went to visit her. She always had some delicious baked good ready to serve me and always invited me in with a smile. The bad news was that she was not available as much as I wished. Either way, that summer she began the process of opening my world to a degree I could have never fathomed otherwise. Her canvas had way more colors than I knew existed. Some of these new colors were light and cheerful. Some were dark and terrifying. Unfortunately, when you mix light colors into dark colors, the dark tends to be predominant.

My second conversation with Mrs. Ray was 10 days following my first. (To set the record straight, I was nowhere near patient enough to wait 10 full days after the first conversation. I had made the trek to her house several times in the days between that first conversation and the second, but no one was home.)

On that stifling July day, I arrived on the back porch around 10:00 in the morning. It was a clear, hot morning, and the sun was already overbearing. I licked my parched lips and hoped she was home so I could get a glass of water. I leaned against the door jamb and looked around for a door bell or ringer, but none was to be found. I lightly rapped on the door frame and peered in through one of the small glass panes. The kitchen was dark and the house was quiet. No one home again. I turned to walk away when I decided I had not knocked hard enough, so I gathered my courage and strength and knuckled up to the door with four hard raps. Again, not a sound inside. I turned to leave when I heard faint footsteps descending the stairs. Marcus Ray opened the door but, unlike his Mom's smile and warm welcome, he just stood there with his arms crossed and a look on his face that said, what do you want?

"Hi, Marcus. What's up?" Why can't I ever come up with the perfect comment that doesn't make me sound awkward?

"Nothing. What are you doing here? Are you lost?"

"I—uh—I'm here to visit with your mom. Is she home?"

He answered with a look of complete confusion. "Why would you want to see her?"

"None of your business. Could you please go let her know I'm here, Marcus?" A rather bold comment for Jacob Ross if I might say.

He shrugged and opened the door to let me in, as if anything else was better than this conversation. His eyes half rolled and he disappeared up the stairs again.

(I didn't see him again that day. As close as Marcus and I became later in our lives, we had a fairly unceremonious beginning. I take that back; we felt flat out disdain for each other.)

"Hi, Jacob!" Mrs. Ray hurried down the stairs. "I was hoping I would see you this week."

"I came by a few times, but no one was here." I added and quickly regretted it.

"We've been busy. All week we've been helping plan the church summer picnic. It was yesterday. Come on in to the kitchen."

"Could I have a glass of water?" The sweat streaming down my face was stinging my eyes.

"It's going to be a brutally hot day. Summer in Kansas, what can I say?"

"Yes, ma'am." It was all I could think of to respond. A stifling hot day in Kansas, and Mrs. Ray looked as cool as the proverbial cucumber. I was sure she never dropped a bead of sweat in her life.

"I don't think anyone will bother us in the kitchen. Seems my family only dares to step foot in this part of the house if food is on the table and it is time to eat. How about some iced tea instead of water, Jacob?"

"Sounds great." I sat in the same spot as last time we visited. There's always comfort in the familiar, I guess. I needed as much comfort as I could muster for sure. Mrs. Ray set the tea in front of me and I immediately drained two thirds of the glass. Man, was it good. She had added mint to the tea. Typical touch.

"Thank you. That really hit the spot."

"Would you like a refill?"

"Yes, please."

With the formalities out of the way, it was time to get down to business.

"Uh—er, Mrs. Ray?"

She interrupted me. "So Jacob, did you think much about last week's discussion?" she said with a smile that indicated she knew our discussion was all I could think about.

"Yeah. Pretty much every minute since we last talked."

"Good."

Good? Why was it good that she had made me think—*obsess*, really? I didn't even know what to say, what to ask. All this chaos was swirling around my mind like some sort of abstract twister. The excitement of this meeting had quickly vanished into confusion. This morning, I had lined out all my thoughts. I knew what I was going to ask and in what order. The perfect path to resolution. But now that Mrs. Ray was sitting in front of me, I may as well have been trying to answer Calculus II questions. I slumped in the chair. My confidence shattered. "Mrs. Ray, I'm lost. As much as I've tried to make sense of all this, I can't. I need guidance. I need help."

"Jacob, let's see if we can make some progress towards that end."

I nodded. It was all I could muster.

Mrs. Ray's demeanor quickly changed from sympathetic to inquisitional. "I'm afraid I do not have many, if any, answers to why you are in the situation you are in. I can't resolve the mystery around your walks, nor your knee pain, and I certainly can't fathom the reasons behind your dreams. But I've been wondering: Are these purely medical incidents? Or is something going on in that brain of yours? I've come to the conclusion that the real question is this: Is something going on that's...*unearthly*?"

I felt my eyes growing wide.

All pretense of formality and, to a degree, civility had vanished from our relationship. At least our relationship as it related to these discussions. Outside of this environment, I viewed Mrs. Ray with courteous respect. In the heat of our conversations, we broke down all barriers and the tone was one of long-time caring friends who spoke honestly and, sometimes, harshly.

"What are you saying to me? I came to get answers, not to be accused of being crazy. Or making this all up."

"I'm not accusing you of anything, Jacob. I just want you to understand my view and, more importantly, my limitations. I can't tell you why you are in this peculiar circumstance. I only know you are. I know this in a very odd way, which I'm sure makes you think I understand what's going on, or that I can possibly cure you." She leaned forward and, with piercing eyes like I've never seen since, said, "But I don't know, Jacob. And I can't cure you."

A spark of anger welled up in me. I'd had enough of not knowing. I decided to try a new tack. "Mrs. Ray, who are you?"

I was breathing hard. I had never in my life spoken to an adult like this. Certainly not one as respected as Celina Ray.

A slight grin appeared at the corners of her mouth, as if to say, Finally, the right question.

She sat back in her chair. You could sense the heat and the tension exit the room. A feeling of comfort moved into its place. "Who am I?"

"Yeah, who are you?" I reiterated.

"My name is Lydia Celina Ray, and I am most recently from Wichita, Kansas, where I lived all of my adult life until we moved here about two years ago." With an absence of emotion, she said. "Settle in, Jake, this is going to take a while."

That comment made me do anything but settle in.

"It is actually good to be home, back in Perryton, Jacob. We've had a rough couple of years, and this move has been good.

"Wait. You grew up in Perryton?"

"Yes, in New Richland. Lived there until I was 15 and then moved to Wichita to live with my Aunt Teresa, my dad's sister. I'd had enough of Perryton by then. Best to get away was how I looked at it. Four years earlier I had lived through the first traumatic event of my life. I was kidnapped out of my front yard. What ensued left two people dead and my family very emotionally scarred. We all recovered but, like a flesh and blood scar, there's always a reminder. A remnant that may fade to some extent with time but never truly disappears."

Lydia Williams. Celina Ray. They were one and the same. I had heard that story hundreds of times in Perryton. I couldn't believe I was sitting here talking to the real Lydia.

Over the next hour I sat in stunned silence as Mrs. Ray told me her version of the story of her kidnapping and the cascade of events that followed. She slid back into a semi-autonomic state as the story spewed forth. As the saying goes, "All's well that ends well." No, not always.

"Johnstone's Freedom Park was named after Mr. Davis Johnstone, wasn›t it?"

"Yes it was. Fitting, for sure. At least people will always remember his name. I can assure you that every single member of the Williams family will always remember Davis Johnstone."

"What happened to Davis?"

"He died in 1979 at the early age of 50. The entire town was in a state of complete bereavement. I found out later that Dad wore a black arm band to honor him for weeks. He loved Davis, and Davis loved my dad. I was living in Wichita by then but came home for the funeral. It was the last time I was here until we moved back permanently."

"What did Mr. Johnstone die of?"

"Brain cancer. Thankfully, he went quickly. The memorial service was at the First Baptist Church, or the First Johnstone Church as people affectionately called it. His dad had been the pastor for decades and retired about a year before Davis died. He was a wonderful man, too."

"I was there a few years ago. For a Christmas pageant," I added to no effect.

Mrs. Ray continued. "Jacob, this is going to seem strange to you, but I'm going to tell you a part of the story that I have only told one other person, and that was my husband. I haven't even told my kids."

I looked at her, confused. "Why me?"

"I'm telling you, because I think it's relevant to your current situation." She shuffled a bit in her chair. You could see her internal debate about whether or not this was a good idea. It appeared I wasn't the only one who felt like I was going crazy.

"I still do not remember being grabbed, you know, on the street that day." She sat up straighter, her body trembling. She leaned a bit forward, eyes riveted on the middle of the kitchen table. She had recessed again. I was not in a discussion with her. She was alone, exorcising long buried demons.

"I was playing in the front yard one second and in the trunk of a car the next. I had no idea how it happened. You can imagine my confusion. I was dangling out of this moving car, half hanging onto whoever grabbed me, half trying to escape. My legs were banging on the road with my knees taking the brunt of the pounding." She began slowly rubbing her left knee as if the pain had returned.

I could relate.

"I was then fully in the car and, again, I'm not sure how that happened. The smell was terrible. The floorboards were covered in trash and beer cans. The stink of the car was only surpassed by the stink of the two guys in the car. I now know their names, Jake, but still to this day, I can't seem to be able to say them out loud. They're just the two guys." She looked up at me but not fully. "It was at that moment that I realized, with terror, that I may never see my parents again."

"Do you know how that feels? A zap of fear courses through your body and mind. My head was spinning and nausea was overwhelming my insides. Clear thinking was not on the menu. The speeding car swerved and then stopped abruptly. My head slammed into the passenger door. They both laughed and spewed terrible language. This was fun for them. They were having a good time. Can you imagine? From my head down to the middle of my shoulders instantly went numb from the blow. I felt a trickle of blood line itself down my cheek. Suddenly, one of the men dragged me out of the front seat and, like a sack of potatoes, hauled me around to the back of the car. My head was hanging lower than my feet and I was covered in road dust. I was all-out crying by now. Through the fog that shrouded me, I heard one of them call me a nigger bitch."

I swallowed hard. It was hard to hear; I couldn't imagine living it.

Mrs. Ray just shook her head and gazed at the wall as if she were speaking to herself. "I will never forget that. I will never forget their hateful laughs. Those words were permanently seared into me. I still hear them echoing in my head from time to time."

"They threw the trunk open and tossed me in without as much as a thought for my safety. My head hit something hard and metallic just as the light was eliminated with the slamming of the trunk lid. Same spot on my head hit that had just the car door. I remember feeling so lost and confused, as if I was dreaming. I know I lost consciousness for a few seconds and then slipped in and out while confined. They also tied my arms and legs, but the worst part was the old, dirty rag they stuffed in my mouth. It was such a violent action that the corners of my mouth split and blood seeped into my mouth. They slapped a piece of duct tape across my mouth for good measure. All the crying had resulted in mucous filling my nose, so breathing was a huge effort. The oil-stained rag remained crammed in my mouth until I was pulled from the truck by my dad. I'm not sure how long I was in there. It felt like a long while…"

Mrs. Ray's words drifted off and she was silent for a few seconds. "Everything I just told you is the same story I told the police and my family long ago."

I nodded. She wasn't going to make me wait until the next time I visited again, was she?

Mrs. Ray finally looked right at me. "Jacob, this next part has not ever been shared with another soul. I even left this out from what I told Mr. Ray. It's never been spoken it out loud."

I swallowed.

"In that trunk, as I was bleeding and struggling to breathe, there was nothing I could do but pray. So I did. I prayed for my dad to save me. I prayed for the two guys to come to their senses. I prayed for my pain and fear to go away. But, mostly, I prayed to God that, if I was going to die that day, He would comfort me in heaven. I prayed as hard as I could. Even as a little girl, I somehow sensed that my life hung in balance."

This didn't seem like that big of a revelation to me.

"But Jacob, there's more. For a few moments, the road noise layered on with my addled state was deafening. I was being tossed around like some loose object in the truck. It was bumpy and loud and torturous. Then, abruptly, in the midst of my prayers, everything stopped.

"Stopped?"

"Yes, it stopped. All the noise ceased and the ride smoothed out. My eyes snapped open. A low intensity glow appeared all around me. My body was vibrating in a very comforting manner. All pain disappeared and my thoughts became crystal clear. I felt as if I was hovering in space, wrapped in a warm cocoon of seclusion and light, temporarily removed from the horrors of my predicament. This was not a dream or a symptom of a concussion; this was real. I knew it then and I know it now. Something miraculous was happening."

"I know that feeling, Mrs. Ray."

"Yes, I know you do, Jacob. At that very moment, absolute calmness washed over me and a voice assured me I would be okay. I was going to be rescued. Jacob, God spoke to me, directly to me. Just as quickly, the glow then dissipated and I was back to bouncing around the open trunk space in state of pain and confusion. The only difference was that I was not scared for my life anymore. Instead, I was scared for the two guys in the front seat.

We both sat there for several minutes, thinking, contemplating. I had absolutely no idea how any of this related to me. How was a 12-year-old supposed to make that leap? I finally broke the prolonged silence. "Mrs. Ray, that must have been so scary."

"It was."

"Bu—but...why is this connected to me?"

"I'm not sure, Jacob, but I just sense that it is." She paused and looked right into my eyes. "I'm really exhausted, Jacob. We will have to finish this up next time you come over."

"No. NO!" I didn't want to be disrespectful, but I wasn't sure I could wait that long again.

"Jacob, I'm sorry. I pray that we will both have clarity soon." And, with that, she cleared my tea glass from the table and walked me to the door, waving goodbye with a weary smile. This time I didn't argue. It would do no good. I simply headed home in silence.

32

JACOB

Refugio, Texas is not a destination town. Not even close. Located at the midpoint between Victoria and Corpus Christi on U.S. 77, Refugio is the same as a hundred other Gulf Coast towns—warm in the winter, hot in the spring and fall, and insufferable in the summer. More humid than an active sauna all year round.

Refugio was originally colonized in the 1830s by Mexican and Irish settlers along the Mission River. The current population is a little less than 3,000 and getting smaller by the day, having shrunk in population most every year since 1960. The townspeople of Refugio, pronounced *Re-fyur-e-o*, are typical small-town denizens—hard working, loyal, and giving. They love their town and love the Great State of Texas even more.

My parents have lived there for going on 14 years. My dad, ironically, answered a call for a part-time pastor at Grace Presbyterian Church of Refugio. Their HR diligence was less than attentive, and Dad was happy to leave Kansas behind the second he got the call.

The feeling was reciprocal for most of Perryton. Mom—who had maintained some friends in Perryton—was not quite as anxious to move, but dutifully followed Dad to Texas.

What choice did she have?

They considered the move a step into paid semi-retirement. Work some, play some, and, with any luck, earn enough of an income to fund their daily existence. The cost of living in that part of the world was not high. Real estate in a shrinking town was a supply-dominated equation, and pastors were often paid for their services in freshly-caught catfish or locally sourced venison.

Pastors in small south Texas towns were generally part-time, not based on the desire of either the congregation or the pastor, but more a function of the church's budget. The churches in Refugio had shrunk at even a faster rate than the population, if you can believe it. The town's population decline, coupled with an aging, dying membership made it so the church was left with a few elderly couples and the rare apathetic young adult who decided not to get out of Refugio right after graduation.

Long story short, Grace Presbyterian was not a thriving church.

Which was exactly what Dad needed. The last thing he needed was some old busybodies doing some digging into…well, into Perryton.

To this day, Mom has never quite recovered from the mess Dad made. She would have just left him—she almost did—but a 60-year-old divorcée without a viable means of self-support was possibly even worse than being married to a man like my father.

Possibly.

So she pulled up her figurative boots and committed to making the best of her remaining years. She reaffirms herself of this chosen course after each and every crying jag. But then she remembers...

Over the past few years, this resignation has been tempered to some extent by a group of friends that collected her into their weekly Bible study, monthly dinner club, and periodic book klatch. None of which Dad has any interest in attending. Mom is glad for that. Imagine if he, as pastor, wanted to be part of the church functions?

But things were rough. More than rough.

If Mom was honest with herself, her greatest regret was not walking hand-in-hand toward the sunset of her earthly existence with a life-long, trusted partner. Yes, she was walking towards that figurative sunset, of course, but certainly not with someone she trusted. She had learned long ago that plans in life are often just that—plans. For some reason, reality always intervenes and kicks the *hoped-for* to the side of the road. Usually using steel-toed boots launched with a great deal of gusto. As a result, the trust that was so tenderly guarded and highly valued is lost, as if one is trying to hold flowing water in a strainer. Trust to never be reclaimed. *It could be worse.*

At least that's what Mom always tells herself. As they say, "A lie you tell yourself often enough can turn into a truth." She never quite believes this euphemism, though, because her life really could be worse.

At least we were grown and gone before the walls completely caved in. When we were little, most people in Perryton thought our family was normal. Good, even. It had taken a while for Mom to open Pandora's box and see what was inside, but when she did, the contents were not pretty. The call to us about Dad's relapse and their hurried departure from Perryton had been a shock to everyone. Including me.

I tried to stay in touch with them, really I did. Mary told me a few weeks ago that she used to plan her calls to Mom around when she thought Dad would be at work. But, with his part-time schedule and unpredictable hours, she heard him answer the phone one too many times. She just stopped calling. Eventually, I did, too.

Mom told me in an email a few weeks ago that those conversations are what she misses the most. Talking to her children. Being part of our lives.

I felt guilty about that for a few days.

But then I remembered.

Parents become estranged from their children in two general ways. One is a slow erosion over many years. A lack of common interests or a lack of collaborative effort. The other is the result of a catastrophic event. The demise of Mary's and my relationship with Dad began with the former and ended with the latter. Luke's once strong relationship was fully imploded by the catastrophic event.

It hit him the hardest.

Either way, our family is completely scattered. Sure, I still talk to Mary, but the rest of them are simply people on my Christmas card list, memories that seem too far, too long ago, too hard to drum up.

And then I got another email.

Mom started by telling me that, at age 62, her life had not played out as she had dreamed it would. Not even close. Living in south Texas, technically estranged from her children, and living with a man who had flushed her respect for him down the drain was nearly unbearable. She reminded me that she was innocent. Sure, she was guilty by association because she had married Dad, but she had nothing to do with it.

She finished by asking a question that made a lump rise in my throat. *"Where do I go now, Jacob? Where?"*

It was a question I ran through my mind over and over on cold, dark nights. A question that seemed to define our relationship, our family's future.

The more I thought about it, the more I was convinced that my mom was okay. Sure, she was upset, but she would never leave.

Never change.

Never do anything about it.

Refugio with my father was where she would finish her life.

33

JACOB

The last time I saw Mrs. Ray that summer was on a Tuesday evening exactly one week before the start of school. I ventured over the fields mid-afternoon and we sat on the back porch in the cool evening air and sipped lemonade. Most of the conversation was a combination of a well-choreographed dance, back and forth, a question asked, a question dodged.

She told me many stories about her life in Wichita, her family, and her faith. I learned that she had met her husband at Wichita State during her sophomore year. When she told me she was 22 at the time, I did some quick math in my head and realized that was a bit old for a sophomore. I asked her why, she told me she would explain later. Always full of mystery, Mrs. Ray.

I laughed when she told me that, on her first day of Psych II, Mr. Ray had forgotten to bring a pen to class so he turned around and begged one from her. Who forgets a pen on the first day of class?

Even I, as a 12-year-old, knew to show up for school with a full bag of school supplies on the first day. Mr. Ray definitely needed Mrs. Ray.

She told me he had asked her out after class and she had said no. And so he kept asking. And asking. And asking. Poor guy! Just as I was starting to feel sorry for him, she told me she finally gave up and said yes. They got married a year later, had all four kids within a decade.

Four kids?

I counted on my fingers.

She saw the confused look on my face.

"Yes, we lost my daughter Adrianna when she was five. It was a few years ago. She was…she was incredible."

"What…what did she die from?" The mere thought of a five-year-old girl dying made my stomach ache.

"Muscular Dystrophy." Mrs. Ray's eyes looked glassy. "Do you know what that is?"

I shook my head.

"It's a horrible disease. She lost her ability to use her legs, her arms, her muscles."

Now my stomach really hurt. And my heart was beating so fast. "Her legs?"

Mrs. Ray leaned forward and put her hand on my knee. "Jacob, what you are going through right now is nothing like what happened to Adrianna. She got sick fast and never really recovered. It's…it's not the same."

I still felt an ache in the pit of my stomach.

"Jacob, I want you to talk to me about your slogs. Not what you do, but what you think."

It was hard for my mind to switch gears. "Why are we talking about my slogs right now?"

"I think the emotional, the spiritual even, is the key to a cure. I want to know what you are thinking as you walk, what your dreams are. I think, if we can figure out that, then *the physical ailments will be cured too.*" She said this more than once.

I obliged.

I told her everything I knew. She just sat there, staring at me with dark, knowing eyes. And then she sent me home again, no more answers, more confused than ever.

I felt as if I had taken three steps forward and about twenty back that summer. Because, as the school year began again, I was in the same place. Morning slogs. Weak knees. And a brain that didn't seem to want to cooperate no matter how much I willed it to.

I arrived home after 11:00 pm.

No one in my family was awake to greet me.

No one said a word the next day.

Had anyone even noticed I had been gone the night before?

34

JACOB

Regardless of what meteorologists say, September rarely, if ever, feels like Fall in central Kansas. Summer is too stubborn. Shorts and t-shirts are still the norm and most kids are trying to absorb as much of the outdoors as possible before the Fall flows into the grip of Winter and forces everyone inside.

And so, after the long and somewhat eventful summer, into sixth grade I was thrust, whether I wanted to go there or not. As I stepped onto the familiar bus at the familiar stop, I basked in the fact that it was my last year in elementary school. I was King of the Hill. (Or at least should have been.) Gimps are not Kings of the Hill in any universe in which we humans live.

It felt as if everyone was numb, as if they were settling in for the long grind. It was as if every ounce of collective energy we had was spent adjusting to daily routine, reigniting the part of the brain that remembers how to learn and, most significantly, battling it out for the all-important social pecking order.

(My rung was low on the ladder. I knew it on day one, and thus was able to save some emotional energy for other pursuits. There was some comfort in sitting on the sidelines.)

Day after mind-numbing day passed until I was lulled into the oblivion that nothing would ever change. Until, during the third week, the unexpected occurred. Or maybe I should say the event was anticipated, but the timing was unexpected. It was a Monday morning at 10:15; class was dismissed for recess. The summer had not been kind to my athletic ability so I no longer joined the hoards streaming onto the playground for a game of anything, much less my beloved kickball. If my classmates were indifferent to me when fifth grade ended, they were now completely oblivious to my existence.

I was left to spend my 30 minutes of recess each day trying to find something, anything, to do. That day, Mom had given me an out. Luke had left his science book on the table as he had raced toward the bus, and so Mom had hastily thrown it into my backpack. I had forgotten to give it to him, so I decided to use my recess time to deliver it. (Altruistic of me, I know.)

As everyone was zigging left out to the playground I zagged right down the hall toward the front of the school. One of the oddities of our school, due to a strange two-phase construction plan created to manage tightening budgets, was the set of two storage closets that were erected side-by-side where the middle and elementary schools V'ed together behind the shared administration offices. The storage closets were not necessarily strange, but the fact that they were built with about a 10-foot space between them was a bit odd. This 10 x 10 area served no purpose and, if some motivated builder had used his wits during the construction of the second building, this space could have been eliminated in lieu of a much larger contiguous storage area. But, alas, the City of Perryton employed no such worker, and the space sat there untouched, unused, mostly unnoticed.

Why does this useless zone between the storage closets matter?

It matters because of the events that take place over the next five minutes. Luke's science book in hand, I exited our building fully intent on a leisurely, 40-foot walk over to the middle school building where I would deposit the book on Luke's science teacher's desk and waste a good 10 minutes of recess time in the process.

My plan was interrupted.

The first noise I heard as the heavy glass door settled shut behind me was a whimpering sound emanating from the useless zone. I thought it was a hurt animal due to the high-pitched, almost rasping tone. I quickly realized I was wrong. Three stilted strides landed me in front of the open space, staring directly at Jimmy Polanski in the flesh. Jimmy had the collar of some hapless kid's stretched out t-shirt in his clutches and was rearing back with his right fist. By the looks of the boy's red and puffy appearance, it wasn't the first shot either. He was half on his knees and half hovering off the ground as Jimmy lifted him while simultaneously delivering the blow. His head snapped back like a piñata nailed by a baseball bat. Jimmy howled in delight. The recipient howled in pain.

His attention turned to me.

Oh, shit.

"What the fuck are you staring at, gimp-boy?" Jimmy spat in my direction. "Keep on walking."

I stood frozen in place.

"Go! Now!" The look in his eyes was nothing short of frightening. I was convinced Jimmy intended to kill this kid. A kid two-thirds his size who was probably guilty of nothing more than being in the wrong place at the wrong time.

The same place I appeared to be.

I flinched at the thought of the end game for this poor kid. I had every intention of leaving the scene of the crime, knowing full well I was already next on the Polanski hit list, and this wasn't going to help my cause. I took one step toward the school doors, trying to tune out the kid's cries. Then I snapped to a halt.

If I walked away, this kid was a goner.

If I walked away, I was most certainly next.

If I walked away, I would be carrying a barrel full of guilt with me even as I labeled myself a target.

It was at that moment that my sixth-grade year changed. I decided none of these things were going to happen. Right then and there, I decided I was done with Jimmy Polanski. With his bullying. With his cruelty. With my own fear.

I turned back around just as another blow was delivered. The limp victim was bleeding from his nose and mouth. He took deep sobbing gulps of air, as if the mere act of breathing caused intense pain. Although still conscious, I guessed he'd soon be out cold. I knew I couldn't do much, but I could possibly stop the beating where it stood.

Or maybe substitute his beating for mine.

"Jimmy, leave him alone." I regretted these words and this stupid idea as soon as they flew out of my mouth. It was now unquestionable that I was soon to meet the business end of Jimmy's fists.

"Jacob Ross, you dumb ass. I'm going to beat you within an inch of your life. I owe you big time and it's about time I paid up." The look of a deranged psycho left his face and was replaced by a look of utter calm. He seemed happy. This scared me even more. Oh, shit, was I in trouble.

Jimmy released the boy's collar and turned to me. I felt victim #1, slightly energized due to my idiocy, scurry away. I never saw him leave. I had developed fear-induced tunnel vision focused on Jimmy's clenched fist.

"I'll give you credit for growing a pair, Ross. I would never have taken you for anything but a pussy who'd run away," he smirked. "Oh, yeah, you're a gimp, so you can't run."

This sordid pun tickled him to no end. He burst out in a huge grin, flashing his crooked, yellow teeth for my gross amusement. He was quickly in my face, grabbing me by both sides of my collar. His breath was horrendous and the psychotic look was slowly moving back across his pock-marked face. He leaned in and sneered, "You're dead, Ross."

I think he meant it.

The other kid's beating had been for general amusement. Mine was for revenge, hate, and jealousy. There was clearly lots of pent-up demand residing in the depths of Jimmy's sick mind.

I never saw the first punch. Not sure if it was a left or a right. What I am sure of is that it caught me square in the middle of my chin. I staggered back a step as my knees buckled, only staying upright due to Jimmy's one-handed death grip on my shirt.

And then, as if to add agony to my pain, my knees began to sing like never before. Not now! I'm not sure if they had ever hurt worse during one of my slogs. Nausea welled up in the pit of stomach. I began to wobble to Jimmy's sick delight.

"Hey Ross, need some help up?" He smirked again, his yellow teeth almost glowing.

Nice guy. He lifted me semi-upright. Enough to have a clear shot with what was sure to be another well-located punch. I saw his fist forming. It was like watching a slo-mo replay. He reached back with his right arm, squeezing every ounce of blood out of his fist. I braced and closed my eyes.

The punch was never delivered.

Instead, I felt him tense up, then jerk back. I finally dared to open my eyes only to see Marcus Ray wrapping his hand around Jimmy's forearm and pulling back with all his might. I thought Jimmy's shoulder was going to dislocate as the full force of his forward movement was first aborted, then yanked in reverse. Jimmy's eyes widened in surprise. *"Who the hell is messing with me?"* was printed on his face. Marcus spun him around with such speed that Jimmy was now the one wobbling in place.

"What the fuck?"

"Leave him alone!" Marcus yelled. "He's tiny and mostly handicapped." Nice compliments, Marcus. I didn't care then, but I would certainly address these inaccuracies later.

Jimmy's first inclination was to turn and hit Marcus. To his credit, he quickly surveyed the situation and thought better of it. Marcus had him by four inches and thirty pounds.

"Leave," was simply all Marcus said, and Jimmy did. His glare said *this is not over.*

Jimmy scampered through the same door I had walked through not four minutes before. I sunk to the ground, trying to catch my breath. My jaw ached, my teeth hurt, and my knees were still humming in a rhythmic pain. I touched the side of my mouth, not surprised to see blood on my fingers.

"What are you doing out here?" Marcus asked, as if I was choosing to get the shit beat out of me.

I gave him the CliffsNotes version of the events including victim #1 as well as a little backstory to my "friendship" with Jimmy Polanski. Marcus frowned and told me I surprised him.

"Why would you help some kid you don't even know?" he asked.

Funny thing is, that is exactly what Marcus had just done in the same circumstance.

I just blinked and wiped the blood on my hands onto my pants.

"Come on, Jacob," he said. "Let's go get you cleaned up."

I said nothing but slowly stood up. My strength seemed to be returning.

"I have to hand it to you, Jacob, taking on Polanski was pretty stupid. But also pretty awesome. I'm sure that kid was happy too. Probably wishes you'd shown up earlier."

I stopped short of the door back into the school and turned to Marcus. "I wish you had shown up earlier, too." I smiled and then stopped. It hurt too bad.

Marcus smiled back. "Me, too, Ross."

I pulled open the glass door and let my new best friend enter in front of me. We were greeted by a horde of distressed teachers standing around a kid lying face down on the tile floor in the hallway.

Victim #1.

I found out later that his name was Tommy Blackshear and he was in fourth grade. His head was turned to his left and his body was twisted back to the right.

It did not look natural. It wasn't.

Mr. Lowden, the principal, later told my parents that Tommy, having escaped a further beating thanks to my moronic heroism, took two steps into the hallway and collapsed to the floor. He twitched for a few seconds and then froze as if someone hit the pause button on the remote control. Not a movement to be had.

Because it happened right at the end of recess when the classes were filing back into the building, several students and teachers had seen Tommy stagger into the school hallway and fall hard to the tile floor as if he was marionette whose strings had been summarily cut. His twitching body had freaked everyone out, followed instantly by his deathly still body, which only accelerated the fear. Blood pooled from his gaped mouth.

Mary Singer had passed out right then and there in the hallway, causing another flurry of activity around her.

And then Marcus and I walked in the doors.

Another flurry of activity, more chaos, as another teacher scurried to get a chair for me to sit down in.

Then, collective murmurs began to rise.

Jimmy.

Jimmy Polanski?

Where is that kid?

Has anyone seen Jimmy Polanski?

***

The assistant principal was sent to collect Jimmy.

I'm sure he dreaded that task. He found Jimmy hiding behind a hedge of Wax Leaf Ligustrums which lined most of the east side of the school property. He was smoking a cigarette of all things. (Have I mentioned that Jimmy was not the sharpest knife in the drawer?)

Mr. Clarkson escorted Jimmy back inside and then, five minutes later, back outside to the circle drive and into the back of a PDP squad car. Abel Polanski pulled up as the squad car was pulling out. He followed them to the police station. I'm sure Abel provided a calming influence on the situation.

The rumble on school property was the straw that finally broke the camel's back or, said better, the straw that finally got rid of Jimmy Polanski. It turns out my bold move wasn't so stupid after all. The school district had had enough of young Mr. Polanski. So had the Perryton police. As I found out later, Tommy and I were just two in a long line of unfortunate punching bags. What was once passed off as youthful mischief had slowly crossed over into criminal activity.

After Jimmy left that day, Marcus and I spent a good hour in the principal's office recounting our own version of the story. The Principal believed us. He knew Jimmy very well. I was cleaned up in the nurse's station and Mom magically appeared to take me home. Who called her? Why did I need to go home? Marcus returned to the regularly scheduled school day.

Ultimately, Tommy was fine. He was driven to the hospital for a few stitches and an evaluation. I think they wanted to watch him for a few hours to see if he passed out again, but he didn't, so the emergency room doctors sent him home. I'm sure small-town protocols were not always sufficient to detect a concussion, which in hindsight, he certainly had. That said, he was back at school a week later.

I was okay, too. My jaw turned a dark purple and then blue and then yellow before finally returning to its normal color. My teeth hurt when I ate for weeks. But my spirit was oddly bolstered.

That day, well, it was a day that lived in infamy in Perryton, a day that was talked about for months, no, *years* afterwards.

Over time, the facts got hazy as firsthand knowledge faded into third party rumor. But two facts remained the same: The first, I never saw Jimmy Polanski again in my entire life. I'd say the brief beating was worth every ounce of pain. Tommy Blackshear later told me he agreed. The second fact was that I never looked at Marcus the same again. He went from a relative nonentity neighbor and schoolmate to a dear friend of almost hero status. He still is one of my closest friends.

(As a side note, I spoke to Tommy for the first and last time in my life a few weeks later. He thanked me for helping him out with Jimmy and I told him it was no problem and anyone would have done it—anyone who was a moron that is. He told me I was his hero, which is strangely ironic considering my stature and gait. His parents even called my mom and dad to thank them, which made my mom proud. In even more irony, I never heard a word of it from my dad, the one who always told us to be strong men, valiant. Sometimes I contemplate how strange it is that Tommy's and my wandering paths crossed in such a significant manner, one that changed my life, but then never crossed again.)

And so went sixth grade. Day after mundane day, broken by one significant event, and then back to the mundane.

Nothing new, nothing different, nothing better, nothing worse.

Until mid-October when I decided to go see Mrs. Ray once again.

35

JACOB

It was mid-October when I finally worked up the nerve. I arrived on the Rays' back porch with mud caked halfway up my shoes. It had rained constantly since Wednesday afternoon and the path to their house was slick with mud. Gooey, sticky mud. The kind you better clean off while it's wet or you will have to hammer it off when it's dry.

When Mrs. Ray answered the door, I had already set my shoes face down on the first steps of the back porch and tiptoed in my socks to give the door a quiet rap. It was 7:30 am, and she was still in her bathrobe, so she told me to make myself at home and went upstairs to change. Rain was dancing off the porch roof. The weather was finally turning to Fall. It was nice to see Summer move on its way.

I grabbed a glass of water and sat in my normal spot at the table. The quiet was a bit bothersome. In fact, it was too quiet and it made me feel unwelcome, like I was disturbing the soul of the Rays' home.

I wished for a little human company to make the intrusion seem less creepy. The early morning light was poking its head through the blinds partially covering the east window, which sat behind the porcelain sink. The horizontal rays were piercing the grayness of the room, lighting up a tunnel across the open space, directly over the kitchen table.

It was a bit eerie, but also amazing.

I sat motionless but for swiveling my head around in slow arcs. I studied what was visible in the light and imagined what was hidden. The kitchen still smelled of freshly cooked food—probably last night's dinner. Tattered cookbooks, a folded apron, flowers from the garden, and beautifully crafted ceramic plates adorned a room that would have impressed even Norman Rockwell. The rays of light ceded to the darkness on the far counter, settling directly on Mrs. Ray's well-worn NIV Bible.

I had no idea what NIV meant, but it sounded special. Even though my dad had been a pastor in the past, the Ross family now attended church only semi-regularly. You would be hard pressed to find a Bible sitting around our house. Church was a socially required function. Mrs. Ray's Bible was obviously used in the fashion intended. I was fascinated. I felt compelled to pick it up and flip through the pages.

What the heck? Mrs. Ray said to make myself at home.

I arose from the table and walked over to the far countertop. The Bible was even more worn than it originally appeared. The cover was cracked; numerous pages were folded on the top corner clearly marking pages of particular interest. As I flipped through the various books and chapters, I was overwhelmed at the number of notes and references Mrs. Ray had scribbled in the columns and edges of the pages. I shouldn't use the term *scribbled*, as her writing was impeccable. Even my young, inexperienced eyes could see she did not just *read* the Bible, she *studied it*. It was clearly part of her being.

"What are you doing?" I jumped with a start. I clumsily spun around with a clear and obvious look of guilt.

Marcus was standing in the doorway in cut-off sweat pants and a Kansas State t-shirt, rubbing the remnants of sleep from his eyes. He straightened up and alternated his eyes between me and his mom's Bible.

"My mom's bible." I wasn't sure if it was a question or statement of fact. I think it was probably an accusation. As if I touched the untouchable. Had I dared enter the space where no one else had been?

I set the Bible back down in the exact spot from which it was lifted, slightly adjusting the angle so it was a perfect placement. I turned back around to find Marcus reaching into a cabinet for a glass and then heading to the refrigerator to pull out a carton of orange juice. Without looking up, he said, "It's her favorite book. She'll share it with you if you want. That's what she does."

I let out a long breath as the tension passed. Marcus poured himself a bowl of cereal and sat down next to me at the table. The overhead light suddenly switched on, and into the kitchen walked Mrs. Ray.

"Good morning, Marcus."

"Morning, Mom," he managed with a mostly stuffed mouth.

"Marcus, would you mind giving Jacob and me a little time alone? Go watch cartoons or something."

"Sure." He picked up his half-eaten bowl from the table and gave me a little pat on the shoulder. He knew more than he let on.

"Put your bowl in the sink."

Marcus stuffed his last few bites into his mouth, then stood up from the table, set his dishes in the sink, and left. I heard the muffled sounds of the TV awakening in the den.

Mrs. Ray gently closed the kitchen door.

She had yet to acknowledge me directly. She wasn't rude; I think she was aligning her thoughts. Unnecessary chit-chat had disappeared from our time together. Coffee brewed and poured, she walked over to the table and sat down in her self-assigned spot.

"How are you this morning, Jake?"

"A little tired, Ma'am." The truth was, I was exhausted. For some reason, my morning slogs had been taking an even bigger toll on me than usual.

"Did you get up this morning to walk?"

"Yes. Normal walk, but not so normal thoughts. I have a bit of a headache. The nausea welled up at the end, but I didn't throw up."

"Hmmmm..." She nodded as she processed what I was saying. "How about your legs?"

"Mrs. Ray, can I tell you something I haven't even told my parents?"

She nodded.

"My legs, they seem to be getting worse. Remember how I said that, after my slogs, the pain would disappear?"She nodded again and reached out to place her hand over mine.

"Well, now, it doesn't seem to go away. It stays much longer, through breakfast and even later. Last Tuesday, I had to sit down to rest as I walked to my English class. It just hurt too bad to walk."

"Do you think you should you go back to see a doctor again?"

"I don't want to. The last time, it didn't even help."

"Fair point," she said.

"I'm scared that, by next summer, I may not be able to walk at all," I blurted out.

Her eyes widened.

"Of course, seeing how things have gone recently, I'll probably still be able to do my slogs. They seem to go on regardless, as if my body opens a space that allows for my weirdness and then slams the door when I finish up the walk."

Silence settled over the table. Neither of us had anything to add. I stared at her and she at anything but me. I could see the cogs turning. I left her alone to think. It was nice to have someone else thinking about this for a change.

My mind drifted. I started to imagine what it would be like to be crippled Jacob Ross. Unable to walk through the hallways, to run downstairs to breakfast when my mom called, to get on the bus.

Would anything be able to heal me?

Mrs. Ray had once said that the resolution of the mental issues would resolve the physical. Did she think the ever-expanding pain in my knees was being driven by my mental excoriation?

She had to be wrong. Although, the alternative was almost worth it. The truth was that my legs were wearing out and I seemed destined for a life of crutches at best and a wheelchair at worst. Maybe, if I accepted this fact and learned to live with it, the mental side of this nightmare would at least disappear.

Was that any better?

It's funny, when life throws you a major-league curve ball, most people swing and miss, then spiral down. It takes a lucky swing to hit the ball or a special constitution to deal with the miss. I'm not sure I had either at that point. I felt the whirlpool beginning to spin and my life slowly, or maybe not-so-slowly, sliding effortlessly into the vortex.

Mrs. Ray stiffened a bit and turned her attention back to me, pulling me out of my internal debate. "Jacob, you go to church. Have you thought about talking to your pastor?"

My pastor?

"No." That was the best I could do. It was truthful because the idea of talking to the pastor had literally never crossed my mind.

"You should think about it."

I wanted to tell her that, when it comes to church, the Rays and the Rosses were on different planes. The Rosses were like many a churchgoer in the Bible Belt. We went to church because our parents went to church, and they went to church because their parents did. Church was just part of the historical fabric.

(In adulthood, I came to the conclusion that the construct of church for most people is no longer based on faithful need for community, but based on secular need for community. Salvation has given way to socialization. And that's certainly what church was at that point for my family.)

But the Rays were different.

I didn't realize or understand it at the time, but their faith was grounded in the Gospels. It was lived out in the desire to help others, a desire to serve others, and a desire to bring church, as defined by a few, back to anything but the brick and mortar ensconced in

199

bureaucracy. If most people could see the fruits of such a labor, I believe "church" would be on the rise, even if the physical structures were on the decline.

At the time of Mrs. Ray's pointed question, I was taken aback. I couldn't, for the life of me, see how talking to our pastor, a complete stranger in my life, was going to move the ball forward. "I don't even know the pastor, Mrs. Ray. I can't dump my craziness on a stranger."

"He wouldn't consider you a stranger, Jacob. Would he?"

Talk about embarrassing.

"Probably." I realized, by the look in her eyes, I had to be honest. "When I go to church, it's hit the pew at 9:15, mentally check out unless I happen to like the song playing, and bolt at 10:15. Our family is in the car by 10:16. We aren't…um…involved."

"Okay," Mrs. Ray responded as if she had moved on to another thought.

"I don't really want to venture down that path. The pastor thing."

"Okay," Thankfully, she seemed to have given up on that idea. "I have another idea, Jacob. Let me sit on what I'm considering for a while and then, if I still think it's a good approach, we can discuss it further next time you come."

Next time. In typical Mrs. Ray fashion, this conversation was over right when I thought she was going to give me some answers. I pushed back from the table and stood up. I had a strong urge to give her a hug. I had not had any physical contact with her since the infamous hospital incident and I was half scared, half curious as to whether touching her would involve a repeat of last time.

I set that aside and leaned over her as she sat in her chair. She knew it was coming and received me with grace and warmth. We hugged tight. It was my way of thanking her for all her time, conversation, and concern. She had taken care of me in a manner that was nothing short of elegant. I held the hug for a few seconds and then stood back up. We smiled at each other as I turned to leave. There was no awkwardness at all.

There was also no spark.

"Goodbye for now, Jacob."

"Goodbye, Mrs. Ray. Thank you very much."

"You are more than welcome. See you soon."

The cold and rain of the walk home was completely obliterated by the warmth I felt inside.

36

JACOB

The day in the empty space between the schools changed everything between me and Marcus Ray.

At the time, I wasn't sure as to why. Was he told to look after me by his mom? Did he feel sorry for me? Was I to be some free source of academic tutoring?

Now I know it was because he genuinely liked me and I liked him. We quickly became true friends—brothers, almost. Marcus and I sat with each other at lunch most of the time. Some of his other, cooler friends sat with us too. At first, they couldn't figure out why I was there, why he was hanging out with a kid like me. The slack-jaw looks he got from these A-listers were priceless. Why would he bother with this withered-up, crippled kid?

But, over time, they became deeply indifferent. They weren't my friends by any means, but they certainly weren't my enemies. Some lowered themselves to including me in their conversations. Some of them were pretty nice once you washed away the jock façade. A few became my closest friends later in high school.

But, at the start, the odd couple relationship between scrawny, awkward me and cool, athletic Marcus probably confounded the majority of the sixth graders.

I will say that I liked it.

Marcus made me feel special in a time when I needed a friend, a lifeline more than anything. As you can imagine, my self-confidence was ebbing far beyond low tide.

Many years after high school, I asked Marcus why he did what he did. His answer both shocked and pleased me. It had nothing to do with the prodding of his mom (although her fondness for me didn't hurt). Instead, his effort toward me was driven, at least initially, by the fact that he could tell I genuinely didn't care for *what* he was (the popular, cool star of the football team), but instead, I cared more vitally about *who* he was.

For me, his athlete persona was clearly unimportant. I just wanted to be friends with Marcus, the person. Once I heard that, I told him my own reasons for working toward the friendship. At first my reasoning was that I was so thankful for his intervention with Jimmy, but then I realized he was more. He was brave and kind and saw me better than anyone else.

He quickly became my idol.

I grew to appreciate his abilities on the football field. Marcus was the sole reason we won so many games in high school and the primary reason we won the State Championship our freshman and senior years. (Don't tell Dad I said that, as he's convinced it was due to the immense tackling ability of the starting linebacker who happened

203

to share his last name.) Truth be known, if the Kansas UIL would have allowed it, Marcus would have been the starting running back for the Bearcats as a sixth grader.

He was that good.

But he was so much more than a star football player.

He was a man of integrity, even at that young age. A man who would change me, press me, help me, make me stronger, make me better.

He was a man that I could—and still can—call my true friend.

***

"Why do you hang around that guy, Marcus? He's gimpy weirdo." Mike Jefferson tried to whisper, but I could still hear it. Clear as day. Mike was the starting quarterback for the Perryton Varsity football team and was probably the second most popular guy in the school. "I know he's Luke's brother and all, but he doesn't exactly fit our mold, does he?"

"What is our mold, Mike? Tell me." Marcus shot back. His voice was much louder than Mike's. Loud enough for me to hear it very clearly.

"Well, for starters, someone who can walk without the aid of braces. Someone who is an athlete and someone who is cool."

"That's not my mold, Mike. Jacob is my friend and has been for a while now. Grab your Webster's and look up the definition if this concept is not quite clear to you." I loved Marcus. Still do.

"Chill, man," Mike said.

"It's just that he's…mmmmmm…dragging us down." Mike decided to get in the last comment. Not too wise.

Marcus turned on a dime and took two steps toward Mike. As if in slow motion, his fists clenched. He took a deep breath. And then he stopped, turned back, and slowly unfurled his hands.

Marcus has always been both kind and wise.

Striding, as only he could, he took off down the school hallway and almost took me out. We both stopped in time to avoid a front-on collision of which I would have taken the brunt.

"Did you hear that?" Marcus asked.

"I…uh…did."

"Are you okay?"

"Yeah, man. Thanks for sticking up for me."

"These guys can be such jerks."

"Yeah, they can. I'm kind of over it. It doesn't even get to me anymore."

"You heading to lunch?"

I held up my brown paper sack. "Yep."

With a slap on my back, Marcus gracefully strolled to the cafeteria, with me, his Igor-like friend, in tow. Marcus and I sat in our normal spots, me unwrapping a turkey-on-white and him staring at a plate of mostly unidentifiable food.

Marcus stood up to grab a milk and I couldn't help but get lost in my thoughts. Lunches should not be lonely—school should not be lonely for that matter. But, for people like me, life was lonely. I tried not to dwell on it too often, but sometimes the thought overwhelmed me. Less than 3 years before, I had been at the cool table. I had been one of the popular kids.

I never would be again.

Marcus came back with a carton of milk, followed by a few of his friends who scooted in next to Marcus and opposite of me. (I'm sure the idea of getting too close to the leper scared them. What if they caught something from me?)

Marcus was the starting running back on the varsity. He dominated every game he played. He was big for his age, but it was his athletic acumen that made him larger than life. Marcus was also extremely fast. He was rarely caught once he got a full head of steam. I didn't miss a home or road football game. In fact, I saw every game until we graduated from high school. I always struggled to mentally connect the humble friend I knew with the beast of a running back I watched on the field. By the time we were seniors, Marcus was 6'2", 215 pounds with state championship level speed. Every scout from coast to coast descended on Perryton for every game played during his final three years. Some games seemed to have more reps from D-1 colleges than actual Perrytonites. This never went to his head. Never phased him at all. Marcus was Marcus. Marcus was, and still is, special.

"You going to finish that?" Marcus asked as he was pointing at the remains of my sandwich.

"Nope. Go for it." Which he did with vigor. The kid can eat.

"Marcus, slow down." The voice came from behind me. Susie. Marcus grinned the patented Marcus grin and ignored her. I turned, my heart rate rising by the second. "Hi, Jacob."

"Uhh…hi." Damn, she was beautiful. No one in the entire school could imagine her hanging out with me, talking to me. The class gimp with the class beauty. I must admit, it seemed weird even to me. I often didn't believe it when I thought about it, but then Susie would walk up and smile that smile and I would know. She read from the same dictionary as Marcus. She was a true friend.

As much as I loved our friendship, I knew it was fleeting.

She was only going to get prettier, and I was definitely not getting more handsome. Or athletic. I knew eventually she'd drift away from me. She would succumb to hormones and peer pressure. She would slowly pull back, stop dropping by to say hi.

I hated that fact.

But I also understood.

Once upon a time I wanted nothing more than to become Susie's boyfriend. To fall in love with her, to have her fall in love with me. At the time, it somehow felt possible, realistic even.

Then, I still wanted nothing more than to be her boyfriend. But it had become even more impossible and unrealistic.

It's funny how things change.

37

JACOB

By nature, the vast majority of 12-year old males are completely oblivious to most of their limited surroundings. A partially-formed brain, combined with an extreme inward perspective, takes most of the blame, of course, but either way, we're just oblivious. And oblivious is a word that could have described me perfectly that winter.

That whole year, in fact.

This was particularly true when it came to life in the Ross household. How could anything be wrong at home? (Other than my strange behavior and physical ailments, of course.) How could anything be amiss with my parents? (They were the same as always—my dad gruff and serious, my mom soft and kind.)

Problems? Those were for other people.

Then my pretty little world exploded.

After 12 years, the Ward and June Cleaver façade of my parent's marriage cracked open, and I quickly realized they were more closely aligned with Al and Peggy Bundy. They loved each other, I'm sure of that. The problem was they didn't like each other very much, or more acutely, they didn't like the way their dreams had played out as they journeyed through life together. Dreams are a dangerous thing. Rarely do they materialize and, when they inevitably don't, who do you blame? The ones you're closest to, that's who.

My dad's dreams certainly did not materialize. There is no way he sat up at night as a child and dreamed of a life as a struggling farmer. (And, for that matter, I'm entirely positive he never even considered a life as a relegated pastor, but I'll get to that later.) Sadly, I never knew what his dreams were, because he never broached the subject.

(After many years of reflection, and a little investigative activity, I lay the issues squarely at his feet. He was a landowner, a fairly accomplished, although currently dormant pastor, had a wife who did truly love him and three kids who caused no significant issues and, in fact, grew to be accomplished in their own right. I'd even tag Luke with that description, at least after many deep valleys. So, why the feeling of failure and, more precisely, why act on it to the degree that the idea of failure becomes that fact of failure? I'll never know these answers. I'll never know what was rattling around in his thoughts. I can merely address the collateral damage.)

Mary had her first inkling of a marital issue in early 1991. I, as I mentioned earlier, was oblivious, until Mary later opened my eyes. (Boy, she had a lot on her mind that year.) The truth was that Dad was too shallow to realize that Mom, a beautiful and wonderful woman, was right there available at home. All he had to do was put a little creativity and effort into his marriage.

Mom was no runway model, but she was a pretty woman who

managed the ravages of three childbirth incidents without too much bodily harm. Wow, that sounds overly harsh. The point is, Dad was looking for someone exciting and unhindered and seductive.

Someone…scandalous.

I had seen Dad and Mrs. Ryan under the stadium stands during the prior football season and had completely forgotten the incident. I was in the Ward Cleaver stage at that point. But Mary knew right away, and that affected her deeply. In the end, it affected all of us deeply. What I don't think people understand is the ripple effect of their selfish decisions. The four other Rosses and three other Ryans were forever impacted in a very negative way.

Trust was never to be healed.

(I never talked to Mom about this act of indiscretion in detail. She only referenced it in the grander scale of marital issues. It was indiscretion number one, and I gather Mrs. Ryan was one of what was ultimately four or five thoughtless transgressions. But none of those transgressions affected Mom—our entire family—as deeply as the last. It was the catapult that sent the Rosses hurling toward south Texas.)

Either way, I was oblivious to it all.

Until I wasn't.

38

JACOB

I did not spend nearly enough time with Susie that Fall.

When she made it to school, we sat together on the bus and visited periodically on the school grounds, but that wasn't enough time. I could never spend too much time with her. I felt better that Jimmy was out of their home, but worried about what impact his absence would have on her. Would her dad take his anger out on her more now?

I watched Susie as closely as I could to see if there were any noticeable signs of a negative change, but she looked to be managing safely, at least there were no outward indications.

(I later found out life was actually better for her without her brother living at home. She did not have to deal with Jimmy and his explosive temper or pick up the wreckage caused by the inevitable shrapnel. Her dad settled into a general funk, as losing Jimmy was harder on him than one would expect, but ironically, they started to do better financially. The saving grace was when a local farming co-op agreed to incorporate their land and provide the Polanskis with an annuity based on a sharecropping formula. Abel no longer had to work the farm. He wasn't anyway. In return, they had enough income to live modestly. Abel, with lots of prodding from Susie, even fixed the place up. New paint, shutters, and plants. Too bad the improvements were all temporary.)

***

I had moved into extreme slogging season. I should recommend slogging for the next X-Games! Frozen ground, sideways sleet, and horrific wind-chill factors. Lots of fun. True athleticism at its finest.

I simply couldn't deny the alien forces behind the morning slog. I certainly was not powerful enough to even try. I just obeyed. As the Borg say, "resistance is futile!" Mom met me every morning at the back door with a warm blanket and a cup of freshly brewed coffee. (I know, 12 is too early in life to start drinking coffee, but it warmed me up and tasted delicious.)

Mom's view on my slogs and my illness had softened. I think she realized her options were to either accept me for who I was or let me drive her bonkers. (On top of this, she was dealing with problems that seemed far bigger than her son's peculiar, ongoing morning activity.) And so, morning after morning, she'd wrap the blanket around my shoulders, lead me to the table, and hand me my hot coffee. Admittedly, I used it more for hand warmth than internal satisfaction, at least initially. I eventually learned to appreciate the rich taste of Columbia's finest brew. I love coffee to this day, mostly the aroma. And the warmth. And the fact that it reminds me of my mom.

Those were the times when we were the closest.

We would talk about everything and nothing. I think I was her stress outlet, in a good way. She was maybe mine too. A person to talk to who listened and responded.

It makes me mostly sad to think about it today.

Because it was also the time where I began to view my mom as a person and not just a mom. She told me stories about her childhood and parents. She shared her own struggles with school and learning and family and growing up. I even learned how she met my dad and how they fell in love.

Ironically, those were some of the best mornings of my life, even with the slogs.

I wish our morning ritual had never ended.

Unfortunately, all good things end way too quickly. It's only the bad things that seem to linger with determined ferocity.

**

I love Christmas.

I know that's trite, but I love the smell of a real (not fake) fir tree, the smell that emanates from an overactive kitchen, the smell of a blazing, wood burning fireplace, and the smell of a cold winter in the air. But, back in the sixth grade, the thing I loved most was the fact that there was no school for a month.

Actually, that's not true.

I was also in it for the presents. Thoughts of what I was going to get were my predominant thoughts for at least 30 days leading up to December 25th. I spent quite a bit of my time scouting the house for hidden presents. I never found one. (Turns out, Mom always hid them on the top shelf of Dad's storage closet in the barn. I should have guessed.)

That year, I wanted a Nintendo video game system more than anything else. (In the years previous, I had asked for anything Ninja Turtle but, that year, I felt too old for TMNTs. But, truthfully, would have been okay with a few more. I had to act older than I really felt.)

As Christmas approached, I became more and more convinced that there was zero chance a Nintendo would be neatly wrapped and placed under the tree. By the 24th, I absolutely knew I was bound for something more akin to coal. Luke acted as if he didn't care about presents. (He really did.) Mary also acted as if she didn't care. (She really did not.)

Mom spent all day in the kitchen on Christmas Eve. She made our typical stuffed turkey, pecan pie, mashed potatoes, and my personal favorite, Ambrosia salad. (Yes, I recognized that Ambrosia is inappropriately called a salad. Only desserts consist of coconut, fruit cocktail, Mandarin oranges and mini-marshmallows. Call it what you want, I ate my weight in Ambrosia salad every year.)

Everything was prepped and sitting snuggly in the refrigerator by about six o'clock that evening, waiting for the next day's final preparation and mass consumption. Mom had it down to a science. As much as she disliked cooking during the balance of the year, she attacked this meal as if our lives depended on it. Mary and I helped as we could.

Peeling potatoes was generally my job. I truly believe the whole orchestration of Christmas dinner made Mom very happy. Sort of a year-end celebration via great food. Dad was in a celebratory mood too. There were not too many pressing chores to complete around the farm and, besides, it was a dreadfully cold winter. Dad took particular pride in a roaring fire in the fireplace. He ignited the first stack of wood by 10:00 in the morning and it was still burning at 10:00 that night. Lots of trips to and from the wood pile. He let me and Luke stoke the fire, but only under direct orders as to how to rearrange the burning logs, as if it could possibly matter when there were eight inches of red-hot embers lying below the iron grate.

After all the food for Christmas's magnificent dinner was safely in the refrigerator, we had our traditional Christmas Eve dinner. Chinese food of all things. (Over the years, I've heard of other families having similar traditions and eating totally unexpected things like barbecue or sushi for Christmas Eve dinner. I'm not real sure how our tradition became Egg Foo Young, General Tso's Chicken, and Beef Fried Rice, but it did and, man, was it good.)

We always got our Chinese food from the Flying Dragon. The Taos were the first Chinese family to make their home in Russell county. Yung and Grace Tao moved to Perryton in the mid-1950s and opened a restaurant in downtown, just around the corner from Emory's Card Shop. Their presence was met early on with some resistance (Who would resist Chinese food? That's beyond my understanding.), which resulted in a few slow business years. My mom told me that, after World War II, all Asians were fairly or unfairly looked at with a bit of skepticism. Of course, after tasting their Chow Mein, most people set their differences aside. The food was so damn tasty. It didn't hurt that the Taos were great people.

The Taos were Buddhist, and thus didn't celebrate Christmas when they moved to the U.S., so having their restaurant open on both Christmas Eve and Christmas day was very natural to them. By the time they had lived in Kansas long enough to get into the holiday spirit, the take-out business was too brisk on the 24th for them to not be open. Even after they became fully active members of the 1st Presbyterian Church, they kept the restaurant open on the 24th. I guess we weren't the only Perryton family with this odd dinner tradition.

We had ordered the exact same combination of dishes for so many years that Peter, the Taos' middle son, always had the exact order prepared, packed in cartons and sitting in a brown paper bag and waiting for us at 6 pm on Christmas Eve. We would arrive at the Flying Dragon shortly thereafter for a warm visit and to wish the Tao family a Merry Christmas.

That was another of our traditions. In my mind, the better of the two.

A few hours later, our Chinese food devoured, we settled in at the kitchen table for a game of Monopoly. Even Mary played. A Christmas miracle. (She usually won, which was probably why she continued to play year after year.) The final piece of the Christmas Eve routine was to line up in front of the TV to watch *A Christmas Story*. Dad in his easy chair, Mom, Luke, and me on the couch, and Mary sprawled out on old quilts on the floor.

Mom laughed to tears every year when the dogs devoured the freshly baked turkey that was sitting on the kitchen table, and Dad fell asleep every year right when the boys started waiting in line to see Santa. To this day, I can't wait to watch the antics of Ralphie and the rest of the Parker family. The tongue on the flag pole is still my favorite.

(Watching this movie on the 24th is still a Jacob Ross family tradition. I hope my kids and grandkids will continue it.)

After the movie, we'd all head to bed. Please notice I didn't say we all went to sleep. Christmas Eve is rarely a night of sleep. Instead, I'd lay quietly, struggling to fall asleep, giddy with excitement, with the most satisfied feeling. I loved my family, I loved our traditions, and I loved the time we spent together. I would replay the day's events in my mind and finally fall asleep with a big grin of satisfaction on my face.

Of course, even on Christmas, 4:00 a.m. came early.

As merciless as many of my slogs had been—both physically and mentally—the worst one of all arrived on Christmas morning. My clock read 4:10 when my eyes snapped open. I slowly rolled out of bed and dressed in a variety of clothes strewn about on the floor. I exited the bedroom without disturbing Luke. I was very used to this drill. Once in the mud room, I bundled up in a coat, leather gloves, wool scarf, and a blue Jayhawk stocking cap.

As I opened the door to the icy wind, I had a flashback to last night's movie and pictured Ralphie significantly overdressed. I smiled my last smile of the day. Of the year, in fact. I stood at the door and listened to the howling wind. If I was to ever assert my free will and about-face back to bed, this was the perfect morning. I remember trying, begging my legs to turn around, to stop this nonsense but couldn't do it. I was like that heroin addict who says *never again* as they reach for their beckoning stash, spoon, and hypodermic needle.

There was no use. I grabbed the door handle, twisted to the left, and walked onto the back porch. The wind hit me first. Not just wind, but gusts filled with sleet. The depth of the wind's force moved me involuntarily around in an erratic motion. It took me a few seconds to gain enough purchase to step off the porch and head to the south field. Walking was a fight and I was in a draw at best. Every two or three steps forward were accompanied by a stammer backward or to one side. I think I would have laid there and slowly frozen to death had I fallen. At the time, that didn't seem like a terrible option.

As I entered the field and began my slog down the furrowed rows, the exposed skin on my face was stinging as if a swarm of giant mosquitoes was having their pleasure with my cheeks, forehead, and nose. What the fuck was going on?

And then my knees began to remind me that the weather was the least of my issues. They began to vibrate deep underneath my kneecaps, expanding outward with each difficult step. As the pain surged, a wave of heat radiated in its draft. The good with the bad. I was sure the warmth would save my life, or at least keep me alive long enough for the pain to gut me before I made my turn.

By the time I turned, I was limping badly. Much more than usual. Previous slogs seemed to be coated in a mystical protection that allowed me to stride with an almost normal gate, as if the assistance was needed to make the slog complete. Once it was gone, I realized that advantage was truly needed. Comforting heat and exacting pain were racing in competition down my legs and up my chest. I could feel the heat pouring out of my collar.

As if the pain and the cold were not enough, there came lightning bolts of ideas and thoughts racing in a scramble around my brain. I could vividly see colors all around me. Sharp, rich hues that snapped with a loud pop as they injected themselves into my skull. I screamed to no one's attention. The wind was too effectively rendering my voice as mute, as if I was on the first row of a Who concert.

My consciousness slowly ebbed, yet my feet moved forward under someone else's power. My toes felt as if they were dragging the frozen dirt as I was shoved down my designated path. That wasn't possible, was it?

And then, because all good things come in threes, a bout of nausea was added to complete a trifecta of pain and dizziness. It hit me like a storm-driven wave breaking over the bow of a hapless ship. It stopped me in my tracks. I bent over, clutching my stomach, unable to keep my insides from exiting my body. But, as soon as I finished heaving, I was dragged forward again. There seemed to be no time for dalliance, even if it wasn't of my making.

My thoughts, if I can call them mine, swirled within my head. The acuity of the pain was like nothing I had ever experienced. But, with the acuity, came clarity. The voices, thoughts, impressions, whatever you want to call them, were trying to tell me something. I knew it for certain and so I grasped for an understanding. I ignored all else and tried as I might to understand what was hidden in the tumult of competing noises. As soon as it seemed the noise was clearing, it would fade back into the fog.

I heard, *"Jacob, you will...,"* and then nothing but static.

I screamed, *"Come back, please come back, tell me what you are saying, help me!"* It was all to no avail.

The field seemed to spit me out onto the hard-packed mud as it had done so many times in the past; only, in this instance, there was no semblance of a soft landing. My knees and the palms of my hands aggravated the frozen ground with all my weight. I flattened out into a sprawl, lying perfectly still. I took several deep breaths and assessed my body. Shockingly, I was relatively intact. I was overtaken by the cold emanating from the ground.

I pushed myself up to all fours and summarily threw up where I've thrown up so many times before. This whole thing was racing very much past ridiculous. I wiped my mouth with the back of right hand, leaving a fair amount of the sticky remnants on my glove. Still on my knees, I rose up to see my mother sprinting toward me. She had never met me outside after a slog. Why now? Something was different. The sleet storm was still raging and the temperature still felt well below freezing. Ice was clinging to much of my clothing, no doubt sourced from my now freezing sweat.

"Jacob, thank God you're home!" She wrapped a blanket around me and helped me to my feet. As soon as I was upright, Dad joined the fray. I put my arms on their shoulders and began to limp to the house like an injured running back being assisted off the football field by a few of his offense linemen. I heard my mom crying. I felt my dad crying.

They had both reached their breaking point.

To be honest, so had I.

They dragged me into the house and helped me to the table.

"Sit, Jake. I'll get dry clothes." Mom turned toward the stairs. "Brian, get him some hot coffee." In any other situation, I would have found my mom ordering my dad around shocking. This morning I let it pass as normal.

As soon as my mom disappeared up the stairs, my dad sat down next to me. "Jacob, this has to end. I don't care what the doctor said. I can no longer stand by and watch you do this."

I changed clothes and drank my coffee. Life slowly reentered my crushed body. Mom and Dad sat patiently at the table waiting for me to gain enough strength to handle their battery of questions. I must have looked like death beyond dead. (Mom later told me that the way I looked that morning will forever be seared into her memory. She can still describe my ghostly appearance in excruciating detail. Whitewashed, almost translucent, skin with black circles totally encompassing my withdrawn eyes, pale blue lips and ears, and countless red, pin-sized welts spread across my cheeks and forehead. Frostbite entered their concerns as well. Within 10 minutes of sitting at the kitchen table, the grotesqueness that was displayed across my face began to wane. Life was not running away from me as it might have appeared.)

"I-I think I need to go to bed." I was really giving up Christmas morning I felt so awful. I rose from the table and stepped over the heap of wet and muddy clothes sitting just inside the mud room door. I noticed scrape marks deeply gouged into the tops of my leather boots. I shivered with the idea that the tops of my shoes may have spent as much time in contact with the ground as did the bottoms.

I'm sure my parents wanted to jump into a frantic discussion about the pros and cons of slogging in sub-zero weather, but I think we all knew that the interrogation should wait, as sleep was my best medicine at this time.

"Of course, Honey. We will wait until you get up to open presents," Mom said as she gently placed her hand on Dad's forearm.

Open presents. Maybe the fact that I was still alive and scarcely kicking was a present enough. I can promise you a Nintendo video game system was the last thing on my mind. Sleep was the first. Well, maybe the second. This completely fucked-up situation I was degrading into was thought number one.

"Get ready, Mrs. Ray, we're about to cut through the preliminaries and go straight to the final game," I whispered to myself as I trudged up the stairs.

I was tired of vague questions and half answers.

I wanted, no, I *needed*, something to change. And quickly.

***

I woke up at noon to the most wonderful aroma. I quickly got dressed and ran to the bathroom to brush the awful taste out of my mouth. I walked downstairs and found Mom hard at work in the kitchen.

"Well, it's about darn time," Luke said. I rolled my eyes at him. The requisite fire was blazing and Bing was crooning *White Christmas* like we've heard a million times. I love Bing Crosby.

"Dang, Jacob, its noon and we haven't even opened our presents yet. What a dweeb." Luke was clearly oblivious to everyone but himself.

I firmly clutched the railing and descended the stairs one stair at a time. Slow but sure, as the saying goes. Mary met me on the landing and I transferred my grip to her. We walked into the kitchen and I sat at the table.

"Are you feeling better, Jacob?" Dad's eyes were full of concern. He set his glasses, along with that weeks' *Time* magazine, on the table and looked me straight in the eyes.

"A little." It was all I could manage.

"It's Christmas, Jacob, but we will need to talk about this. Tonight. We have had enough of this nonsense."

Nonsense? Is that what Dad thought it was?

It was clear the dam had broken.

Mom was crying again. Although she was facing the sink I could see her shoulders gently shuddering. It was not the Christmas Day we had all envisioned.

"What's going on, you guys?" I didn't understand.

"Jacob, Dr. Johnson told us to leave you to your Compulsive Disorder, as he called it. He was sure you'd quickly grow out of it. He said it was a temporary problem." Mom still had her back to me but her words were loud and clear. Compulsive disorder?

"He…he said these morning slogs would stop. They'd go away. But they haven't."

"You…think this is just me being crazy?"

"Jacob, it's not that. When you checked out of the hospital last fall, the doctor came to talk with us. We had wanted to intercept you in the morning before you headed out on your walks, but he said that may cause more harm than good."

"Is this doctor a psychiatrist too?" Mary interjected. Damn good question.

This surprised Dad a bit. He had forgotten she was even in the kitchen and certainly did not expect her to ask such a pertinent question. "Well, no, I don't think so."

"Then why did you take his advice?" I asked. By necessity, small town doctors often wear more than one hat, even if a few shouldn't wear any. I fear Dr. Johnson fell squarely into the latter category.

"Okay, I can see now that perhaps we shouldn't have taken his advice, Jake." Mom said. She sat at the now crowded table. "But honestly, what would you have done had we tried to stop you? Wouldn't that have been worse?"

"I guess he was partially right." I shrugged. "I wish I could stop, but I don't think I can. And I don't think you can stop me."

"We just feel lost and hopeless." Mom was on the verge of tears once again.

"Me, too." I really did feel lost and hopeless. And desperate for change.

I glanced over to Mary who was sitting quietly with her arms crossed, soaking in the entire discussion. I could see her quick and pragmatic brain processing what was being said as well as what wasn't said. She would visit with me later. We would talk on our own. Let Mom and Dad vent, rant, rave, and effuse emotion. It would make them feel better. She would sit with me sometime today, or maybe tomorrow, and the two of us would have a constructive conversation.

Mom took a deep breath, probably to soothe her nerves. "Jacob, we need to go see some different doctors. Maybe an orthopedic surgeon who can evaluate your knees. And a psychiatrist. We can make some appointments in Wichita."

"No, Mom, that won't help." I felt like we'd already been down the doctor path. I was positive the answers lay within me. And with Mrs. Ray.

"Jacob, we're not giving you a choice. It's settled." Dad said in a tone that indicated this discussion was now over. "But, for today, let's enjoy Christmas." Mom smiled and stood up. "How about those presents?"

I stood up and joined them, but my excitement over the presents was long forgotten. While Mom and Dad, and even Mary, noticeably brightened, I sunk further into the knowledge that I was anything but fine. I knew, without a doubt, that the answer to this mean-spirited riddle lay on the mental side of the equation, but there would be nothing I could do to convince my family of that.

I would have to go to some doctors.

To deal with poking and prodding and questions.

To hope for answers that would never come. Let's make the best of the day and go open presents. The sooner we do that, the sooner we will eat. I was starving as all my previous sustenance lay in a frozen puddle on the front driveway.

The gift giving ceremony took all of 15 minutes. I did, in fact, receive the Nintendo I so coveted. Interestingly, after all that time of waiting and wishing, it stayed in the box for several months. I had bigger fish to fry and my ongoing battle was certainly not a game.

My parents knew that. Mrs. Ray knew that.

And, on that Christmas day, I knew the fun and games of childhood were gone. I was in a battle for my sanity.

In fact, for my life.

39

JACOB

The Rays were gone most of the holidays.

As bad as the weather was, I'm not sure I could have made it to their house but I sure wanted to. I needed to talk to Mrs. Ray about what happened on Christmas.

Mr. Ray, Marcus, and the girls came home a few days before school fired back up, but Mrs. Ray stayed in Wichita to care for a college friend who was in the final throes of ovarian cancer. She died in mid-February so the Ray family drove back to Wichita for the funeral. Mrs. Ray stayed a few days longer to help with the post-funeral matters, so overall she was gone two months. I tried to be understanding and patient, but you can imagine how hard that was for a 12-year-old.

She finally arrived back in Perryton on the last day of February and, while I was chomping at the bit to go see her, I still had to wait. While I hadn't had another morning like Christmas morning, I continued with my daily slogs. As they wearily watched me trek out and back every day, Mom and Dad became more and more determined to make the doctor circuit around the Midwest.

I went along with it to placate them, even though I knew it was a hollow endeavor. (I discovered later in life that a parent's capacity for tireless belief as it relates to the welfare of their children is damn near limitless. You'll do whatever it takes and accept no answer other than what you want to hear. It's the epitome of that deeply innate parental desire to protect your child at all costs.)

Mom made seven appointments with various orthopedic and oncology doctors. Since we were roaming the state—and out of state—to visit specialists, the trip took five days of driving with the last day being the return trek. All six orthopedic doctors performed consistent examinations. They began with a lot of questions, then dove into testing my reflexes, flexibility, and motion, and performing a visual evaluation of my gait. My limp was pretty bad, but I tried my best to walk with a casual appearance. I wasn't too effective. Lastly, I was subjected to a rudimentary MRI.

I never went into the details surrounding my morning slogs, as I knew that would have caused the doctors to quickly refer us to the psych ward. Mom apparently agreed because she never brought it up.

The exams usually took about two hours between the doctors and the techs. This does not count the hour or so that we sat in the reception area waiting to see the doctor in the first place.

Seven doctors. More than 25 hours in doctor's offices.

And still no answers.

Five of the doctors returned with the same general diagnosis. *The structure and stability of Jake's legs, and particularly his knees, looks completely normal and there is no reason for his difficulty walking or the described pain.*

What kind of diagnosis was that? Did they think I was limping for fun? But, each time, the doctors scowled and said they simply could not tie my affliction to any medical facts. Two of them even suggested that my issues were psychosomatic. I had never heard that word before but quickly concluded they thought it was either a mental issue or that I was making up the whole ordeal. My parents knew the latter was dead wrong and refused to believe the former.

The sixth doctor, Dr. Martinson, who practiced in an orthopedic specialty hospital in Des Moines, was a bit sharper than the others. I liked him. He did not talk to us as if we were from outer space. He seemed genuinely concerned. (I remember him vividly to this day. Dark eyes, big round glasses, a caring demeanor. I can't recall any of the other bone doctors we saw on our tour. Dr. Martinson was hugely tall and rail thin. I found it funny that an orthopedic specialist would be so bony. The hair on his head looked as if it had not been combed in months and its wildness was surpassed only by his eyebrows. I couldn't help but stare. But I also couldn't help but like him.)

Unlike the other doctors, Dr. Martinson noted what appeared to be faint stress lines running laterally along the femur, tibia, and to a lesser degree, the fibula, all emanating from where these bones intersect below the knee cap. Dr. Martinson had never seen anything like these markings. (Why didn't the other doctors question these faint lines? As medical professionals, you would think they would have noticed them.)

I knew exactly what they were as soon as Dr. Martinson saw them. I felt them every time I slogged, which led to the inevitable vibrations and pain in my knees. I imagined those markings as the places where my leg bones flared outwards as my legs pulsed. Although Dr. Martinson saw the lines, he had no medical answer to my problem. He asked us to get back in touch with him if the symptoms got worse and he'd re-evaluate.

Another dead end, it seemed.

My last appointment was with an oncologist that specialized in bone cancer in children. This was Mom's idea. I thought it was a bit of a Hail Mary. The oncologist's name was Dr. Silas. She was probably in her 30s which I'm sure gave my parents pause as to her experience. All I remember about her was that she was very pretty.

She poked and prodded and concluded with a battery of blood tests. I felt like I had been attacked by a horde of vampires leaving numerous holes inside both elbows. I checked my neck in the mirror just to be sure. The results came in about a week later. All negative. I was healthy as a horse in the eyes of every single one of those doctors.

Only they were wrong.

Every single one of them.

40

JACOB

I left our house bright and early on Saturday morning and made a bee-line to the Rays' house. The dirt path out of our property was relatively clear, so the footing was sure enough. Steam roared out of my mouth and nose with each breath, and my ears were numb before I reached Old Potato Creek, which was still frozen over. By the time I hit the Rays' back porch, I was rubbing every part of my body to motivate circulation. Mrs. Ray was standing at the back door as if she was expecting me.

She engulfed me with a bear hug. "Pretty cold, isn't it?"

"Yes, ma'am. I'm mostly numb from just the walk over here."

"I can tell," she said.

Mrs. Ray was warm and comforting. Her touch initiated an emotional feeling that's hard to describe. So different from a hug from my mom. A mother's hug is infused with a visceral love and caring that only a parent can have for their child. Mrs. Ray's hug was also a feeling of love and caring, but more on a level that said *I know what you're going through and I will be with you until the end.* It felt amazing, nonetheless. The love I needed most at this time. I stepped back and looked her directly into her eyes.

"Thanks, I needed that."

"I thought you might."

She smelled of lilac, like the bushes my mother had planted out next to our barn. That smell memory is vivid to this day.

I plopped down at the table and rubbed my arms and legs furiously. A pot of freshly brewed coffee was dripping its last drop and beckoning us with its addictive aroma.

"It's been too long, Jacob. Tell me, how have you been?"

The past two-and-a-half months had seemed like a lifetime. "I'm okay."

"And what about your slogs?" I immediately cringed at the thought of Christmas morning. I wanted to tell her everything at a hundred miles an hour, but knew full well she'd hold up her traffic cop hand and tell me to slow down and start from the beginning, so I did. The story did not take too long as most days were the same. I told her about our holidays. I told her about my Christmas presents. I updated her on school. I told her about everything but the Christmas slog.

My nerves settled and it felt nice, comfortable even.

"Well, that all sounds great. I'm also glad you and Marcus are friends. He tells me you are one of his best friends."

I was stunned to hear that but happy as well. I had assumed it was a little more of a one-way street.

"I like Marcus. He's not like the other jocks, sorry, I mean athletes." That elicited a smile. "He's real, if you know what I mean?"

"Yes, I do. He's a wonderful young man."

I smiled.

Then Mrs. Ray's demeanor shifted noticeably.

"Let's talk turkey." I had never heard that term before. It made no sense to me. Truthfully, it still doesn't. "I want to know about your slogs."

The fear I felt after my Christmas morning slog washed back over me. I felt sweat dripping off my forehead and was tempted to run, to stay silent. But I forced myself to talk. If anyone would be able to help me, it would be Mrs. Ray.

"Okay…" I began.

She interrupted me. "I'd like to particularly hear about the Christmas morning walk."

If I didn't know better, she would petrify me.

"How?"

"Don't ask, Jacob," she whispered. "I don't have an answer. I just know. More accurately, I *feel*. I was up early on Christmas morning. We were in Wichita at my sister's house. I always have a hard time sleeping in any bed other than my own. Anyway, I was having a cup of tea when you came to mind. Anxiety spewed up from the depths of my brain. It was almost painful. I immediately knew something was wrong. I immediately knew it was about you. It's not like I had a clear and precise vision—I had no details at all because the knowing was a blur. But I knew right then you were in a dreadful situation. I felt it."

She stopped and we stared at each other. I think we were both trying to process this admission. My adolescent brain couldn't come close to understanding.

"I was too far away to do anything, to help you, so I just prayed. I prayed hard, Jacob."

"What's going on here, Mrs. Ray?" I swallowed hard. "It's like we are...we are *connected*."

41

MARY, 2015

"Jack, I really want to do this." Mary was standing in her apartment kitchen slowly, if not mindlessly, stirring homemade ham and bean soup. It smelled intoxicating. It was Jack's favorite. She set the large wooden spoon across the top of the Caphalon pan, picked up her glass of wine, holding it securely with both hands, and repeated herself. "It's really important to me."

Jack stood up from the bar that separated the kitchen from the den and walked around into the kitchen. "Okay, honey. I'm all ears."

She smiled at their inside joke. Jack's DNA had worked overtime to imprint his aunt's trademark on his head and the result was his ears were a bit grander than most men enjoyed. Mary thought he was incredibly handsome either way—especially when his loose curls waved over the tops of those giant ears.

"I want to go to Phoenix to surprise Jacob. I can take a week off work and hop on a red eye, just show up at this house. We can even get Margie in on the ruse so they are ready for us. What do you think? Will you and Liam be okay without me for a week?"

It was no longer an idea. It was going to happen. The game was afoot.

"We'll be great." He put on his most dramatic pout face. "We'll miss you, but we'll survive."

Mary jumped up and planted a kiss on his lips.

"Margie will love helping you plan it. You two will have a great time planning the subterfuge. I'll, in turn, plan a week of guy heaven with Liam. Pizza, soccer, beer, and smoky pubs."

"Very funny."

Dinner, if soup and a bottle of 2009 Quintessa Cab can be defined as dinner, was outstanding.

Almost as good as the wrestling match in bed afterward.

42

JACOB

"*Connected*...yes. I think we are connected in some way, Jacob." Mrs. Ray smiled and patted me on the shoulder.

"But how?"

"I don't understand it any better than you do. Truthfully we may never know how. But I do think we will eventually determine why we have been connected in this way." She paused. "I just know we are connected so I can help you through your situation."

"I hope so." My voice sounded desperate.

"How I am going to help you is still a bit fuzzy to me, but I do know for a fact that you're here for a reason. We are together for a reason." She paused, as if she was contemplating what to say next. "And, Jacob, I believe what you are going through is significant for reasons still unknown. But we have no choice but to continue to unravel this mystery, to push forward."

"I don't know how much longer I can push, Mrs. Ray." I was tired. So tired.

"Let's start by talking about Christmas morning."

I walked Mrs. Ray through the Christmas morning slog in as much detail as I could remember, which it turns out was quite a bit. She sat quietly with her hands folded in her lap. She nodded periodically, otherwise was still and attentive.

"So, you haven't had any other mornings like this since then?"

"No. Everything since then has been normal." I stopped myself. "Do you think maybe that was the worst I'll ever have? Like it was rock bottom and now I'm going to start getting better?"

Mrs. Ray frowned. "Maybe. But I have this feeling it will get worse. I just sense it."

This stunned me. I felt tears well up behind my eyes and it was hard to breathe. "That…can't be right. I can't take another morning like Christmas morning, Mrs. Ray."

The tears began. Confusion and fear ripped into my brain. I briefly felt like I was in the middle of a slog.

Maybe she was wrong?

I hoped so.

But she had never been wrong before.

I limped back home, oblivious to the hostile cold weather, my mind a whirl of terrifying thoughts.

Maybe she was wrong.

Maybe I shouldn't be spending time with Mrs. Ray if she was going to say things like that. And then I quickly corrected myself. Even filled with fear and anger, I knew right then she was my one lifeline in the world.

43

JACOB

I woke up with a start, sweating profusely.

My mouth was bone dry. The glorious feeling of the delicious lasagna my mom had made for dinner the night before faded abruptly. My alarm clock read 3:35a.m. *What is going on?*

I was literally pulled from my bed.

I know no one pulled me, but that's the best description I have, as I surely was not volunteering to get up so early. When the clock registers earlier than 4:00 a.m., it is not early in the morning; it's more like late at night. It was immediately clear to me that the normalcy that defined my slogs for the past few months was now shattered. Nothing about how I felt at that moment was normal. The next three hours were not normal either.

Right then and there, I had a smoldering feeling Mrs. Ray was absolutely dead-on.

I walked—more like was *pushed*—outside.

The breeze increased in effort and was pushing against my back. Tears began to flow from my eyes as I knew I was about to yield to the malevolent power behind my slogs. I envisioned a large, black scaly creature with sharp teeth and claws. He was laughing at his position of power and my position of powerlessness. A slog monster, if you will. He then reached forward with the sharp nail attached to his pointer finger and forced me forward.

I was a puppet without strings.

I took one step forward, then another. I didn't want to. That didn't matter. I stared at my feet, trying to will them to stop. After a dozen plodding steps I looked up and spotted a small, bright light floating just above the ground at the far end of my selected corn row. The unknown light did not move; it just pulsated slightly. Diamond-shaped glints burst from this bright dot as my vision was fractured by my tears of anguish. I grabbed the bottom of my t-shirt and swiped my eyes dry. The light was now a well-defined dot. This perfect circle of intense white light was so out of place it gave the impression of being a well-crafted special effect. It stood motionless.

I did not.

Step after uneven step, I trudged ahead. On cue, the pain in my knees increased, followed by the tangled thoughts borne on electrical jolts. I tried to fall in my tracks hoping to clutch the ground as if it was an anchor. Each time I was propped back up against my own desires. Maybe the puppet strings were simply invisible. Halfway down the row, I began to lose consciousness as the artificial thoughts pounded the inside of my skull. It felt like the inverse of being pelleted on the head during a hail storm. The floating light grabbed my attention, keeping me from blacking out. *Was the lighted disc larger because I was closer to the end of the row or was it growing in size?* I tried to focus on the answer, but the chaos in my head rendered my ability to reason ineffective.

I finally approached the far end of the plowed row. My clothes were sopping wet with sweat. So much for the cool breeze. The fog in my head cleared enough for me to realize the strange light had grown in size and intensity. It was now as bright as one of those search lights used at a car dealership grand opening, only this beam was not pointed up into the sky; it was pointed directly at me. The hovering origin appeared to have grown to the diameter of an ordinary dinner plate. The diameter of the beam itself widened as it extended toward me until it matched my height.

A perfect fit.

It seemed strangely alive, as if it had depth and substance. The light then encompassed me. The beam did not extend more than a foot or two past me as if darkness swallowed the stream of light in its entirety. The shaft of light folded back onto itself forming a perfect convex terminus. I was neither blinded nor bathed with discomfort. Conversely, the spherical enclosure was strangely refreshing and comforting.

I stopped sweating.

All of my pain and distress evaporated.

I remember thinking that was the best I had felt in two years. With that soothing thought, all my anxiety vanished. I had morphed into an extremely happy 13-year old.

Then I blacked out.

JACOB

Mr. Ray slammed the door to the back porch and crouched down next to me.

He stared at me for three beats as if he was trying to figure out who or what was piled on the porch in front of him.

"Jacob. Good Lord." Mr. Ray stared at me with a look waffling between terror and disbelief. "Marcus, go get your mom."

I opened my mouth to try to talk, but no words came out.

Mr. Ray's face faded to black.

The next several days were a hazy dream.

I later learned Mr. Ray had carefully cradled my head in his hands and taken my pulse. That Mrs. Ray had screamed when she had seen me, that Marcus had called 911, that they had all spent 10 agonizing minutes waiting for the ambulance as they tried to figure out what had happened to me.

My mom later told me she had arrived at the same time as the ambulance had, that she had seen the scratches on my legs, my pale skin, the fact that I wasn't moving and hardly breathing, and she had also screamed. Then Mrs. Ray had held her as the EMS loaded me into the ambulance. She was in such a state of shock that she hadn't even moved when the EMT asked her to ride with us. Finally, Mrs. Ray had drug her over to the back of the truck and helped her climb inside.

I remember nothing from that ride. Not the lights, the sirens, the frantic EMTs as they tried to take my vitals, to figure out what was wrong.

Nothing except blackness.

A blackness that would take days for me to climb out of.

JACOB

I was in room 303.

The nurse told me I had been unconscious for the better part of two hours while in the ER, so they had finally moved me up to the pediatric wing. It was a semi-private room and I occupied the other half of the room I had landed in the last time I had been admitted to Russell County Hospital. At least I was getting a good view of all aspects of the hospital.

Dr. Morton had already come by several times to check on my vital signs, as did Dr. Rajal, the closet thing Perryton had to a neurological specialist. Both hovered at my bedside, whispering in urgent tones. You would have thought the two doctors were trying to solve the mystery of string theory as presented in a Mandarin text book. They tried. They really did. But, in the end, they were completely and utterly clueless.

Mom, Dad, Mary, Marcus, and Mrs. Ray had stood vigil in the waiting room. My mom said they had commandeered a corner and sat together playing cards, praying, and munching on microwave popcorn. (Luke had better things to do, namely, hang out with his friends, which only served to drive a larger wedge between us.)

Mary later told me the layers of emotion in that waiting room ran the gamut. Mom was at her emotional breaking point, often bursting into tears as Mrs. Ray wrapped her in yet another hug and patted her back. Dad spent half of his time in a state of disbelief, as if he knew at any moment he would wake up from that nightmare. The other half of his time was spent trying to determine who he should blame. Marcus spent the days tossing a miniature football up into the air and catching it, biting his lip as if he were about to cry. And Mrs. Ray, who was clearly shaken to her core, spent the day in pensive thought.

I now know she spent that week planning her next move.

It was clear to everyone in that hospital that something needed to change and change in a hurry.

That first night had been a long night. My mom sat by my bed. I remember fragments of time, seeing her pacing the floor, her eyes wild with worry. The shroud of paralysis that enveloped the hospital staff had now squarely settled over me. Over my whole family, in fact. No one had any idea of where to go next. Glimmers of conversation struck my consciousness.

Mayo Clinic.

Nothing we can figure out.

Need a specialist.

How are we going to find the money for that?

I remember my parents arguing in hushed tones about how tight money was, how we just couldn't pick up and move the whole family, how maybe we could figure it out there.

"I cannot believe what I am hearing," my mom said. "Money? Money is your concern? What about Jacob? Your son." What had been fuzzy alertness moments before turned crystal clear with each sentence that came out of my mom's mouth.

They were fighting over me.

"I'm just saying, Susan." Dad was trying to whisper but wasn't succeeding.

"I know what you're saying and I'm not buying it. Damn it, Brian." Mom interrupted.

"We can't spend what we don't have."

"A weak argument, Brian. If the doctors think we should go to *Mayo Clinic*, we go to *Mayo Clinic*." Mom glanced at me. I continued to fake sleep.

"We have catastrophic coverage, Brian. They'll surely cover something like this. We can scrape together the balance." Her words drifted off and then picked up again. "Maybe if you quit spending money on all that unnecessary football crap you covet so much, that might start the kitty."

"But that's Luke..."

"I don't care about Luke right now. He is perfectly healthy and should be second to Jacob in your cares and concerns, but I see he isn't. You are fucking disgusting."

My heart rate sped up and I heard beeping coming from the monitor. *Calm down, Jacob.* I heard footsteps going toward the door and a door slam, then Mom's quiet sobs as she sat down next to my bed.

I swallowed hard and did my best to remain completely still.

Not only was I destroying my own life, but it seemed I was destroying my family as well.

***

The next morning brought no change.

I was still in and out of consciousness, my head pounding, my body aching and unable to move as I was hooked up to three IVs. The only difference was that I was often alone. Mom and Dad came in occasionally, but often glared at each other before escaping to the waiting room where they were certainly fighting.

I felt the room shrinking, as if my world was pressing in on me even tighter than it had before. Mom and Dad were clearly not happy with each other, and I began to feel a sense of guilt about everything. After all, this was all caused by me. If only I could have just stopped it, made it disappear.

In one of my more alert moments, I remember Mrs. Ray and Marcus walking in, telling my parents they would take a rotation so they could go get something to eat and shower. Mom had argued, like any mother would do, but she had relented. "It's fine, Susan. I will watch him closely."

"But what if he wakes up?" Mom's eyes looked panicked.

"I'll be right here, Susan. He will be fine until you get back."

And I was fine. I drifted back into blackness, hardly noticing that Mrs. Ray and Marcus sat by my bed, held my hand, sang church hymns.

Mom came back.

"Thank you, Celina."

Mrs. Ray stood up and gave her a strong hug, the kind that is part care, part support. Mom clearly needed both. "I am so sorry for all of this. I feel as if I am partially responsible."

"No, Celina. It is not your fault." Mom pulled away. "I will never feel that. Think that."

"I—I'm at a loss."

"Me, too. I can't believe I let this happen. I have stood by and let my son degrade into this." She waved her arm in my direction. "What kind of mother allows this to happen?"

Mrs. Ray stepped back and looked at my mom firmly. "No, Susan. You can't go there. You can't begin to think things like that. It will tear you up."

"I—I've been so weak."

"How so?"

"I just kind of let this all slide. I assumed you would help him, that he'd grow out of it, that he would figure it out." Tears were now streaming down Mom's face. "I never imagined it would come to this."

"Neither did I, Susan." Mrs. Ray sat down in one of the mauve armchairs by my bed.

My mom hid her head in her hands and cried.

"Susan, can I pray for you?"

"I…I would like that very much."

I fell back asleep to the sound of their whispered prayers, and for the first time in months, I felt a niggling voice whisper in my spirit that maybe, just maybe, I was going to be all right.

***

By the third day in room 303, I was feeling much better. I had downed four cartons of green Jell-O and a juice box. When the doctors came in and admitted they were stumped (a hard step for an ego-filled doctor to take), I didn't take it too hard. After all, everyone seemed to be stumped by me. (They didn't need to admit ignorance though. It was obvious to everyone who was paying attention.)

Marcus walked in, carrying the same April 13, 1992 issue of Sports Illustrated he had been carrying around since I had arrived at the hospital. Why are waiting rooms the elephant graveyard for old, dog-eared magazines? The cover showed Bobby Hurley in action as the Duke Blue Devils won another basketball national championship.

"You're awake, kid!" He smiled and came over and patted me softly on the shoulder.

Mom stood up next to me protectively. "Careful, Marcus. He is still very fragile."

"You don't look good, Jake, but you don't look too bad either." Marcus moved aside as Mary walked into the room. She marched right around the bed and hugged my neck. The metal stand holding my IV bags wobbled back and forth as she hugged me, but she had no regard for their presence.

"Jacob Ross, don't you ever do anything like that again." Mary's voice was stern, but she was smiling.

"Hi, Mary," I croaked. "Mom, can I have some water?"

Marcus hopped up and poured some water out of the turquoise jug that sat on the side table. I chugged it and asked for more.

"Marcus and Mary, Jacob is very tired. So say hello and then we're going to let him rest."

Marcus and Mary both nodded but neither of them made any movement to leave.

"I was just trying to explain to Jacob why he is here. He seems to not remember much from the last few days." Mom patted my foot and smiled.

"Yeah, man, imagine how I felt seeing you all crumbled up on my back porch, white as death." Marcus chimed in. "You terrified me."

"How long have I been here?"

"It is Monday afternoon," Mom said. "You've been here about a day and a half."

"When can I go home?" I wrinkled my nose. "The view is nice, but the food here is atrocious."

"We'll have to visit with Dr. Morton on that one." Mom looked worried. I could tell she wasn't going to let me have any freedom for a long time. "In the meantime, rest. We have plenty of time to sort everything else out."

She was wrong about that. We didn't have plenty of time. I felt like I was dangling at the edge of my sanity and, if I didn't have answers soon, I was going to end up right back here in the hospital. Or worse.

46

JACOB

I hung around the house for the balance of June. Mom pretty much demanded it. The mood at home had noticeably changed. The lingering angst was still palpable—ending up in an unconscious heap on your neighbors' back porch will do that.

The only difference was the additional undercurrent of animosity between Mom and Dad. If it had been there in the past, and according to Mary it had, I hadn't noticed it.

But I did now.

Over the course of that month, I rarely saw them together. I never heard them speaking—at least in conversational tones. I heard lots of raised voices muffled through their bedroom door. The air was filled with tension.

"Jake," Mom sat down next to me on the couch. "Are you okay?"

"I think so."

"I'm so sorry for all of this. Your health. Our discombobulated family."

"It's not your fault, Mom."

"I just…feel so bad that I can't fix this."

"There…is nothing you can fix." Mom was the Toyota Camry T-boned by the 18-wheeler. She never had a chance to avoid the collision.

Mom pulled me into a hug. "I love you, Jacob."

"I love you too, Mom." It was all I could say. It was enough.

(Part of me is glad I didn't know all the reasons for Mom's fretfulness at that time. I would have worried more. But part of me wishes I had known. Maybe I could have changed something? Because when I did find out, it was too late. Like that Camry, I didn't stand a chance.)

I limped up the stairs and stopped in front of Mary's room. I could hear the radio playing the latest *Nirvana* hit. I started to knock, then pulled my hand back.

Mary would certainly know what was going on with Mom and Dad.

But did I really want to know?

Ignorance is Bliss ultimately lost the debate with *I Can't Stand Not Knowing*. *I Can't Stand Not Knowing* then knocked on the door and entered Mary's room when given permission. (In hindsight, I wish *Ignorance is Bliss* had won that argument. It would have made that summer more bearable. But hindsight is 20/20, isn't it?)

"Hey Jake, what's up?"

"Just hanging out at home like always. Mom doesn't want me out of her sight."

"Can you blame her?"

"No, I guess not."

"So, how are you doing?" Mary tried to keep her voice casual but I could tell her words were anything but.

"I'm—I'm okay."

"Have you visited with Mrs. Ray recently?"

"I went last week. Mom drove me over because she didn't trust me to walk the whole quarter mile."

"And?"

"Well, it's always fun at Mrs. Ray's house. Last week she made me coconut cream pie."

"But?"

"Well, I guess it feels like we are running in place. Nothing ever changes. Nothing happens.

"What do you guys talk about? What does she say to you?"

"A lot of times it's just meaningless stories about stuff I've done, about you guys, and what I want to do. But sometimes she asks hard questions. And sometimes she tells me things about herself."

"She's your shrink," Mary said with a tone of humor.

"Are you saying I'm crazy?" I tried to laugh it off, but part of me wondered if Mary was right. I sure was acting crazy.

"I was kidding, Jake."

I shrugged it off. "Last week, she did say there is someone she wants me to meet. Someone she's known for years who was helpful to her at one time."

"Did she say who it was? A name?"

"No." I turned to Mary. "But I'm going to go.

"When?"

"I'll ask her tomorrow. I'm going over there to see Marcus."

Mary stared at me like I was withholding information.

"I can't tell you when, Mary. Mrs. Ray can be very mysterious. Sometimes I wonder if she is holding something back. We'll be talking and she will look like she's about to say something out of the ordinary, or maybe important, and then she'll stop."

"Do you think she's keeping a secret?"

"I don't know. I know she's really honest with me, so I'm not sure why she seems so guarded. I've asked her to tell me what she was about to say, but she just smiles, shakes her head and says *Later sweetie, it'll make more sense later.*"

"Has later ever come?" Mary was frowning now.

"I wish. I know there is a whole bunch of later to drop on me at some point in time. I'm waiting for that day."

I went quiet. I didn't want to tell anyone about Mrs. Ray's secret, but I felt compelled to tell Mary. Like she needed to know.

"Okay, Mary, If I tell you something, will you promise you will tell no one? Not a soul."

Mary looked at me like I was crazy. "You can trust me, Jacob."

And so I told her. About Mrs. Ray's kidnapping and particularly the bizarre events in the trunk, about how Mrs. Ray felt like my situation was similar, how we felt this connection.

Mary sat in stunned silence. For several minutes.

"Do you believe Mrs. Ray?" Her words were soft.

"Of course. The story of her kidnapping and Davis Johnstone's heroics are known by everyone in Perryton."

"I know that. That's not what I'm talking about. Do you believe the story about what happened in the trunk?"

"I do, Mary. Because…this is going to sound weird…because I have felt it. That connection. That energy."

Mary looked pensive.

"I know it's weird, and I know it sounds crazy, but it's real to me. I know it's there. That's why I keep going back to Mrs. Ray. I know she is the key to my answer."

Silence invaded Mary's room as she sat back and processed all she had heard. The wheels were grinding. "I believe you, Jacob."

"And?"

"I think you're right. Mrs. Ray is the key."

"And?"

"And what, Jacob?"

I got frustrated. "That's your comment? That's all you have?"

"What do you want from me? I am lost as you are, maybe more. I just don't know what to say."

We both sat still and gathered our thoughts.

"Mom and Dad are no help, Mary. Mrs. Ray helps a little, but not really. I have no one to talk to about this." It hurt to admit this to anyone.

"I'm sorry, Jacob."

"Mom wants to help, but doesn't seem to be able to. It's like she's unable to function around me. She tries—she really does—but a hot bowl of soup is not a cure."

"She's a wreck, Jacob. Her baby boy is a sci-fi movie and she can't turn it off. She has no idea how to deal with it, with you. She wants nothing more than to help, but that's as likely as you running in the '94 Olympics."

"Real funny, Mary."

"Sorry, that's not funny. I'm sure it sucks not to be able to fully use your legs."

I nodded. She was right. It really sucked.

"Just…give Mom a break. She's really weighted down right now."

"By what?" I asked.

And then it came, the reason I wished *Ignorance is Bliss* had won the earlier debate.

"What world do you live in, Jacob Ross? Don't you pay attention?" Mary rolled her eyes at me.

That was painful. Had I been so caught up in my own problems that I had become oblivious?

"Are you sure you want to know, Jake?"

I nodded.

Mary proceeded to tell me about Mom and Dad's disintegrating marriage, the financial stresses of our farm, and the, at least in her mind, imminent implosion of the Ross family. All separate topics, yet connected. Basically, my parent's marriage was falling apart.

If I really thought about it, I knew.

I had ignored it, but I knew.

Then, Mary dropped the bomb. "Also, Jacob, Dad is having an affair."

"What?" I was on the verge of tears.

Mary reached out and grabbed my hand. "It's true, Jacob."

"You're wrong, Mary. You have to be wrong."

"I'm not wrong, Jake. It's true." Her voice was gentle.

"I...I assume Mom knows?"

"She knows."

Another gut punch. My head was spinning. An affair? How could my dad do this to my mom?

"Is...is Mom okay?"

"Not really, Jacob. It's a wonder Mom hasn't burst into flames. She is obviously a lot stronger than any of us give her credit for."

The tears came. I couldn't stop them. The real world was crashing down on me with incalculable weight. I was getting crushed.

What a nightmare.

47

JACOB

A county carnival—both mysterious and glamorous for a 12-year-old. The caravan of dilapidated trucks arrived unexpectedly at the Russell County fairgrounds, setting up elaborate rides, flashing millions of lights—attracting kids like bears to honey. Every kid under the age of 16 was instantly begging their parents to drop them off with a pocket full of money, ready to eat too much junk food, ride the spinning death traps, and have the time of their lives.

I was no different. As sick as I was, I wasn't going to miss it.

On July 15th, the barren, dusty fields surrounding the fairground pavilions were empty and silent. By the evening of the 16th, the entire area was alive with sound and light.

Mom dropped Marcus and me off at 6:00 that evening. She slipped me two ten-dollar bills, and I slid them into my pocket. It was a big step for her to let me out of the house and, more specifically, out of her sight.

"Don't tell Dad I gave you those." It was all she said as we hopped out of the car and walked towards the arching entryway into this mystical land of excitement. The magical words *Carnival–Rides, Lights, and Fun* were embedded in the arch and lit up by countless colorful, blinking bulbs. I wanted to stop and soak it in, but Marcus would have none of it. He wanted to get in there as fast we could.

"How do your legs feel, Jake?" Marcus asked as we settled into the end of the ticket line.

"Well, I hadn't thought about them until now, so thanks a lot." I smiled and punched him in the arm.

"Sorry, man."

"I'm kidding." I had to laugh. He thought I was serious. "They hurt, always, but I'm too excited to care right now. Let's get our tickets and head to the Rock 'n Wrecker. I bet it's still the scariest ride they have."

Marcus did not respond. I noticed a bit of a frown cross his face, just briefly. A struggled smile reappeared.

We finally arrived at the front of the booth and were greeted by a woman who appeared to want to be anywhere in the world other than where she was at this moment. "How many?" she said in a droll voice.

"I'll take 10 dollars' worth."

"Me, too." Marcus slid a 10-dollar bill on top of the one I had just placed onto the indented tray and under the glass separating Miss Sunshine from the masses. The woman slid 40 faded green tickets back out through the slot. Only her fingers extended beyond the glass barrier, enough to make me think of overly wrinkled sausages left on the grill too long. Her chipped finger nails were painted with a bright purple lacquer that badly needed a touch-up.

Marcus and I turned and headed into the jungle of lights and noise.

"What first?" Marcus asked.

"I don't know. How about some food and then we can hit the rides?"

We veered left and followed our noses. Most of the food was to the left and most of the rides to the right. Straight ahead were the arcade games. We would start left and work our way around. Great plan.

The good thing about carnival food is that none of it is good for you so you can't make a bad decision. (Not to mention there are no parents present to apply the guilt.) We chose French fries as an appetizer, greasy sausage with grilled onions for an entrée, and powder sugar-dusted funnel cakes for dessert. For good measure, we settled on a mound of blue and pink cotton candy for the road. (It sure tasted good going down. Didn't sit so well once it got there.)

With grease smeared on our hands and powdered sugar dusting our t-shirts, we moved toward the middle of the carnival grounds. Time for some arcade games. We traded turns sending rubber frogs off of steel catapults to hopefully land in shallow dishes, all of which were perfectly lubricated so there was no way for the frog to gain an ounce of purchase. We didn't come close to winning a single time. The hunt was much more fun than the kill.

"We're almost out of tickets, Jacob." Marcus said. "And I have to pee."

"Okay, give me 10 bucks and I'll go back to the ticket booth and get some more. I'll meet you at the rides. Let's hit the *Rock 'n Wrecker* first."

"Okay." Marcus was already walking toward the restrooms. "See you in a few."

I wound my way back through the myriad of arcade games and popped out behind the ticket booth. The crowds were pouring in. Opening night was going to be profitable for the carnies. I circled the booth and walked with purpose to the back of the expanding ticket line.

As I stopped at the back of the line, I heard, "Hey, Jacob."

I turned around to a voice I recognized immediately, furiously dusting off the remains of the funnel cake from my shirt. "Susie."

"Did you just get here?" she asked.

"I've been here a while. Marcus and I spent the last hour eating junk food and losing money in the arcade." Another great thing about being young is that eating junk food is a badge of honor, not a demotion in social status or a prelude to a lecture on clogged arteries.

"I can tell by your t-shirt," she remarked with a broad grin.

"It was good at least," I said with a hint of embarrassment. I finally removed all the powdered sugar from my International Harvester t-shirt, feeling not-so-grubby for the effort.

Susie looked great. Cut-off shorts, flip-flops and a too-small *ZZ Top* tee, which nicely accented her growth spurt. I was a mental mess. One look at her turned my brain to jelly.

"Get in line, you can come ride with Marcus and me."

"What about Laura and Lindy?" Susie looked behind her to two girls and waved them over.

Laura and Linda both shook their heads no.

"Marcus is waiting for me." I said it loudly so they would hear.

They both shrugged and walked up and handed me more cash to buy tickets. Of course they wanted to go if Marcus was there. Marcus to the rescue once again.

Would Susie have gone with me even if her friends didn't want to be seen with a quasi-gimp? I believed she would have either way.

I combined Marcus's and my money with Susie's and extracted 60 tickets from the sausage fingers, being extremely careful not to touch them. As I passed out the tickets to the group, we headed off to the rides. I was very nervous and a tad queasy, either from the thrill of Susie or the fast food battle raging in my stomach. Still, I tried my best to bury my limp and walk like I had no physical cares in the world. I didn't pull it off. Susie didn't seem to care so I slowly regressed back to my normal awkward gait.

We found Marcus despite the crowd.

"Hi, Susie. Laura. Lindy."

"Hi, Marcus." Laura and Lindy almost twittered.

"We'll slip away and leave you alone," Marcus put his hand to my shoulder and leaned it to whisper. I didn't even have to respond because within 10 seconds he had melted into the crowd with Laura and Lindy. Good friend, that Marcus.

"Susie, I'm glad you're here."

"You said that already," she teased.

"Yeah, you're right. Maybe I'm double glad." And there it was: my typical reversion back to dumb responses.

"I'm glad I'm here, too, Jacob. I've missed seeing you. It was a hard spring and the summer vacation started off kind of rough, too, but life has gotten better lately."

I left her comments alone, hoping she would explain more. She didn't.

"Want to ride the *Rock 'n Wrecker*?"

"I don't know, Jake. It looks pretty scary."

It did look pretty scary, but my mouth led my brain into action as soon as I realized my manhood was on the line. I had to ride it. Couldn't even let Susie talk me down. The Rock 'n Wrecker was the most feared ride at the carnival. It had been for three years running and was back to win the award for a fourth year. It was a rickety contraption that had probably undergone no significant maintenance for years. As with all carnival rides, it was held together with duct tape and bailing wire.

(How these rides ever got sanctioned, I'll never know. Maybe someone was getting paid off handsomely, but at the time, I didn't care.)

The *R&W*, as we called it, was five extended arms with a large, triangular shaped bucket at each outer end. This bucket sat six people, two to a side, and spun independently from the arms. As the ride spun in a clockwise direction, the arms began to lift and lower, all the while sending the manned buckets into a spinning frenzy.

It was awesome.

It was scary.

And it was not a ride to be on after a full meal of fried food.

A raspy speaker mounted in the middle of the ride blared a continuous loop of 80's rock greatest hits (Get it? The *Rock n' Wrecker*?) with the audio clarity of a drive-in movie. The *Wreck* portion of the name was a tribute to the way one felt after riding this contraption. I could tell by the line of kids exiting the ride that wreck was an appropriate description.

Susie and I reached the front of the line just in time to be nervously seated in the final open bucket. Marcus and crew were the first group on the ride, so they ended up being right behind us. A mullet-wearing carnie with indiscernible tattoos walked counterclockwise to every bucket and checked on the metal lap bar by halfheartedly pulling upward. They all seemed to lift a bit, probably more than intended by the manufacturer, but the carnie didn't seem to care. And we certainly couldn't act like we were scared.

"Hold on, Jacob, it's about to get fun!" Marcus yelled. He didn't have to worry. Susie and I both were clenching the lap bar as if we were trying to wring it free of water. With a grin exposing less than a full complement of teeth, our carnie friend wiped his mouth with a handful of his *Motorhead* t-shirt and shoved the accelerator stick shift forward, ramping up the central motor which launched the *R&W* into a heartless and ever-dizzying frenzy.

The first two turns were bearable. (I'm guessing they weren't full speed, and therefore the buckets turned quietly.) All hell broke loose after that. By the end of the third revolution, the monster was in full attack mode. The buckets were fully spinning as if death to their occupants was the primary goal. The arms were lifting and lower in a herky-jerky fashion. Back to that maintenance issue.

All this would have been bearable and survivable if not for a profuse stream diesel exhaust that blew into my face with each turn. Every revolution, the engine's struggles amplified and, with each amplification, more foul-smelling fumes where spewed. Was I the only one on the ride encased in this brown cloud? Maybe not, but I was the only one where the cloud set off a chain reaction. Increasing waves of nausea wracked my stomach. The grease in my stomach raged with enough ferocity to decide that exiting my system was the best way to solve its immediate problem. And exit it did. I felt the waves of spasms in my diaphragm lurch with every turn of my bucket. I knew what was coming, or should I say going, and slammed my right hand over my mouth. This was about as effective as boarded up doors in a Zombie movie.

I glanced at Susie and she was painted with part fear and part enthrallment.

She was enjoying herself.

That was about to come to an end.

The last two spasms were so strong I was worried about splitting my gut in half, and so it was a mild relief as my stomach began to empty itself. All the surrounding noise disappeared and I was in a silent, slow-motion nightmare. The stomach spasms waned immediately but were followed by violent chest heaves as my four-course junk food meal ignited a greasy stream of vomit up my throat. As my palm was blasted with the full brunt of the greasy stream, my hand flapped open like the starting gate at the Kentucky Derby. Up and out the shoot. Initially, my hand deflected the stream into my lap but then physics took over. The force threw my head back and the discharge was free to fly.

I was in terror.

Susie was in repulsion.

The stream passed across her chest and launched itself up into the air and then descended squarely in the bucket occupied by Marcus et al as they passed under the arc of vomit. The smell was immediate and potent. Made the diesel odor fade to the background. The sounds around me, from Def Leppard's *Pour Some Sugar on Me* (how ironic), to Susie's screaming, to the screeching from Marcus' tub returned.

I caught a glimpse of the carnie who was about to fall off his chair in utter laughter. I'm sure he'd seen it before. I would have thought he would immediately stop the ride, but he didn't. Instead, he sat back on his clean little chair and enjoyed the chaos.

It finally ended as the carnie reached forward and pulled back on the accelerator allowing the *R&W* to grind to a slow and painful death. My bucket settled into a slow rocking motion, seemingly unwilling to completely stop.

"Susie, Susie, I'm so…

"Don't say a word, Jacob Ross. Just get me out of here." I couldn't tell if she was mad or just disgusted.

I slumped to the men's room to try to clean up and stared at myself in the mirror. I had just lost Susie, probably Marcus, and most definitely his posse. With one carnival ride, I completely sealed the deal on my pariah status. Not even Marcus could save me.

I did my best to clean up and then headed for the front of the carnival grounds, trying to avoid Susie, Marcus, and anyone else I knew.

No such luck. Just as I reached the ticket booth, I heard my name screamed behind me. I turned to see Marcus heading my way. By the looks of him, he had avoided the Ross puke-shower. He was clean as a whistle.

"What do you want, Marcus?" I asked.

"You're my ride home, Ross." As if he couldn't get a ride with a half a dozen other friends. "Besides, I wanted to be sure you were okay. Holy crap, Jacob, that was unbelievable. How did you have so much puke in your system? You were the *Old Faithful* of pukers."

"Marcus, I'm sorry."

"You're sorry? Half the people on the ride are sorry." The jokes kept coming. I knew what he was trying to do and it worked. A little.

"How am I ever going to face these people, or any person in the entire town, again? I'm destined for social hell."

"Naw, it'll be forgotten by the time school starts."

Just then, my mom pulled up in the *LTD*. A grand sight for extremely sore eyes. She waved out the window and I waved back rather weakly. She opened the passenger window and leaned across the front seat. "Glad you're here so I didn't have to wait. Get in guys. You too, Susie."

Susie?

"Thanks, Mrs. Ross. I appreciate the ride." I turned to see Susie standing behind Marcus and me. She didn't look very good, yet she looked great. Dust had encrusted the puke splotches on her shirt and sadly, her hair. She shrugged her shoulders as if to say *all is forgiven*. She smiled slightly as she walked past me and got in the front seat. A smile that changed everything, healed everything.

"Jacob, what in the world..." Mom interrupted our moment.

"You don't even want to know, Mom. I just want to go home."

"Are you okay, Jacob?"

"I'm fine, Mom. Just go."

We drove the rest of the way home in silence.

48

JACOB

"Marcus tells me you guys had a lot of fun at the Carnival," Mrs. Ray said as she folded her apron into a perfectly neat square, set it on the counter by the drain board, and sat down at the kitchen table, obligatory cup of hot tea in hand.

"Yeah, it was fun," I responded. "Until ... well, I'm sure you heard."

"Jacob. You are not the first person to throw up on a carnival ride, and you won't be the last. Pretty embarrassing though, I would imagine." It didn't take special powers for Mrs. Ray to come to that conclusion.

Marcus grabbed a *Gatorade* out of the refrigerator, unscrewed the cap, and chugged half the contents. He then wiped his mouth with his sleeve, clearly much to Mrs. Ray's chagrin.

As he walked out of the kitchen, he grabbed his stomach and feigned throwing up. He then burst into laughter.

"Marcus Cameron Ray, that's disgusting and mean. Get out of this kitchen right now."

"I'm sorry, Jacob," Mrs. Ray said. "I'm sure he didn't mean it."

"I'm sure he did. Besides I would have probably done something similar if the shoe was on the other foot."

Mrs. Ray simply smiled, then returned to a somber state as she broached the topic we both seemed to be avoiding.

"Tell me, Jacob, how have your morning slogs been?"

"I seem to have settled back. But I still go. It's not over, and I can't help but wonder if and when another bad one is coming."

"I've been wondering the same."

"I am not sure if I can take another one."

"I have an idea. But, before I get into that, let me tell you a little story first."

JACOB

My slogs continued to be mild, almost a non-event. Brush your teeth, wash your face, eat a bowl of cereal, have a 4:30 a.m. slog, and you're ready for another productive day on the farm. Even my dreams seemed less invasive for a while.

I hadn't had a blackout slog in months.

My headaches were minimal at best.

All in all, life was not too bad. (Relatively, of course. I had learned enough in my short time on earth to believe this was the beginning of the end. I knew it wasn't. There had to be a point to all this. A climax to the weirdness. And I knew without a doubt there was no way that all I'd been through could merely end with a slow tapering off.)

Over the past three years, I had had three frighteningly bad slogs. Slogs that either put me in the hospital or close. And so, even as things got better, I prepared myself for the worst. I knew something bigger, and more frightening, would come. The floating light was the start of something, not the end. How *something* is defined was a mystery.

Mom surprised me with a set of compression knee braces. (One of those surprises that was much appreciated but also showed how far I had sunk.) They were made from thick, sturdy neoprene, supported down both sides with hinged, steel flanges. To put them on, I slid a tube of black rubber up over my knees and then tightened them to tolerance with two Velcro straps above the knee and two below. I imagined myself an all-American offensive lineman preparing to block for Marcus in the national championship game, the braces hidden underneath my cropped football pants. Which, in hindsight, was a bit stupid considering my size and lingering disdain for the sport of football. But hey, whatever works to get you through. These braces probably helped more mentally than physically, kind of like a placebo.

The Bearcats won their district and made it deep into the 2A Kansas state playoffs. We were the second to the lowest classification, but still, it was an impressive run led by a 7th grade running back. Marcus ended up running for over 1,800 yards in just 13 games, adding 25 touchdowns for good measure. That was the worst statistical year of his high school football career, too, which was pretty amazing. My best friend, the football star.

(Luke had a good year too. He led the team in tackles. The loss in the semi-finals was devastating to both Luke and Dad. They mourned all the way through Christmas, if you can imagine. Marcus moved on from it the very next day.)

Susie and I, well, we had the bus. I looked forward to those rides to and from school more than I looked forward to anything. Periodically, she'd venture over in the cafeteria and we would eat lunch together as well. We also had two classes in common. Not that I was tracking my time with her or anything.

I didn't realize it then, but I now know that, even in those innocent days, social pressure was starting to divide us. She still had a strong thread of warmth attached to me, and in her own way, she clung to our friendship longer than most people would have. But I found out later that, in those years, she vacillated mightily. Peer pressure was a very powerful force. We are all jockeying for outward position and inward esteem. Those middle school grades are a difficult time in anyone's life, and especially for someone like Susie who had so many struggles at home. I made things harder for her.

In hindsight, I should have cut her loose, but I didn't. I couldn't.

And she should have walked away from me. But she didn't.

And now, we are both very grateful we clung to our true feelings, to each other. Susie had no idea at the time what a profound impact she had on me. Marcus was my pillar; she was my beacon. I truly believe the two of them together kept me alive.

This time in our lives was a source of many discussions and much laughter in years to come.

50

JACOB

Luke was back into football preparing for his junior year. Spring practice finally got him out of the *we lost in the state playoffs* funk. Yes, that's right, it took him that long to recover. (I'm not sure if Dad ever recovered. Other than dinner, I rarely saw Mom and Dad in the same room at the same time that year. All was not good on the home front.)

My chats with Mrs. Ray became fewer and farther between. I still saw her periodically, but those sessions where more akin to a status check. She knew deep down that our ordeal was far from over, but she also seemed to sense that we had a little break. A calm before the storm. And so, for those few months, I spent more time at the Rays' house just hanging with Marcus than seeing her. Truthfully, when I was at the Rays' versus my own home, my anxiety level was lower. Between Dad's growing absences and indifference and Mom's blooming bitterness and anxiousness, I needed a place of refuge.

The Rays offered this haven and I gladly accepted.

Seventh grade unceremoniously ended with a quiet thud. I hopped, as best I could, off bus #346 having said my goodbyes to Susie. We swore to get together over the summer. We really wanted to and had all sorts of hopes that it would happen. But we also knew life was changing and we had no expectation for what the summer would hold.

"Bye, Vernon. Have a fun summer."

"Bye, Jacob. You, too. Get better. I want to see you back on the bus in September having grown a few inches and running around like you used to, okay?"

"I'm planning on it, Vernon." I turned to face him as he was shutting the door. We both waved goodbye. We both smiled. I stood at the bus stop as #346 pulled away for the last time that year. The dust wrapped itself around my legs and settled to the ground for a long summer sleep.

Bye, Vernon. Have a fun summer.

(Little did I know that Vernon certainly would not have a fun summer. Instead, he would spend it working two jobs in Des Moines just to make ends meet so he could come back to drive us in the Fall. He worked construction during the day and bartended at night. A tough life. Vernon was our bus driver for two more school years, then he just up and disappeared. When the door opened on the first day of 10th grade, Vernon was not behind the wheel. I must have looked totally confused when the new bus driver opened the door. I stood there for a few seconds as she beckoned me with her eyes saying, *get on the bus, I've got a schedule to keep.* I even checked the bus number to be sure it was the trusty #346. It was. *Where was Vernon?* As it turns out, no one knew what happened to him. On that late August day when the district bus drivers reported to the school district's bus barn, Vernon was absent. It was like he vanished from the face of the earth, never to be seen or heard from again. To this day, the story behind the disappearance of Vernon the Bus Driver remains a Perryton mystery, never to be solved.)

But that day, I knew none of what was coming.

I just knew it was summer.

And I had no idea what the next three months would hold.

51

JACOB

"Jacob, get the front door!" Mom yelled from the kitchen. She was propping the kitchen's swinging door open with her foot, turning oatmeal raisin cookie batter over in a metal mixing bowl wedged under her left arm. "I've got my hands full."

It was summer. Which meant I was home and Mom was hovering.

"Got it!" I responded as I waddled down the stairs. "I'm coming, hold on!" I yelled to whoever was knocking on our front door.

"Well, hello, Jacob, you look like you just crawled out of bed."

I was struck mute. I stood still for 10 seconds staring at Susie Polanski standing on my front porch. "What are you doing here?"

She blinked several times.

"Oh, man, sorry, that sounded terrible. I'm just shocked to see you." I moved back to hold the door open for her. "Hi, Susie. Come in.

Can I get you a drink?"

Boy, was I off to good start.

"Hi, Jacob. I spent the last week fixing up an old 10-speed I found in the barn and thought I'd try it out. Works like new. I got here rather quickly." She leaned the bike against my porch and walked in the door.

As she walked by me into the cool of the living room, I realized how bad I certainly looked. I had taken a quick nap after my morning slog and had been in the process of knocking out a few chores. Needless to say, I wasn't looking overly attractive. I was wearing mismatched shorts and a holey t-shirt and had unfortunately forgotten to put on a ball cap. My hair must have looked like I stuck my finger in a light socket. Later confirmation in the bathroom mirror proved my assessment had been correct.

Susie, on the other hand, looked great.

Amazing, actually. Her thick blonde hair was pulled back in a pony tail that danced around her shoulders as she walked. No 70s rock band tee this time, though. The slight sheen of perspiration did nothing to detract from her looks. (Of course, she'd look good to me covered in dirt and rags.)

"Have a seat." I pointed to the living room sofa before I pushed through the door into the kitchen and smiled at my mom.

"Who was at the door?" Mom inquired.

"Susie Polanski. She was out riding her bike."

"Oh, was she now?" Mom added with a wry smile. "Go back out there and I'll bring you both some iced tea."

"Thanks, Mom." I turned and started back to the living room, stopping before the door to do my best hair combing with my fingers. I heard my Mom chuckle.

"Mom's bringing us some iced tea."

"What's she cooking? It smells great," Susie said as the smell of the cookies baking in the oven followed me out of the kitchen.

"Oatmeal raisin cookies. My favorite. I'm guessing a few will make their way out here with the tea."

"Let's hope."

"Did you fix the bike yourself?"

"Yeah, it was easy. Not too much to do. I think it was Jimmy's bike from a few years ago, but he never rode it. Or at least I never saw him on it. Needed air in the tires, a little oil, and a seat adjustment. Even with all the rust, it still rides pretty well."

"How are things at home?" I ventured into this subject without much thought. I was still nervous and taken aback by Susie's presence. We'd known each other forever, but she still made me feel all jittery. (The jitters went away as we got older and were replaced with good old-fashioned, highly-active hormones, a few of which were definitely starting to bubble to the surface the second Susie sauntered through the front door that afternoon.)

"Not great. Dad seems to be sliding into a state of permanent sadness. His life is not happy. He doesn't even say much to me anymore."

"I'm sorry." What else could I say?

"He putts around in the barn all day drinking *Coors Light*. So I'm kind of on my own. The good news is that I shop for my own food, so I can eat mac & cheese every day."

"Nobody can help you out?" I suggested. It seemed like a pretty good response.

"We can't afford hiring help, so I run the errands. I do it early so Dad can drive me to the store before he drinks too much."

"Well, I'm glad you're here."

"I've been lonely." Three words that could tear out my heart in an instant.

"So, Jacob, how are you doing?"

"Okay, I guess." I glanced quickly at my knees. That said enough.

Susie stayed for about two hours. Her visit made my week. We covered a bunch of random subjects from 8th grade, to the 4th of July parade and fireworks, a little teenage gossip, and this year's carnival, a subject that was less painful now than it was almost a year ago. Finally, she said good-bye and headed off on her new-to-her bike.

It was the fastest two hours in the history of my life.

"How is she?" Mom leaned against the door jamb into the laundry room as I closed the door.

"I feel like she needs help." Everyone in town knew her circumstances and also knew how strong she was.

"What if we asked her to dinner once or twice a week?"

"Great idea!" *Hell yah in spades was what I said internally.*

"I'm sure you think it's a great idea," Mom smirked.

(Understatement of the year. That summer will forever be known as the *Summer of Susie.* We ended up spending much more time together in the years to come, but that summer and the weekly dinners that started that day will always be very special, to both of us.)

Mom was true to her word. Every Friday night Susie was the Ross's dinner guest. The meal was served promptly at 7:00. Mom always made a fuss over the menu. Most of the time, Susie rode her bike over as soon as she could get away, but sometimes, when her dad was gone, we would go pick her up in the *LTD*. I liked when we picked her up because that meant she didn't have to leave by 8:30 to avoid darkness. I can guarantee you no one at her house noticed what time she was coming home.

I can also guarantee that I was never fashionably caught off guard again. I showered, combed my hair, and even wore matching clothes. Okay, so it wasn't *YSL*, but not bad for a 14-year-old farm boy. (As a side note, I noticed Susie dressed better as the summer went along, too. Sundresses and sandals by August. She was clearly maturing well past my station in life, but I was still too young to notice. Or care.)

Susie spent one glorious night in late July with us. Mom told me later that her Dad had been thrown in jail for a few days due to missing a court date related to a *DWI*. Mom couldn't fathom Susie staying alone in her house, so she invited her to stay over. She slept in Mary's room as Mary was gone at some academic camp for the long weekend. I wasn't too focused on those unimportant details, simply on the fact that Susie was sleeping just a few feet from me.

It was quite possibly the most exciting night of my young life. I laid awake until probably 3:00 a.m. The idea of Susie sleeping in the room next to me was too much to bear for my young mind. I learned that day that falling asleep at 3:00 and waking up at 4:00 for the daily slog is not conducive to a night of quality rest.

I was dead tired all the next day.

Yet still I slogged.

It was an easy day, thankfully. I was back by a little after five, greeted at the back door by Mom and a cup of coffee. Same old routine every day. I went back to bed as soon as I finished my coffee and fell asleep immediately, not waking up until around 8:00. I dressed, washed my face, and threw on a *Cardinals* ball cap before heading downstairs to the kitchen. I wasn't going to risk a bed-headed greeting from Susie.

Before I even reached the kitchen, I heard muffled laughter. I breached the door only to find Mom and Susie grinning at each other across the table.

"Good morning, Jacob," Mom said.

"Morning, Mom. Morning, Susie."

"Do you want some breakfast? Susie and I have already eaten."

"Sure. Thanks," I responded as I sat at the table between Mom and Susie. My knees were aching a little and felt a bit unstable, but I was not going to wear my braces. Not in front of Susie.

My mom placed a plate of eggs and bacon in front of me and I began to shovel it in. Susie smiled.

"What are you smiling about?"

"Nothing really. Just enjoying the morning. Your mom and I had some fun discussions."

Oh crap, that can't be good. Moms love to tell ultra-embarrassing stories about their kids and I'm sure Susie got an earful. "I'm not sure how to respond to that."

"No response needed, sweetie, just girl talk." Mom winked at Susie.

Susie winked back.

I finished my breakfast just as Susie stood up. "I need to go. Dad may be home this morning and I need to do a few things around the house."

My heart sank. "Are you coming back soon?"

"I'll come on Friday. As always."

Just six more days until more *Susie time*.

"Jacob, walk Susie to the door and I'll clean up the kitchen." (I have to hand it to my mom: She knew what she was doing. She had a real soft spot for Susie. And for me, of course. I think she had secret wishes of a blossoming romance.)

Susie turned as she walked out the door. "I'll see you later, Jacob. I had fun. Your mom is wonderful."

"She is, thanks."

Susie then turned and gave me a warm hug. She whispered in my ear. "Jake, you always have been and always will be my special person. You know I don't care about what other people care about. I'm just glad we're friends." She then kissed my cheek and quickly turned away, descending the porch steps onto her bike.

I stood in the middle of the porch, feeling as if I was floating in place, and watched her pedal away.

That summer was amazing. Better than amazing. So amazing I just don't have the words to describe it.

52

JACOB

The euphoria of the *Summer of Susie* quickly shattered.

About a week after Susie's sleepover, I returned from a fairly gentle slog and was not immediately met at the back door by Mom. Instead, she was sitting at the kitchen table wearing her light blue terry-cloth robe. Her hands held a cup of coffee and her head was on the table. Next to her hands, sat a steaming cup she had obviously poured for me.

It was clear something was wrong.

She lifted her head up and her eyes were wet and swollen. She must have been crying a great deal.

"Sit down, Jake," she whispered wearily.

I began shaking as I plopped into the chair. I didn't want to hear what was coming next.

"Your dad is moving out of the house." She didn't soften the blow. She just threw the bomb out on the table and its explosion floored me. I honestly did not process it at first. What kid could? This is something no kid expects, although in my case, I should have. The signs had all been there.

"Why? Why is he leaving?" I probably sounded angrier than I should have.

"Jacob, I'm sorry. I can't go into the whys right now, but we can chat when I have better control of myself," Mom added with finality as she rose from the table, crying again as she left the kitchen.

What the fuck, I mumbled out loud. Then the why hit me. All the puzzle pieces just slipped into place and I knew right then that Mary had been right.

My ears were ringing from the bomb. I immediately got that full-body tingling sensation of shock and disbelief. Stress fell on me like a downpour. I forced myself up from the table. My coffee went untouched. Mom's did too. I literally sprinted out of the kitchen and up the stairs to Mary's room. As I hit the top step, I could hear raised voices slipping out from my parents' room. The confirmation of everything I had been avoiding the last few months piled onto my shoulders. No knocking this time. I burst in unannounced. My startled sister unwrapped herself from her bed and sat on the edge, feet firmly planted on the floor. She knew me well enough to know something was serious. She also knew enough about our family to guess why I was frantically waking her in tears of agony.

"Mary, do you…"

Mary raised her hand and interrupted me. "Yes, Jacob. I know. I knew this was coming." She reached over and rubbed my shoulders.

"It can't be true. These are our parents. This can't happen to us!"

I blurted out as I sat down next to Mary on her bed. She wrapped her arm around me and pulled me close. I must have felt like a small child to her. Mary was four inches taller than me and equal to my weight. She was normal in size for her age; I certainly wasn't. I started crying. She did, too. We sat on the bed for a good five minutes in complete silence other than the sound of our hushed sobs. I didn't want to let go. Mary was now my anchor and the one person I could count on. Everyone else seemed to have failed me. I feared if I let go, so would she.

To this day, Mary has never let go.

Needless to say, the remainder of the summer was a nightmare in the Ross home. Dad did, in fact, move out on the same morning Mom dropped her bomb on me. Mary and I heard him thud down the stairs and out the back door. He then started up his car and squealed down the driveway. He did not step foot back in our house for about a year. It felt like five years, in retrospect. (No matter what pain a kid has in his life, nothing measures up to that of having their parents separate or divorce. The downward spiral it creates is irreversible. And, for me, it was worse considering my illness.)

The last two weeks of August also brought home the reminder that my life was not returning to normal. I was lulled into a false sense of comfort and hope as a result of so many consecutive months of soft slogs. Mrs. Ray was even moving to the hopeful side of the ledger. That all changed on the last Saturday of the month, four days before school was to start its fall semester.

The previous night was Susie's last Friday supper with the Ross family. (It was just with Mom, Mary, and me. Luke had spent 24 hours a day in his room since Dad's departure.) I waited for Susie on the front porch so I could intercept her before she walked into our house. I heard her tires crunching on the caliche road before

I caught sight of her. I stood up and walked a few paces forward. She skidded to a stop next to me. Sweat was gently rolling off her forehead. Her blouse had a dark line down its back. It was a hot August day in central Kansas.

"Hi, Jacob." She was always so easy-breezy calm.

"Let's sit on the front stoop for a minute," I said. "I need to tell you something." I spent the next 10 minutes telling her about my parents.

"I'm sorry, Jacob," she whispered when I finished. If anyone understood family problems, it was Susie.

I felt better for telling her. To a degree, it was good to let it out of my system. Bottling up a toxic event can end up polluting our entire body. Purging helps. Purging to Susie also helped to bond us closer. After what she had lived through with her mom and dad, we had a commonality to share. From that day forward, she opened up to me about her mom and dad and the impact her situation had on her life. It didn't come all at once, but over the years, I've heard a lot of the story. Parents can sure screw up their kids' lives. The scars from which never come close to fully fading.

Dinner was fine, if not subdued. Having Mary and Susie for dinner cheered up Mom, it seemed. I was sad because I knew this was the end of the *Summer of Susie*. Friday nights during the Fall are all about football, even for those of us who hate the game. Susie had made the cheerleading squad, so she would be at every game from that day on.

I went from having a weekly dinner with her to watching her social life bloom from my not so glamorous seat in *Bearcat Stadium*.

Susie didn't completely disappear from my life.

But it certainly was not the same between us again for quite a time.

53

JACOB

Evil hides in the shadows and dimness of light. It paints itself as benign even though it's a raging, malignant cancer. Evil wants to lull you into dropping your defenses and then, at just the right time, pounce like a lion on the weakest of elands. Evil is infinitely patient; therefore, it wins the long race. This patience reared its ugly head that Fall in a way I never expected.

It started with a normal, fun Saturday.

I spent a bit of time with Marcus and Mrs. Ray. We played games and talked about the coming school and football year. There was no counseling, none seem to be needed. Then, that afternoon, Mom, Mary, and I went into town to buy the last bits of school supplies. (We bought supplies for Luke, too, since he was holed up in his room. I felt very sad for my brother. Dad was his hero and his brother in football arms. He lost that in a blink of the eye. The impact on his motivation for life and school was negative.

The impact on his motivation for football can only be described as miraculous. He took all his hurt and pain out on the football field. He was an unstoppable, tackling maniac.)

I talked Luke into having dinner with us that evening, the first time in ages that all three children sat at the dinner table together. What a weird family. For the second time in as many days, the meal seemed to brighten up Mom. We finished the evening with a few games of *Parcheesi*. Luke won them all. He always seemed to win everything in those days.

I finished the evening in front of the TV. Luke was already snoring when I walked into the room to go to bed. I undressed and removed my braces and crawled into bed. I thought about my Mom and Dad and how our happy little family had dissolved into…this.

I had no answers. I cried myself to sleep.

I was jolted awake at 3:55 a.m. from another episode in the series of vivid and frightening dreams. I dreamed I was flying, almost soaring through the starlit night sky. I sped forward, held aloft by a cool, comforting wind. I felt strong and alive, with no pain or anxiety. I was filled with a feeling of well-being. Suddenly, as if I was a plane running out of fuel, I began to slowly drop in altitude. The cool breeze ceased and the night air thickened as it rose quickly in temperature. I had left the splendor of the countryside and struggled to maintain flight over a blight-ridden city. The high-rise buildings were charred and dilapidated. Fires were raging up and down the streets and dead, bloated bodies were strewn everywhere. All the light from the abundance of stars was blotted out.

As I continued to lose speed and elevation, the stench of burning meat filled my nose and burned my eyes. I was choking from the odor and smoke as I was now tumbling down a large, wide boulevard maybe three feet off the ground. All the lush grass and majestic trees that had once beautifully lined the median strip, were now charred and bent over as if mimicking ugly, black crows digging for worms.

It became clear that, at any second, I was going to crash chaotically into the cement. I always do. Indistinguishable faces stared at me from behind a broken window. Several of the people—at least I think they were people—were unemotionally on fire. Blank, dead eyes pierced me with guilt. A large mass of writhing blackness appeared at the intersection ahead. This amorphous being, best described as an absence of light, let out a piercing sound that then began to form random words and sentences. None of the sounds made sense, at least not at first.

I finally lost all power of flight and careened into the street just like a freshly-shot white-winged dove smacks the ground next to a watering hole. I folded into a loose ball and rolled, leaving chunks of skin behind. I slowed to a clumsy stop and stood up. I was covered in bleeding street burns from stem to stern. The pain was unbearable. I looked up and the shapeless blob was upon me, looking down at me. Its words were now crystal clear. He said, *I have you now, Jacob Ross. Oh, the fun we will have together.*

And that's the moment I woke up.

I scrambled for the light next to my bed to confirm I was not actually bleeding from my many scrapes. I was not; my skin felt like it was on fire, but it looked untouched. I was soaked from head to toe with sweat. No dream had ever felt so real to me; well, at least up to that point.

I quickly turned off the light and forced myself to get dressed. I threw my sopping wet t-shirt into the dirty clothes bin and left my room, my heart still pounding in my chest. I knew the night terror was no fluke. It was no normal dream. I remember it with renewed chills to this day. The message it sent me was devastating.

I hit our dark kitchen as if I had stepped into a tidal pool, being sucked out the back door and into the wheat field with a ferocious effort. My entire body was immediately wracked with pain and nausea. I took two floundering steps and was violently thrown facedown into the furrow. I barely managed to rise to my knees as the entire contents of my stomach exited my nose and mouth. My body shook feebly, rocking back and forth. I was waiting for permission to stand up. Permission from whatever someone or something was controlling my mind.

The giant blob from my dreams entered my conscious.

Then permission came.

I didn't hear it spoken, but I felt it implanted in my mind. I stood much like the *Weeble* Jimmy Polanski accused me of being. I slowly gained my footing and balance and proceeded forward. My steps were labored and seem to hit the dirt with a resounding thud, each time sending pain up my legs through my knees and into the core of my being. I wanted to stop but couldn't. I wanted to die but couldn't do that either. On I slogged, heading west down the much-tilled trench. The only silver lining was a complete lack of electrical thoughts. My mind was clear except for the dream that seemed to be playing on a loop in my mind. I believe this clarity was provided so there would be no interference with the intent of the night's slog.

I reached the far end of the field and turned to return home. The return trip looked like it was miles of a rut carved in the dirt. It was much further than the outbound trip. I took a deep breath and prayed to no avail for an end to my living and breathing hallucination. Good*ness* had completely deserted me and left me to be devoured by Evil.

Unexpected thoughts slipped in between the nightmares: this wasn't the end of Jacob Ross. I had a life to live. I had Susie to love and Mary to thank. I had Luke to reconcile with and Mom to care for.

I felt myself straighten up, and for the first time, start to fight back.

I didn't know how I was going to overcome, but I did know that I wasn't going to die in the middle of our family wheat field.

I was going to survive.

I was going to overcome.

I teetered again, fighting my collapsing muscles. Each step was very arduous, but I walked on. The wind grew still and all the night sounds were sucked out of the air. I felt an unseen presence. I knew the blob was about to announce its terrible existence.

I was wrong.

Far away at first, but quickly approaching, a dim light grew in intensity. The same light I tangled with last summer. It was back. Only this time, it didn't feel evil. Instead it felt…different. Hopeful, even. The dish-shaped light hovered 10 feet in front of me, pulsating in both sound and light. We both stood motionless as if preparing for a gunfight at high noon. Who would flinch first? I guess I did.

"Who…or what are you?" I shouted at the top of my lungs.

The disc didn't respond other than to simply move closer to me. Just as before, a concentrated beam of light began to emanate from the disc and surround me in a globe of energy. The air grew cool and my pain vanished. I was hovering off the ground imprisoned in a ball of light. Was I in *shitstorm* part two? Was I going to end up in the hospital again?

Then, just before total darkness engulfed me, I heard another voice, a voice I instantly recognized as the same voice I heard a year and a half ago. *Jacob, you will be fine. I will care for you.*

I woke up some time later at the foot of our back porch, partially tucked under our scraggly bushes. It was still dark, but the morning sun was peeking over the horizon. The sounds of movement were clear inside our kitchen, so I knew Mom was probably making my coffee. My clothes were damp from both sweat and dew.

And then I realized the strangest thing of all: I felt wonderful. All the pain was gone. I had unreasonable energy and, most importantly, I felt a sense of calm and peace. I could recall every facet of that morning's slog down to the tiniest of details. The floating globe's voice and message still resonated deep within me; both frightening and comforting. Last night's horrific dream was vivid in my memory as well.

Opposite feelings, opposite emotions, all crashing into each other.

Up the stairs I walked with a bounce in my step. Mom must have heard me coming as the back door opened. There she stood with a cup of coffee in each hand.

"Oh my, Jacob, what in the world happened this time?" she shouted as both cups tumbled from her hands, shattering upon impact.

54

MARY, 2015

Heathrow Airport was a zoo, even at 7:00 a.m. on a Thursday. Jack dropped me off at the curbside check-in for British Airways. Liam was fast asleep in the backseat carrier, so I touched his face, hugged and kissed Jack, promised to bring home lots of souvenirs, and headed into the terminal. I took a deep breath and steeled myself for the myriad lines that necessarily accompany all travelers these days. Particularly on international flights.

Line number one was waiting for the BA attendant who manned the check-in desk inside the lower portion of the terminal. Curbside check-in stretched a good 50 feet, so I took my chances inside. The line was long but moved quickly and, within 10 minutes, my bag was checked. Travel purse in hand, I set off for line number two at the security checkpoint. This checkpoint line reminded me of the lines I waited in at Six Flags over St. Louis as a kid. The line extended past the serpentine design of the markers that guide you into the boarding pass and passport confirmation station. Once through that line, it was back into a third line to half strip down, get eyeballed by some high school graduate, and have the contents of my carry-ons run through an x-ray machine.

There must be a more efficient process. I made a mental note to obtain the needed security clearance to access the preferential line.

Still, I had made it. With enough time to get a latte before I boarded. All-in-all, not too bad. With my latte in one hand, and the day's London Times under my arm, I walked the labyrinth that is the main terminal walkway until I arrived at BA Gate 15.

I was going to see Jacob.

It felt strange to even contemplate. Strange, but so good. I missed him.

Boarding was announced, and I reassembled the Times and moved to the boarding standard indicating where to line up for access to the plane as called. Just as I was stepping onto the plane, my phone pinged.

Have a great trip, love you...Liam. I laughed at Jack's attempt at text message humor.

Will do. Love you, Sweetie. Tell your dad I love him too, I replied.

Then I turned my phone off and settled in. My flight departed Heathrow on time and I spent most of the flight sleeping and reading. Excitement on a flight is not a good practice. I had learned that from experience.

Thirteen hours later, the pilot announced our initial descent into Phoenix's Sky Harbor International Airport.

And so the butterflies began.

55

JACOB

"Good God, look at you!" Mom grabbed me and pulled me into the house. I had no idea why she was so upset. I felt great.

It turns out I didn't look so great.

In fact, Mom said I looked like I was one slippery step from death's door. Nice comment, huh? Mom escorted me into the bathroom to see for myself. I barely recognized the face looking back at me. My normally dark brown hair was now sandy blonde with singed, grey ends. My brown eyes somehow changed to a pale grey-blue, and my once freckled skin looked to be bleached smooth and clear. I looked five years older, as if I reappeared from my latest slog magically teleported to the end of my senior year. All this cosmetic change was worsened by the smears of dirt and blood. The dirt I understood, the blood I didn't. I had streaks of dry and crusted, deep-red blood hardened down my cheeks from my ears and surrounding my lips and chin from my nose. I have no memory of bleeding or even the feel of the blood running down my face.

I looked awful.

The strangest part, by far, was a slight glow around my body, like a faint aurora. I turned off the light and, in the darkness, my skin glowed. My mom gasped, then turned the light on and off several times. It looked like my glow-in-the dark *Frisbee*. A faint greenish tint. (As a side note, I revisited the bathroom about an hour later and again switched off the light. No glow. Whatever was causing the full-body halo had disappeared.)

"I think we need to go to the hospital, Jake," Mom stated as we walked back into the kitchen.

"No, Mom. It didn't help last time and it won't help this time either."

Mom stared at me in resignation. "But shouldn't we at least get you checked out?"

"Mom, you saw what happened in there just like I did. No one is going to believe us. And no one will have a clue what to do."

"Jacob, what's happening?"

"I wish I knew, Mom."

"Well, at least shower and eat something while I think this through. I'm going to call Celina."

"Okay," I headed up the stairs and then paused and looked back at my mom. "Mom, the weird thing is that I feel great. Something happened out there and I feel better."

"You don't look better, Jacob."

"I know. I'm okay, though."

"Are you going to be okay in the shower? By yourself?"

"I'm fine. I promise." I came back downstairs 20 minutes later with a killer appetite. I plopped down at the table as Mom placed a plate of pancakes and sausage in front of me. Great timing. I ate with uncontrollable lust as if it was my first meal in days.

"You do look better. Are you still feeling okay?" Mom inquired.

"I feel pretty good, particularly now that I've eaten."

"I hate to ask this question because I'm sure I don't want to hear the details, but—what happened this morning, Jake? What did you go through to look like this when you came back to the house?" Mom said, pointing her finger at me to emphasize the word *this*.

I relayed the events of the morning in the wheat field with as much detail as I could. I purposely left out the dream from the night before. Mom listened intently between audible gasps and a few interjections of *oh my word*.

By noon, my rush of adrenaline had waned and I was back to normal physically. The braces were fitted back to their proper place. I spent a good hour in the bathroom staring at myself. I looked like the same old Jacob, just enhanced a bit as if I was made up for a movie. Cleaning my face and hair made me look more my age, but there was still an almost indescribable change that made me look older, as if I had had the growth spurt I desperately wanted and, quite frankly, should have had by now.

But the next day was the same.

Well, except for the singed ends of my hair. Those disappeared with my next haircut, one done my mom in the kitchen so a hairdresser wouldn't ask why my hair was burned.

I never knew what happened. What caused the burning, the

bleeding? And I never felt the worse for wear.

That alone was possibly the most frightening thing of all.

56

JACOB

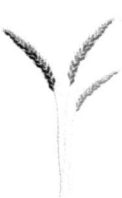

My mom had called Mrs. Ray after my Sunday slog, so I knew I owed her a visit. And, since the new school year began on Tuesday, Monday was my only option.

"Hi, Jacob. Come in and sit down." She stepped aside, having opened the door to let me enter. "Your mom called me."

"I know."

"But I already knew. I woke up with a start about 4:45 yesterday. I could feel the conflict. I could feel your pain. I knew it was happening again. Not in detail, but close enough."

"So you felt it?" It was so strange.

"Yeah, I felt it." She gave me a grimaced smile.

"It's so strange. There is a connection between the two of us I just don't understand."

"I don't either, Jacob."

"I guess I'm just starting to wonder why. Why you and me? And why am I the only one slogging myself to death while you lie peacefully in bed?" I was halfway out of my seat gripping the table's edge. It felt unfair to me. I knew I shouldn't have been taking it out on Mrs. Ray, but I was mad.

"Jacob, honey, I've often thought about this as well. It's totally unfair." She paused. "The only thing I can think of is that what happened to me in that car trunk is similar to what you experienced during your slog last year. The light, *the disc*."

"What do you mean?"

"Maybe...maybe someone or something wants to send you—or us—a message."

"It happened again last night," I interjected.

"You saw the light again?"

I proceeded to tell her about the light, the feeling it gave me, and what was said to me. I also replayed my dream. All in great detail.

57

JACOB

Mrs. Ray settled in to her seat and folded her hands in her lap. She looked squarely at me and started to talk.

"Melvin Standard was born in one of the infamous two-story row houses that was part of Cabrini-Green, a housing project initiated in the early 1940s by the Chicago Housing Authority as a public housing project. Cabrini-Green was located on the North Side of Chicago, but not too far north of downtown. Some people now call it the Slums, or the Projects; by either name it's a tough place to live and survive. Guns, gangs, and drugs were prevalent; education was not. Do you remember a TV show call Good *Times?* Jimmie Walker and his trademark "Dy-no-mite!""

I nodded.

"That show was set in Cabrini-Green. Their on-screen lives were happier than the normal residents', though, I'm sure. Cabrini-Green was not a nice place to live. Melvin's parents moved to Chicago just after World War II, when his dad returned from the European front. They were one of the first families to make Cabrini-Green their home. Money was tight and Cabrini-Green houses were affordable. It was a nice place to live—for a while at least—but, over the years, deterioration set in and the neighborhood slid into disrepair. The Standards only lasted about 15 years before they moved.

Melvin was born in 1943, the oldest of four kids. The Standards were very strict—they believed God and church first, school and family second. Which meant that any trouble was dealt with swiftly and corporally. All four kids toed the line. Monday through Friday everyone either worked or went to school. Evenings were for family dinner and homework; excellence in both was a requirement, not an option. Saturday was a day of fun, but they worked hard at this too. Sunday, as you can guess, was spent at church. No arguments, no exceptions.

Melvin obliged.

Had no choice.

But he didn't necessarily like it. He always said it seemed too formal and repetitious to him. Same liturgy, same hymns, or at least they sounded the same to him, and same sense of guilt. The First Baptist Church of Chicago was not his favorite place. The only part of Sunday he looked forward too with joy—other than the tuna noodle casserole served in the basement dining hall—was the pastor's sermon.

He was enthralled when Pastor Clark took front and center. Something about his booming voice, his stern countenance, his soft words would cause Melvin to immediately stop squirming and sit rigid. He absorbed his every word and mannerism. How this man captivated the audience was a thing of beauty. How he had them hanging on every word was a pure art form. Melvin didn't always understand the deep biblical message, but he sure recognized the weight of the words.

As he grew into his teens, the sermon's subject matter began to come into focus. The power of the pastor's delivery never waned and, as Melvin sat there listening to those words, he decided his calling was to be the next Pastor Clark. He was going to be a preacher. And he was going to learn to captivate an audience just like Pastor Clark did.

There was only one road block: he had no desire to be schooled as a theologian and certainly had no propensity to study the Bible as a means to an end. To be sure, he knew the Bible better than most—how could he not? Osmosis alone handled that issue. He felt called."

I stood up and filled up a glass of water and then sat down. "This is all interesting, Mrs. Ray, but what does it have to do with me?"

"Hold on, Jacob. You'll see in a few minutes," Mrs. Ray continued. "Melvin, never short on smarts or determination, decided to shortcut the process. This epiphany hit him shortly after his 16th birthday as he lay in bed one night. There were not deep voices from above or bright lights announcing the idea. He simply decided it and, from that point, it was a fact of coming to life. He was going to start his own church following his own rules."

"By this time the Standards had moved to Wichita and settled in a middle-class neighborhood. Melvin's dad was a First Line Manager in a very large, very successful cattle stockyard, processing receiving herds from Texas to Montana for shipping to the East Coast. It was a good job for a man whose skin was not the color of most of his peers. His boss, as well as the owner of the stockyard, were devout Christians who firmly believed a man's worth is on the inside. Delbert Standard proved them correct every single day. In return, they treated him as they would wish to be treated."

"Melvin finished high school as did all of his siblings. Three out of four of them went to, and finished, college. A huge accomplishment. The 60s were not easy on any of them, but they persevered. *Thrived* is a better term.

But Melvin was an exception. He never got the image or feeling of Pastor Clark out of his system. The idea of following in his footsteps as a career choice never left him. The million-dollar question was how to become a theologian without any formal training. The answer to the million-dollar question was to just jump off the cliff and see how hard of a landing he was in for. Well, it didn't kill him, but it bruised most of his body.

Melvin, all of 20 years old, talked a struggling landlord into allowing him rent, to use the term loosely, an abandoned warehouse in the City Center section of Wichita. With no congregation, next to no money, and absolutely no idea what he was doing, the Evangelical Baptist Church was launched in July 1962. He had just taken a gargantuan leap of faith.

Outwardly, that first day of business was the high point for the initial two years of EBC. By July 1964, Melvin had run out of money numerous times, gone to bed hungry many nights, accumulated a flock of maybe 10 people (15 if you counted the winos who snored through the Sunday Service), dodged an eviction notice or two, and had his utilities turned off and on so many times you'd think he was in a ping-pong match with Wichita Power.

"If you asked Melvin, the first two years were a smash hit. Heck, its doors still opened every Sunday morning at 8:00, didn't they? He'd tell you he had become a member of the neighborhood, that the warehouse had been refurbished using Standard elbow grease, which was part of the renegotiated lease terms. Furnishings, such as disparate pews and chairs, a podium and a large steel cross, were donated along the way. But the best part was that he was able to preach. And preach he did. Melvin had a gift to go along with his dream. He did not stomp around the stage, waving his Bible in the air, as if he was he was acting in a made-for-TV movie. His approach was the opposite. He'd slowly pace the stage, stopping often to emphasize a point or clarify a passage. The power was not in the act; it was truly in the delivery of the message. He oozed serenity and honesty. His congregation, even as it grew into the hundreds, believed because he believed. He loved the Lord and the people in the pews knew it with every fiber in their collective bodies.

He had become his own version of his hero, Pastor Clark.

"And what does this have to do with me, Mrs. Ray?" I asked. I was honestly very tired of just sitting still and listening.

"I'll get to that, Jacob." She paused. "Melvin has been a dear friend of mine for about 30 years. You're looking at one of the 10 people that was sitting in his congregation in those early years. I was in awe of his abilities and the message he spoke. I attended his church until its last days. My aunt lived a few blocks from his church. Remember, I told you I left Perryton to move to Wichita soon after my kidnapping. My aunt attended too. She asked Melvin to work with me as I was having grave problems with the aftermath. It's funny—for a while the kidnapping was a bit of a non-event, but as I grew older, I began to struggle mightily. I now realize he is connected to us, to this."

I shrugged. This was getting weird.

"Over the next 10 years EBC grew substantially. It topped out at over 250 congregants. But, even with more people sitting in the pews, money was always an issue. Most of the regulars were poor and struggling. I believe everyone tithed as much as they could, but the collection plates were never full. Melvin didn't care. He was doing exactly what he had envisioned that night lying in bed some 16 years before. He stretched every dollar even to the point of providing funds for other local ministries. Volunteers helped him fill the roles of janitor, maintenance man, and yard boy. He lived and breathed EBC and it cared for him in return."

"But it didn't last? You said you went there until its last days. What happened to the church?" I was anxious to move the story forward.

"Ahh, so you are paying attention."

"Yes ma'am. I'm listening. I want to know how Mr. Standard is connected to me."

"One of life's adages is that success breeds jealousy and jealousy breeds destruction. This adage, sadly, hit Melvin right square in the face. Some of the local pastors grew jealous of EBC's success, watching their congregational attendance flatten while his grew leaps and bounds. I mean, after all, it's all about numbers and dollars, right?"

"Well, I'm not sure."

"Yes, you are, Jacob. I can tell by your puzzled look you don't agree. I sure don't and I know Melvin didn't. But his competition, as they viewed themselves, saw it otherwise. It's amazing how many pastors and church bodies become *Pharisaical*. Money and power begin to push the true meaning of the Gospels to the background. Human nature, I guess. Anyway, these pastors dug a bit into Melvin and his church and soon discovered that, not only was he not educated or ordained, but he was not even a paying member of the Baptist Convention. Up to this point, EBC was too small for anyone to care. Not anymore. One thing led to another and the Baptist hierarchy ultimately swept in and stripped Melvin of everything they could.

This was devastating to his congregation. Not the revelation that

he was a rogue minister—they didn't care about his credentials—
but that he was losing his church. Very few understood it and even
fewer liked it. After all, wasn't he doing God's work? In lieu of a
long-drawn-out proceeding, the Baptist church offered Melvin a
deal. The long and short of it was, stop being a pastor and we won't
grind you into smoldering ashes. Nice, huh?"

"Yeah, I'll never understand how adults work. I mean, he was
helping people."

"I know, Jacob, it's so sad. Deep down he knew this day of reckoning
was going to come. Melvin was steeled to the verdict and, with the
grace he exuded for the prior 12 years, moved on with his life."

"What did he do after he lost his church? It doesn't seem very fair."

"You're right. It wasn't fair. Our whole church felt it was terribly
unjust. He spent the next year living with various congregants,
winding down the church, and deciding in which direction to take
his life next."

"So, what did he decide?"

"Well, Jacob, that's where this story gets interesting."

"All right, tell me more."

By the shimmer of her eyes, I could tell she was about to get to her
favorite part. Soon to be mine too.

58

JACOB

"Even with the implosion in his life, Melvin still saw me periodically. I'd seek him out when the anxiety would flare up over my kidnapping. It was akin to the experience that many soldiers have upon returning from war. I would start having memories of the events, panic attacks even. He'd schedule a formal session, but when the time was up, we'd continue talking. He often bounced his latest career ideas off of me. Most were reactionary. None were worth doing in my mind.

One day during this period, I was having an unusually bad day so I called Melvin and, like he always did, he came over immediately. I was married to Paul by that time and we had a small house not far from where EBC once stood. When Melvin walked in the front door, I noticeably flinched. He smiled and asked what was wrong. I don't remember my exact answer, but it was something like *you've changed*.

What I meant was that there was something different about him. He looked exactly the same as he did the last time we were together, but I felt a change. I felt as if he was different in some instinctual way. Paul looked at me like I was a bit off, but he was not connected to Melvin like I was. We sat outside on the back porch as we always did. Tea-sipping and small talk behind us, I pointedly asked him *what was different.* He answered with a question. *What do you feel?*

I wasn't sure what I felt, but I did know something was different. He then proceeded to tell me what had happened to him not one week prior."

Mrs. Ray got up to refill her water and then sat down.

"I'll give you the short version, Jacob, since you've already been sitting here for an hour. Melvin had developed a bit of insomnia due to the stress of his situation and one night he was lying in bed awake. He often spent those middle-of-the-night hours alternating between the forced planning of his future and deep prayer. Anyway, that morning around 3:00 a.m., Melvin felt his fingers almost brush up against the answer as if it was within his grasp. He caught himself physically reaching his arms out to grab this idea as if it was tangible. On his knees, he rocked back and forth. Sweat was flowing from his body.

A light suddenly appeared in front of him. The light seemed to be emanating from nothing; it was just there floating in front of him for a few seconds and then it reached out and engulfed Melvin, physically lifting him from the wooden slats. A warm comfort invaded his being. At that point, he knew all was going to be right. His world was about to gain absolute direction. A layer of static was intertwined with the light and slowly penetrated his chest. The static spoke to him. Its heat grasped him and he heard, *you are mine. I am proud. Goodness needs you. Continue your work and you will want for nothing.*

He told me that day that he didn't exactly hear the voice with his ears or his mind; he heard it with his heart, as if it was planted in one fell swoop. The light immediately vanquished. The warmth endured. Melvin laid on the porch staring up at night sky, watching a series of comets grace the darkness. He now knew his path. Clear as a bright summer day, he saw his mission and he grabbed it with an energy and vigor that few men can muster.

"Who spoke to him? God?" I was feeling way out of my league.

"Melvin wasn't sure. Was it God? Was it an angel? Or was it a merely a messenger for Good? Whoever it was, his goal for the rest of his life on earth was determined. He knew from that day forward that his job was to help as many people as he could and intercept as many indifferent lives for Good before they were swept off the table by the influences of Evil."

"Do you think this light was the same thing that protected you when you were trapped in the trunk?"

"Yes. I'm sure of it."

"How do you know for sure?"

"After Melvin told me his story, he hugged me. Hugged me in a way I had never been hugged before or since. It was a hug energized with caring and salvation. As he held me, all my anxiety and stress streamed out of my body. I felt it. I can still feel it. From that point to this day, I have never had another moment of anxiety about the day I was kidnapped. I still remember the event, but it's as if I am remembering a movie that I've seen enough times to have all the scenes memorized. It was like that day with Melvin cured me. He extracted my illness."

"So how does this relate to me?" I still didn't understand why she was telling me all this.

"Jacob, I'm not sure why, but it's so clear to me that you and Melvin are also connected. I think I first realized it the night we found you so sick on our back porch. I was sitting alone in your hospital room and it struck me that maybe Melvin could help you like he helped me. I'll admit I wasn't completely sure until you relayed the story of the previous morning's slog and the bright light. Now you confirmed it with last night's repeat performance. Melvin was selected to protect me. Melvin and I have been selected to protect you. To guard you from Evil and make sure whatever special purpose you have been gifted with is an instrument of Good. I believe you are on the side of Good*ness*, a significant player in Good*ness's* plans, and that is why Evil is interested in your demise."

"That sounds a bit crazy," I paused, not wanting to offend her. "I mean, an epic battle between Good and Evil is video game stuff."

"But Jacob, think of it this way, Evil needs your cooperation. It needs your help. Evil's plan was to make you slog your way toward it. I imagine things would have been a lot worse for you had you not had help from the other side, the Good side. You'd probably have broken a long ago."

"Awesome. So basically Evil is making me slog and the only thing protecting me from sure chaos is…a Good *Light*?"

"Pretty much, Jacob."

"Awesome." To be honest, this was way too much for a 13-year-old to take in, much less process. It would take years of rehashing before I truly understood what Mrs. Ray said that day. Unfortunately, I didn't have years to figure it all out, so I had to take the leap of faith. A leap of faith based on my gut reaction to the story and my trust in Mrs. Ray.

"So where is Melvin Standard these days?" I asked. It seemed I was going to meet him; the only open issues were when and where.

"I don't know for sure. I lost track of him after I left Wichita and moved back home to Perryton."

"You lost track of the man who changed your life?"

"Yeah, it's a long story, Jacob, but life happens. It happened. But I do know some people in Wichita that will know how to find him. My guess is he's still just trudging forward with his mission in life. I just need to find out where. It shouldn't be too big of a problem to solve."

"Do you think he'll be able to help me? That he'll want to?"

"Don't worry, Jake. He'll help. That's not even worth fretting over."

Mrs. Ray stood up from the table and I knew immediately what that meant. We'd been sitting at her kitchen table for three hours and I was tired and stiff. My knees were starting to hum. I needed to get home.

"Well, it's been interesting, Mrs. Ray. See you later!"

As I walked home, I realized I wasn't even sure what I had just heard or agreed to. But I also knew I didn't have a choice but to try. Something had to change. I wasn't sure what, but something.

But, in the midst of that epic struggle between Good and Evil, I did know one thing for sure: I needed to go to bed.

I needed sleep.

I needed the dreams to stay away.

And I needed a break from slogging.

But it was not to be.

59

JACOB

I was struggling to stay aloft.

An unseen weight was winning the battle, against all my efforts and all my hopes. The graceful lines I carved through a blue and orange sky were now jagged discords similar to those of a WWI bi-plane spinning toward the ground after a losing effort in a dogfight. A fiery crash seemed inevitable. As I left the comfort of the countryside and entered the burning city of my dreams, my anxiety ascended commensurate with my loss of altitude.

The buildings were still burning, a perpetual fire fueled by the remnants of a once great city. Flames were dancing out of the building's windows and storefronts. Dead bodies were strewn everywhere, rapidly becoming food for the scavengers of the skies. Some bodies were twitching, most were silent, all were charred beyond recognition. As I flew low and between the buildings, the heat built but not to the same degree as the stench that emanated from burning and rotting flesh. As I looked left and then right through the holes where window glass once lived, I saw hazy figures dart and flit in the shadows created by the billows of black smoke. This scared me to no end. I began breathing with great labor and sweating profusely. My dreams were always the same, yet subtlety different. Same story but the scenes were ever so slightly different. Once again, I lost the battle of flight and slammed into the ground at a low angle, allowing my body to scrap and roll for 20 or 30 feet. Skin left and blood appeared. Pain followed. I couldn't move for several minutes, then I slowly unfurled myself and stood up in the middle of a main thoroughfare.

It was one of those streets with a large, wide, grassy median that bisects the opposing traffic lanes. The median was now mostly dirt and dead grass. The trees were charred black, lifeless but for the random flames eating the last of their withered leaves. The eerie silence was broken by a guttural whirling sound that had no apparent origin. With the advance of the noise, I felt and saw countless shadow figures closing in on me. They didn't rush toward me but instead they twisted and turned in the distance, closing ranks in an almost imperceivable rate.

Yet, I knew their goal. I was their goal.

I spun on my heels looking for an escape. There was none. The burning buildings were closing ranks too. The wide gaps that once existed between each structure were narrowing and the tongues of fire were multiplying, all soon to form a cohesive blockade that would surely become impenetrable.

I looked skyward as the approaching sound creaked like contorted steel as it flowed over the heights of the burning buildings. The writhing, black mass was gaining speed as it imitated some macabre waterfall following the sound into the arena formed by the closing buildings. All remaining light was blotted out. The thick, viscous feel of darkness was set to attack me where I stood.

I was the object of its desire. I had nowhere to go, nowhere to escape to.

My eyes snapped open. 4:05 was glowing on the face of my alarm clock. I had never in my life been so happy to wake up, even at that ungodly hour. As before, I pulled off my soaking wet t-shirt and tossed it into the dirty clothes basket. I almost skipped out of my room and down the stairs.

My slogs were not nearly as frightful as my dreams.

Even if they were inextricably tied together.

60

JACOB

I was steeled for an awful slog. How could it not be after the dream I had just had?

I was wrong. It was easy and quick. I was back at the kitchen table eating my sugar-encrusted Cheerios in no time. I alternated between thoughts of Pastor Standard and my nightmare. What would it hurt to visit with him, that is, if Mrs. Ray could locate him? Maybe I could tell him about my dreams and he'd be able to help me escape.

I decided to take as many notes as I could about my dreams, even the small, incoherent fragments, so I'd be able to remember every detail. Maybe the act of writing would help me to conjure up other bits and pieces, even if too many slivers of my nightmare series were not possible to recall.

"Hi, Jacob. You're back earlier than I expected." Mom walked through the swinging door into the kitchen. "I don't even have your coffee ready."

"Easy morning." And that was the end of that topic.

"What do you want for breakfast, sweetie? You pick it and I'll make it." She glanced down at my now-empty bowl of cereal and pointed. "That is not breakfast for a growing boy."

"Wow, really? Anything?"

"Anything reasonable and that I have ingredients for. I see your mind conniving."

"Okay, how about scrambled eggs and bacon?"

"Pancakes too? I have some batter left over in the fridge."

I wasn't going to argue with that. My morning was starting off well, despite the horrific dream.

Don't get too excited, Jacob. You know better than to expect a good day.

Good self-counsel.

Because I did, in fact, know better.

61

JACOB

One thing I've learned over the past two years is to never, ever take your eye off the ball. As soon as you get comfortable and let your mind wander, a line drive nails you in the bridge of your nose. Cartilage cracks, blood flows, and to your knees you crumple.

I've been hit on the bridge of my nose a few times. You would think I would have learned my lesson, but I've had so many ups and downs followed by horrifying events that any ray of sunshine was worth grasping for.

After my conversation with Mrs. Ray, I grasped for Pastor Standard. I admit that at first I was skeptical, but after a few days of contemplation, I was sold. I believed he was the answer. (As desperate as I was, I would have probably believed anyone or anything was the answer, but at the time, I didn't think of it that way.)

I asked Mrs. Ray every time I saw her. Had she found him? Had she located Pastor Standard? And every time she just shook her head and said, "Be patient, Jacob. Be patient."

I was tired of being patient. I wanted to yell *Why not? Try harder. Don't you know I am out-of-mind desperate?* But I knew it would do no good. Mrs. Ray had promised me all would be solved in time. Not my time, but the right time. I was merely along for the ride.

I'm sure the idea of patience and due time was right, but for a teenage boy, it was torture.

Pure torture.

62

JACOB

"Jacob, I've found him. He's in North Carolina. He is still running roughshod over the established church community." Mrs. Ray was standing on our back porch at 6:00 p.m. on a Wednesday in December. She was shivering cold, clearly having dashed out of her house in a hurry. "He was so excited to hear from me. He didn't have long to talk so I gave him the abbreviated version of your story and he wants to talk more. He's going to call me on Saturday."

She was breathing hard and trembling by the time she got it all out.

"Come in, Celina, get out of the cold!" Mom yelled over my shoulder, almost shoving me aside to make a path into the kitchen. Mom closed the door behind Mrs. Ray and gave me one of those looks that clearly said, *where are your manners?* I was too stunned and so happy to think about something as insignificant as manners. After all, were we at Cotillion?

Mom ushered Mrs. Ray to the table and started making coffee as Mrs. Ray filled Mom in on why she had come over. The background story on Melvin Standard was watered down quite a bit. The crazy stuff was left out. Smart move. My mom couldn't have handled it just then.

Then, as if I wasn't standing there, they sipped their coffee and caught up on local gossip and talked about how their lives were. As impatient as I was to hear about Pastor Standard, it was also nice to see Mrs. Ray and Mom in a normal situation. It reminded me of what great people they were. Of how much normalcy both had missed out on.

After about an hour of chitchat, Mrs. Ray rose from the table and said her good-byes. Mom lent her an overcoat for the walk home. As Mrs. Ray was about to step onto the porch, she backed up a few steps into the kitchen, closed the door, and looked at Mom. It wasn't a look of two friends visiting; it was the look I seen a hundred times at her kitchen table. She had switched to Jacob-needs-help mode.

"Susan. I need to ask you a favor. I need you to take a leap of faith."

Mom recoiled slightly. I think she knew something was coming that was related to her peculiar son. "What is this about, Celina?"

"I want to take Jacob to North Carolina with me to visit with Pastor Standard. I think he may be of some help in understanding what's happening with him."

Mom then shocked me to no end. I thought she would argue, she would say no, she would question. Instead, she showed no hesitancy, no desire to argue, no look of surprise. It was as if she had given this a preponderance of thought. She merely said, "Absolutely. Whatever you think is best, Celina."

"What? Just like that you say I can go?" I blurted, shocked she had simply acquiesced.

"What will Dad say?" I responded, almost in defense of her indifference.

"Honestly, Jacob, I don't care. I trust Celina's judgment and I know you need help. If you think this might help you, then you should go. Dad lost his chance to have a say in this the day he left our house."

I was taken aback. Also, I was impressed. Mom had a whole lot more backbone than I thought.

"All right, then, I guess we're going to North Carolina, Jacob."

"It looks like we are."

"I'll call your mom and fill her in on the details after I talk to Pastor Standard on Saturday."

"Sounds good."

Mrs. Ray smiled and walked out the door, leaving a quiet in the room that only the absence of Celina Ray can create.

"Jacob, look, I would never normally let you head out to another state to meet a complete stranger. But we are not in the world of normal, are we?"

"No, Mom, we're not." I knew exactly what she meant.

"Plus, I trust Celina."

"I do, too. Mrs. Ray will take good care of me." I started to chuckle. "I know her well enough to pity the person who crosses her."

"I agree, Jacob. Don't you dare cross her."

We both laughed.

I smiled as I fell asleep that night. My mom was awesome.

***

"Jacob, Mrs. Ray called this morning and wants you to come to her house this afternoon. She wants to visit with you about next month's trip to North Carolina."

To say I was excited was an understatement. I was more excited for that trip than I had ever been for Christmas or my birthday. Part of my excitement was driven by the hope of progress. The idea that I could be cured and maybe, just maybe, get my life back. I found myself daydreaming of a life of pain-free, healthy legs. A life devoid of slogs and wicked dreams. A life where I grew to a normal size and participated in normal activities. The anticipation was numbing me with exhilaration.

"What time does she want me to come over?"

"She said to come any time after 3:00."

I was on her porch stoop at 3:01, knocking on the back door with unbridled gusto.

"Hey, Jacob." Marcus opened the back door with a sandwich in one hand and a glass of milk in the other. "I'll tell Mom you're here. Sounds like a road trip is in your future, huh? I wish I could go, but Mom said I can't miss school. You're so lucky."

"Want to change lives with me, Marcus?" I used my best smart-ass voice.

"No thanks, Jake." He smiled. I laughed. We had the kind of camaraderie that could withstand snarky remarks.

"Hey, Jake, can we go back to your house after you and Mom are done and go through the pre-Algebra homework? I need some help."

"Sure. I haven't started it yet, so we can work through it together."

"Thanks. I appreciate it." Marcus downed the milk, grabbed an apple out of the ever-present and ever-full wooden bowl that was a staple of the kitchen table, and exited the kitchen just as Mrs. Ray walked in.

"Hi, Jake. Sit down, please. I have great news. I visited at length with Melvin and he is eager to meet you. He did not promise anything miraculous or even react much to our conversation. I think he was processing it all. You have to admit, this is not an everyday story."

She was dead right there. "But do you still think he can help?" I was almost begging.

"I don't know, Jacob. I don't think anyone knows, but it's worth a try, isn't it?"

My previous high was significantly lowered with three words. *Worth a try.* She sounded very unsure of a positive outcome from our meeting. What if we went through all of this and nothing changed?

"Worst case scenario is we have a fun trip together," she paused. "And at least then we'll know that this isn't the answer. There has to be one out there even if this isn't it."

I felt a feeling of complete and utter deflation come over me. The last thing I wanted to do was take a road trip with Mrs. Ray for no good reason or outcome. (No offense to Mrs. Ray, she's great and all, but that long in a car with a grown-up was not my idea of a fun time.)

My shoulders slumped. "Don't get dejected, Jake," she said. "Let's let this possibility run its course. You never know what will happen. And, at this point, the worst thing we can do is just do nothing."

She was right about that. At least we were doing something.

Feeling dejected had become a significant part of my emotional life—I had lived the last few years waffling between the peaks of hope and the valleys of failure. As soon as I had a peak moment, it seemed to be shattered by the certainty of the valley. To say the least, I was used to it. I steeled myself for disappointment, all while allowing myself a moment of hope.

"When do we leave?"

"Two weeks. Melvin has a bit of travel next week so we can't go sooner."

Two weeks.

A long time to wait.

But I had no choice.

"Okay, sounds good, Mrs. Ray. I'll get Mom to make the arrangements with the school. How long will we be gone?"

"Don't know for sure. Let's plan on a week."

A week.

That was a long time to be gone for nothing.

Of course, if it worked, it would be worth it.

I stood up and walked across the kitchen and through the door into the living room. Marcus was still eating. "Marcus, let's roll. Grab your math book and let's get this over with."

We walked the path to my house in relative silence. Marcus was pretty good at knowing when to talk and when not to.

And that was definitely one of those times when I needed silence.

Our homework took about an hour. Marcus picked up the concepts fairly quickly—he was a lot smarter than he gave himself credit for. He proved that by the time he graduated from high school.

63

JACOB

The quiet of my bedroom was comforting.

Although it was early evening, the sun had all but disappeared. I half-heartedly cleaned up my side of the room. Luke's side was, as always, a mess. I quickly decided to give up with the cleaning, knowing it wouldn't do much good and instead stretched out on my bed to contemplate my upcoming trip.

Was it going to be a waste of time?

My mind wavered. One moment, I began to hope. Mrs. Ray was encouraged. She thought this could be the answer. But then voices of doubt crept in. Was I wasting a week of my life? Would I spend 20 hours in the car each way chatting with the mother of my friend for…nothing? I wavered back and forth, my emotions roller-coastering, before I reminded myself I had to be positive. This was my only hope—my last hope, it seemed.

I stared at my wall, thinking, worrying, contemplating.

The wall started to darken, to look fuzzy, to look like…bricks.

I looked around me. Where was I?

The bricks began to morph into each other, entwining themselves into a single mass, creating a circular wall that imprisoned me. I stood up in time to see smoke-colored beings back off behind the interlocking walls, as if their duty was now done. What looked like an enormous, black amoeba was trailing over the towering building tops in numerous, pulsating ribbons. With great speed, the dark beings descended and reformed themselves into a singular vibrating mass. Dark grey contrails extended off the ribbons. It was both fantastic to watch and frightening to be part of. The black mass oozed laterally until it became a prison within a prison. There was no escape. The moving wall stood 25 feet high and rippled like the currents in the ocean. The smell was noxious. I was frozen in place. My prison began to close in on me.

Then, in absolute clarity, a voice boomed above me, *I am here for you, Jacob. Let's play, shall we?* Death was not going to come quickly, but it was surely coming.

My heart rate rose.

I looked for an escape, clawing at the wall.

Suddenly, the wall gave in. I awoke with a start, clenching my comforter. Had I fallen asleep?

I couldn't have been asleep for long, as it was still dusky outside and I was not completely soaked with sweat. Still, my heart pounded in my chest; the dream remained vivid in my mind. I realized with sudden clarity that my dreams were getting slightly clearer and shorter, as if they were rapidly moving toward a conclusion. I was pretty sure the conclusion would not be fun and games, but the mere fact that it was closer, and thus almost over, brought comfort.

I was no longer entering into my dreams by soaring over a beautiful countryside of unknown location. That had disappeared as I had jumped directly into act two of the nightmare. I sat up in bed and pulled my knees to my chest. They felt good, really good, but I knew things could change quickly.

I headed downstairs to get something to eat, as my empty stomach was beginning to growl. The kitchen was dark, cold. Had I missed dinner during my little nap? Or had my mom simply not started making it yet? I turned, trying to shake off the mental debris left behind by my dream and saw that the illuminated desk clock read 7:42.

7:42.

I opened the fridge and there was my answer. True to form, Mom had placed all the leftovers in two clear Tupperware bowls, neatly stacked on the bottom shelf. I didn't bother to heat either bowl, I just unsnapped the blue and yellow lids and dug in. Meatloaf, mashed potatoes and green beans. There was a hint of warmth in the center of the meat loaf, so I hadn't missed dinner by too long. Man, was I famished. I left nothing but a single bean uneaten. I have my limit on green items for dinner.

"Hey, Jake, about time you got up. I see you found dinner." Mary walked into the kitchen. "Good meatloaf, right?"

"Are you saying you ate with the family tonight?"

"What family? It was just Mom and me." I could see a hint of pain in her eyes.

"At least Mom didn't have to eat alone."

Mary responded with a look that was both contemplative and pained. "Do you think I've been retreating too much, Jake?"

I stared at her, "We need you, Mary. You're the strong one around here. Come downstairs more often." I punched her on the arm to lighten the mood.

"Okay, Jake. You're right. I do think I need to be more involved. Especially with Mom in such a bad place."

I didn't want her to be too hard on herself. "I just miss you, Mary. I know Mom does, too."

I carried the dirty Tupperware to the sink, rinsed them off, and placed them into the dishwasher. I poured another glass of milk and sat back at the table. I wrapped my hands around the cold glass. It felt good. Almost reassuring in an inane way.

"So, Jacob Ross, how are you doing?" Mary asked in a joking manner.

"Oh, just fine, other than pretty much everything."

"Everything, eh? Want to talk about it?"

"Yeah, I think I do." But where do I start? I guess it doesn't matter so, with scribbled notes in hand, I started with my series of nightmares and ended with the plan to drive to North Carolina to see Pastor Standard. In between I told her about my dreams, my fears, my plans, my hopes, and she listened.

We sat there for more than two hours.

Then, just as I thought we were finishing up, Mary looked me in the eyes and dropped the gauntlet: "Jacob, you can't go to North Carolina with Mrs. Ray. It will kill you. Literally. I'm not sure you've thought this through."

"What are you talking about?"

Then she told me.

I wasn't able to sleep for even a moment that night.

64

JACOB

I arrived at the Rays' before seven the next morning. I didn't shower after my routine slog or even stop to eat breakfast. I merely changed into a clean t-shirt and shuffled out of the back door, telling Mom I had to talk to Mrs. Ray. Right now.

The frozen dew crunched under my feet as I made my way to the Rays' back porch. I stamped them as hard as I could to knock the dirt, leaves, and melted frost off my shoes.

"What is going on out here, Jacob? It sounds like you're playing a one-man game of basketball." Mrs. Ray came to the door, still in her bathrobe.

"Sorry, I was trying to get the ice off my shoes."

"Come on inside. Do you want some breakfast?" She was already pulling a frying pan out of the cupboard.

"Sure."

"Scrambled eggs okay?

"Yes, ma'am." My mouth was already watering.

"So, Jacob, what brings you here so early?" She sure got right to the point.

"I have something to tell you."

"Alright. Let's hear it." She pointed toward the coffeemaker percolating on the counter. "Help yourself to the coffee."

I grabbed a mug out of the overhead cabinet next to the sink, added a bit of milk, and filled the balance of the mug with steaming hot coffee. Man, it smelled good. I returned to the table and sat in my usual seat. With both hands, I absorbed the heat and breathed in the aroma. For a few seconds, I was somewhere else.

"Jake, what did you want to tell me?" She asked with a spatula in one hand and the other hand on her hip.

"I can't go to North Carolina."

"And why not?"

Mrs. Ray stood in silence as I explained what Mary had said. She chewed on the information while slowly folding some milk and cheese into the very well beaten eggs. Finally, she looked up and simply said, "So, Mary thinks that, if you're not at home in your own fields at four a.m., you won't be able to slog, and if you don't slog, that evil will gain a power hold?"

"Pretty much." It sounded crazy.

Mrs. Ray stood there for several minutes, thinking. "You know, Jacob, I think Mary might be right."

"So, you don't think she's crazy?"

"No, I don't. I'm a little upset with myself for not thinking of this as well. Heaven help us, Jake. We are so out of our league."

Not exactly what I was hoping to hear. "I'll tell you, I'm sure I have no idea what to do, Mrs. Ray."

"Neither do I." She paused for a few seconds. "You know, Jacob, we are covering new territory. Not only new, but weird and probably life-threatening. We have no choice but to trust."

"Trust who?"

"Why, Good, of course." She turned back to the stove and adeptly poured the egg mixture into a cast iron pan coated with bacon grease she spooned out of jar. On an adjacent flat griddle, she began lining up strips of bacon. The smells were becoming intoxicating. My stomach roared with approval.

"There's only one thing to do, I suppose. We'll cancel the trip to see Pastor Standard and ask him to come to Perryton. I think he'll do it. The real question is when."

"You think he'll come here?"

"I hope he will. I'm still convinced he is the answer. Or at least part of it."

I took a deep breath absorbing this new information.

Would he really come all the way to Perryton to help me?

And was he really the answer Mrs. Ray was so sure he was?

I jolted in my chair as the kitchen door kicked open and Mr. Ray walked in wearing a faded green robe and slip-on house shoes that looked like they had traveled many paths over many years.

"Good morning, Jacob. Didn't mean to startle you." He said with a pat on my shoulder. He probably thought his wife had adopted another son.

"Good morning, Mr. Ray." I looked at the settling door, anticipating more Rays to follow.

He kissed his wife. "Nothing gets those children up this early. Not even the smell of Celina's world-class breakfast. Their loss, wouldn't you say?" He poured himself a cup of coffee and sat down.

"Yes, definitely their loss."

Breakfast was served and all conversation ceased. The only noise was the clanging of metal utensils on ceramic plates. Mr. Ray and I finished at the same time and laughed out loud as we set our fork down into the middle of our plates in concert.

"Man, was that good, Mrs. Ray." I wiped my mouth on a cloth napkin, no paper for Mrs. Ray, and stood up. "Thanks so much for the food."

"You're welcome, Jake. I'll let you know when I speak to Melvin. All will work out as it's supposed to be. I truly believe that. Do you?"

I said yes, but didn't feel it. I know that things don't always work out, and I certainly didn't know what the definition of "as it's supposed to be" is in this world in which I now live. Not sure it meant happily ever after for Jacob Ross.

65

JACOB, 1998

Sleep evaded me as it had for the past nine years. Would I ever be normal? The kind of person who fell asleep at night and woke up refreshed the next morning?

I didn't think so.

But I was learning to deal with it. In the grand scheme of things, a little less sleep at night doesn't change much. I stared out of the bedroom window of my upstairs apartment and into the darkness of night and my mind continued to ping pong. I have a bad habit of rolling my torrid memories over and over in my head. The vividness of those events presented an almost cinematic experience.

And I was okay with that. The tribulations of my childhood made me who I became. They drove me out of Perryton, never to return. I know one thing for certain—that was definitely for the best.

Her warmth was exhilarating, only exceeded by her smell. I breathed in deeply, and snuggled her into me, like two spoons tucked in drawer. I listened to the cadence of her regular breathing as my left arm rose and fell with the tempo of her movements.

She slept soundly, like any normal human at 2:00 in the morning, especially one who had been on the road most of the previous afternoon. Just lying next to her was simply heaven. I had known the depths of hell on earth so I had pretty good measure on such things. My thoughts were chaotic, rushing in and out like a tropical storm. I had a lot to be thankful for, I really did.

No more slogs.

No more nightmares.

No more pain coursing through my legs.

Having all that in the rearview mirror was incredible, life altering, but even that paled next to the feeling of having her asleep next to me. Several times I started to disconnect our warm bodies, and each time her reflexes pulled me back. I quit trying. Smart guy.

At that moment, my life had landed exactly where I had hoped it would since I first laid eyes on Susie Polanski on Bus #346. Through all that time and all my travails, she had stuck with me. Lots of people came back into my life, as if we had been friends forever. She had never left. Our bonds were too tight. Our experiences too similar. Mostly we have an energy that connected us and won't allow any distance to interfere. I am grateful for our instinctual connection. Right then, I was overwhelmingly grateful to be lying alongside Susie.

On nights like that one, my lack of sleep seemed to be almost a blessing. Why would I want to sleep when I could experience her with all my consciousness? I tried not to think about how many more of these nights we would share with each other, as I lay awake, wishing for forever.

A subconscious sensation told me our time together was limited.

I shoved that feeling away as quickly and forcefully as possible.

"Hey, you're awake, aren't you?" she whispered as she slowly broke through sleep's grip.

"Yes, as always." I brushed her hair from her face. "I'm sorry I woke you."

"I just wish you were able to sleep more, Jake. It can't be good for you."

"I'm okay. I would much rather cuddle up to you with all my senses on high alert, than be dead asleep." I had never been so truthful in my life.

"You're sweet," she said as she slowly wiggled closer to me. By that time, I was unquestionably wide awake and beginning to tingle.

"Come here, Jacob Ross," she said. "I'd like to show you how sweet I think you are."

Who was I to argue?

66

JACOB

Melvin Standard arrived in Perryton, Kansas on March 23rd, 1994 to no fanfare or celebration. He simply drove into the Rays' driveway in his dull green '88 Chevy Impala on a cool spring Sunday afternoon. Mrs. Ray and I were waiting on the front porch, trying to act like his arrival was no big deal.

Of course, it was a huge deal.

Mrs. Ray had told me it hadn't taken any major cajoling to convince Melvin he was needed in Perryton in the worst way. (Truth be known, he told me later he would have gone anywhere at any time to help her. She was as special to him as I was to her.)

Having pulled his world's belongings out of the car's trunk, Melvin closed the lid, stretched his stiff muscles, and turned a deliberate 360-loop, taking in the beauty of Midwestern farmland. Satisfied, he clutched the two suitcases in his grip with his overflowing briefcase pressed tightly under his left arm. He looked like an impeccably dressed door-to-door salesman about to foist a vacuum cleaner on an unsuspecting housewife. Three steps towards the Rays' front porch, and Mrs. Ray vaulted down the steps, arms extended and grinning from ear to ear.

"Melvin Standard, aren't you a sight for my tired eyes? Here, give me a suitcase and come in." She handed one suitcase to Mr. Ray and extracted the briefcase without a second word of warning. They strode happily into the house and sat in the living room, putting an end to Marcus and Cynthia's time in front of the television.

"Turn off the TV please, and meet a dear old friend of mine," she commanded.

With proper introductions, the room was cleared as Mrs. Ray and Pastor Standard sat across from each other, Mrs. Ray in her favorite rocking chair and the pastor in the center of the couch. Mrs. Ray patted a seat beside her, indicating that I should sit down.

Mr. Ray, Marcus, and Cynthia quietly slipped out of the room; they knew how badly we needed to get down to business.

"Celina, how long has it been? I'm guessing 18 years at least."

"I think that is about right. Too long, I think we can agree on that, don't you?"

"Definitely too long."

She stared at his face as if she were taking account of her old friend. "I have to tell you, Melvin, if it really has been 18 years, you're not too much worse for the wear," she paused, a smile cracking across her face. "Okay, so your hair is a bit thinner and greyer, but I guess mine is too. You look great!"

"Life is taking its measure," he said, "but all-in-all, we're faring okay."

"I think we are giving life more than we're taking," Mrs. Ray said. "Lots of road yet to travel."

"I hope so."

I tried to focus as Pastor Standard and Mrs. Ray made small talk. He told us how he had spent the last three days traveling as a tourist from Raleigh, North Carolina, stopping in Knoxville, Tennessee; Bowling Green Kentucky; Rolla, Missouri; and Wichita, Kansas. Melvin said he needed the time to shake off the dust from his latest *Pharisaical* rumble.

He told us how he had stopped and visited colleagues and old friends at each stop along the way, hoping to re-energize his batteries. It had worked and so he came to us ready and refreshed.

He turned and looked straight at me. "Jacob, we are going to take on Good and Evil, the three of us. You just wait and see."

Just then, Mr. Ray reentered the living room with a serving tray neatly stacked with cheese, crackers, and three plastic glasses brimmed with iced tea. "How about a little snack?"

"My word, today's a landmark day. Paul Ray engaged the kitchen." Celina laughed. "Not his strong suit for sure. Must want on the good side of the pastor."

"Thank you very much," I said, trying to remember my manners before grabbing a slide of cheese.

"Tell me a bit about yourself, Jacob," the pastor said.

He turned to me and I felt the weight of his stare. I knew I had to be honest and upfront if this was going to help, to work. I took a deep breath and began to tell my story. I told him about my slogs and all the related issues. I told him about the dreams. About my knees. About the strange connection between Mrs. Ray and me. It was a difficult task. It was an emotional task and I felt myself growing weary, exhausted even.

When I finished, Pastor Standard put his hand on my knee. "That's quite the story, young man. I'm not sure what to do about it, but I'm going to pray and think, and we will come up with something."

"Yes, sir." I did my best to keep my voice from shaking.

Melvin suddenly looked 10 years older than when he arrived earlier in the day. He was slightly slumping and dark circles appeared below his reddening eyes.

Mrs. Ray must have also noticed. "I think we should call it a day, Melvin. You must be worn out. Jacob, why don't you head home and come back over in the morning and I'll cook up a big breakfast just like you like it." She paused. "I think we will all feel better in the morning."

Tired as I was, I actually wanted to keep going.

I felt like I was so close to answers that I didn't want to stop now.

But I could tell by the look on both adults' faces that it had been decided.

And so I headed home, anxiously awaiting the events of the next day.

***

I felt a conclusion on the horizon. The idea, or hope, of an end to my situation was comforting in weird way.

It was a frigid, but mostly calm, morning, as I descended the back porch steps for well over the thousandth time. I headed northwest into the wheat field. It was going to be a good year for wheat if our crop was a proxy for the entire state.

The Ross farm was now under the management of Cummings Consolidated Farms, the same co-op that managed the Polanski farm. It was an economic arrangement for both parties. They manned all the required efforts, whether planting the crops, fertilizing, harvesting, or the million other things required on a working farm.

That morning's slog was of no consequence. Simply an out and back with no strangeness in sight. Much like 99% of all my other mornings. How does the 1% completely devastate the 99%? It did in my case and it wasn't close. This morning's thoughts were my own. I had 40 minutes of clear, concise thoughts. This clarity of thought greatly solidified about a year earlier when I accepted my situation, quit feeling sorry for myself, and decided to fight for a resolution. Mrs. Ray was my fortitude.

I had a few important questions whose answers would certainly launch me toward an understanding at least and a resolution at best. *What is controlling me and my morning slogs? Why has it lasted so terribly long, almost four years? Am I strong enough to break free of its grip?* And lastly, *Are Mrs. Ray and lately, Pastor Standard, my answer?* I had pondered these to no avail. I would keep after it.

I knew I kept feeding the hidden monster and it seemed to like it so much it might never leave. Were my slogs its major source of daily nutrition, or did these morning dances among the furrows turn me into some sort of court jester for its sick entertainment? I was sure it was going to eventually tear me open. It already had its hands wrapped around my throat only to squeeze on those rare, dreadful mornings. I was positive there was an end game. There had to be. Whatever had me captive was doing all this for a pointed purpose. A purpose that would only successfully end with my destruction. I needed to overcome it. Tall order.

Once again, I returned home with all questions and fears and no answers.

67

MARY, 2015

The Boeing 767 seemed to taxi halfway across the city of Phoenix before it came to a rest at Gate B25 in Terminal 4. It was clear that every single person on the plane was antsy and tired from sitting for so long as the plane burst into a dull roar as soon as the intercom hurled an audible ping indicating that the jet had stopped at the gate. The walkway immediately filled with the occupants from the aisle seats, lowering the overhead compartments, reclaiming their belongings.

I smiled at the man next to me who was telling anyone who would listen about how glad he was to be getting off the plane. I felt the same. My exit out of Business Class was orderly and quick. It felt good to walk briskly and feel the pumping blood reactivate my muscles. The closer I got to baggage claim, the more impatient I felt. I couldn't stand another line, another wait for my suitcase.

I was too excited to see Jacob.

I couldn't wait to hug his neck, to see for myself what was going on in his life, and if his "everything-is-great" stance was really the truth. Most of all, I couldn't wait to see his jaw drop to the floor when I walked in his front door.

I was giddy with what was sure to be a fun day. (And I had absolutely no premonition of what was coming. None at all.)

My luggage slid down the metal tongue that jutted out of the ceiling of the lower level, and I was relieved to see no visible damage. A quick walk from baggage claim to the Hertz counter and I rented a red, 2014 Maxima with the life saver known as GPS. Three more lines, ten more minutes of paperwork, and I finally exited the rental car portion of the airport parking garage heading out onto the vast freeway system of the Southwestern U.S.

I was not in London anymore, that was for sure.

68

JACOB

Luke was oblivious.

Did he even know what was going on with his brother over the past three plus years? I put on a clean t-shirt. After all, I had to make a good impression, or so I thought. Kind of dumb in this scenario. I sat back down on the end of my bed. I was shaking. I was scared. I was sure this was my last chance and we were going to completely miss the target. How do I handle myself with Pastor Standard? A million questions and doubts flooded my mind. I thought about crawling back in bed, but that was the same as quitting. I had been through too much to quit. My bedroom door slowly opened, and the hall light drifted across the floor, hitting me before I noticed.

"Scared?" Mary asked as she stood with her arms folded in the doorway. She looked ominous with the light flooding from behind, making a dark persona out of my older sister.

"Yes, most definitely. I'm shaking," I admitted.

I stood up and walked toward Mary. She met me halfway and embraced me with a tight hug. My fear disappeared. My confidence flickered to life. She did what Mary always does. She made a dreadful situation better.

"Thanks, Mary. I needed that."

"I know you did. Don't tell anyone, okay?" she said as she softly slugged my shoulder. "This is a good day, Jacob. Persevere like never before, will you, please?"

"I'll try, Mary, I'll try."

I left her standing in my room as I turned down the hall. I would persevere, but would it be enough? We'd see.

***

I hadn't even walked onto the Rays' porch when the smell of bacon stopped me in my tracks. Man, did it kick start my appetite. The door was propped open so I let myself in.

Pastor Standard was already at the table with a huge, steaming mug of coffee in front of him. He was wearing khakis and a blue dress shirt; way nicer than the sweat pants I had thrown on when I had gotten home from my morning slog.

"Hi, Mrs. Ray. Hi, Pastor Standard. You guys are up early."

"Why, hello, Jacob!" Mrs. Ray turned from the bacon pan and smiled at me.

"Hi, Jacob. Have a seat." Pastor Standard pointed to the chair next to him.

"Hope you're both ready for breakfast. There are about five

minutes before the eggs will be ready." Mrs. Ray smiled as I nodded vigorously. I was always ready for breakfast at the Rays' house.

"So, Jacob, while we wait for this food, let's have a little talk." Pastor Standard looked me right in the eye. "One thing my many misadventures have taught me is that Evil is like hunger. You're hungry, because your stomach is empty. You're evil, because your soul is empty."

He sure got right to the point.

"Anyway, Jacob, Celina—er, Mrs. Ray—and I have spent hours discussing you and your situation. And, while I'm not entirely sure I know what's going on, I do know this feels like an epic battle between Good and Evil."

I nodded, my words caught in my throat. "What does that mean?"

"We don't know yet, Jacob." Mrs. Ray walked over and set a heaping platter of bacon in front of us.

I fought back the urge to cry. If they didn't know, what was I doing here? I wanted to reach for bacon, but my arms remained at my side. Something didn't feel quite right. I was getting an amplified humming from within my legs. The feel of a familiar friend with awkward timing.

"Are you okay, Jacob?" Mrs. Ray looked concerned.

Pastor Standard looked at me, perplexed. "I—uh, I feel it too, Jacob. I feel it, too."

"You feel...what?" My words were slow and forced.

"What do you feel, Melvin?" Mrs. Ray was frowning at us, clearly worried.

"Celina, I feel something. A humming. A connection with Jacob here." Pastor Standard didn't seem to think this was concerning or strange, but, instead, he seemed excited.

I took a deep breath, focusing on my knees when a zap of energy—that's the only word I can think to call it—visibly leapt out of my body and collided with Pastor Standard. The force seemed to shake him, to hit him, and push him backwards.

I knew right then that he was either the answer to all my prayers or the manifestation of my worst nightmares. I wanted to believe he was good because of his relationship with Mrs. Ray, but I was not willing to dive head first into a swimming pool when I couldn't tell how deep it was.

I made a mental decision to reveal my cards slowly.

I may not be wise about much, but I was wise about my predicament. Wise enough to pace myself for success or retreat.

"Pastor Standard?" My voice was shaky, small. "What is happening?"

"Do you know what Evil is, Jacob?" Melvin asked as innocently as if he were teaching a high school geography class.

I laughed out loud. Mrs. Ray sort of did as well.

"I'm pretty sure I've taken this test before." I have no idea what gave me the audacity to be a smart ass right then, but the words slipped out.

"I'm sure you've heard and answered that question many times, Jacob. But I believe we have to understand Evil to defeat it." Pastor Standard's voice was getting stronger, steadier, even as mine grew shakier.

"I really don't know. I'm sure that whatever is driving...this whole thing...is evil. Nothing good would ever be so cruel."

"You're probably right about that, Jacob. But what is your definition of Evil?" Melvin persisted.

I wasn't ready to answer more geography teacher questions. "I'm sorry to be so slow, but I don't know the answers to your questions."

"To be honest, Jacob, there probably isn't a right or wrong answer. Let's attack this another way. Without evil, what is good? How would we measure good, or evil for that matter, if the opposite didn't exist?" Now he was really getting pastoral on me.

The humming in my knees intensified like a jolt and I shot up from my chair, almost turning it over on to the floor. "Stop! Just stop. I've had enough already. I'm sick of theoretical questions. I'm sick of philosophical discussions and mostly sick of going nowhere in a hurry."

Where had that come from?

"Now Jacob, Pastor..." Mrs. Ray started to inject.

"No, Mrs. Ray. Don't lecture me. Of all people who should understand what I've been through and the toll this weirdness has taken on me, it should be you. I am so tired of talking. Let's do something or do nothing, but the idleness of the in-between is about to drive me crazy."

It had happened.

I had finally cracked.

I then started laughing. The laugh of a person who is laughing so they don't cry. I was sure I was already crazy, or pretty damn far down the trail to the front door of the asylum. "No offense, Pastor Standard, but it is time to either win or lose at this mad game. Can you help me, or not? If you can, let's get on with it. If not, then please leave." I was shaking where I stood, looking from

Mrs. Ray, who was again speechless. I swallowed hard, sure I would be grounded for life if my mom ever heard about this outburst, in front of a pastor no less.

Pastor Standard stood up from his own chair without an ounce of emotion on his face. He put his hands on my shoulders.

"It's okay, Jacob." He smiled at me, making it clear no apologies were necessary. "I appreciate your bluntness. I can tell your emotions run deep and are very painful."

I nodded.

He was definitely right about that.

Then he continued. "What do you want, Jacob, and what do you want me to do?"

"I want you to cure me. I want you to give me my life and health back. I want you to wake me up from this miserable, depreciating existence so I can be normal. Please, that's all I ask. I just want to be better!" I was shouting again.

Not a peep came from his pursed mouth. He simply stood and stared at me. He looked down at the floor and then slowly raised his head. His eyes told me first, but were quickly followed by his voice. "I'm sorry, Jacob, but I don't think I can do that."

"What?" The dam broke again. "Why are you here, then? Why can't you just hug me and pull all this poison out of me like you did for Mrs. Ray?" My arms were wide open and flailing as I was inviting his hug right then and there. The magical hug I had dreamed of since Mrs. Ray told me the story of her cure. I wanted him to engulf me and rid me of my pain, nightmares, and slogs all in one fell swoop. My energy was entirely drained.

He looked at me with a sad silence.

After several minutes, I sat back down in my chair with an audible thud of resignation. "What good is any of this? I'm trapped in my own private hell and will forever be viewed as a gimpy outcast."

"Jacob, I can't cure you with a hug or a snap of my fingers or even with the stroke of some magic wand. I'm not that powerful, and whatever resistant influence or influences that have a hold of you *are* that powerful." Pastor Standard sat back down beside me. I would soon learn that nothing ever outwardly excited the Pastor. He was the epitome of calm under fire. No matter how I manically thrashed and yelled, he would sit quietly and, when I was spent, respond in the most serene voice.

"This is a three-way battle, Jacob, and neither Celina nor I are combatants. We can help, or at least I think we can, but you, and only you, have the fortitude to resist Evil and pull free of its grip."

What was he talking about? I had to resist all of this? I had to cure myself?

He removed his glasses and rubbed his tired eyes. "It's you against Evil, Jacob, but like I said earlier, it's a three-way battle. You obviously have help. It's clear that you've had goodness on your side the entire time. And the two of you form a very formidable team."

"If good and bad are not flesh and blood or visible or even…" I paused without a way to describe what I wanted to say. "I don't know how to finish my sentence. I feel it but I can't say it."

"You're right that they aren't physical beings. Good and Evil are not tangible; they are transcendent."

"What does that even mean?"

"They are not of our world or out of the range of human experience. Mystical in a way. Think of them as invisible forces that are everywhere, yet nowhere. Two forces that exist without any tangible proof of their existence. They live, if that's the right word, in a thin layer that shrouds all humanity, poking and prodding to find the select people who can further their causes. Evil is focused solely on making humanity evil, and goodness is focused on making people good and protecting the good people from evil. A more difficult two-pronged effort. Basically, they battle each other for our souls."

And I thought Mrs. Ray was confusing. My tiny brain was about to explode like an over-stuffed Thanksgiving turkey. "Pastor Standard…"

"Melvin. Please, Jacob, call me Melvin. I dislike the formality."

Calling an adult, especially one as old as Pastor Standard, by his first name was way out of my comfort zone. I couldn't imagine what my mom would say about that. But he had asked me to, so I tried. "Melvin, I think I follow you to some small degree, but how does this help me? Quite frankly, what you have described makes me think it is hopeless."

"Not hopeless, but surely difficult. You will never defeat Evil in the way we understand victory. Being victorious in our battle is simply not falling prey to the malevolent intentions. We are victorious every minute or day that we remain on the side of virtue."

"Why me, then? I'm a 14-year-old nobody who lives on a small farm in Kansas."

"You are clearly special and worth having as a participant in this ageless battle. Sometimes the least obvious people are the ones who are chosen for the greatest tasks."

Suddenly I was a secretly-chosen superhero. "So what you're saying is that a kid who lives in a cornfield in Kansas and hobbles around in a state of complete cluelessness was magically chosen for an epic showdown between Good and Evil? I don't think so." I paused for a minute, gathering my thoughts. "I've been dealing with this for almost four years and have not moved the pawn one square forward on the chess board. I'm worthless and ineffective. If what you're saying is true, then Evil has me exactly where it wants me and that's completely out of the game."

"Do not say that, Jacob." My words seemed to scare the pastor.

"What does it matter if I say it? I am thinking it." I responded.

"It matters greatly, Jacob." Pastor Standard wiped a tear from his eye. "It matters greatly."

JACOB, 2015

Mom turned 63 years old last Monday, and none of her kids were there to celebrate. I'm not sure whether she viewed it as a celebration, especially with us gone, but I did. I felt a bit guilty having not talked to her in three months, and not reaching out to wish her happy birthday, so I called her hoping to catch her home alone.

I got lucky.

She quickly explained that Dad was off attending to one of his pastoral duties. We had a good conversation. I always enjoyed our calls, but it wasn't the same as sitting at the kitchen table with a cup of coffee in hand and talking. I still missed those times. Strangely, I missed the relationship we had during *Great Slog Era*, as I not-so-fondly call it.

We talked for 10 minutes or so, catching up on small, everyday things. I would never admit this to her, but part of me was still mad at her for accepting her self-imposed fate. Most of me still loved her dearly and prayed for her happiness, don't get me wrong, but I was also a bit angry still. I probably always would be.

Mom said she spoke to Luke on that morning and that he seemed to be doing well. It was hard to tell sometimes because he painted his world with the bright colors of optimism. Those words may seem light and bright, but they are not generally accurate. Luke's life had been a series of bad decisions, whether in his career, with his finances, or in his choice of wives. In some ways, one fed the other. I blamed my dad. Mary and I may have survived and, in her case, thrived despite my dad's dalliances, but Luke's scars ran too deep. It had been hard to watch his life fall apart.

I used to cringe when I received a call from him.

They always seemed to come at the most inopportune times. His name would pop up on caller ID in the middle of the night, while I was on vacation or at one of the kids' events. I'd hold the phone at arms' length, as if that would help the name on the screen disappear, and I would argue with myself on whether to push the answer button. I always did.

And then regret it as I spent the next 30 minutes discussing his latest issue, his latest problem. It all seemed to revolve around his very unlucky number, which was three. Three marriages and divorces, three job losses (that I know of), three bankruptcies greatly accelerated by the two previously mentioned threes, and three stints in rehab. He lived with Margie and me twice during some of those tumultuous times. I was holding my breath for the third. It had to happen, didn't it? After all, three was his unlucky number.

I will say, he seemed to have crossed over the summit and was coming back down the mountain of crap he had lived on for so many years. He had been employed by the same computer hardware company for the past few years and was spending and saving appropriately. He had a steady girlfriend Mom approved of, albeit based on a very low bar. Lastly, and most importantly, he'd been sober for five years. I loved Luke. I missed Luke. Yes, the same Luke who spent years sharing a room with me, torturing me at times, grating on my last nerve.

I think the good times growing up together somehow had begun to outshine the bad. All I could do at that point was shape the future and try to have a relationship with him from that point forward. I prayed that someday we would find a way to get past our past. It would be hard, but what worthwhile endeavor isn't?

I shook myself back to the present. Mom explained that she was doing well but I didn't fully believe her. I heard it in her voice. She was forever protecting me, shielding me from what was sure to hurt.

Before I hung up, I asked her to come to Phoenix to visit. She said she would. She knew I meant for her to come alone. Neither of us needed to say it though. I considered asking about Dad, but I didn't have the energy to hear the answer. We finished our call and hung up.

I spent the next hour sitting on the edge of my bed and staring at the floor.

Myriad thoughts engulfed me. Myriad emotions too.

Life can be unnecessarily cruel, to say the least.

70

JACOB

Pastor Standard and I called it quits.

I was wrung out.

I knew it; he knew it; we both knew it was time.

Mom and Mrs. Ray rejoined us, and the conversation turned a little more upbeat. Pastor Standard accepted a cup of coffee and began to chat pleasantly about his efforts in ministry. He was as committed of a person as I had ever met or have ever met since that day. All his money and time seemed to go into the people who lived in his community.

I sat there, trying to focus, trying to hear what he was saying to Mrs. Ray about his church business plan, his life, the successes, the failures. And, while I was too exhausted to focus on every word, it became clear that Pastor Standard lived his life firmly cemented in the fight against Evil. Evil was summarily getting its ass kicked by a tiny, greying man who looked like a tax accountant.

A surge of belief swept over me and absorbed itself into my very core. Suddenly, I knew for certain why he was sitting at my kitchen table.

I knew why Mrs. Ray was in my life.

I knew I had a fighting chance.

I still didn't understand why I was an important cog in this battle. But I was.

It was early afternoon by the time Pastor Standard and Mrs. Ray left. I decided to take a nap. I could feel my knees starting to assert themselves and hoped a rest would allay the inevitable.

My bed felt reassuring and sleep came quickly.

So did my nightmares.

***

The afternoon sun was all but blotted out by thickening smoke. Only a few dusty slivers of light reached the intersection that was soon to be my prison. The downtown buildings that surrounded me were shifting forward as their facades began to peel themselves from the steel understructure. As the sheets of brick left the host buildings in their wake, the individual bricks began to split along the edges of each panel, all the while sewing themselves into the adjacent panel like some ghoulish zipper. Within minutes, the disparate layers of brick were melded into one continuous framework, closing ranks in a suffocating manner. The surrounding air grew palpably dense and, with each breath, I felt the acidic stench of smoke rush into my lungs. I would soon drown as surely as if I was sinking into the depths of an ocean.

Welcome back, Jacob. It's good to see you, my boy. A gravelly voice whispered to me from nowhere in particular; the sound was dispersed in the air as if it had been waiting for me to arrive in this specific location. The declaration didn't disappear as one would expect, instead it hung sticky in the air, almost reverberating like a deathly echo. The black, viscous ribbons crested the top of the wall and began to swiftly descend. The flowing masses were barely visible in the fading light, yet shimmered as they undulated downward. I was to be engulfed as if I was a prehistorical mosquito in the deadly trail of unrelenting tree resin. It took all my strength to remain conscious due to the diminishing air supply accompanied by the growing stench that continued to settle on the boulevard like a dense seaside fog.

I began to wobble with weakening knees and fleeting muscle control. The black amoeba was lapping at my feet. I was sure I would crumble to the ground, but something, someone seemed to be holding me upright against my will. The dark mass sent small, slender tendrils up my legs and around my waist. I was powerless to do anything but watch this horror show unfold before my eyes. My body began to quiver violently. The lead tendril lightly touched my neck as if it was teasing me before my imminent demise. The finger-like projection lapped onto my shoulder leaving a grey sticky residue in its wake.

I screamed, knowing it would be futile, but hoping that somehow, someway, someone would come help me. Save me.

"Jacob. Jacob. Wake up!" The amoeba disappeared and I was being shaken by Mary in an almost vicious manner. She had both hands on my shoulders and was twisting and shaking me with all her gusto. "Jacob! Stop. Come back to me."

My heart pounded in my chest even as her words soothed my terror.

"Another one of your nightmares? I could hear you from my room,

Jacob. You were yelling and thrashing."

"Each one goes longer than the previous one," my voice trembled. "Each time Evil gets closer to me. This time he almost caught me."

I sat up on the bed and rubbed my face. The nightmare was still very real and concise. This nightmare series was playing out in an almost physical manner. It was tracking something. It was telling me something. That something was the final dice roll of this sick and deadly game I was a part of. Evil and Good had spent four years setting up the board game, it seemed, and I could sense they were finally ready to play it out.

"Mrs. Ray called when you were sleeping." Mary reached out and put her hand on my shoulder.

"I am tired of talking, Mary. Tired of it all."

"Well, it's not like you can just put your head in the sand like an ostrich, Jacob."

"Why not?"

"Because I won't give up on you, that's why." With that, Mary stood and left my room and I stood up to shake off the groggy remnants of my latest nightmare. It didn't work. I flipped on the bathroom light. My messy hair was in dire need of a comb and I needed to pee.

I finished up, splashed water on my face, and reached to turn off the bathroom light and head downstairs, stopping to take a final glance in the mirror. It was then I noticed a small blob of shiny black goo on my left shoulder. I froze in horror. The blob left a grey, slimy film on my t-shirt as I pulled it free. I rubbed the greasy mass between my fingers and brought it to my nose. The odor made my knees falter. It smelled of dead and decaying flesh.

My nightmare was much more real than I imagined.

What was I going to do now?

***

"I don't think that is a good idea, Mrs. Ray. I really don't think so. It will do more harm than good. I don't want to endanger him." I paused, desperate for Mrs. Ray to drop her silly idea.

"Jacob, I think it's your only choice. Someone has to go with you, to see what's going on."

"I don't know. I've always done them alone"

"Well, that's going to change, Jacob. Tomorrow." My mom walked into the room just as I resigned myself to what Mrs. Ray was saying. I held up my finger to indicate I was almost done.

"Fine, Mrs. Ray. I'll do it. But don't blame me if it all goes south." I hung up and turned to face Mom.

"What was that, Jacob?"

"Mrs. Ray wants Pastor Standard to go with me on tomorrow's slog. She thinks he can help resolve my affliction easier if he sees me in action. My words, not hers."

"And what do you think about that?"

"I'm not sure I have a choice. Mrs. Ray seemed pretty adamant." I paused. "Plus, I guess at this point, what could it hurt?"

I walked away, unable to stop thinking of the small, black blob I had found on my t-shirt. A massive quiver shot up my spine. No, at this point, things really couldn't get worse, could they?

***

I woke up three minutes before 4:00 from a dreamless night's sleep.

I threw on my clothes not so carefully piled at the foot of my bed, waved good bye to Luke, in case the morning went terribly wrong, and scooted out of the house. Pastor Standard was waiting for me on the back porch bench. He was dressed in all black, including his stocking cap. How did looking like a cat burglar help?

"Hi, Pastor Standard. How long have you been waiting?"

"Since 3:00. I didn't want to chance missing you."

"Well, I'm here now," I shrugged. "Let's go."

My expectations for the morning were rather low. After all, it was likely that all Pastor Standard would see was me roaming the wheat field.

"You know, I doubt you'll really see anything, Pastor. Probably just a normal morning."

"For some reason, I don't think it is," he eerily replied.

I did not like that response. How could he possibly have any inkling about what was to transpire? I never knew if a slog would be routine or not.

"You ready?"

I nodded. It felt strange to have company.

We walked past the barn and out to the wheat field in a muted silence. I was too scared to say a word. I believe Melvin was too. The ground was wet from yesterday's rains making the well-worn path slicker than normal. A slippery path and gimpy legs are not a good pre-battle combination. I was limping much more than normal. The humming in my legs had started when I stepped off the porch and was now amplified to a dull roar. I was in pain and we had barely cleared the barn. Adding to my physical predicament, the waves of an unknown origin were bombarding my mind. My head was full of static and noise. Nothing made sense. The din was deafening and I was beginning to feel waves of nausea ripple through my gut.

It appeared that Pastor Standard had been correct.

As we approached the head of the selected furrow in the wheat field, Pastor Standard placed his right hand on my left shoulder. He didn't squeeze or pat my shoulder; he merely set his hand in place with his fingers extending to my collar bone. I was startled at first, but just as quickly his presence became comforting.

Within seconds, a massive electrical current shot into my body, whipping itself in tornadic fashion through my torso. I shuddered as my knees buckled and my muscles weakened. Just as quickly the jolt exited with an audible swoosh. Pastor Standard backed away and I crumpled to the ground. I expected my old friends to take over— Mr. Heave, Mr. Headache, and Mr. Excruciating Pain—but they were nowhere to be found. I slowly gathered my strength and wits, rising to my feet. The pain was gone, as was the fragmented noise.

I felt rejuvenated and my thoughts were crystal clear.

I turned to Pastor Standard. "What happened?"

He looked at me and blinked several times. "You know what happened, Jacob."

And it dawned on me: I did know.

Perhaps subconsciously, probably reluctantly, but I did know exactly what had happened.

I was ready to proceed.

71

JACOB

Susie Polanski had already dealt with more strife in her young life than any 14-year-old should have to. A wildly dysfunctional family, a self-interested mother, and a maniacal brother, not to mention her alcoholic father; although to Abel's credit, he had stuck around. So far.

After a normal day of school, Susie and I had headed home in row four of our school bus. The afternoon was cool and comfortable enough for most of the bus windows to be dropped open. The fresh air was crisp and blew through the bus in an unruly fashion. Susie battled to keep her hair from whipping into a tangled mess. I thought she looked perfect. I always did. We talked about nothing important, but it was everything to us. The chatter of best friends.

Vernon pulled off onto the shoulder next to the drive which led into Susie's farm and stopped next to the well-worn mailbox with Polanski on the side. The right rear-view window barely missed sending the metal container into orbit. Another of Vernon's bus driving skills, I guess. I never saw him hit one mailbox in all these years, but he was often within centimeters of taking one out.

"Bye, Jake, see you tomorrow." Susie smiled back at me as she floated down the bus aisle. Her smiled seemed a bit forced.

"Bye." I was so smooth with my creative response.

As always, she turned slightly as she started up her drive and waved to me, no smile this time. I waved back.

Susie lifted her bike up out of the grass behind one of the large Cottonwood trees that lined the entryway and straddled the seat. The bike made the trip to and from the bus stop a lot easier for her. She rode her bike back up the windy road with a purpose and burst into the front door.

I couldn't help but feel a sense of foreboding.

"Vernon, stop!" I yelled as I scrambled up the bus's aisle. "Let me off! I need to get off right now!"

Vernon looked up at me through the rearview mirror. "Sure, Jacob."

The bus slowed to a stop and I jumped off, yelling "thanks!" to Vernon as I hit the ground and started after Susie.

I turned right onto the driveway and ran as best I could the entire length to her house. I was hoping for a bit of the Flash to reappear. I was sweating profusely, and breathing even harder, as I stopped just short of the front steps. Luckily, my knees mostly left me alone. I limped onto her porch and immediately rapped my fist on the front door. The feeling of danger was swirling inside me.

"What are you doing here, Jake?" Susie scolded as she swung open the front door.

"I… uh…I don't know. I guess I was worried about you."

"You were?"

"Yeah, I felt like something was wrong."

Susie's eyes darted back and forth, and she bit her lip. "Jake, I can't find my dad."

"What do you mean?"

"He's not here."

This seemed like a normal thing to me, especially for someone in Susie's situation but she looked so scared, so small.

"Can I help?"

She shrugged. "You know he'll be furious if he sees you here."

I nodded.

"Look, if he comes in, you should run. Like sprint home."

I nodded again. Susie was worth a good sprint.

She pointed up the stairs. "You look upstairs and I'll look down?"

The master bedroom, although a stench of a mess, was empty. The equally filthy bathroom was vacant as well. The odor was so sour I was compelled to pull my t-shirt up over my nose. It did not help very much. How did Susie live in this place?

The remainder of the upstairs scavenger hunt ended in the same manner. No sign of Mr. Polanski. No explanatory note either.

I walked back downstairs and found Susie standing in the middle of the kitchen.

"What now, Susie?"

"His truck is parked at the end of the driveway so he couldn't have gone far." She bit her lip again.

Susie grabbed her jacket to head outside. She cupped her mouth and yelled at the top of her lungs, "Dad! Dad! Where are you?" Again, no response came her way. Running short on options, we decided to check one last place. Susie walked around the back of the house to the dirt path which led to the barn.

Susie suddenly stopped dead in her tracks. "Jacob, it's been a long time since I've gone into the barn. Funny, because it was once my retreat, or maybe hiding place is a better word. When life got too loud or mean in the house, I'd sneak out the bedroom window, shimmy down to the back porch, and run into the barn."

The cavernous structure was inviting like an old friend. I loved old barns—the sweet smell of the hay and the silence of towering, resonant lofts. The barn was a mixture of grays and blacks, periodically interrupted by slices of light that found their way through the cracks and crevices every aging barn endures. For a moment, I allowed myself to imagine that Susie and I were the only people alive and she allowed me into her private haven.

And then a shiver settled into my spine.

An uncommon smell invaded my senses. For a moment, I wondered if it was possibly cow and horse manure, but that wasn't quite right. Besides, the Polanski's barn had been void of farm animals for close to five years. I saw Susie grasp the wooden supports for the permanent ladder which led up to the hay loft. Left foot first, then right, she ascended. I followed her up as the smell grew stronger. So did my fear.

Just as I crested the top rung the pungent odor slapped me in the face. She stopped just ahead of me, frozen in place, blinking several times as if begging her eyes to overcome the darkness of that loft.

A pair of work boots came into my focus, boots not sitting on the loft's deck, but hanging in midair.

My mind was not processing what I saw.

I stood there for several more seconds, blinking, thinking, analyzing.

Then it hit me.

I grabbed Susie by the arm and flung her into my chest, trying my best to protect her from the scene in front of us, hoping she wouldn't have this image ingrained in her memory for the rest of her life. Her father, the only person in her family who had not yet left her, had done just that.

I couldn't help but stare at him as I fought to keep Susie from doing the same. Her dad's work boots swayed ever so slightly, as if the last of the energy escaping his body was propelling his feet back and forth. His back was facing us so his face was not visible, which was probably a blessing. From my perspective, looking up at this figure, he looked headless, as if the hastily made noose was jutting directly out of his shoulders. His neck, sufficiently snapped, was hanging forward as if he was perusing the ground below his feet.

Susie screamed, loud, agonizing.

I pulled her to me, pulled her down the ladder, desperate to get away. Together, we half descended, half fell back down the ladder onto the hay strewn floor and stumbled out through the barn door, back into the afternoon sunlight. In later years she told me she had seen more than I had suspected.

We ran to the house and burst through the back door.

"Susie, we have to call the police."

She nodded, in a daze, so I grabbed the phone off the wall.

"911, how can I help you?"

"My friend's dad, he's dead. Or at least I think he is—he's hanging in the barn, in the loft. I think he committed suicide, I don't know. I'm not sure." I sounded like a crazy person. I knew I did, but what else could I say?

It took them about 15 minutes. The longest 15 minutes of my life as I held Susie in silence.

Neither of us knew what to say.

But the silence was soothing, healing even.

That day, we forged a bond that would never leave us, never tear us apart.

72

JACOB

I was ready to proceed, sort of.

I looked at Pastor Standard's calm, reassuring face and said, "I think this slog is going to kill me."

"No, Jake, I think it will make you live."

Make me live?

What did that even mean?

He put his hand on my back and gently nudged me forward. I took two steps toward the wheat field on the hard-packed dirt that led into the soft, clumpy furrows. I stopped and turned around. Pleading one last time for Pastor Standard to grab me and tell me I could go home. Those words didn't materialize. His eyes actually said the complete opposite, and I knew in my heart I couldn't go back anyway. I hadn't been able to resist the force that drove me to go on these slogs on my own.

I certainly wasn't going to be able to resist now.

I turned back around and slogged forward. The first few steps felt no different than normal, but with the fifth or sixth step, my surroundings began to change. The plowed dirt below my feet started to shift, threatening the limited purchase I currently enjoyed. The stalks of wheat sprang into action. As if a great wind erupted, the wheat was arrhythmically tossed side to side and across the furrowed path. I remember thinking that was strange as there was no wind to be felt. The air just stood there, thick and still, even as the wheat danced.

I forged ahead. I was still clear of mind and devoid of pain, a fact that made me feel unrealistically hopeful. I took a dozen more steps and that hope faded. Fighting through the frenetic wheat crop became more difficult and, with every step, I sensed small electrical shocks licking at my legs. They were invisible at first, but three steps in, the miniature lightning bolts became a miniature light show. For a moment, I was strangely entertained, interested in seeing the lights, the novelty of a new slog.

But then the pain set in.

It was as if each lightning strike zapped out of the field, forcing me ahead in agony. I turned once again to beg for Pastor Standard's help, but he was not in sight.

Had he left me alone?

I looked desperately for someone—anyone—to help me. Then I remembered Melvin telling me I was in the middle of a three-way fight. Good had my back, or at least I hoped it did. With that insight, I moved forward. The disjointed movements of the wheat plants suddenly began to move in a more coordinated manner, much like the choreographed high-kicks of a chorus line.

This was not normal.

It was also not unplanned. I stopped in my tracks and stared at the plants. They seemed to grow thicker and taller in size and their leaves began to stick together, weaving themselves into an impenetrable curtain. I was being imprisoned by the wheat field. I could neither see over the top of this curtain nor escape.

The last openings sealed shut with frightening speed just as I heard the guttural sound from my dreams. The noise was indiscernible at first, but soon I knew that, once again, the mass was marching towards me.

I was on the edge of the abyss falling forward.

My prison became a circular wall of quivering leaves and branches. They seemed to sense the mass approaching as well and appeared to bow down to cut an easy path through which the amorphous being could enter. The world grew hazy, dark even, as if the night sky was creating a form of camouflage that allowed Evil to blend in with the surroundings.

I seized up. My clarity of thought vanished.

I just stood there, frozen in the wheat field for what felt like hours. I didn't know what to do, how to leave, how to escape. The blackness began slowly ringing our gladiatorial pit, projecting its own version of a stare down. Its voice became audible. It was giving me an ultimatum. I either become a leader in his army or vanish into the earth where I stood, never to be seen or heard from again.

I almost acquiesced.

Gave up.

Gave in to Evil.

But then a picture of Mary and Mom and Mrs. Ray flashed into my brain as if it were implanted right there at that specific time. Good had not left me. Neither had Pastor Standard. I gathered a modicum of their collective strength as if it was injected into my mind through some of the many incongruent thoughts I had experienced during so many of my slogs.

"Stop this madness! Stop right now!" I screamed. "I am not like you! I am not evil! I am a good person and refuse to be otherwise!"

My body was shaking and soaked in sweat. The black mass slowed its encroachment and blindly stared at me. *"Jacob, my son. You know not what you're saying. I am the way to the life you want to live. I am the answer to your pain and misfortune. Together we can do wondrous and bountiful things. Just say the word and we are as one."*

The smooth words were addictive. They wrapped around me, luring me in, giving me hope for a way out. I wanted to give in to its offer. At that point, I would have done anything to escape, to stop.

I wanted to be folded into this dream.

But then sharp reality hit: this was not a dream. It was the final, unwritten episode of my nightmares. And it was Evil, not Good, that was starring in the show.

I pulled away—I had to. I felt an intoxicating counter tug. I pulled harder, fighting toward Good, even as Evil pulled.

I was being tugged back and forth, stretched, tried by the fire.

I fell to my knees and begged at the top of my lungs. "Help me! Please come and help me!" I was pleading for the comfort of the lighted disc that had met me on this very field. The warm light of Good that would engulf me and protect me from the lies spewed from the mouth of Evil.

The wall of blackness began to undulate and a sickening sound began to emanate from its being. A laugh so hideous that my fear escalated. *"You sad, pathetic boy. You have a power that very few possess, yet you are unable to comprehend your power, much less its potential."* What had felt like hopeful words just minutes before now felt ugly.

Being nice had not worked, so Evil did what it does best and spewed forth threats and derision. *"This is your last chance to assume your rightful place. We have been together every morning for your past four years. I've nurtured you. I've protected you. I have shown you pain and confusion only few have ever seen. And I've done it all for a reason. Now you know this reason. You have been chosen by me. Invited into the great battle beyond mortal comprehension. We can together spread darkness and disease throughout mankind, drawing in more and more weak souls and ripping the flesh from their rotting bones for our ultimate victory. Man is weak, Jacob Ross, but you are not."*

I admit it, I was tempted.

Curious even.

But hearing my name called out by this mass of Evil snapped me to attention. I wasn't having a nightmare, I was living out my greatest battle. I had a choice. I could turn to Evil, or I could stand firm to my conviction.

Evil felt so easy, so simple.

But Good felt…right. I am a good person. I do want to help others. I will not fade into false promises.

The undulating circular wall stood 10 feet off the ground and was eliminating most of the diminished starlight. Darkness was upon me. I had no other bullets in my gun so I stood motionless. I refused to beg or stare at the ground. I also refused to give in. If this was my last day to live as a normal Jacob Ross, I was going down with my head held high and my soul intact. I closed my eyes and prayed. Not to be rescued—I knew it was too late for any heroics—but for my family, for Susie, for Pastor Standard, and Mrs. Ray.

And mostly for myself.

Because, without some major intervention, I would never be able to hold the fort against this swarm of Evil.

***

Mrs. Ray had followed Pastor Standard to my house that morning.

She told me later she had no idea why she had done that, but she had felt compelled, unable to stay in bed.

She had stayed far enough behind him to not be seen or to disturb his concentration. She knew she couldn't disturb either of us. She sensed it was an important day, an important slog.

Once Pastor Standard and I had left toward the wheat field, she had seen a light on in my mom's kitchen and knocked. Not that she had anything to say that would magically make Mom wash all her stress away, but at least she could be there, to sit with her friend and be comfort.

My mom had already made the coffee.

I later found out that they had spent the following hours in an anguish of prayers and tears. Drinking coffee, praying for the epic battle that was taking place just a half a mile away.

And while I didn't know they were there, praying, I sensed it.

I knew I was being bolstered by more than just my own prayers, than by Pastor Standard, but by others who were willing to stand in the gap when I needed them most.

73

JACOB

When I opened my eyes, I noticed the morning light was peeking over the heaving walls of my incarceration. Had the sun already risen?

I was standing in the middle of a 20-foot wide circle as the mass was moving slowly inward. It seemed to be enjoying the delay in the inevitable. It was clearly willing to bide its time.

I was not.

"Get it over with, will you? I am not giving in, so you may as well end it right now." Something in me was suddenly brave, unmoving.

The writhing, black form said nothing. We had both made our decision, so what was there to say? The morning sun was casting a few flickering shadows that allowed for a sense of space. My vision was clearer but there was nothing to see, only the blackness of Evil that had covered the makeshift wall in a sick imitation of tar. Tar that rippled and moved both upward and downward, ever changing over itself as if it was a collection of a thousand living branches.

I looked at my watch. Why I looked right then, I don't know. Maybe it a macabre sense of wanting to know the exact time of my demise, or maybe it was just something I did out of a bored tick. Whatever the reason, I realized it was only 5:30 and the sun could not possibly be on the rise above the horizon.

Yet I clearly saw light.

Big, bright, shining light.

Where was the imitating sunrise emanating from? Then I saw it. The hovering disc was back. Pastor Standard had been right; I wasn't alone. The intensity of the light increased and I began to hear an audible hum as it approached.

The wall ceased its affront. Almost instantaneously.

It began to recede, to back away, as if the golden disk was now issuing commands.

My mind was alive with questions. My body was tingling with hope. The writhing tendrils froze in place as time seemed to stop. I held my breath. The glowing disc's light was breaching the wall at such a high angle that I knew it was very close. The rays pulsed as if a million small bursts were rapidly shot from the dish. The humming increased, as did the intensity of the light. The black circle then began to move again. The entirety of the wall began to flow downward to its footing and then fold underneath itself as if it was winding tighter and tighter. The circle began to enlarge and the walls began to shrink.

It was definitely backing off.

The attack had been aborted.

It was silent no longer as the wall's folding motion released a high-pitched metallic shriek. Was it in pain? I hoped so. I watched in stunned silence as if someone had accidentally hit the reverse button on the DVR. The world was flowing backward. With every reduction in the wall's stature, more light spilled over the top and bathed the inside of my prison. I reached up to the sky as far as possible trying to touch the oncoming rays.

The light rays quickly paralleled the ground and the top of the disc came into view. I cannot adequately describe my feelings at that moment. Elation, euphoria, even ecstasy does not do justice to how I felt. My trauma—my pain—was finally over.

I knew it that instant.

The glowing disc cleared the top and stopped in mid-air. The intensity of the light was so acute I was rendered virtually blind, blind to the point that I could not see the last of the retreating mass. But I didn't care.

I never wanted to see the face of Evil again.

74

JACOB

Months later, my mom told me that, as they drank coffee that dark morning, Mrs. Ray had a violent, sudden flinch. She tensed up straight as a board and expelled a breath of closure.

Mom and Mary had both seen it and flinched as well, but for a different reason. Mrs. Ray scared and confused them. What was wrong?

"It's over," Mrs. Ray said, wide-eyed and breathing heavily. "I feel it. I have enough of a connection with Jacob to feel a thin thread of his being, and that thread is not broken. In fact, I think it is growing stronger."

They told me she had been so certain, so sure.

"Where is he? When will he be back? Should we go out there, Celina?" My mom had been panicked. The fact that her baby had been outside, fighting the battle of his life, while she sat and drank coffee filled her with a mixture of fear, disbelief and, when she heard Mrs. Ray's proclamation, tentative joy.

"No. If I am correct, let's let Jacob play this out. I know it's a lot to ask, but sit patiently for now. Can you do that, Susan?"

Mom hadn't wanted to.

She had wanted to race out there, to help me, to be with me.

But Mrs. Ray seemed so sure, so certain.

"Do I really have a choice?" Mom had responded while clutching her coffee tightly. After four years of daily pain and not knowing if I was going to return from a morning slog, sitting there in the safety of her kitchen was all she felt she could do.

She trusted Celina.

And she trusted me.

75

JACOB

The intense light wrapped itself around me and warmth infused my body. I was immediately void of fear and pain. I knew I was safe. I knew exactly what was comforting me, what had pulled me back as I was about to fall into the vast nothingness of evil.

I wanted to shout *thank you*! but I couldn't talk.

And something in me told me it didn't matter.

The connection was sufficient. As I was lifted off the ground, my wrecked body went limp, and consciousness quickly slipped away. Before my mind shut down, I heard a strong voice begin to say, "I promised I would care for you. Your faith…"

***

Consciousness returned and I realized I was no longer in the wheat field.

Where was I? Where was Pastor Standard? Was I even alive?

I did the required check to see if all body parts were present. They were indeed. My vision slowly cleared and I blinked several times as I found myself staring up toward the sky. I felt pretty good. My legs were not aching and my mind was clear. I sat up and leaned back, using my arms as support, and looked around. I released a slight chuckle when I realized I was sitting smack-dab in the middle of our barn. The hard-packed dirt floor smelled better than anything I could describe. The smell of familiar covered in the smell of safety.

I had made it out of the wheat field.

I was alive.

And I was, seemingly, safe and sound.

I gathered my legs under me and stood up.

I had nowhere to go other than home.

***

For many years I was curious to know what Melvin had heard and seen while waiting for me to reemerge from the wheat field. When I finally pried the story out, he said he had watched me enter the wheat field from about 20 feet behind my left flank, not sure if he was really seeing what his eyes were showing him. He stood like a vigilant sentry as I stepped into the field. From his vantage point, the wheat field appeared to be a river flowing out of its banks after a tropical storm. The leaves and stems were whipping in all directions as I plowed forward. A shroud of mist had settled over the field, engulfing me more and more with each successive step.

He remembers anxiety. A feeling of panic thinking he couldn't lose sight of me even as the mist enshrouded my body.

He remembers light. As if the entire path through the field had been lit with thousands of small electrical jolts crisscrossing the furrow.

He remembers watching those jolts attack my legs, my body.

He remembers darkness.

Melvin could not hear the sounds of my battle; he could only hear prolonged silence. Painful silence that indicated nothing. The wait to see who or what emerged from the conflict was excruciating.

His long wait was finally interrupted by a low rumbling noise emanating from the wheat field. The humming sound was rising up from the fertile ground as if it was slipping out from beneath the thick fog that had blanketed the field. The rhythmic purring was growing louder as it came toward him. For the previous hour, the ocher-colored fog had settled over the ground and sat frozen in place. It began to move. The segment of the fog which sat directly over the furrow that led me into the field started to swirl in a tight circular pattern, much like the exhaust from a jet engine. The tight spiral grew larger as the pulsating noise increased.

Melvin's reflexes took over and he began to step back from the edge of the field. The fog began to part, unfastening vertically from the outer edge of the fog bank and peeling back into the field. A still, indistinct light appeared deep in the fog. As the light's intensity grew, so did its diameter. He then realized it was gliding toward him, soon to escape from the clutches of the fog and the field. This had to be a sign of success, didn't it?

Light is never associated with Evil, is it?

Melvin had backed up 30 paces from his sentry position when the disc burst through the final remnants of the fog. It stopped in place as if allowing him to fully understand what he was seeing. It wasn't working. Did he really see a hovering, intense light exit the wheat field? The light was as bright as any object he had ever encountered, yet the area around the object was not illuminated. The ground below it was still covered in darkness. The light was tightly contained around what was an almost perfectly round orb. The light was not allowed to escape, as if the purpose was to make the orb clearly visible as opposed to lighting a pathway.

The intensely glowing sphere began to move toward Melvin. He felt no threat. His instinct told him he was not in jeopardy, so he stood his ground. *Where is Jacob?* he said out loud. The globe passed within 10 feet of him. He felt no heat and, just as the ground below the orb had remained black, he was not illuminated by the light. As it floated past, he realized the lighted sphere was roughly five feet in diameter. Melvin started to turn away to protect his eyes from its brilliance when it slowed to a dead stop next to him. The emitted light began to dim, allowing him to see the outline of the sphere. The outer shell appeared to be composed of a translucent skin that swirled like a raging ocean.

Melvin leaned into the orb and could see the faint outline of my motionless body. He knew that instant that I was safe. That I would be okay. The glowing orb then re-amplified its intensity, causing Melvin to again avert his eyes. It resumed it course down the hard dirt path toward my house.

He stood there for several moments, afraid to move.

And not sure what to do.

***

I walked out of the barn into the morning's awakening sunlight. The world had a different feel. It had a different look. Colors were brighter and sharper, as if cataracts had been removed from my eyes. Four years of travails had apparently eroded my senses without me even noticing the effects. I jumped onto the back porch steps in one, graceful leap. That was amazing. Strength that had been absent for years was now beginning to course through my muscles.

Don't let me be dreaming; please let this be real.

Mom simply stared at me when I walked through the back door. Her mouth moved, but no words came out. She immediately jumped up from the table, shoving the chair back in her wake. Around the table she spun and grabbed me in the most tender, yet ferocious, bear hug.

"Jacob! You're safe!"

I found myself in the middle of a group hug as Mary and Mrs. Ray joined the fun.

We all sat at the table, ready for what would be an epic debriefing. They were looking at me like I was some alien novelty about to break into a song and dance.

"I'm fine."

"Fine?" Mom scowled at me. "We wait for hours as you're out there doing who knows what and you're *fine*?"

"I—uh—I'm not completely sure. But I think it's over. I think whatever happened out there…basically…cured me." I was stuttering, not truly believing what I had just said.

"What does that mean, Jacob?"

I shrugged. "I guess Good overcame Evil, and I am the beneficiary."

Mary said nothing; she just squeezed my hand as if she was never going to let go. Mom looked at me, blinking. Mrs. Ray just smiled and didn't say anything. She sat there calmly staring at me like she has done so many times before. Her hands were neatly folded on the table.

After what seemed like an eternity, Mrs. Ray reached over to me. "We are so glad you're back with us, Jacob. I think you're right. This is over."

I squeezed back. Could it be true? Could I be...normal?

Mrs. Ray suddenly looked up. "Where's Melvin?"

I looked around the table. "I don't know. He was right behind me when I entered the field, but that is the last time I saw him."

"You know he is a big part of the reason you're sitting here right now. The reason you are seemingly cured of your affliction. Without his faithful strength to augment your powers, things may have ended differently. The two of you melded into a dominant force."

I wasn't sure what exactly she was saying, but I later understood perfectly. We then heard Melvin step onto the back porch.

76

JACOB

Four a.m. and my eyes flew wide open.

Oh no. Had everything that happened yesterday been…a lie?

Was I really up again to go slogging?

I stayed in bed for a few minutes, waiting for the familiar tug to get up, to get dressed. But it never came.

Apparently my muscle memory had not quite received the notice that I no longer needed to get up this early. Because, while I was awake, I definitely wasn't feeling the urge to slog.

I tried to fall back asleep but to no avail. I lay in bed for a while rehashing bits and pieces of the last four years. I still, even with all of my thinking and talking and praying, couldn't understand why.

Why me?

Why then?

Why that?

I finally got out of bed. Not to slog, just to be up.

Mom was awake when I walked into the kitchen. Her schedule would take a while to adjust back to normal too. She would eventually get there. One out of two of us wasn't so bad.

"Can't sleep either, huh, Mom?"

"No, sweetie. Too many mornings sitting at this table waiting for you to return." She answered, tapping her finger on the wood tabletop as if I didn't know which table she meant.

(There are times I still miss that time in my life. The conversations. The sense of urgency that comes with the possibility that life will not last as long as it should. We still visited after that, but a certain connection was missing. It went back to Mom and teenage son, and let's face it, that's not normally the recipe for heartfelt dialogue. That said, our early mornings were still special. By the Fall, Mom was back to waking up at a more reasonable hour. If she did wake up early, she'd find me sitting in the kitchen. We would fall back into our pattern of dialogue. The discussions flowed easily. A few silver linings emerged from the four-year shit storm. My opportunity to know my mom on a deep, intimate basis was easily the one I cherished the most.)

"I'd sure like to sleep a few hours longer. Kind of a pain now that I don't need to get up so early."

"It will come, Jake. I'm sure of it."

Mom and I sat at the table until the sun came up, drinking coffee and talking.

***

The two most significant events of the summer between 8th and 9th grade were, for me, at the opposite ends of the spectrum. One was the miraculous physical changes I reveled in, and the other was Dad's reentry into our lives.

It started innocently. My mom asked us kids to be available for dinner on a Saturday night in mid-July. I didn't think much of it. I arrived first, followed by Luke and Mary. The scowls on their faces flashed their excitement. It didn't bother me at all. At least up to that point. We piled into the kitchen and sat at the table. There was a feel of nervous energy in the air. Mary later told me she knew when she sat down and looked at Mom that something bad was coming.

I guess I was too naïve to read Mom's face.

"Mom, what is going on?" Luke barked.

"Can you help me set the table?" Mom seemed distracted.

I widened my eyes and looked at Mary and Luke who both kept their faces neutral. Mary was a good faker, but Luke commenced to expel his energy by tapping his fingers on the wooden tabletop. This did nothing but amplify the tension. We knew something was coming, but I had no earthly idea what was about to blow up in the middle of the Ross family dinner.

"Okay! Dinner is served!" Mom set a huge platter of roast beef on the table and went back into the kitchen for a bowl of mashed potatoes.

I dug in like a man possessed. I was starving, shoveling food into my mouth without noticing that Mary sat as still as a statue and Luke merely poked as his food with a fork.

"Ahem." Mom let out a little cough-like whimper. "I have a bit of significant news, and I wanted to tell all three of you at the same time."

The B-52 opened its cargo doors and out poured the ordinances. "Your dad is moving back into the house tomorrow."

There it was. Nine simple words that had a profound impact on our family, and not a positive impact. Mom's head swiveled from one of her children to the next looking for any kind of reaction. At first, and seemingly for five minutes, the three of us sat there in complete silence as if someone hit the mute button. Luke broke the angry silence. He slowly pushed back his chair as he stood up from the table. He wiped his mouth and dropped the napkin into his chair. The napkin floated comically slow, acting much like a starter's flag. When it gently landed in position, the explosion went off. Luke raised his right arm over his head, gaining as much leverage as possible and proceeded to slam his fork into his dinner plate. It was a direct hit. Gravy-covered mashed potatoes exploded upward and outward. The slab of meat flipped off the plate and landed upright against the salt shaker, gravy slowly dripping onto the tablecloth. I flinched, then froze, with my fork in mid-path to my mouth. I wasn't sure whether to laugh or stay quiet. I wisely chose the latter. It was hard though as both Mom and Mary had splatters of potatoes and gravy across their shirts.

"Well, that's just fucking great," was all Luke said as he stormed out of the kitchen. I'm sure that conversation hadn't gone quite like Mom envisioned it.

"Luke, come back here," Mom feebly asserted. Luke ignored her. He stomped up the stairs as the slam of his bedroom door reigned over the silence.

Mom then broke into tears.

"What did you expect, Mom? Dad ripped Luke's heart out, and now you expect him to take this bit of news in stride, maybe even thank the two of you for righting all the wrongs of the past?" Mary

389

bluntly and accurately assessed.

"I don't know, Mary. I just want to be a family again."

"That's never going to happen, Mom, and deep down you know it.

Mom only nodded her head.

My brain started to function again. Part of me was sure I had misunderstood Mom, yet deep down I knew I hadn't. Now it was my turn to be pissed. "I agree with Mary. This isn't going to work. Dad left us. He left in the middle of a crisis where you and I needed him the most. I don't want him to come back. Ever. Do you hear me? Never, ever."

The words poured out before I really had time to think about them.

But I meant them. I really did.

I looked at Mom and saw she was noticeably digging for those magical words that would make us understand her position. Why she was allowing it? (I now understand what was surely the desperate feeling of loneliness. I sure didn't then.)

"I'm scared to be alone," Mom stammered. "I'm scared to have you all move out, and then what do I do?"

"Get on with your life, for God's sake, Mom." Mary appeared to be madder than I was. "Maybe the excitement of the unknown is better than the bitterness of the familiar. No, not maybe, it absolutely is."

Wow, where did she come up with that? She was dead on though. Mom should have cleared the slate and moved ahead.

But she was too weak. It dismayed me then and it still does today.

"I'm sorry. I've made my decision, and your dad and I are going to give it a shot."

"He will do it again, Mom." Those were Mary's last words as she quietly exited the kitchen leaving Mom and me sitting in the middle of the kill zone.

"Jacob, please tell me you understand."

"I can't, Mom." I couldn't understand how this tragedy in the making was so clear to three teenagers, yet to an adult it was the correct and rational choice. I rose from the table and went upstairs. I decided to go to Mary's room as I was sure Luke was about to blow a gasket and I wanted none of that. It was about an hour later when I heard Mom cleaning the kitchen. Her wonderful meal went into the trash.

I was so very sad.

***

Our home life was an utter catastrophe.

Mary and Luke rarely left their rooms and I wasn't much more adventurous. If I did venture out, and Dad was anywhere to be seen or heard, I turned right back around and went to my room. Our house was one giant eggshell. Luke, Mary, and I were converted into unwelcome strangers in our own home. At least in our own minds. Dad tried to reconcile at first but gave up after a while.

Mary's prophetic comment about Dad never changing came true during the summer after my senior year in high school. Old dog, same old tricks and all that. The next Mrs. Ryan emerged and, true to a small-town rumor mill, leaks sprung from this overly-used boat. During my first and only year at Wichita State, Mom discovered the truth, as did Dad's employer. You can imagine their delight. Apparently, Dad's earlier dalliances were kept much more under wraps. (Maybe that was normal in the pre-social media days.)

Dad's final episode was not so clandestine.

By the summer of 2000, we had all had enough of small town Kansas, and Perryton agreed. They'd had enough of the Rosses. Mom and Dad sold the farm and most all their possessions, packed the balance in the LTD, and left Perryton.

It was sad considering the roots we had planted so deeply over the many years. But they had no choice. They roamed around Texas and Oklahoma for a few years before finally settling in Refugio. I'm guessing it was the first stop where Dad's past didn't catch up to him.

In some ways, I'm glad.

Yet, while all this drama ensued, I felt amazing.

My strength and stamina suddenly rushed back to me. I loved it. I grew several inches and gained 25 pounds. By the first day of ninth grade, the new and improved Jake Ross looked and felt a few years older. In three months, I had made up for the four years of physical idleness.

Over the summer, the only people with whom I came into contact had the last name Ross or Ray. Mrs. Ray told me she was expecting such a change. Marcus was amazed and was begging me to join him on the varsity football team. Mom and Mary were quietly thrilled for me. Luke was indifferent, and my spurt was one more thing that scared Dad about his youngest son. All in all, I felt physically wonderful. My mental well-being was a different issue.

After her dad's suicide, Susie had left town for the summer to live with relatives in Omaha. Mom had told me that she arrived back in Perryton at the end of the summer and was living with the Marconi family. They had six children, so what was one more? I had spent that summer longing for her. I missed her. In fact, I didn't hear from her or see her during that entire summer.

Which means she didn't see me.

She didn't know the Flash had pulled a Lazarus.

She didn't know the Flash was back.

***

On the first day of school, I leapt off the front porch, ran the distance to the bus stop, slammed on my brakes, and looked back at the length of my skid mark. I rode to school in complete oblivion.

I gracefully walked into Perryton High as a young man who stood 5'11" and weighed a very solid 185 pounds.

No one recognized me. A few people looked directly at me but with only a faint hint of recognition. I may as well have been a transfer student from Mars.

For the past few years, I would walk these halls daydreaming I was a normal teenager. That Susie would look up and see me, a brawny teenager instead of down at a shriveled-up kid. That I could compete with all the older jerks who hit on her with regularity. I had severely misjudged her criteria, but regardless, as I entered the school that day, I finally thought my dream of Susie walking arm-in-arm down the crowded hallway of Perryton High School could be a possibility.

I immediately started my search for Susie.

It didn't take long to find her. She was in the middle of a growing circle of students who wanted to talk to her after her summer-long absence. I approached the energetic crowd feeling less confident with each step. The eighth-grade Jake's mindset began to take over. The mindset of a small, physically underdeveloped kid. (It took me several years to put that vision away to the back of my conscious. That Jake pokes his head out periodically, even to this day.)

The circle seemed alive with all the kids jockeying for position. The beacon that was Susie Polanski stood at the bullseye on this dart board. She looked even more beautiful. Her hair was longer and she had developed a touch of maturity in her appearance. Understandable after what she had endured. *You age quicker in the middle of a shit storm* would become one of our favorite expressions. I stood on the periphery, clear of all the bouncing heads between Susie and me. That felt great. I finally caught her eye and smiled the best smile Jacob Ross could muster.

She looked away without a glimmer of recognition.

Then she turned back, and as if no one else was in the hallway, shouted "Jacob Ross, is that you?"

I just smiled what was likely the goofiest smile I'd ever smiled.

Susie started to part the sea as she worked her way through the crowd. I heard many people's remarks as I waited for her. *Jacob Ross? I don't see him. What is she talking about that runt for? No gimps around here that I can see.* Those comments would have hurt me last year, I dismissed them now with only a slight twinge of pain. The outer rim of the mass of humanity finally parted and out shot Susie.

"Jacob, it is you? I didn't recognize you at first." She smiled. "Look at you. What happened to you?" She jumped into my arms. It was the greatest single day in the history of Jacob Ross. The entire school watched as Susie Polanski outwardly professed her affections for the gimp. The hall went silent and then started to empty as the first bell rang. I didn't want to let go and probably wouldn't have unless Mr. Lowden, our esteemed Principal, had not walked by and told us to get to class.

"Are you okay, Jacob? You've changed so much. You've grown so much. How did this happen?"

"Let's get together after school and I'll bring you up to speed. There is a lot to tell you about the last four years and about this summer."

"Okay." Puzzled doesn't adequately describe the look on her face.

Susie and I rode the bus home that afternoon, both getting off at my house. We spent the next four hours on the front porch as I walked her through the *Great Slog Era* and this summer's aftermath. She asked a few questions, but mostly sat enrapt.

"How did I not know any of this?" she asked as I ran out of words and steam. "I thought your affliction was an incurable disease. I was afraid to bring up the subject for fear of embarrassing you."

I shrugged.

Her face turned stern. "I should be very mad at you for not sharing this with me, but I can't get mad at you, Jacob."

"Other than my family, only Marcus and his family knew the details. Truth be told, Mrs. Ray saved my life. She's the reason I'm cured and sitting here with you."

I had fallen completely and utterly in love with Susie long before that day.

But that day sealed the deal.

As the sun set, and I knew I had to get inside to do homework, Mom volunteered to drive us back to the Marconi's house. I got out of the car and walked Susie to the door.

"Jacob, thanks for telling me your story. I will keep it just between us."

"That's probably for the best. You'd get committed for being crazy otherwise."

She then said good night and took one step toward me. I could feel her brush lightly up against me. The combination of our heat and her smell were intoxicating. Standing on her tiptoes, she whispered into my right ear, *"I have always loved you for who you are, not what you looked like. But I am glad you're well again."*

Then she put her arms around my neck and nervously kissed me.

My first kiss.

Mom just smiled as I sat down in the passenger seat. I have no recollection of the drive home. It took me a while to fall asleep that night.

***

By the end of October, the barrage of questions and strange, sideways looks subsided to a trickle, and my school days fell into a much-welcomed routine. I don't blame anyone for feeling a bit apprehensive about my quantum change over a single summer. The wide berths in the hallway were understandable.

I finally acquiesced by 10th grade to Marcus's incessant pleadings to play football, but was so far behind everyone else in the nuances of the game that I was limited to mop-up duty. Things changed my junior year. A light clicked on with the help of Marcus's unending tutorials.

For two years, I was simply required to take the snap and accurately pitch the ball to Marcus Ray and then watch him turn the corner ahead of a floundering defense. What an easy job. I rarely handed the ball off to the fullback and even more rarely stepped back to pass the ball.

Marcus was named first team All-State for four straight years.

College coaches from around the country made regular treks to our games to try in vain to persuade him to commit to their school. We would routinely sit in his living room with six offers spread out over the coffee table and discuss the pros and cons of each school. Mrs. Ray would feed us and Mr. Ray would sit quietly and take it all in. Mr. Ray believed it was Marcus's choice so he kept his opinions to himself. On signing day, Marcus donned the cardinal and gold of Southern Cal. He was happy, I was proud, and his mom and dad were both. He played three years for the Trojans before going to the Arizona Cardinals with the fifth pick in the 2002 NFL draft. Six years as an elite NFL running back provided complete financial freedom for the remainder of his life.

As can be imagined, Marcus and I ran in very different circles after high school, but we never lost touch. I received one or two calls a week from wherever he was at that moment. I think I was his anchor to remain grounded in what was important. We talked very little about sports and mostly about life. There is a reason we both now live in the greater Phoenix area. We've always been drawn together and always will be.

***

I was greatly dismayed the day Mary left for NYU. Scholarship in hand, and the world to conquer, she left Perryton in her wake, never to return. I visited her in New York during my freshman year at WSU and she came to Wichita soon afterwards to attend a wedding of a high school friend. Other than that, we went seven years without seeing each other. We talked periodically, but it was not the same. Fortunately, our gravitational pull would not allow us to grow too separate. We were drawn back together even though we had been divided by the Atlantic Ocean for many years. I'd love to see her again soon. I miss her. I believe she misses me too.

I graduated from high school in May of 1999. I was more than ready for the next phase of life. Problem was, I had no idea what that phase entailed. I ranked number two in my class, but it sounds better than it really was. We only had 17 kids in our graduating class, so technically, everyone was in the top 20 of their class. Marcus graduated number four, and Susie was in the middle at number eight. Most of our class drove out to Cedar Bluff Reservoir after the graduating ceremony and spent the entire night drinking around a bonfire. That was the last time I ever laid eyes on all but three members of my graduating class. A graduating class of kids with whom I had traveled 13 grades. Childhood proximity breeds very little I guess.

77

JACOB

I decided to enroll early at Wichita State University and begin classes in June. Another excuse to be away from home. Marcus left at the same time for sunny California. Susie stayed behind in Perryton and worked as a waitress at Downtown Diner over the summer. She still lived with the Marconis, but that arrangement was coming to an end. She drove the 150 miles to WSU most every weekend to see me.

Yes, we stayed together. From that first kiss on the first day of 9th grade, through every high school dance, every game, every class, everything.

During her visits to Wichita, Susie and I spent a lot of time talking about the future and about the past. She opened up about her family, facts that both horrified me and filled me with a sense of relief. I shared with her, too. Her early childhood was happy—as best she could remember. Her first memory of a crack in the façade was the anger and fits of rage exhibited by Jimmy. She had no idea why he got so angry and why he took it out on her.

Her dad's failures in life and his failure to have a life outside of the choking grip of Perryton was funneled directly into Jimmy. Her mom protested vehemently, but her complaints were answered with the same cruel treatment. Susie remembered her dad stomping around the house and yelling, fueled by a fit of alcoholic afterburner. The topic of most of his rants centered around the fact that he didn't leave the piece-of-shit town when he was 18 years old. He'd cuss at his brothers all the while enraged about the life he could have had. It was so nice of him to metaphorically wipe out the existence of his kids.

Periodically, the rage manifested into physical abuse. Again, aimed primarily at Jimmy and then diverted to Susie's mom if she intervened. Many Sundays at church were skipped as bruises were given time to heal. Susie believed her dad saw the root of his failures in Jimmy; he saw himself in Jimmy and wanted to lash out in anger. After all, you don't blame yourself, when an able-bodied personification is right in front of you.

Particularly one half your size.

More than once, Susie would walk into Jimmy's bedroom, only to find him bleeding from the latest altercation. At first, she could comfort him, but that became impossible after a while, as his crust grew thicker and harder. All this was compounded by the complete adoration with which Abel showered Susie. If Abel viewed his wife and son as a symbol of the immovable anchor holding him in Perryton, Susie was his view of sunshine and opportunity. Jimmy hated his dad for obvious reasons. He hated his sister because she wasn't hated by his dad. Cycles like this do not spin upward, only downward, and Jimmy's spun hard and fast. As he grew older and stronger, Jimmy began to fight back and the violence escalated. To his credit, he avoided confrontations at all costs, but Abel's addled mind was often set on the warpath for no valid reason.

Mrs. Polanski eventually had had enough. In the middle of the night after Abel passed out, she packed one suitcase, snuck downstairs and drove away. It was only a few days after our brief conversation at the concession stand. Susie heard her bang her suitcase on the stairs, so she followed her mom out the back door and onto the driveway, only she was too late. Susie stood in complete darkness and watched the tail lights of Mrs. Polanski's car disappear down the winding road that led to her mom's freedom. Was she going to the store? Was she visiting a friend? Would she be back soon? Susie made up a lot of scenarios until the absolute realization sank in that her mother had left her. I could both empathize and sympathize. I also felt my own anger boil up.

Abel's drinking accelerated and the beatings increased. Jimmy didn't miss all those school days because he was sick or expelled, as the rumor mill indicated. He missed because he could not physically get up and out of his house in the morning. Listening to Susie recount this tragic tale brought the legend of Jimmy Polanski into a very different light. As the years have passed, I moved more to the sympathy side of the ledger. How horrific and how cruel his life had been! Abel Polanski, due to his complete inability to deal with life's unfair trade, completely ruined one person—his son, for God's sake—and deeply and irrevocably scarred two more.

Part of Jimmy's legend grew throughout Perryton, particularly among his peers, because of all the fantastic stories that circulated about his whereabouts after he was sent away. Rumors surfaced, swirled around the school, and then died, only to be replaced by the next imaginative piece of speculation. The most popular rumors were that Jimmy was shipped off to a federally-run institution for the criminally insane only to be trained as a CIA hit-man, or that he was forced to enlist in the Marine Corps only to become a hero in the Gulf Wars before dying from a well-placed IED, or that he escaped from the Perryton jail and made his way through Mexico before joining a Columbian drug cartel. The truth was much more simple and sad. Susie had never told anyone this story and probably never recited it again.

Her dad had apparently received a letter from the Kansas Juvenile Correctional Complex that ignited an afternoon drinking jag. Susie arrived home later that sunny afternoon to find Abel passed out on the living room couch and the KJCC's letter wadded up on the table. She straightened out the paper and read its contents. She read it three times to be sure it wasn't misread. It wasn't. Due to the weight of unbearable grief, she dropped into the exact same kitchen chair in which she would sit after finding Abel swinging from the rafters.

The true story of Jimmy Polanski post-Perryton lasted three months. He was shipped off to a regional detention center, and then on to the KJCC in Topeka, where he was discovered by a guard during his morning walk through the facility. Jimmy was lying face up in one of the communal bathrooms, vacant of any life. Bruises, cuts and bloody edemas made him mostly unrecognizable. The official findings indicated he died instantly from a blow to the head with a blunt instrument. No perpetrator was ever charged and the matter was quickly forgotten. People are not too concerned with the lives (or sad endings) of the Jimmy Polanskis of the world. The unofficial facts surrounding Jimmy's death were that the single blunt force was at the end of many a series of other blunt forces. It seems Jimmy's rage was directed at the wrong person. The truth is that Abel Polanski killed Jimmy as sure I'm sitting here. Susie felt the same way.

The revelations of all our demons, as well as our joys, came in many episodes over the summer. They were often intermixed with tears, but the exercise was healthy for both of us. We usually lay together drained of most all our mental and physical energy. Not drained enough that we didn't enjoy each other before absolute exhaustion turned off our consciousness.

78

JACOB, 2015

Phoenix can have some of the most debilitating weather during its never-ending summers. (Unless you like living in an oven, I suppose. Then it's wonderful. I guess I've gotten used to it so it doesn't bother me that much.) What I do love are the winters. Most of the country would laugh at the thought of describing our weather as related to winter. High 60s during the day and mid-40s in the cold of the night. Margie and I take the kids and dogs for a walk every day, relishing the magnificent sunsets and chill in the air that beckons the need for a pullover fleece.

It has taken me a little over a year to write these memoirs. I know that sounds snooty, and I don't mean it to, but calling it a book is giving more credit than is due. I have no better term. Just before Christmas last year, I opened a long-buried box stashed in the recesses of our attic and dug through the contents. I sat on one of the attic's joists and rifled through a few old family pictures, trophies, and awards that were piled randomly within the cardboard box. I quickly picked through each item and dismissed them just as quickly. That is, until I found my journal that documented the *Great Slog Era*. Believe it or not, that four-year portion of my life has mostly faded from my day-to-day thoughts. I've tried my hardest to make it fade.

Flipping the pages of the journal allowed all the suppressed memories to spring forth. It was a rush of dreadful anxiety laced with warm memories. I decide right then and there that organizing the disparate entries in the journal into a comprehensive narrative would do me wonders, much like writing them in the first place. I think it worked. It was cleansing to relive that time. The fact that I still see Marcus and Mrs. Ray on a regular basis rendered their parts of the story rather unemotional. The fact that I work closely with Melvin had the same effect. The fact that I have not seen Susie Polanski in 16 years took me to my knees when her memories and stories flooded back into my consciousness. I was overcome with her smile, her feel, her warmth, and her taste.

I will never come close to getting over Susie Polanski.

Ever.

She was my first love, and that love sank its barbed hooks into my core being and they will never shake free. I feel pangs of guilt by simply admitting this weakness as I truly love Margie and have since our second date. It is just different. If I had the balls to discuss this with her, she'd probably agree. All the other characters in my story were and are benign. Susie was way past visceral.

I painfully remember the last time we saw each other. It was the Spring in my Freshman year of college. When the Fall semester at WSU started, her trips to see me began to slowly wane. She enrolled into the Topeka Community College System to take basic core courses and allow herself the space to plan her next step. We had both assumed those steps would be in concert with mine.

It was not to be.

Two months into the school's Fall term, she dropped all her classes and left Topeka altogether. She had met two girls from Kansas City at TCC and they became fast friends. I never meet either of them so I can't hazard a guess as to what the attraction was. I guess it doesn't matter. The three of them packed all their belongings into a car and left for Florida. They traveled up and down both coasts, living off odd jobs and enjoying the fruits of wild oats finally sown. I no longer heard from her, the regular calls became irregular, and then ceased. I was unsuccessful in contacting her and had no direct way to try to locate her.

I finally heard from an old friend that Susie had called and told her she was leaving school and going to Florida and that, under no circumstances, should she tell me where she had gone.

That stung. Deeply.

From there the story got murky. The three of them finally ran out of money or energy and she apparently returned to Perryton in February of 2000. Under the cover of darkness, she collected six months' worth of farm Co-op checks, now in her name, the last of her needed belongings, and left before the sun rose. She eventually sold the farmhouse and the two acres it sat on and had the monthly share-cropping checks forwarded to an unknown address. She rolled into Wichita that next morning around 11:00.

I was sitting in the Ablah Library between classes when my phone rang. I stared at the caller ID, not believing my eyes. Susie P was printed on the face of my phone. I punched the accept button and heard nothing on the other end.

"Hello, Susie?" My voice was pleading. Was it an accidental call or maybe not even Susie? "Susie, are you there?" I repeated.

Still nothing, then I heard a faint breath. "Jake. Hi, it's me."

I was flooded with emotions and relief. I was happy and then outraged. I was hopeful, yet deep down I knew what was coming.

"Susie." I paused, unable to get out the words. "Where are you? Where have you been?"

"Let's meet for a bit." The use of "*for a bit*" further confirmed my dread. "You pick where."

"Sure, how about Smitty's?" I mentioned a bar where we had spent hours talking the previous fall.

"No, too many memories. Anywhere else will work."

"How about one of the benches in Lincoln Park? Do you remember Lincoln Park, just a few blocks north of Smitty's?"

"I'll be there in five minutes." And she hung up. *No goodbye or can't wait to see you*, nothing but a dial tone.

I was scared to death. Six months ago, we had talked about marriage and a life together. Now I watched as if my time with her was sand slipping through my fingers. I gathered up my books into my backpack and walked toward Lincoln Park. I was alone in the world, as I struggled to maintain an appearance of calm. I crossed 21st Street, walked past Smitty's, and soon arrived at the park.

I entered through the namesake gate and immediately saw Susie sitting on a bench not 25 feet away. I stopped in my tracks. It was Susie, but it wasn't. *What has happened?* Every emotion I had for her boiled over. I felt sick. I fully expected an encore of my knee aches and slog ailments. Luckily, they stayed away. That was the only positive thing that happened that day. At about 10 feet she looked up and directly at me. Embarrassment flooded her face. She burst into tears and buried her face in her hands. I watched as she released months, or maybe years, of pent up feelings.

"Susie, what is going on?" My brain was churning without developing any coherent thoughts.

Her crying slowed and she settled down. She raised up again and met my stare. Had it only been half a year since we last laughed, held each other, and she looked at me with those intense, sensuous eyes? She now looked tired and worn out. Her beautiful eyes had dulled and darkened. I was crushed. *Where was my Susie? Where was the love of my life?*

"Jacob, I am so sorry. What have I done?"

I had no possible answer. I could only repeat "What is going on?"

"I...I just snapped last Winter. Years of hate, rejection, and anger exploded and I ran away. I ran away from you. Don't ask me about the details because I will not tell you. I want you to remember me as I was before."

"You are not making sense, Susie. Why wouldn't I remember you for all the years ahead of us?"

She placed two fingers on my lips as if to stop me from saying something stupid. "There is no time ahead for us, Jacob. I am leaving Kansas today and will never, ever return. I don't know where I'm going, but it will be alone. You look truly great and I hope your sickness stays in remission. Go live the life you deserve. I don't deserve you and you shouldn't want me."

"But..." I was panicking then. "I do. I do want you. I do. I don't care about anything you've done. I just want you back."

She was slowly shaking her head. The sand was about to end its path between my fingers. I was spinning out of control. I couldn't lose Susie, not after all we'd been through together and all we've planned together.

It seemed I didn't have a choice.

"You are best friend, Jacob Ross," She wasn't making any sense. "You are my first love and the man that makes me the happiest. I hate myself for this, but I must go."

She rose from the bench and began to walk away. I grabbed her hand to halt the inevitable. She stopped and turned slightly towards me. Her sad eyes were filled with tears and she said, "Please let me go."

You age quicker in the middle of a shit storm echoed in my mind. She must have experienced some nuclear shit storm. Although I did release her hand, I never really did let her go. She still has my heart held captive. Much more than I thought when I entered this dusty attic looking for the last of the tree ornaments. More pangs of guilt rippled through me.

I haven't seen her since.

I doubt I ever will.

***

Melvin disappeared shortly after I was cured. No thanks needed; it was just part of his fabric. I sought him out in my depression over Susie. After Susie walked out of Lincoln Park, I returned to my apartment and packed up my scant belongings. I proceeded to leave Kansas as fast as my old '76 red Camaro could move down the highway. I drove nonstop to Phoenix, knowing that was the last recorded address for Melvin. He was still there. It took me a while to find him. He was surprised to see me get out of the Camaro as I parked in front of the People's Non-Denominational Church of

Phoenix. We hugged, laughed, and reminisced. I told him about Susie and me beginning in ninth grade. I finally told him I needed help. I had no idea what I wanted to do, nor what skills I had to accomplish anything worthwhile. His face lit up.

"What do you mean, Jacob Ross? You have an innate skill very few people have, and you're in the right place to exploit that skill. That special skill was on display to its grandest on that dark morning in your family's wheat field. You are home now. Let's get to work."

***

The PNCP has followed the trajectory of all of Melvin's other churches. Lots of high-highs and a few low-lows.

But we all knew it would be his last church. Mine, too.

Melvin said he was too old to move again.

Celina was too tired to move again.

And Marcus was too integral to the city of Phoenix to be allowed to move.

Yes, that's right. The Rays and Pastor Standard moved out to Perryton with me. And our rag-tag church council spent quite a few late nights in strategy sessions. What could we do to maintain the integrity of the work we perform in the neighborhoods in need? After so many years, we had hundreds of families that relied on us and, quite frankly, we relied on them. Family is an overused term, but that's what they were.

Which meant, when things got tough, I couldn't leave them in the dark of night.

***

"Jacob, come down here! I need your help!" Margie yelled.

"Be down in sec!" I answered, as the computer was powered down. Her timing had been perfect, calling me down just as I had typed the last sentence in my memoirs. It seemed complete and straightforward... finished. I'll let you be the judge of that. Either way, I am emotionally ready to be done and get back to the present and future. The unknown always seems to need more attention than the already known.

I threw on my last remaining K-State sweatshirt. It was so old and threadbare that the purple had turned grey and the term sweatshirt hardly applied. My last thread of physical connection to my home state, I guess. As I turned left on the landing, I heard voices echoing up. I froze in space. The voices came again and I was absolutely sure. I bolted down the remaining stairs two at a time and sprinted into the living room.

"Mary?" What a surprise. She was exactly who I needed. Margie stepped back as I engulfed Mary, lifting her off her feet.

"Whoa, Cowboy, you're going to break my spine!" Mary objected, but not too hard.

I looked at Margie and the expression on her face told me she was part of the ruse. "Wow, you guys surprised me!"

"You two sit down and get caught up," Margie said. "I'll go finish up dinner."

"Jacob, you look great. Margie looks great, and the kids are huge compared to the last time I saw pictures of them."

My joy suddenly waned. "Mary, why are you here? What's wrong?"

It seems like when I see Mary, I start expecting the delivery of bad news.

"Not a thing, Jacob. After you surprised me for Liam's birthday, I've wanted to do the same. Margie was more than game, so we planned the surprise."

"I need to call Marcus and Mrs. Ray. We can have a cookout to celebrate our reunion. Melvin will insist on cooking the burgers."

We sat up well into the night covering every known subject. I got current on Liam and David and their life in England. I couldn't help thinking of the shy, introverted sister I had known so many years ago in Perryton, Kansas and how she blossomed into the international art expert. (We saved talking about Mom and Dad for the end. Why put a damper on such a perfect evening? The discussion was short, as what was there to say that hasn't been covered ad nauseum?)

We finally headed to bed around 1:00 a.m.; after all, we had a celebratory picnic to plan and execute as well as many more topics of discussion. I was a happy, very content camper as I snuck quietly into my bedroom.

Tomorrow would change that.

But, for that evening, life felt…complete.

***

"Good morning, Jake."

"Good morning, Mary. I am so sorry for keeping you up last night. You have to be so jet-lagged."

"Normally I would be, but for whatever reason, I feel fine. I wouldn't have missed our discussion last night for anything in the world."

"Grab some coffee and I'll fix you some breakfast."

"How long have you been up?" Mary asked, knowing the answer anyway.

"Since just after 4:00. I have already read the paper, had coffee, and worked on next week's sermon."

A frown washed over her face. "Still can't sleep to a normal hour, can you? I'm sorry."

"Don't be. On one hand, it allows me time to myself to work or plan the day; on the other, it reminds me of how blessed I am. I could be slogging the corn fields, right?"

I made bacon and eggs, with toast, strawberry jam, and a big bowl of fruit. All things that Mary rarely eats, but she ate every bite and explained that the British version didn't hold a candle to mine.

"What's on the agenda for today?"

"I have already talked to Melvin and Marcus, and we decided on 4:00 for the cookout. I need to go to the store to get a few things and then swing by the church for a short time."

"I'd like to go. I would love to see your church."

"Don't expect much. It's a bit of a mess and sits in a not-so-great part of town."

"I don't care. I still want to join you."

"I would like that."

Mary and I spent the remainder of the morning, and part of the early afternoon, running errands and stopping by PNCP. She met a few of the crew who happened to be working on a Saturday, got the grand tour, and generally soaked up the feel of a bootstrap operation. I did not mention our nameless benefactor; I didn't feel Marcus would mind. We talked at length about the other local churches finally catching wind of our presence, and the predicament that was gaining momentum. Mary, as always, had some valid thoughts and outstanding ideas.

We pulled into the driveway at half past two. I grabbed the groceries out of the back seat as I began to make the mental list of items to knock out before the burger crowd rolled in at four.

"Marg, we're home!" I yelled as I kicked the door closed with the heel of my boot.

"In the kitchen."

A chill set over me, and I looked at Mary. "Something is not right." We entered the kitchen to Melvin and Margie sitting at the table. Both were distraught. Both were stained with tears.

I knew immediately.

I just knew.

"Oh, Jake," was all Margie could mutter.

Melvin added. "She died peacefully, Jacob. She went to her room this morning to take a nap and never woke up. Marcus and Cynthia are at her place now, making arrangements. He didn't sound good on the phone. I think he needs you, Jacob. He said she was talking about her Jacob Ross all morning as if she had you on her mind at the very end."

I dropped the bags on the counter and ran out the door.

***

I spent the weekend with Marcus and Cynthia. Melvin took over Sunday duties and Mary stayed with Margie and the kids. I was shattered. The invincible Celina Ray was gone and, with the wink of an eye, I had lost my anchor in life. The anchor that had kept me from floating adrift at sea for the past 20 years. Melvin may have been the final piece of the equation that defeated Evil on my behalf, but Mrs. Ray was the heart and soul of my battle.

A part of me shriveled up and the bitter ashes were tossed to the sky.

I have known two Celina Rays. One was the woman I have written so much about. The warrior who took in an eroding adolescent and saved his life. My life. I loved that woman intensely. The other was the woman I got to know as the kindest, wisest, most caring person I have ever met. Her compassion for her family was limitless, only slightly greater than her single-minded focus on the betterment of our beleaguered congregants. She worked tirelessly with Melvin and me. My success was born from her efforts. I will never fully recover from her loss. My brother and I sat together in the celebration of life and in the misery of death unexpected.

***

The funeral was set for 3:00 p.m. on the following Wednesday at the People's Nondenominational Church of Phoenix—where else? I helped Marcus and Cynthia finalize the arrangements. Mary and Margie managed the flood of people arriving to honor Celina one last time. We all walked through those preceding days more akin to zombies idly roaming the countryside. I was so very happy for Mary's presence. Her strength was exactly what I needed.

By 2:30, all the chairs in the makeshift sanctuary were full. We scrambled for everything and anything to sit on, lining the back walls with these resources. The last wave of arrivals was relegated to standing where floor space provided. Over a thousand people overwhelmed our capacity. I'm sure the city would have objected in theory, but not in spirit. We finally started the celebration at 3:30.

I stood from my chair on the dais and slowly walked to the lectern. "Thank all of you for attending this celebration of one of the brightest lights to ever grace another's life. Celina would be humbled and embarrassed. Maybe a little excited too. I'll ask her that later."

I was more nervous standing in front of a crowd than I could remember. It was mostly PNCP's congregation, for heaven's sake. I spoke in front of them every week! But, that day, my stomach flip-flopped and I felt light-headed. My initial words sounded wooden and canned. *Where was the Jacob Ross of old?* He suddenly arrived with a little assistance from a dear friend. I paused to take a sip of water. A tried and true way to reset the theatre. It worked. I then heard a pale whisper in the recesses of my mind. *"Relax, my love, you've got this."*

Celina to the rescue one last time.

My nerves unwound and my head cleared. Time to eulogize.

After two deep breaths, I looked out over the crowd. There was an emotional tightness in the air. My stomach began to reignite, I decided to jump into my prayerfully prepared eulogy. So, I began. "To a large degree, I stand here in front of all of you ashamed of myself. Ashamed because I cannot adequately express what Celina Ray means to me, means to you, and means to everyone who has had the great pleasure to cross her path. I'm sorry. I'll try for fitting words by starting with a story. A story I have kept significantly to myself over the years, although a few people know bits and pieces. Many of you know that Mrs. Ray and I have known each other for a long time. It was quite obvious. What I want to convey is how we came to know each other and what that meant to me, and I believe, to her.

"I met the Rays when I was an 11-year-old farm boy in central Kansas. Perryton, Kansas to be exact. Paul and Celina Ray bought the farm directly behind my family's farm.

I believe that the Rays did not select that farm to buy. I believe they were directed to buy that farm. They were placed there, and she in my life, by the grace of God. By age 12, I was squarely on a debilitating path to an early death. Mrs. Ray would have none of that. She took me under her care and charms, providing me with hope in what I thought was a hopeless situation. You see, I was dying. Not in the conventional sense, although the result would be the same. I was dying, because pure Evil had decided I was needed to fight its dark battle against all that is Good. As strange as that sounds, and I know it does, it is the truth.

I would have sunk under the pressure of my physical and mental pain without her. Mrs. Ray and I had threads of experiential bonds. Bonds that only she could coalesce to. She provided me with a backbone when I was nothing more than a scared child; she gave me a beacon of light when it was the darkest; she single-handedly turned my fear into confidence and success. She wound our common threads even tighter. She saved my life, then launched my life. She has saved many lives since then too."

A raucous "amen" was raised for the first sound since I started speaking.

"Amen is right," I echoed. "I'm guessing she launched many other lives afterwards too. I know she did." I paused again to gather myself.

"I loved Lydia Celina Ray. Period. No exceptions. She was family, maybe more so than my own. Since then, I have spent thousands of hours being graced by her wisdom. Some day we will continue those discussions."

I paused again and gathered my thoughts. Looking out over the group of mourners, many of whom were still in a state of disbelief. I asked. "Why are we on this earth? This crowded earth where it seems everyone is out for themselves and the rest of us better beware. I believe the answer is painfully simple. We were put here to make life better for the people we love and, more importantly, the people we don't. To take care of each other when the world we live in would rather chew us up and spit us out, that is if our world even cares to notice. I believe that with all my heart. Melvin Standard taught me this practice, but it was Celina Ray who instilled this belief deeply into Melvin and me. Not necessarily the mechanical act of caring, but the tender art of caring, art thoroughly salted with selfless love and affection. She took us to another level.

"I cannot adequately express what Celina Ray means to me. I'm not sure any of us can. But I think we all know the answer because it resides in the deepest reaches of our being. Hold that feeling tight. Let that feeling guide your thoughts and actions. If we do that, we will adequately express what Celina Ray means to all of us. Amen, and may God bless all of us, and may God continue to love on Celina Ray."

Many mournful and joyful tears and hugs followed. The last of the congregants and friends shuffled out of the sanctuary after an hour of personal stories about Celina. Many I had heard before and enjoyed again, and many I had the pleasure of hearing for the first time. I was a worn-out wreck as I closed the church and let Margie drive me home. We ate as a family and retold stories. I tried to get Marcus and his sister to join us but they were understandably too emotionally spent. He told me later that they also sat around the dining room table, eating in celebration and reciting family stories, much as we had.

Sleep came fast that night.

THE END

EPILOGUE

Evil and Good do not move in time. They have no calendar or watch. Chronology means nothing to them. They simply float in the fourth dimension. That's why the human need to "get this over with" is irrelevant to them. Do not base your actions on the temporal because man's invention of time cannot replace the eternal, any more than the material the can replace the spiritual. Never let your guard down, Jacob.

Sage words of advice. Celina Ray scripted these six sentences on a post card and handed it to me the day before I left for Wichita State. Appropriately, we were sitting at her kitchen table. The card is now a little yellow, and rather tattered, but her impeccable penmanship has weathered the years. I found it in the same box in which my journal was lying in wait. At some point, I had slipped it behind the front cover of the hardbound journal for safekeeping. Everything has been returned to the cardboard box, except this note. I now keep it in the lap drawer of my old desk at work. I am not sure why, but it seems like the right thing to do. I don't need to read the crafted text any more, as I have memorized it word for word. I have begun to repeat it to myself in the early mornings when I awake with a start, just before I walk down stairs to the kitchen. The nausea hasn't quite resurfaced yet, but the faint humming in my knees has begun to put me on notice.

Susie was right; I was only in remission.

Acknowledgments

For all the people that helped in this process:

To Erin MacPherson for a whole host of reasons, not the least of which is agreeing to take on the formidable job of editing a book written by a first time writer, who quite frankly, knew nothing about the process and little about what he was doing. Thanks also for the hand holding, graceful edits of needed deletions, soft landings on debated issues and a gentle leash to guide me to completion.

To Marla Taviano for copy editing in the midst of ministry work on the other side of the world.

To Sandra Shellum for being bold enough to read an early draft with a critical eye.

To Taylor Fleming and Lindsey Engleman for providing strength and motivation in all I've ever accomplished since the very day you guys were born.

And most importantly to my wife Sandy, who is and always will be the gentle and not-so-gentle driver behind everything I do. Thanks for reading my work in process, encouraging me to soldier on, designing the cover, creating the book's layout and generally being my partner in crime. All my love.

ABOUT THE AUTHOR

Soul Survival is the first book written by Craig Fleming, a writer, artist and business owner. A sequel to Soul Survival is in the planning stages.

Craig and his wife, Sandy have lived in Austin, Texas for twenty years.

www.ingramcontent.com/pod-product-compliance
Lightning Source LLC
Chambersburg PA
CBHW071220250626
47163CB00001B/59